FOXFIRE'S LEGACY

"There has always been a great mystery among my people. It is simple enough: once there was a Ler rebel . . . The rebel's name was Sanjirmil, which in your speech signifies natural spontaneous combustion—will-o' the wisp. Foxfire. Those Ler who were with her descended into the Warriors of Dawn, who later dwindled and vanished. There were Humans, the Klesh, whom the Warriors enslaved and bred into many pure types. We are going to Monsalvat to talk with some Klesh, who are the only link with that past . . .

"Sanjirmil set forces in motion that made the Klesh and separated them from both Ler and Human. The stories claiming th⬛⬛ ⬛⬛jirmil was victim not perpetrator have ⬛⬛⬛ ⬛⬛ back to one common source—M⬛⬛⬛⬛ ⬛⬛ Klesh. I have tried to past-m⬛⬛ ⬛ have gotten is a radia⬛⬛ ⬛⬛⬛⬛ ⬛yond that is a cur⬛⬛ ⬛⬛⬛⬛ ⬛⬛swer is there. . ⬛⬛⬛

The Day of the Klesh

M. A. Foster

DAW BOOKS, INC.
DONALD A. WOLLHEIM, PUBLISHER

New York

For Eugene

FIRST PRINTING, OCTOBER 1979

1 2 3 4 5 6 7 8 9

DAW TRADEMARK REGISTERED
U.S. PAT. OFF. MARCA
REGISTRADA. HECHO EN U.S.A.

PRINTED IN U.S.A.

1

"Anyone who reaches a new world must conform with all the conditions of it."

—A. C.

The Summer labor fair on the outskirts of Kundre, on Tancred, had been an established feature of the country for years past counting, reaching far back into the days of ancient tradition when Men alone ruled the world Tancred. The coming of Ler-folk in the latter days had, in its due course, changed much, as always, slowly and subtly, but not Kundre, and not the fair. It persisted. It grew, for nothing remains the same: and the fair, which had begun as a hiring place for harvest helpers, had slipped back into summer, then early in the season, almost into spring, encompassing more trades, jobs, specialties, finally virtually everything. Most importantly, it had become a place where young people seeking change might choose and hope to be chosen for many tasks, long and short, near and far, on-planet—or off it.

The cities of Tancred were uniform and uncosmopolitan: Kundre, by the fair, was not appreciably different from its sisters, Bohemundo, Isticho, Athalf, Ricimer and Amand. The fair, on the other hand, evidenced diversity and difference; there were star-captains, laborers, entrepreneurs, hiring-bosses and foremen, all of several kinds of creature: Humans, in egg- or teardrop-shaped craft; Ler, in windowless, featureless spheres; and, typical of this sector of space, Spsomi, foxy, sharptoothed humanoid beings who resembled lemurs or galagos, but who were not, technically, primates at all, being descended from an unspecialized carnivore closest in form to the raccoons and pandas of old Earth. Spsomi took to space in asymmetrical slipperships whose shapes were never repeated and remained difficult to describe for they most resembled doodlings in three dimensions, smoothly finished

5

and gracefully curved, broken by exterior piping and conduits, as eccentric as the ler ships were featureless.

Odor, sound, sight; contrast and difference filled the region of the fair. Cooking proceeded in booths scattered over the fair grounds. There were also dust, odors of beasts, chemicals, scents to repel and allure. Prospective employers set up their placards and tables and glowered at one another—Humans in all-purpose coveralls or spacesuits, or pajamalike utility garments: Ler in *pleths,* like nightshirts, or in loose tunics and pantaloons; Spsomi in vests and loincloths, which were patterned in ornate designs and worked in colors of jarring disharmonies. There were sounds of motors, the wheels of carts and barrows, cries in several languages, fragments of incomprehensible words, and music—accented, rhythmic human forms, accentless, formalistic Ler music, erratic, syncopated Spsomi tunes and jangles.

The place of the fair was an open, spacious plain set among distant, low hills. To the west, opposite Kundre, a river made a broad sweep, enclosing the field within a long curve of tall trees. There, along the river, the ships grounded.

From those hills, by way of Kundre, had come four young men, all of an age alike to wander and explore, to see new things, new lands, or to sight the invitation and return, sobered by a secret self-knowledge: Ilver Quisinart, Grale Cervitan, Dreve Halander, Meure Schasny. Their distinguishing characteristics could be noted at a glance: Quisinart was lanky of build, long-nosed and querulous. Cervitan was long of trunk and short of leg, thick and stocky, with smooth contours in the heavy bones of his face. Halander was unremarkable in any degree, unmemorable, bland and neutral as a store manikin. Schasny was wiry and delicate, small-featured. Otherwise, they were similar in skin tone, eye color, hair texture and color, and general shape. Humans were now as uniform as Ler; there was only one race of man, with only minor planetary variations.

All were acquaintances, loosely friends, but of somewhat differing origins. Quisinart was from an experimental commune; Cervitan the sole child of a herdsman; Halander the middle child of a merchant family; Schasny the youngest of a family of landtenders. None had futures that were both desirable and assured. And it was for such as these that the fair by Kundre had existed since time immemorial.

The four passed a Spsomi booth, surrounded by a half dozen of the slender, foxy creatures, who were at that moment all talking at once in their sputtering language with its accompanying gestures, slow-motioned as the deliberations of sloths, but also frantic; measured nervousness. The Spsomi looked their way, and foxy, delicate muzzles bared needle teeth in the Spsom version of a smile. Drooping feeler-whiskers waved, preposterous curved ear-trumpets waggled, opened and closed, swivelled independently. Behind was a sign, crudely lettered, which proclaimed, "Fame—its fortune, in employ the Great Capitan Iachm Vlumdz Shtsh. Sojourn Pstungdz, Whulge, Tmargu, SfaDdze—bonded pipemen: 9 their-places." While they watched, one of the Spsom bent to a communications device set out on the table, listened, raged back at the device as if the voice in it came from there, not somewhere else in the field of the fair, and then peacefully walked to the sign and changed the number 9 to a 6.

Quisinart gaped in open wonder; Cervitan stared. Halander frowned. Meure Schasny looked at the four-digit hands, which waved, gestured to them, motioned, beckoned. Each digit was tipped with a ridged nail, which in the course of normal wear shaped itself to a needle-sharp point. He made a polite sign to the Spsomi, continuing past the booth.

As they passed on beyond the booth, hopefully out of ear-shot or notice of the furred Spsomi, Cervitan remarked, "No fame there—all one sees on a Spsom ship are the interiors of conduits."

Quisinart asked, "What are the pipes for? They don't seem to discharge anywhere." Quisinart greatly admired the man-of-the-world air possessed by Grale Cervitan.

Cervitan answered, "No one knows, that I've heard. The Spsom don't tell—all they want to do is hire someone else to clean them—it's considered to be a job suitable only for convicts, outcastes, and offworlders. All I know is that they have to be kept spotless. Some are dusty by nature, others get greasy. All smell funny, or bad. They are cleaned both in flight, and on the ground. There you have the extent of my knowledge concerning Spsom pipe and conduit."

Halander interjected, "No fortune, either. Pay is computed on the basis of 'lays,' which is a fraction of the net profit of the voyage. The rub comes when the lay gets 'adjusted.' They add a lot on; food, taxes, bonuses, antibonuses, ship stores, stipends, garnishments. One is indeed fortunate to arrive ahead at all, that is, owing the furry devils nothing."

"What, no money for liberty?" asked Meure, in tones of mock outrage.

"Absolutely none," answered Cervitan. Fardus shipped with them two years ago, and had to swab conduit the whole trip. Never saw a thing. And they put him out on Lickrepent for debt and he had to work his way back here, almost begging. As it was, there was fuss enough; the Spsom captain threatened to fricassee him, but the Lerfolk on Lickrepent would have none of that. At the least, they paid him out."

Quisinart asked, incredulously, "Would they really have eaten him?"

"Never a doubt." Cervitan said the last with all seriousness, but he also flashed a quick glance at Halander, which Meure saw. The true answer was that they probably wouldn't have, although there were enough stories going around about the Spsomi to that effect that Quisinart would believe it.

Here they passed by a small, semipermanent office, with a signboard in the window listing inbounds, outbounds, and ships currently grounded on the field. There were three rows, showing status, and three columns, showing race of the crew. The four strolled over to examine the listings. The first column listed human ships, the second, Ler, and the third, Spsomi.

Halander read aloud, "*Zahed* and *Zain* are departed, as are *Assiah* and *Sadran*, which left yesterday. *Baal Chalal* and *Aur Chasdim* are yonder in the field. *Nistar* is also down, here, but is awaiting parts and is not in commission. *Tiferet* and *Merkava* are known inbound, with *Zemindar* and *Kavannah* reported."

Cervitan commented, "Little enough there to work with. *Baal Chalal* is a scow, and *Aur Chasdim* is worse, according to rumor. *Nistar* is an excellent ship; well-run. That's why her Captain took her out of commission. Most would order the part and fly on. *Tiferet* I've heard mentioned, but the others I don't know. *Zemindar* . . . Hm . . . probably not so good, either."

Halander squinted at the listing for the Ler ships, and continued reading, "Let's see what the Lerfolk offer spacewise . . . Ah. *Dilberler* is gone. A shame. That's a good ship. *Forfirion* departed day before yesterday, in the company of *Gennadhlin Srith*. *Tantarrum* and *Holyastrin* are still here. *Murkhandin* and *Volyasmus* are reported. And the Spsom? Let's see. . . . None have left recently. *Thlecsne Ishcht* is down, as are *Vstrandtz, Warquandr* and *Ffstretsha. Mstritl* is due in next week."

Cervitan commented, "*Vstrandtz*. That'll be the ship of Iachm Vlumdz."

Halander asked, "Do you know the other three?"

"*Thlecsne* is reportedly a privateer. There's a war going on, the far side of Spsom space, so they say, so it could be on this side, doing some trading of raid-booty. *Warquandr* is a scheduled liner, and I think *Ffstretsha* is a tramp for hire. Watch that one! There's no telling what kind of work they'd get into."

They passed onward, aimlessly drifting in the fine warm afternoon from place to place, passing booth, stand, field-table and outdoor restaurant alike. At the hiring booths, some advertised tasks which were elaborately specified, listing duties, responsibilities, hours of employ. Some went further, and added elaborate pay scales and types of promotion ladders, as well as pension plans. These were also equally exact in their requirements for prospective candidates. Others advertised more simply, even to the point of deliberate obscuration. These simply promised "good money" for "hard work," specifying neither the task to be performed, nor the employer for whom it was being performed. These they sensibly avoided; the conventional wisdom held that employment so advertised would, of necessity, be either illegal, dangerous, risky, underpaid, or any combination, possibly all four simultaneously.

They visited a small emporium specializing in roasted sausages and foamy, pale beer, settled themselves in a convenient booth, and took a relaxed lunch, each sitting quietly to himself and savoring whatever revelations the day at the fair had brought them.

Meure Schasny was, in a word, bored. Aside from sightseeing, they had accomplished little this day, and the next ones promised more of the same. He knew that as long as they contented themselves with sightseeing and sign-reading, they were unlikely to go anywhere in any employ, dangerous or not. Finally, seeing the bland expression of Cervitan, the blank face of Halander, and the gullibility of Quisinart, he said, "And so? After the sausages, what do we plan to do?"

Halander ventured, not even surprised, nor bothering to reflect upon his answer, said, easily, "No problem there; Kundre is within walking distance, and there are always a number of footloose girls there. I move that we address ourselves to the town and avail ourselves upon them, of course allowing nature to dictate the turn of events."

Cervitan agreed, finishing the last of his beer. "I would have said as much. I agree. Let us proceed with all dispatch."

Quisinart pulled his nose and asked, "Could we not go down by the river and look at the ships? I never saw one closely before. Perhaps we might get some ideas there as well."

Halander and Cervitan glanced at Quisinart with expressions of disdain, but Meure agreed. "Indeed! A good idea. I agree with Ilver, for once. We two will stroll along the riverbank and interview crewmembers, if they will talk with us, and you two can return to Kundre and satiny flesh."

Cervitan lowered his heavy brows and glowered. "One moment. The satiny flesh is by no means certain; and anyway, how will you two know what to ask? You are babes in the woods."

Quisinart ventured, "I can tell a regular fellow from a rogue, and I intend to sign on with no Spsom, whatever their promises."

Schasny agreed, "And I will do likewise. We will have to start somewhere, and," here he hesitated, ". . . prosper or suffer as circumstances will come to dictate." It was brave, nevertheless, he regretted saying it immediately, for it had established a certain relationship with Cervitan that could not end but in one of them losing face.

Halander tossed down the remainder of his beer and said, agreeably, "Well, that settles it. We shall go look at ships and converse with crews. And afterwards, if nothing has come of it, can we take ourselves to the city?"

"Agreed," said Meure, and with that, the four of them arose, settled their bills with the cook, and set out in the direction of the place nearer the river where the spaceships were grounded.

The fair proper had always oriented itself on the side of the field nearest to Kundre. But as one proceeded westward through the temporary structures of the fair, the fair soon fell away and the grounds were merely open field, fading away to the riverbanks. From Kundre, the ships were hardly noticeable, abstract artifacts by, or under the distant row of riverside trees. From the fair, they were little more, but out in the open of the fair grounds, they began to assume shapes of a greater distinction. Schasny found himself glancing upward, now and again, so as not to be surprised by another ship settling in.

Nine spaceships were arrayed, following the broad curve of the river; from the far distance, they had seemed small and insignificant, but as the four walked across the open, the ships grew in size and importance. The nearest ship was the Human spacecraft, *Nistar*, awaiting parts. No point in going there. They were obviously not going to sign on anyone for a while. Although deactivated, the scene was far from being over-relaxed. A pavilion had been erected before the entryport, and members of the crew were engaging in an afternoon buffet with some ladies of Kundre. It was all very sedate, orderly, and impressive; the green of the branches and overhanging fronds of the riverside trees, the gold-brown color of the dry summer grass, and the deep green with which the ship *Nistar* had been painted. They were close enough to read the name and origin placards attached over the entryport: *Nistar*, and below, *Port Callet, Samphire*. The crewmembers they could see were suave and polished, making elegant gestures effortlessly, and in full-dress uniform. The four walked past, trying to appear inconspicuous. Surely such a craft did not recruit actively on a back-country world like Tancred. They would want able spacemen, merchant officers, pursers. It was, as such craft went, rather small. Schasny suspected that *Nistar's* cargo was usually valuables, money, jewels, wealthy people who could go visiting. He sighed, hoping the others would not hear him. That was something like what he wanted, but which seemed, here and now, light-years away.

The next ship was a large Spsom ship, without a nameplate. From its naked armament-blisters, however, they could deduce that it was most probably the *Thlecsne Ishcht*. This one was shaped in an asymptotic curve, the pointed ends elevated. It also carried noticeably more than the usual number of exterior pipes and conduits, and was colored a sooty brown. The pipes had probably once had color of their own, as was the custom with the Spsom, but the paint appeared to be either burned off or worn off. They kept a certain distance from it, not wanting to be suspected as spies; but they saw no activity. Nevertheless, *Thlecsne* conveyed an impression of wary activity; a faint hum could be heard from somewhere underneath, and none of them doubted for an instant that it could spring into furious life then and there. They passed on, hoping they had not been noticed, but sure that they had been.

Somewhat farther down the irregular line of ships was a smaller Spsomi spacecraft, considerably smaller than the *Thlecsne Ishcht*, but considerably more open. This one seemed to be shaped into a rough crescent, although one end was higher, shorter, and more sharply curved than the other. It was a dull coppery color, but it seemed clean and well-cared for, the exterior piping was maintained after the full rigor of the Spsom custom—each pipe was garishly painted in bright, prismatic colors, so far as any of them could tell, each differently. As they drew nearer, they could make out, under the tangle of piping, an open entry port. Over the port, with its attached stairwell, several ideograms in the Spsom manner were painted. To the side, another legend they could read: *Ffstretsha, Imber, SfaDdze*. By the stair, a single Spsom had opened an inspection plate in the hull and was taking readings on a portable device which he would attach at different points inside. Satisfied, so it appeared, with the measurements, the Spsom disconnected the device and turned to re-enter the ship. An ear swivelled around, followed by the foxy head. The creature stopped, halfway up the stairs, as the four approached.

The Spsom spoke first, distorting the language in the peculiar way Spsomi did when speaking a human language.*

"Yis, yis—y'r wis'n watt?"

Cervitan, who seemed to have a little knowledge of the odd creatures, repeated the question for the rest, " 'Yes,' he says. 'What do we wish?' "

"To look at the ships," volunteered Quisinart.

The crewmember seemed pleased, for both ear-shells now rolled around to point at them. It said, "Vv'ri gidd, yis, v'ryvry gidd. Pit wvi nid nnu ppeypmnneuw. (h)'eff gidd ppeypm'n frr'm Vfzyekhr; sle-vess, yis."

Cervitan repeated, "He says that's very good, but they already have pipe-men, slaves from a world he calls 'Vizyekher.' I don't know where that is. Probably a long way from here."

---

* Spsom distorted non-Spsom speech in numerous ways, not limited to grammar and phonetics. The least of these effects was due to Spsomi mouth structure—which forced most of the formants of speech to occur forward of the palate. This, in turn, lent a whistling, spitting quality to Human or Ler speech. Further, Spsomi had few resonance cavities, so their speech sounded timbreless and flat.

Meure Schasny said, glancing upward and around at the exterior piping which encompassed the Spsom ship, most of which seemed large enough for a person to slither through, "We are sorry to hear that. We are still looking for work, though. We won't touch anything. We had never seen one of your ships close before. Thank you."

The Spsom wrinkled its brow in concentration, and answered, making a serious effort to speak correctly, "Wirk yi went, yis? Fff . . . gu erundt thirr, bbehend ddhi sh'p. Lirmin thirr, nid two merr. Inskild, yis? Go-u see Lir-men, bey dhii rrver. New m'st gou. Ness t'telik 'f yu. Gid dey, yis?"

The Spsom turned and sprung upward into the ship, through the hatchway and out of sight. They hoped, out of hearing.

Schasny shook his head. He said, "That's our speech?"

Cervitan answered, "That's nothing! That one spoke it very well, indeed. The last was the most important. It said, 'Work you want? Go around behind the ship and talk to Ler. They need two more, unskilled.' "

Schasny said, "That's what it sounded like, all right."

Then the four looked for a long time at each other. Halander finally broke the silence. "Ler, behind a Spsom ship. Grale, what do you make of that?"

"Charter, likely, if they're really with this ship."

Schasny added, "Can't hurt to ask. All they can say is no."

They stood for a moment, irresolutely, looking at the Spsom ship, the late afternoon shadows now gathering around the curves of the hull, and farther, over by the riverbanks under the trees. And at each other all over again. Then they set out in the direction the Spsom had indicated, being careful to keep a distance from the hull of the ship and the fantastic network of piping that surrounded it.

Beyond the ship, the dry-grass meadow sloped gently to the banks of the river. Overhead, tall Aoe-trees formed an overarching, lacy canopy, which was just beginning to stir with the evening breezes, for which Kundre was justly famous. Beyond the tree trunks was the river, the water slow and opaque. And on the riverbank was a small group of Ler, sitting quietly and talking among themselves. Two Spsom were also with the group.

As they drew closer, they saw subtle differences between these Spsom and the one they had talked with at the ship's entryway; these were more reserved, moving about very little. They also seemed to be outfitted more completely—the open

vests the Spsom seemed always to wear were carefully ornamented with little strips and tags of gray hide, and the more
imposing of the pair wore also a design in wire on one shoulder that suggested the piping encompassing a Spsom ship.
That one also wore a gold armband on its upper arm.

Spsom, no matter how much one saw them, were a form
of life that men never became accustomed to. It never had
been that they had been incomprehensible culturally, but that
their physical proportions sat wrongly on the human conceptual framework; they simply didn't look *right*. To start with,
the limbs were two-jointed in the middle of the limb, so that
there were three sections, rather than two. This was accomplished by an elongation of what would have been ankle or
wrist bones. The feet were digitigrade, with a short, bony
spur projecting backwards for stability. The hands were four-
digited, but arranged two by two, permanently opposed.
However long the evolutionary path had taken them, Spsom
were a very long way from their natural origins. Legs completely adapted for running and leaping, and arms and hands
modified into highly specialized organs of grasping.

The body trunk was short, and the limbs were long; an
overall impression of them would bring to mind such terms
as delicate, wiry; sometimes, gangling or awkward. More,
they had retained their fur, from their days as pure animal; a
short, dense pelt of a neutral, slightly ruddy, brown, with
darker accent lines along the face and shoulders, and a
lighter stippling along the flanks and thighs.

The hand was quite different; it was virtually palmless, and
consisted chiefly of the four digits, normally carried two-by-
two, opposed. And last, the head. Spsom faces were narrow,
triangular, slimming down to a narrow muzzle, incorporating
nose and upper jaw. It seemed almost foxlike, until one considered the large eyes, the swell of the skull, and the highly
mobile ears near the top of the head, constantly in nervous,
yet measured motion. Spsom looked more like animals than
some animals did, yet they always conducted themselves in
what could only be called a civilized manner; i.e., they spoke,
they read and wrote, they flew spaceships and lived in cities,
and also made a low-key form of war upon one another. More
rarely, upon other races.

As for their relations with Humans and Ler, there was a
difference. Where Humans and Ler saw similarities in each
other, Spsom saw the differences. Ler they treated respectfully, carefully neutral, at a distance. Humans they liked and

lost no opportunity to associate with them, circumstances allowing.

Besides the two Spsom associated with the group, there appeared to be three Ler, two Elders, judging by their long hair, and an adolescent, dressed in loose tunic and pantaloons. The Elders wore the traditional *pleth*, or overshirt.

The four young men approached the group cautiously, not knowing which person to address; the adolescent, the Elders, or even the Spsom. Grale went first, followed by Meure and Halander, with Quisinart bringing up the rear. When they had effectively joined the group, Cervitan stopped, looking about a little uncertainly, trying to select the best one to begin with.

The Elders solved the problem for him. Of the two, one was fuller-figured, more round. The other was thin and saturnine. The round one said, "You are here for work? To sign on with us?"

Cervitan answered, "Yes. We heard there were some places left, and would like to look into it."

The Elder said, "Straight enough. So attend: we lack two places yet, and will depart when we have them, at that moment. I will describe the offer of employ, thus: *Daorman*,* that is to say, general porterage and housekeeping assistance, serving, cooking. Pay is the customary rate for unskilled *daormen*, and the term is for the duration of a voyage to a certain planet, and the completion of our duties there. You may select return to Tancred, or as customary, first-port-of-call. We do not go to make war, nor settle vendetta, therefore hazard rates are inappropriate. We intend to exhibit prudence in danger, as applicable. It will be about a year, local, more or less. Do you have your cert?"*

Cervitan answered for the group, "Yes, we all have them."

At this point, the smaller, and less-dressed of the two Spsom said something in his own speech, a sibilant whispering, broken by labial stops and dental aspirates, uttered in general, as if addressed to no one in particular.

The adolescent Ler now stepped forward, between the two Elders, and indicated Cervitan and Quisinart. Closer now, it

* A temporary servant, hired for completion of a specific task or mission. No status change is implied. General work to the task at hand is suggested, but sometimes clerical duties were also performed by "temporaries," on a renewable contract basis. In this case, "Porters" might be the best translation.

* Cert: A document issued by the local prefect, stating that the bearer may act responsibly in his own behalf.

seemed to be a girl. She said, "These two, the one who speaks, and the one in the back, will not be suitable, according to Adjutant Iflssh."

The Elder nodded, and added, "Therefore I withdraw my offer to the two individuals indicated." He turned to the girl. "The others?"

"Acceptable."

Meure now spoke, "Why are they not acceptable?"

The girl said, "Scent. Spsom have sensitive noses and can predict general demeanor. We want no one that is too bold, nor one who is not bold enough. These two are thus; no dishonor intended, but we cannot use you. You two remaining are fine, if you find the conditions correct and in order."

Meure said, "They are correct as far as they go, but much remains to be seen. We know nothing of your project or mission, nor how it is organized. Can we not hear more?"

The girl glanced once at the first Elder, then turned back to Meure. It was a girl all right, very slight in build, almost weak. Nor was she pretty, or full of the robust tomboyness of the average Ler girl. She said, "We have chartered this available ship, the *Ffstretsha*, of the Spsom owners, to transport us to a certain world, and there, to various points on its surface as required. And then back to the nearest Ler world, where your group and mine will part company. We intend to return to our proper places by scheduled liner. The *daormen* we hire from this world will be expected to perform odd jobs aboard ship, primarily porterage on the planetary surface. One among you will operate communications equipment. This is, you may say, a scientific expedition to gather facts. That is all. You may consider our group a fact-finding organ, one that would settle a long-standing question among my people."

Halander asked of her an odd question. He said, "Why Tancred? I mean, why hire here, and not someplace else?"

"Why Tancred? Because it happens to be along the way there, that's all," she replied, as if surprised.

Halander said, "Oh," and was apparently satisfied with the answer, but Meure thought, *They could charter a Spsom ship anywhere at all. They go everywhere. But Tancred is the last of the settled worlds, I know that. Beyond us lie only the colonial worlds, and the wild ones. And the Spsom don't voyage outside much, at least, not in this part of space. They come from inside ordered space, and if Tancred is on the way there, then there is outside.*

Meure asked, "Does this world have a name?"

The girl answered, "It is called Monsalvat."

The name meant nothing to Meure, nor to any of the rest of them. It sounded like a corruption of a Ler name. The four looked at one another, missing the girl's attention, which was on them intently. The name didn't register. Meure turned back to the girl and the Elder.

"Very well. I apply for the position of Daorman."

Halander added, "And I also."

The Elder paused a moment, glanced at the two Spsom. The smaller one nodded, quite humanly. The larger one, with the fine shoulder decoration, said nothing, made no gesture. He seemed oblivious to all of them. The elder now turned to a small valise on the ground, bent, opened it, and retrieved two sheafs of paper. "These are your contracts. Thumbprint, please." Meure placed his thumb at the place indicated. Halander, after a moment's hesitation, did likewise. The Elder then separated the sheaves, handing one set to Meure and Halander, one set to the girl, and one set the last, to the smaller Spsom, who turned and sprung off in the direction of Kundre.

The Elder now said, "You are signed on. You may enter the *Ffstretsha* immediately, if you have no further errands to run."

The remaining Spsom also turned and departed, without a word, striding off around a projecting corner of the *Thlecsne* and disappearing. Meure Schasny and Dreve Halander looked at Cervitan and Quisinart. All this had happened too fast, and there seemed nothing adequate to say to fill the silence. Cervitan managed, "Good luck, you two! We'll be on the next one!"

They finished their short goodbyes, and Cervitan and Quisinart started off back in the direction of Kundre. Meure and Halander started uncertainly for the entryport of the ship.

The Elder who had talked before now walked straight for the ship. The remaining one stepped forward and said, "Come along, now. All are aboard, save us. The *Liy* Flerdistar* can be explaining your duties while the Spsom crew is securing the port. We are ready to leave. Surely . . . Is there something else?"

---

* *Liy* is a title-of-reference used where an order of nobility is implied. In this case, for an Elder to so refer to an adolescent, it could only mean that the girl, Flerdistar, was of a Braid of very exalted status on her homeworld, the Ler equivalent of near-royalty. *Liy* should thus be rendered as Demoiselle.

Meure answered, "No, no we are ready, as well. Let us be off." But as he walked toward the *Ffstretsha*, he looked back, more than once, at the receding figures of Cervitan and Quisinart. They did not look back.

Meure reached the outthrust entry-ladder and saw that he was indeed the last one to enter the asymmetrical Spsom ship, the *Ffstretsha*. He could see inside; only the Spsom crewmember, apparently the same one they had talked with earlier, was there, waiting in the passage beyond the port for him to enter. Meure climbed the unfamiliar, wide-spaced treads, grasped a projecting lip of the port, swung into the alien ship, and stood aside.

He was in a short passageway which joined another not far ahead. He felt a sense of vertigo, a strangeness; this, already, was an alien world, of course. Impressions crowded his perceptions: the light in the ship was soft and indirect, with a yellowish tinge. There were various odors and scents—the acrid flavor of the tanned leather the Spsom habitually wore, and the scent of the creatures themselves, ever so slightly sweet, like bread, or perhaps cookies. And sounds: there was a faint hum that told the ship was already energized, and over that, a mindless little tune hummed by the Spsom as he went about his task of closing and sealing the port. He realized that he did not know which way to go in the corridor ahead.

The Spsom crewman spoke into an intercom in his hissing, sputtering language, and then turned to Meure.

It spoke slowly and deliberately, knowing that Meure found it hard to understand. "B'spoke yu b'fore, eotside. So yu came wif'us, efter all. Virry gid ey thingk, yis, virry gid indid." The Spsom indicated itself. "Vdhitz. Ey. Mesellf."

Meure looked closely at the Spsom called Vdhitz, trying not to stare. He saw bony, strong hands, wiry, lean limbs covered in dense, short fur; a figure larger than himself, and definitely more sure of himself. Where skin was exposed, it was a dark color, not black, but a very dark brown, dry and dull. The pointed muzzle, the sharp, white teeth, the ridiculous mobile ears, the fine whiskers which he could now see, all those things shouted "animal" to him, but the gesture of the hands and the intelligence of the expression said "person" more persuasively. Meure pointed at himself. "Meure," he said. "Meure Schasny."

"Myershtshesny," Vdhitz repeated, pleased with his success in communication. He pointed at the corridor ahead, and then to the right. "New yu go therr. Yu wirk fir the Lirmen, net thee Spsm. Shee will tell yu whet yu hef tu doo." He stopped, then added, "Kell un me. Ey kenn hhelp."

Meure started off toward the corridor, and turned to the right as he had been told when he got there. He looked back. Vdhitz was busy at some task, manipulating controls on a panel which he had opened. Meure turned and walked ahead.

The main corridor had a flat floor, of some dark, resilient material, like rubber, but not rubber. The walls and ceiling merged into one, smoothly curving. The corridor itself veered to the right, then curved around sharply to the left, as if detouring around an obstacle. In the middle of the detouring curve back to the right was a door, and voices. He went in.

The room was a spacious compartment, with curved walls and ceiling like the corridor, and lit by the same type of indirect lighting, soft, shadowless, yellowish. Meure thought of a day when the sky was covered by a fine, high overcast. Yes. The Spsom homeworld must be cloudy, cool. Perhaps the dominant race of Spsom originally came from a region of rounded, eroded rocky defiles and canyons. Perhaps. He did not know. 'Rrtz, the world of the Spsom, was incalculably far away.

Here, there was a table, integral with the material of the floor, translucent, moulded, obviously manufactured, yet with an air of nature to it, as if it were a form of peculiar rock which had just happened to be formed to that shape and size to fit in this room, now.

There were already seven people present, seated or standing according to disposition, for Meure could sense no order in their placement. There were four Ler: the Liy Flerdistar, who reminded him ever so slightly of poor Quisinart, but with infinitely more reserve behind the thin, bony face, the two Elders he had met outside, and another adolescent, with still, perfectly regular features. There were three Humans as well: Halander and two girls. One of the girls was strongly built, but smoothly contoured, with a reddish tint in her brown hair, cut short almost after the manner of the Ler adolescents, and with a warm, tanned tone to her skin. The other was slender and delicate, pale-white. She had large eyes, dark hair, a full mouth. The first girl seemed bored; the second, apprehensive and nervous. And Halander obviously was pleased with circumstances. *So*, reflected Meure, *am I*. Both girls were attractive, after their own fashion.

Flerdistar noted Meure's arrival and waited for him to find a place, patiently. There was absolutely no sense of time in her manner whatsoever. Meure, nevertheless, felt an embarrassment for being the last and hurriedly found a seat by the table.

The Liy Flerdistar began, "Good. We are all present. I will make the introductions and we may then go about our tasks, which for the moment are simple enough." She indicated the Ler Elders. "These respected Elders are Rescharten Tlanh, whom you may regard as the leader of this, ah, expedition." She nodded toward the heavier Elder, the one who had spoken first outside the ship. "And Lurtshertan Tlanh." That was the thin one. "The *Didh* to my right in Clellendol Tlanh Narbelen, and I am Flerdistar Srith Perklonen*. The Forerunners are Meure Schasny, who just entered our common room. The other young man is Dreve Halander. The girls are Audiart Jendure," here she indicated the strapping girl with the reddish tint in her hair, "and Ingraine Deffy." The thinner girl shook her head, briefly, nervously, a motion that made her loose, cascading hair ripple.

Flerdistar continued, "The Spsom you will see little enough of. Shchifr is Captain. He wears an iron medallion on a chain around his neck. Mrikhn is Astrogator. That one is small and dark. Vdhitz, who was by the port as we entered, is First Officer—Technician. Zdrist is Second Officer—Overseer. There are two natives of the world the Spsom call 'Vfzyekhr.' They are in the ducting and I know not if they have names, or what the custom of their world is.

"Your term begins now and will continue until such time as we are successfully off the planet to which we are going. Some of you will doubtless wish to continue your employment and provision will be made then. The rest will become passengers and must pay, just as we. You can elect to return to Tancred, or first port of call otherwise, which I do not know now. Until we land, your duties will be simple: rationing and housekeeping. There is concentrated foodstuff and facilities for preparation in your compartment, which is to the left. We occupy the cabins to the left. Audiart Jendure, whom we have appointed head *Daorman* until planetfall, has our schedule. Otherwise, you are free to do as you feel inclined, in the time remaining. Do you have questions?"

---

* Ler surnames reveal occupation, or profession. *Narbelen* is a contraction of the phrase *Narosi Bel Ghenaos*, "ninth thief its-family (Braid). Similarly, Perklonen indicates "first historian family."

The girl, Ingraine, said softly, "We are to go to a world called 'Monsalvat'; how long will we be on the ship?"

Flerdistar answered, "It is a long voyage, but we go straight, with no stops. The Spsom tell me six weeks, perhaps eight, depending on currents. Yes, it is long, this way. Spend your time well. The *Ffstretsha* is a small ship and there is little room for us to impose upon the other. Now let me tell you a thing about Spsom and their ships. It will be true on this one, and on any other you may ever ride: outside this cabin, you may go anywhere freely where you see an open door, or open passageway. You may not pass a closed door. Custom varies as you must know. Do not pass through a closed door. Do not knock on it for entry. If you must pass, you must wait. This is the only prohibition I lay on you."

Halander asked, "Is there anywhere we can see out?"

"Only from the cockpit and the wardroom. You will see very little of either, if anything. What would you expect to see? It is only space. The Spsom instruments transmit a coherent image, but the view is not different at night. For the most part, the Spsom areas will stay closed-door. Remember what I said. There are serious consequences to you first if you disregard this. Is that all? Good. I believe Miss Jendure has the schedule. After the supper hour there will be tonight a short honorary visitation with Captain Shchifr. The Elder Rescharten and I will attend. Schasny, you stand by for service there if required."

The Ler girl turned and quickly left the room, followed by the rest. Clellendol was last. He arose from his seat with measured, careful movement, taking a look about the whole room, noting each of the four remaining, making some unknown assessment of each of them. They each felt slightly uncomfortable under that reading glance; a scion of the Ninth House of Thieves*, indeed. And then he, too, slipped into the quarters Flerdistar had indicated were the cabins of the Lerfolk.

It could have been an uncomfortable moment for them,

---

* Ler, with the thoroughness typical of their kind, had instituted Braids to perform what might have been left to accident on Human worlds. The various Belen Braids did actually steal, as their hereditary occupation. Of course, under elaborate and traditional restrictions. Members of the so-called "dark Braids" were often called upon by others for their unusual skills, so it is not particularly unusual, in the Ler context, that such a person as Clellendol would be included on an extraordinary undertaking.

when they were left alone, but Audiart did not permit them time to think about possibilities; she immediately began explaining what they had to do, in a quiet, sure voice. Her manner was carefully respectful, distant. Meure kept sneaking glances at the other girl, the slender one, Ingraine, and as he noticed also, so did Halander, but at the same time he appreciated Audiart's taking charge, and risked more than another look at her.

Then she took them into their own quarters, of which there was little enough to see; a narrow corridor, an odd sleeping room of six enclosed bunks, three on one side, three on the other, stacked atop one another. There was a tiny, but complete, even luxurious bathroom at the end, and the kitchen and locker were next to the door into the common room.

Audiart indicated the bunks. "I suppose we can pick as we will. I claim no authority, but there appears to be room for all. The two extra we can use for storage. We all have little enough."

Meure looked closer at the stacked bunks. There seemed to be enough room within for a person to sit up without bumping his head. Access was gained by a narrow ladder, and a sliding opening presumably at the head of the bunk.

Halander ventured, "Are we to follow the custom of the Spsom in the matter of open doors here as well?"

Audiart started to say something, stopped, began again. "The practice seems understandable enough," she said, carefully neutral, and not at all warmly. For the time being, there was no open invitation here offered to Dreve.

She indicated a small locker. "Liy Flerdistar has provided us with a generous stock of clothing. I fear it is after the Ler fashion, but there is quite a bit of it on the shelves therein. Take what you desire—it is all plain and discreet and should fit us all reasonably well. Go ahead and use it; it comes with the job. Now—we should get things ready for the supper hour. Them first, and then us. Come along now, we can settle dividing up the clothes and selecting the bunks afterward. Schasny, you may have to pick a bunk, at least. I don't know how long you'll be up in the wardroom."

Meure said, "I'll take top right."

The rest agreed. Then they set to the work of getting everything in order. In the small space, everything seemed to fall into place quite smoothly. The supplies were all where they were supposed to be, the equipment was in working order. In fact, they were well into the work, and starting to work efficiently together, before Meure thought to ask something that had just popped into his head.

He was standing by the door, getting ready to take the bowls into the common room, when he turned to Audiart, who was then making some adjustment to the cooker. There was only a small lamp over the counter, so the entryway was quite dim. He looked at her, the light outlining her short, straight hair. He said, "When do we leave, Audiart?"

She made the adjustment, turned away, to the counter. She answered, "Didn't you know? We left when you came aboard. We've been in space for several hours, I should guess. We're well away from Tancred by now."

After supper, Meure left for the wardroom. Audiart had told him what to do there, and how to get to it. It was simple; a short way along the main corridor, up a ladder, down another short corridor, and up a short stair. The door was open.

It was a common room similar to the one below, only somewhat smaller, and different. The walls were interrupted by screens giving views into space. Between the screens were shelves of drinking bowls with elaborate handles, ornamented plaques, framed mottoes or certificates written in the Spsom ideograms. There was room for four or six, and that was all.

Meure recognized the Spsom Captain from the description Flerdistar had given: the medallion. The Astrogator was not present. Presumably he was flying the ship. Vdhitz was the other Spsom. Meure entered without knocking, as he had been told, and stood by the doorway, his hands behind his back.

They were talking, Rescharten Tlanh and the Spsom Captain, Shchifr, with Flerdistar and Vdhitz translating by joint effort. Sometimes they would discuss a point at some length before rendering the offered statement, going either way.

Meure did not understand much of the discussion, and the Spsom end was incomprehensible, so he did not listen very closely. They seemed to care not at all what he overheard or didn't. So he took the opportunity to look at the screens showing the view outside the ship. The stars moved. First, the fields of stars shown in the viewscreens drifted slowly past, the obvious effect of their motion through space. They also moved slightly along the other axes, as if the ship itself were changing its orientation in space. It was a motion not unlike that of the sea upon a boat, save that it was slower, a differ-

ent rhythm. Meure watched one screen in particular, until
something intruded on his field of vision from another. He
looked. There, to all appearance off on the rear quarter of
the ship, was another ship visible in the screen, flying formation with the *Ffstretsha* across the oceans of space: he recognized it. The accompanying ship was the *Thlecsne Ishcht*.

2

"*Imagine, then, how I gloried in the flow of the
silken waters about the ship, in the fantastically im-
material outlines of the hills, in the gloom of the
frondage of the forests, in the curves of the cobra
coast, in the sinister stories of wreak and piracy
which haunt that desolate abyss through which we
were steaming, where for nine months of the year
one can scarce distinguish between sky and sea, so
dark and damp is the air, so subtly steaming the
swell; while beyond, as in a hashish dream, arose
the highlands, provinces all but unknown even to
the civilized inhabitants themselves. There, primrose
to purple, was the promise of undreamed-of tribes of
men, strangely tattooed and dressed, with awful
customs and mysterious rites, beyond imagination
and yet brutally actual, folk with sublimity carven of
simplicity and depravity woven of the most complex
madness.*"

—*A. C.*

The remainder of what passed for conversation between
Rescharten Tlanh the Elder and Shchifr the Spsom Captain
passed by Meure unheard and the proceedings unseen. He
kept watch, as unobtrusively as possible, on that rear quarter
viewscreen, watching as the erratic motion of the *Ffstretsha*
would, from time to time, bring the ominous outlines of the
Thlecsne into view. The privateer neither advanced nor
dropped back, but maintained its position carefully. The
Spsom Captain, Vdhitz, Rescharten, Flerdistar, all must be

aware of it. They could not but see it, just as he; yet they were totally unconcerned, therefore they knew it to be an expected condition. Meure then wondered indeed about their destination, that they should be accompanied by an armed warship in order to go there.

Shortly after, he sensed that the momentum of the meeting had been lost and that affairs had been completed. The two Ler arose from their places and bid the Spsom goodbye, for the moment, and left. After a moment's hesitation, Meure followed them.

The girl seemed preoccupied with something, perhaps fatigued; Meure did not think it best to ask her overmuch now. And Rescharten? He thought even less of asking the Elder. They returned to their quarters, through the ladders and corridors, in silence. At the common room, they found the other Ler adolescent up, studiously reading from the leaves of a reproduced text. Rescharten ignored the boy and passed directly into his own area, closing the door. Flerdistar passed for a moment, as if she had intended to say something, but Clellendol ignored her presence entirely, and after a moment, she, too, passed through the doorway into the Ler living quarters, not without a glance back, an unfathomable expression on her face.

Meure now felt the events of the day pressing time upon him. He was tired. He also saw no reason to remain, and reached for the handle of his own compartment door.

On a second thought, he turned and said, "You know that we are accompanied."

Clellendol looked from the book and turned a disturbing, direct glance onto Meure. "The *Thlecsne?* Yes, I know." The boy pushed his chair back and stood slowly, laying the sheaf of reproduced pages on the table.

Meure asked, "Why should a privateer fly formation with a small chartered liner?"

The boy smiled, not unfriendly. "A privateer? Yes, so it was told. Actually, it's something rather more than that; *Thlecsne Ishcht* is a commissioned warship of the Spsom Federal Naval Force, and a very special class at that. It has, so they tell me, the general plan and size of a frigate-class vessel, but more the armament of a cruiser."

Meure felt a sudden spasm of awe. That these people were wealthy enough to charter an entire Spsom ship, and a battleship as well . . . He said, "Your party hired both ships?"

Clellendol shook his head. "Hired them both? No. Not

even Flerdistar could arrange that. The *Thlecsne* is the request of Shchifr . . . No. Say no more. There is more to this
than a night's talk will cover. I dare say the Spsom first Officer may already have warned one of you. Aha, it was you.
Well, there's no cure for it, Schasny. Let it soak in—we've
the time for it, and I want no panics."

Clellendol indicated the sheaf on the table. "Here. This will
tell some truths about where we are going. You will need to
know something. And stay away from the *Liy* Flerdistar. Ask
her nothing."

Meure ventured, "She is yours?"

Clellendol yawned, stretched like a cat. "Quite to the contrary . . . I mean in quite another sense."

"Why me, of the four of us?"

"You seem to have your head screwed on right, that's all."
The adolescent Ler spoke with a certain impatience, as if
Meure were deliberately avoiding what he had been trying to
suggest all along. He added, "I have made contact with a certain Spsom, who shares my apprehensions. I see from your
expression that he has also approached you. Read what I
have left you and, in your leisure time, speak with Vdhitz,
however difficult it is to listen to Spsom speech. Become
aware. There is need for it."

Clellendol turned and went to the door of his quarters. He
glanced at the papers, once, to be sure Meure did not miss
his intent, but he did not wait to see if Meure picked them
up. Meure had not missed the pointed invitation, although he
seemed sure that he was not overtly being asked to join a
conspiracy as such. He gathered the papers and took them
with him.

Inside, all were asleep already, or so it seemed. There was
only a weak glow of a night-light by the cooker. He looked at
the bunks. All were dark, the sliding doors closed. All was
quiet. He felt a small moment of relief. It seemed that Halander had not yet succeeded. Meure looked again. All the sliding panels were closed, save the one he had picked. He had
no idea whatsoever what lay behind them, nor the number of
occupants therein.

Meure climbed the narrow ladder to his bunk, leaned over
into the opening, climbed within. Inside, it was surprisingly
roomy and comfortable, furnished in considerable detail and
evident quality. Immediately inside the sliding panel door,
there was an upholstered shelf; the bed proper lay at a
slightly lower level. Along the walls were cabinets and

shelves. The light came from a ceiling panel, but there were other lamps as well, cleverly recessed into the walls. Looking about, he found a panel of switches that controlled the lights; he also noted that there was another panel on the wall, with odd receptacles, for which there were no instruments in evidence. Spsom entertainment devices? Communication system plug-ins? He did not know. The switches did not feel right to his hands, and from that he knew it to be a standard Spsom compartment; but other than the odd feel and action of the switches, there was no alien feel to the compartment whatsoever. He felt perfectly at ease, completely at home.

After some experimentation, he found the switch that controlled the ceiling panel, and when he had found what was ostensibly a reading lamp, he turned the ceiling panel off. Inside the shelves, he found blankets, but no pillows. He then undressed, wrapped himself up in the blanket, and rolled another up for a pillow. And remembered a sheaf of papers. He was tired, and hesitated for a moment, wondering if he shouldn't just go to sleep and forget about the article Clellendol had given him. He yawned, sighed, and picked the sheaf up resignedly. He thought he would look it over before he turned the light out.

The first section was a dry text about the known features of the system of which the world Monsalvat was a part. Meure read through it quickly; it appeared there was nothing notable about the system at all. Nothing? He read through the section again. Nothing of particular interest. There were six planets, one habitable, one other technically habitable but not exploited. Monsalvat was the Third from its primary. The other world was called Catharge, the second planet, and was hot and dry and rocky. There was no gas giant in the system, a fact that struck Meure as a little out of the ordinary, and the primary was a close double of K6 stars, again, rather odd, but nothing to cause alarm. The system was both exceptionally stable and apparently very old, judging by the metals percentage in the spectra of the two suns, which were as close to being identical as would seem possible.

There was no evidence of intelligent life forms in the past of Monsalvat. There was native life, sure enough, but the Human discoverers of the system had found no trace, no artifacts, no ruins. It was a fact that had given them much pause, and Monsalvat was set aside for further study. And before final conclusions could be drawn, there had arisen an

unexpected need for a whole world, off by itself, and the
planet had been colonized in an odd and rushed manner.

There was a break in the text. Then the description started
again, rather more now in earnest and less in the abstract.

"... (It read) ... Monsalvat, a rather watery world, has
four land masses of near-continental extent: Kepture, Cantou, Glordune and Chengurune. The last is the largest, and
Cantou is the smallest. The total land area, including known
offshore islands, represents nineteen percent of the planetary
surface. This land mass has, to all evidence, been insufficient
to close both poles off simultaneously to free circulation, so
Monsalvat lacks evidence of planetary or even hemispheric
glaciation, even though all continents, save Cantou, show evidence of light glaciation in their geologic layer systems, but
therein was found no synchrony.

"The climate, therefore, is rather even for the degree of ax-
ial tilt to the plane of the ecliptic (twenty-eight degrees),
this being due to the moderating effect of the large amounts
of water in both liquid and gaseous form. ...

"... If the climate could be said to be even, the weather
is a different matter altogether; Monsalvat has a day of
twenty-two standard hours and a small satellite that exercises
little tidal influence; therefore the weather is strongly varia-
ble, if one may speak conservatively. In the equatorial and
sub-polar regions, it is violent, characterized by high winds on
the surface and rapid change. In the South Polar part of the
world-ocean, with no land masses or major undersea rises,
waves and individual storms can sweep completely around
the planet. In temperate regions, storms are much less fre-
quent, but change is more manifest. In a deep atmosphere,
with a high content of water vapor, there is considerable activity of cloud formations as a result. Curious though it may
be, Monsalvat is not a rainy world. Little precipitation falls,
considering the water vapor content. This has been attributed
to the general freedom from atmospheric dust which is characteristic of the planet. Consequently, from the surface the
sky, when clear, assumes a deep blue-violet color. Clouds can
range from white and gray, with a yellowish tinge, to orange,
depending upon the angle of light from the double primary.

"As one researcher subjectively described it, the light of
Monsalvat possessed a most peculiar quality—piercingly clear,
yet also possessed of a sense of fluidity apparent to the eye,
the presence of a medium, something more than just air.

Rays and beams slanted through the layers of sky, with its stirred curds and streamers of clouds, and always there was subliminally the sense of constant change, ferment, activity, that eventually began to wear upon the nerves. 'One was always looking around, over one's shoulder, behind. The background was never still long enough for one to be sure there was not some activity transpiring against it.' "

Meure yawned and turned the page. There was more, a section delving into planetary features at a highly technical level. Meure found most of it indigestible. He glanced through the data, nodded to himself. Nothing about Monsalvat was extraordinary at all; he could summarize it easily; a little larger than average, a bit lighter in mass. Monsalvat was a watery world of stormy oceans and a planet of pedestrian proportions. There were no great ranges of high mountains, although lower ranges were common. The oceans were deep, but not abysmally so. So far, it sounded pleasant, perhaps a resort world. A place of relaxation, retreat from more pressing affairs. He turned the page.

Here was a section, extracted from some other tome, on the history of the planet, and this he read more closely.

". . . in 9223, the Klesh People, who were Humans who had been artificaly racialized into a number of pure strains by a long-degenerate splinter faction of Ler, were removed from the planet Dawn and transported to Monsalvat, which had been reserved for them alone. At the time, they were considered too divergent culturally from the common Human institutions to mix freely, and were to be segregated in the system of Monsalvat to allow them time to adjust. Since no one could be considered wise enough to select among the various breeds and races of Klesh, they were left to fend for themselves, under a planetary governorship which was to maintain order and encourage peaceful habits.

". . . The history of the settlement on Monsalvat can only, in retrospect, be regarded as one of the great failures of mankind. Nothing in human or Ler history compares to it. Governor after Governor, administration after administration, all were posted to Monsalvat, with the same result: while learning the rudiments of survival, the Klesh also grew ever more recalcitrant and barbaric with the years. In time, they came to regard themselves as a destiny-blighted race, fit for nothing save the endless skirmishes, enslavements, crudities, and general barbarisms upon the surface of a planet far removed from their origins.

". . . All Klesh, whatever their type, possessed a curious view which they never gave up; none ever longed for the planet Dawn. Moreover, there was no memory whatsoever of their condition before Dawn. No folktales, no legends, nothing. The Warriors of Dawn had utterly erased their connections to the past. The result was a ferocious longing for the future, a detestation of all Ler, and a contempt for the rest of humanity. Aside from these qualities, the average Klesh may also be distinguished by his dislike (at best) of all other Klesh breeds not his own.

". . . It had been assumed that the isolation of Monsalvat would keep cultural shock to a minimum, and that general regulations would prohibit unscrupulous traders from capitalizing on their needs for the artifacts of civilized society. After a time, however, the regulations fell into disuse; Monsalvat was too far out, and the (here the text had not reproduced correctly, and a section was blotted out) . . . approaches too dangerous, and the Klesh themselves remained too faction-ridden to assemble the organization necessary for their own move into space.

"In the meanwhile, the various Klesh types flourished and declined, intermingled and crossbred, died out and were reconstituted in the eternal ferment of the planet. The number of surviving Original Breeds (the Klesh word is *Radah*), of course, declined exponentially through time, but new breeds were constantly arising in the flux, to produce in turn even more varieties than there were in the beginning (it was said that there were over 500 types of Klesh when the ships were loaded on Dawn). All, of course, claim equal merit. This process has continued to the present time. Curiously, little, if any, homogenization has occurred on Monsalvat. The culture—if it can be called that—of Monsalvat at the least agrees upon one point: that racial purity is the utmost aim, and that mixed men are to be avoided as pariahs.

". . . In 9403, the Arbitrator's post fell vacant and was not filled. Within the year, the tiny enclave of civilized society was inside an armed perimeter, and the Governorship was effectively at an end. By 9405, all remaining Humans were off Monsalvat. It may be added here that the surviving members of the mission were rescued by armed warship, an astounding turn of events not seen since the Tau Ceti Crisis of 5225.

". . . Traders, explorers, various academic bodies continued to make sporadic visits from time to time, but, over the years, these contacts became even more hazardous, and in consequence, the visits declined. Monsalvat is no longer a port of call. Now and again some ship passes by, perhaps a rare landing is attempted; the results of these brief visits tell the same tale—the Klesh seem to have stabilized as to number of types, but the life there is as hazardous as it ever was. Conditions remain chaotic, if not anarchic."

There was a simple map, followed by another section discussing the various Klesh types, their numbers, locations, habits. This information was wryly preceded by a caveat that it was sadly outdated and would probably no longer be true, for anyone foolish enough to attempt a landing on Monsalvat. Meure read the descriptions with amazement and wonder, made fearful by the range of variation among creatures very like himself, ultimately sprung from the same soil. Humans, he reminded himself, now showed little more variation than the Ler. But there, he read of races on Monsalvat whose members were well over two meters in height; others were hardly more than a meter. Some were so pale and unpigmented that their veins lent a bluish tinge to the skin: others were colored a dull carbon-black. Some were hairy enough to be considered furred; others were totally hairless. Every conceivable variation occurred on Monsalvat. Some persisted, none seemed to gain any permanent advantage, and none seemed able to dominate any major section of either of the four continents.

Meure placed the papers on a nearby shelf and turned out the light, pulling the covers up. Monsalvat! He had forgotten it, of course. It had been a tiny datum in the history courses in school, something to forget. The place where men still had races, a concept so savage and barbaric he found he could not imagine it. And they were going there, directly there, not just visiting, but for a purpose. Meure felt sleep coming, and did not resist, despite the feeling of apprehension that had entered his mind.

Sleep was not peaceful. He tossed and turned in the compartment, certain he was disturbing the others. But all remained quiet and dark, and each time he went back to the uneasy sleep. Finally, he began to dream. At the first, there were merely disconnected fragments, symbols, images. They would flit into view, and then vanish, permutating into something, someone else.

Then, quite easily and unexpectedly, the transformation took place and his dream became coherent, as vivid as reality. He was in a palace. That was clear. Not very luxurious, he thought curiously, but he knew that to be a subconscious comment. It was a palace, all right. A place of stone, great dark stones, heavy and massive, cut and dressed and fitted together without mortar. It was a palace, and it was his. He could move at will. But he also knew it to be a prison in some subtle sense. There was one of whom he was aware who served, but who was to be feared. Meure knew this, but did not comprehend. He was pacing back and forth in an anteroom. Then, shifting, he was in a deep vault under the palace, or fortress. There was light from pitch torches set in crude metal sockets bolted to the stone walls. He paused uncertainly . . . He was about to do something. Something he feared, something . . . dishonorable, so it seemed. Something his mind would not form an image of. He feared unknowns, and alternatives surrounded him. But there was a horrible bright emotion of triumph mixed with the fear and the horror, a feeling of a revenge to come, an emotion so raw and direct that Meure almost woke up. He returned to the dream, sensing that he was losing it. He held something in his hand, something cold and metallic and sharp, almost cutting his hand, so tightly did he grip it. He set a deadfall in a doorway, then stepped within. Inside was an ornate mirror, and he turned and looked in the mirror, as if for a last look. A block of stone was poised to fall over the doorway. He looked, and the image would not form. He tried harder, he had to see, in the dim red light, what he looked like. And at last, something cleared, and Meure felt himself floating upward into wakefulness. But he could see the face in the mirror, he could see: it was the face of a stranger, an utter stranger. It was a sharp, harsh face, full of lines around the eyes and mouth, framed in curly red hair and marked by a neatly trimmed full beard and mustache, the same wild red color as the hair. A hard face, angular and bony, but small, too. The eyes were squinting to see in the light, but there was a leer of triumph, too, an evil smile. Clenched teeth gleamed.

Meure Schasny awoke in a clammy sweat, eyes staring. Something with the eyes! He had looked from the mirror, downward . . . he could not remember. The thread had broken. For an instant, fully awake, he felt an odd paradox often noted by persons who have had an especially vivid, enigmatic dream, an oracular dream: that the memory upon awakening was stronger than the dream-experience itself. The red-haired man, the harsh, sharp face of a roughneck, a brawler. Familiarity hovered close, immanent. Meure almost knew the man. A shivering sense of unreality passed over him, as a chill: he knew the man—he *was* the man. And yet at the same time, he wasn't. He was also himself. He felt as if he could almost remember a name . . . Meure Schasny had never personally known a red-haired man in his entire life. The sense of immediacy began to fade. Meure heard small noises from the other parts of the communal cabin. The others, they were now rising, up and about.

Meure did not think of himself as overly introspective, and he filled his time with things to do, reasoning that the curious dream was no more than that; a curious dream, and that his attention to it would wane after a time. He did not speak of it to anyone. Not Halander: he would think Meure a mooncalf. Not Ingraine Deffy, who had already put on one of the overshirts in the locker. Not Audiart . . . not yet, at any rate. Certainly not to any of the Ler present. They were polite enough, but also very distant; Flerdistar and Clellandol were also occupied with one another in a way Meure did not understand, as if they were studiously avoiding one another. In any event, neither seemed interested in anything deeper than the most superficial contact with him.

Day-cycles passed aboard the *Ffstretsha*. Audiart donned the Ler clothing, as being more comfortable. Halander followed, and then Meure, too. He visited the wardroom on the upper deck several times, once just wandering around. The view through the vision screens remained the same in general features as the first time he had seen through them: blackness, distant points of stars, slowly moving past, and in the rear screen, the ominous bulk of the cruiser *Thlecsne*, although at the last viewing it seemed that there was more of the rolling and pitching motion visible in the screens, and that the *Thlecsne* in particular seemed to be rolling rather heavily, almost laboring. . . . Meure did not understand how Spsom ships operated, so he admitted that he could not interpret the rolling motion as anything relevant to himself. But he kept thinking of the image in his mind of a ship, rolling and pitching on the heaving surface of a very rough sea.

A change began to be visible among the Spsom as well. Meure's first impression of them all alike had been one of relaxed competence, knowledgeable professionalism; they seemingly ran the smallish ship *Ffstretsha* without visible effort or interpersonal friction. The Captain reigned; the Astrogator flew; the Overseer kept the unseen slaves busy, and Vdhitz saw to the general functioning of the ship. To be sure, the change was subtle. But it did seem as if the crew were now in a hurry more than at first, that they were going to additional effort. The doorway into the bridge stayed closed more often, and then all the time. Then the wardroom was closed off. Vdhitz, when seen, seemed to be slightly in a hurry.

And the dream remained in the back of Meure's mind. After some time, several day cycles, he sought out Vdhitz in the Spsom's usual location in the after part of the ship. No closed doors stopped him; he went farther and farther back. The curving passageway hid the view ahead, and grew narrower. At last, it opened up into a cramped circular chamber. There, Meure met a most curious scene.

Vdhitz was bending over a still form lying on the floor, an odd shapeless form which Meure's mind at first refused to resolve. Behind Vdhitz stood another similar creature, looking down, unmoving. Beside the creature was Zdrist the Overseer, bearing in one hand an odd device, part handle, part glove, open at irregular intervals, a handle for a thin rod; presumably a Spsom weapon, although Meure could not see what its function was. There were no openings, nor anything appearing to be a projecting device.

The two creatures were apparently the natives of Vfzyekhr. The one standing was about half the height of a Spsom, completely covered with a deep pile of off-white, colorless dull fur. It had two legs, two arms, both short. It seemed to possess a head and neck, but he could make out no other features; the fur covered everything. After a moment, Meure could not be certain the creature was even facing him.

He waited. Vdhitz stood, spoke quietly with Zdrist, who answered. Then, both spoke in an undertone with the remaining Vfzyekhr, who made only a slight rocking motion from side to side. Then the two Spsom conversed again. Vdhitz reached to the side, to a wall panel high up, touched a lighted button. At the back of the compartment, where Meure had not seen a door or any suggestion of one, an iris formed, and then opened to full dilation. The Vfzyekhr turned about and scampered up into the revealed silvery passageway beyond, apparently crossing the axis of the opening at a right angle, where it turned and waited. Zdrist manipulated the device on his hand, and removed it, handing it to the other Spsom. Vdhitz took the device, and Zdrist climbed into the opening with the Vfzyekhr. Vdhitz closed the opening; then caused another opening to form off to the left and low. Into this he thrust the still form lying on the floor. It was only when he had completely finished his task, including stowing the antennalike device, that he turned to face Meure.

He said, "Eh hef been brectising speeking. Yur speetsh. Eh hhowp it iss bbeter now, yis?"

Meure unconsciously fell into the Spsom frontalized accent, "Oh yis, much better."

Vdhitz motioned with an ear-trumpet to the back of the compartment. "We lusst one of our Vfzyekhr now. Very bed, thet. Zdrist will now hef to hellip, in the tubes. If we lose the other one, Eh will hef to sweb them."

"What did the . . . ah, Vfzyekhr die of?"

"It was hurrt, frem the worrk."

"Injured?"

"Yis, yis, the word. Eendzhur'red. It is verry rough now, bed spess here, *verry* rough. Denjurous! End there iss a sterm now too."

Meure ventured, "I see motion in the screens in the wardroom; it seems rougher now than when we started. Is that what you mean? We can't feel it in the ship."

"You will, soon. If it gets stronger. But wee egsbected something lek this. But not so rough."

"What do we do then? Turn back?"

"The Kepiten will hef to speek with the Lirmen. Eh don't know; they hef alreddy ped, end, eh, eh," he laughed, a short, barking chuckle, "Shchifr hess alreddy spendt dit. A SSpsom-spi shipp iss elweys in debbit." He reflected for a moment, then added, "Et's thet Demm plenet Minsilvet, ef kurs. Thiss iss a pert of spess we evade, ehh, how you seyyit . . . lek the plegg!"

The large, expressive eyes tracked off Meure for a moment, moved randomly, unfocused, as if Vdhitz were reflecting on some internal vision. At last the attention returned, and he added, "Spess iss net emmpity, end ets different from one pless to another; one pert iss smooth, enother reff, still enother full of udd mutions, whish we learn . . . Thiss pert sims to heff the werst of ehf'rrything."

After a time Meure asked, tentatively, "I wanted to ask you if Spsom ever had dreams."

"What iss 'drim' word signify?"

"Visions when you sleep; you see them and live them, but it is all in your mind."

"Aha—sa. *Mstli*. Yis." The Spsom said no more, and Meure could sense a subtle disapproval, as if dreams were an area Spsom did not discuss. Vdhitz added, almost off-hand, "You hedd one you den't enderstend, eh?"

Meure nodded. Vdhitz said, "Heppenz ell the temm in these perts. Ell peeples err trubbled by semething eround here, sem mere, sem less."

Meure started to speak, but Vdhitz motioned him to silence. "Tell me net of it. It iss fery bedd ferm among erselfs. You can tell it to the Liy, perhepps she will see into it end tell you whet she sees."

"The Liy Flerdistar?"

"The semm. She does something lekk thet, su eh hear."

Then he turned away and became busy with indeterminate tasks, as if he found the subject distasteful and wished no more with it. He had recommended Meure to Flerdistar in the same way one would suggest a purveyor of a vice which one found distasteful. Meure, in his turn, did not wish to make the Spsom angry at him, and so turned and left, without pushing Vdhitz further on the subject.

That evening, after the hour of supper, and after all his chores had been finished, Meure put on the cleanest overshirt he could find in the clothes locker and sought out the Liy Flerdistar. She was not within the suite; neither was Clellandol. He went out into the hallway; *Ffstretsha* was a small ship. There were only so many places where she could be.

Up to now, the ship had been quiet. There were, however the Spsom ship propelled itself through space, no sound effects attendant to the process. Once out in the empty corridor, away from the rest of the people, though, he became conscious of a sound, a series of sounds, a family of sounds, he had not heard before. They were faint, hardly discernible; mostly unrecognizable, and coming, so it seemed, from the ship itself. Meure listened. He could not identify the sounds.

He passed along the passageway toward the front of the ship, climbed the ladder to the second deck. The door to the control room was closed tight, and a dull red light shone above the doorframe. The wardroom door was open, though, and a light was coming out of it. As Meure moved toward it, Clellandol stepped out, looking back into the wardroom. When he saw Meure, he said something unintelligible back into the room, a phrase with the trilling, buzzy quality of Ler Multispeech. There was no answer from within. Clellandol passed along the passageway and disappeared down the ladder, saying nothing more.

Inside the wardroom, the room was empty, save for one occupant: Flerdistar. There were two mugs on the center table, both still steaming.

Meure had not thought the Ler girl attractive since he had seen her, and aboard the ship, she had not grown any more so. She was thin, almost bony, and unlike the slender human girl Ingraine, moved with no grace at all. Further, Meure had been put off by her imperious manners, and had avoided her as much as possible. Now, close, across the table, he could see her directly; her skin lacked tone, her mouth was thin and colorless, the eyes dull gray and slightly watery. What made the physical impression of her even stronger was the fact that she was wearing an unusual garment, such as he could see of it; it was a loose diaphanous blouse, open-necked and translucent, so that the body underneath was suggested. She sat with her elbows on the table, her body leant forward, as if weary. There was none of the usual precocious belligerence in her now.

Meure asked, "Am I intruding . . . ?"

Flerdistar answered, voice soft, controlled, but tired. Meure felt fatigued himself, just hearing the overtones in it. "No. Ask what you will of me."

Meure looked again. He could see through the cloth quite easily. There was little to see. Ler girls were nearly flat-chested as a rule, and Flerdistar was more so than most. The figure he saw was slight and boyish. Or rather childish. He began, "I do not know the forms to say this . . ."

She waved one hand, without removing it from the table, signifying that forms were inapplicable now, for some reason.

". . . One of the Spsom crewmen told me you could interpret dreams. I had one, on this ship, that lacks all meaning, and I wondered if you could help."

She smiled. "Interpreting dreams, now. There's what we need . . . No. As such, that is not what I do. I am a past-reader. I listen to the present, which is full of the ringing echoes of the past. I sift words, tales, things which literalists say are distorted, not true, but which have once been true. And gradually, line by line, I can reach out . . . and touch it. See it, very much as it was in reality. I can, if given long enough to work on it, reconstruct things people think they have forgotten."

"Why are you here, bound for Monsalvat?" Meure asked of her.

"There has always been a great mystery among my people. To you it may not have any meaning at all. Many Ler feel similarly. It is simple enough: once there was a Ler rebel. It had been assumed that she remained one, judging by subsequent events, but there was always the disturbing tale that she wasn't. There is more to it than that, of course. If she wasn't, why then did the rebellion occur, in her name. The rebel's name was Sanjirmil, which in your speech signifies natural spontaneous combustion—will-o' the wisp. Foxfire. But those Ler who were with her descended into the Warriors of Dawn, who later dwindled, and vanished. There were Humans, whom the Warriors captured, mistreated, enslaved, and bred into many pure types, and who lost. We are going to Monsalvat to talk with some Klesh, who are the only link with that past."

Meure objected, "Well enough. Everyone has heard of the Warriors, and their Klesh. But time! There is a long time between the Klesh brought to Monsalvat and the time of Sanjirmil. They would not remember her; she was gone, having lived her life probably before the Klesh-breeding started. And by all accounts, even more has happened since they have been on Monsalvat. Ferocious events, to them, at any rate. You may be fortunate to get anything coherent out of them at all, much less a memory thousands of years old."

She looked blankly back at Meure. "No, it's not like that. What I weave into a coherent whole seems to the untrained to be random noise. But we know two things: we *know* them. Not speculation. Sanjirmil set forces in motion that made the Warriors and the Klesh, and separated them both from both of us. And the other is that all of the counterstories—that Sanjirmil was victim, not perpetrator, have been traced back to one common source—Monsalvat and the Klesh. I have tried to pastread elsewhere, and all I have gotten, I and all the other pastreaders that have gone before me of the House of Historians, is a radiant point from Monsalvat. Beyond that is a curtain we cannot pierce. So the answer is there, buried in the collective memory of the legends of the people."

Meure looked askance at her. "Why not ask Ler who were the wardens of the Warriors after their resettlement? After all, you do have a recall we do not."

Flerdistar shook her head. "Not so easy. We did that first. All we got from that was that there was a secret about the origin of the Warriors which was known only to certain of their number. This cult was never divulged to any Ler who guarded the remainder of the Warriors. We are prone to keep secrets. It is our nature, and I can tell you that there were Warriors who autoforgot to preserve their secret, even though by then, it was largely gibberish to them. Another problem was the Warriors themselves; they were not really Ler any more, but something else. Not Human, either. The radiation of Dawn was slowly loading them with lethal mutations. We are rather sensitive to that, you know. So that much of what we could get to by relay-memory was lost, even more so than among Humans, who would at least retain traces of the events, built into the fabric of their legends, unknown to them. No. The Warriors were a dead end. And they never revealed their cult internals. So we switched to Humans. And there, it is as I have said—either we get the official account, which we suspect, or we get Monsalvat."

"Why is it important, after all these years, centuries?" Meure asked, genuinely perplexed. "What difference does it make whether she was really a rebel or not? It was done, that's all."

Flerdistar looked directly at Meure. "It involves a very basic question about the nature of . . . being itself. Something more than Humanity, than Lerdom, than intelligence. Something Basic. Long, long ago, in your own history, a struggle to define it took place. You have forgotten it, so I will not burden you with it. But therein was no victory, for one side apparently was uninterested in defining the issue, and let the others have their say. Everything we are, you and I, goes back to that. Everything. And yet every time anyone even tentatively feels around this, there is a nagging suspicion that the other side was right."

Meure said, "What difference does it make. So they were right: then we'll change."

"It goes beyond that. If they who lost were really correct, and theirs was the more accurate view of reality, then all of us, in their terms, are insane, and have been, and will always be. But I have said much here that is far beyond you; indeed, most of it is beyond me, too. I am only repeating much of what I have heard. I am an investigative vehicle who searches for one kind of truth. And I will try to read your dream if I may. Speak of it."

Meure felt off balance, distracted by the abrupt turns of mind; he had felt a trace of the same feeling when talking with Clellandol. Almost as if, in the cases of both, their attention was . . . somewhere else. But where? He decided it didn't really make too much difference. He almost was glad her attention was divided; that he was not getting the full benefit of her attention. He began, "Everyone has dreams, but most are nothing out of the ordinary; an occasional nightmare, and we are purged. But this was . . . clear, like it was really me, but at the same time, not me, either. Someone else; I was in a castle, or a fortress—it was all made of dark stone. It was very confusing—I was the master of that place, but I feared it, or someone in it. Almost as if it had become my master. Then there was a shift, and I was in a deeper chamber, underground. It was damp, in the air, but the stone was dry. I was going to do something I feared very much, but that I knew was necessary. There was something in my hand, but I can't tell you what it was; it . . . it was sharp, but it was not a knife. I don't think it was solid. I saw myself in a mirror, and I wasn't me, I mean not the real me in front of you now. The person I saw was red-haired and had a beard. He was like the laborers who drift in and out of the Fair at Kundre. A rowdy, a roustabout, a roughneck. I was in great fear and a sense of wrong, but what dread thing we would do was to be anyway. Then I woke up."

Flerdistar looked away from Meure, her eyes focused on something very distant, something probably beyond the walls and doors of the wardroom. She said, without shifting her attention, "Understanding proceeds fastest when phenomena are sorted into related groupings; even if one's initial array is partially incorrect, the order inherent in the system suggests corrections until an approximation is reached. Dreams are also phenomena, and can be grouped. If you are not a student of this branch of knowledge, I will not bore you with the classification system currently in use; it will be sufficient to say that your dream does not arise from unsatisfied yearnings, unresolved conflicts in you; nor can it be déjà-vu: the anticipation of the future, for you are obviously not red-haired and show no inclination toward that coloration."

"How do you know . . . ?"

"A rather simple deduction: I am a stranger, of an alien race, female—if your dream were wish, you would already have forgotten it—you would certainly not tell it to me, nor would you seek interpretation, for you know the meaning already."

"True, I suppose . . . but when I say the 'I' of the dream was red-haired, I do not mean of the red hair of the Humans of today, but of old: Bright red, not the auburn-brown, say, of Audiart. That was significant to me, why I could remember it."

Flerdistar turned her full attention onto Meure now. If there had ever been any distractions in her mind's eye, they were wiped away without effort. Meure felt exposed and naked, because of the sudden attention, the full weight of it, made even more noticeable by the childishness of the girl, the watery eyes, the thin figure. Many of the old terrors of the strangeness of the Ler returned to haunt Meure then; they were adults who grew old and gray and seemed to retain the values and appearance of children; and they were also apparent children who possessed an eerie adulthood far beyond real adults.

She said, carefully, "It's that it's you, not that it has red hair."

Meure said, "But that's what I'm trying to tell you: it's not me. I didn't think anything was wrong with the dream until I saw the mirror—and I knew it wasn't me."

She replied, still focusing her full attention on him, "But you didn't know it until you looked in the mirror, eh?"

"Well, yes . . . it was—wait—too clear for a dream, like any I've had before. It was as if I were remembering it. Yes. A memory."

"What was your name?" She asked without warning.

"I can't remember it. It's just on the tip of my tongue, I know it, but I don't. I ought to know it, because I can feel it even now, hanging over me, like a threat. . . . It's a simple name, with one meaning. I can sense that. I just don't understand it; we never had barbarians on Tancred. . . ."

Flerdistar interrupted Meure, "It didn't come from Tancred, your dream. I know Tancred's history probably better than you. In fact, it was because of that history that we recruited there, rather than, say, on Lickrepent, or Ocalinda." She sighed, and some, not all, of the intense regard departed. She reflected, "Humans have become bland and normal in the last few thousand yearlings; I mean that you seem to have become as immune to history as we are. People lead ordinary lives, accomplish their ends without causing vast miseries, griefs. Gone are the great wars, the mass movements, the prophets. Tancred happens to be a product of this period, and is blander than most worlds."

Meure said, "Well, isn't that what people have been striving for all these centuries. Ler used to complain that Humans were too erratic; now that we're orderly, is that a fault, too?"

He expected a hot retort, perhaps a reprimand. Instead, Flerdistar said gently, more than he imagined she had in her, "I meant no offense . . . Ler history, such as there is of it, is smoothly contoured largely because we wish it that way. We are a cautious people. Historyless history is our nature; it is manifestly not yours, and when Human history becomes as smooth and uneventful as ours, then we expect to see other things in connection with it. You are . . . unbalanced, somehow. Peace and contentment you have attained and kept; but your total population is declining, and you are no longer opening colonial space."

"I know these things; it's no secret, either. But no one would trade his heart's-desire for a maybe-glory . . . particularly on someone else's concern."

"Well, enough, then."

"What can you tell me about the dream?"

"As I told you, this is not my specialty. I know about some of it, as one might say, by fortuitous accident. There are certain parallels . . . let me say that if I were a witch of the ancient times, and you were of my tribe, I should tell you that you had been possessed, that you should perform the appropriate rites in the secret places known to the wise men of the tribe. But of course I am not a witch, and you and I are not Stone-age tribesmen squatting before the fire."

"I don't understand what you are trying to say."

"I don't know, myself. I can put it in one context, and it comes out coherent, but when I try to put it into contemporary reference, I see a recursive pattern of contradictions."

"Explain, Liy Flerdistar; I am completely lost."

"Just so: possession. To the savage, that covers a lot of things which we classify another way and come up with a family of ills, we civilized creatures. But even if we admit such a thing, after all our civilizing, we now have to admit that we no longer have the mechanisms to cope with the .001 percent real thing. I read your event as contact with someone else, and that you should protect yourself from that influence; contact increases susceptibility."

Meure thought a moment, and said, "It would seem there is little enough I can do; as you say, I no longer have the refuges of the savage, and in addition, I am on a spacecraft bound for a destination I did not choose. Shall I apply to Shchifr to turn about and avoid Monsalvat?"

The glittering attention returned, burning. "Why do you say that?"

"It's where we're bound."

"You should hope it's not from there."

"I was reading about Monsalvat, before I had the dream. Are there red-haired Klesh?"

"There once were, long ago . . . There is much here that I like not . . ." She broke off, suddenly, as if she wished to say no more.

Meure pressed the Ler girl, daring just once. "What else?"

"Monsalvat is a planet of chaos, compared with the rest of inhabited worlds. Little better than anarchy reigns there. But other than its unusual history, there is much more—the whole region of space about it has a bad name: communications devices, fool-proof, don't work there, or rather *here*. Ships are stressed, broken up, never seen again. We fly aboard a Spsom ship because no Ler ship can approach it—here is one of several places where our Matrix Drive doesn't work."

"Somebody got in, once. They brought the Klesh to Monsalvat."

"We don't know about that period. Only since. What we know now is that it's a region of unusual turbulence, unusually strong. Like a region of storms on a planet's ocean. We are in such a storm now, and we are in great danger. The only reason we have survived so long is that *Ffstretsha* is small. *Thlecsne* had to break off days ago; it was being severely overstressed, and was near being disabled. Their Captain disengaged."

"Ours didn't?"

"Not that Shchifr wouldn't, if he could. No. It's that he can't. Spsom ships, of course, use a different system from Ler ships', but they are like ours in that they have no contained power source, but rather tap forces of space to generate momentum. Like sailing ships."

Meure said, "Like sailing ships . . . No power?"

"They have drive systems to land and take off in a planetary system. Nothing more. For distance work, they tap outside forces, just as a sailing ship uses its sails. And we are now in a situation analogous to a sailing ship in a great storm: we cannot turn, and we cannot stop. To turn would stress the sails, dismast us, and roll us out under the waves. To take in sail will allow the following seas to catch us and swamp us from behind."

"But you said *Thlecsne* disengaged . . ."

"Our last communication with *Thlecsne* was to the effect that soon after she disengaged and hove-to, the storm driving us abated in their region and they were able to proceed normally. They were damaged and had to turn to the nearest port. Believe me! Shchifr has tried. In fact, they have worked at nothing else."

"Do you know where we are headed?"

"Where else? Monsalvat, more or less, the last fix we got, at about twice the normal top speed of a Spsom ship. Can you not hear the ship groan with the stress? Can you not see in the screens the tossing and rolling? Look! Listen!"

Meure turned from the Ler girl and looked into the viewscreens; now the stars, the starry background, which had once swung to and fro, back and forth, with an easy motion, as if from a ship on a sea, moved jerkily, erratically, with sudden unpredictable lunges, after which the motion of the ship seemed in the screens to be uncharacteristically mushy, as if it were not answering its controls properly. Another thing impressed itself upon him; no longer was the medium of space empty, a mere vehicle for impulses. To the contrary, space itself seemed muddy and roiled; disorganized violent rippling motions were passing across the field of view of the viewscreens. Simultaneously, Meure listened to the ship, and the odd sounds he had heard earlier. The sounds were still muted and subtle, but now he could hear them for what they really were—the sounds of Spsom alloys in protest. He looked back to Flerdistar.

She said, "We don't yet feel them inside the ship; the system that generates the sensation of gravity negates that motion of the outside and we do not feel it. But we will, soon enough. By my reckoning, sometime tonight. Things are wearing out, being carried away by wavelike surges outside."

Meure heard the words, and digested their dire import, but somehow he failed to derive any emotional sensation from them. They were in great danger, trapped in some kind of storm, a violent cyclic alternation of the stuff of space itself, they could not apparently get free of it, and the ship was slowly being torn apart, being driven down upon Monsalvat . . . He saw that it was true, but he did not fear it. He said,

"Then they, the Spsom, are all in there." He gestured toward the bridge, where the door was closed.

"Yes. I know no more than that. Shchifr is reckoned extraordinarily skilled in ship handling, and *Ffstretsha* is built for strength according to the Spsom Canon, however odd it seems to you and me, in appearance."

At that moment, although neither one of them had heard any sound, Vdhitz appeared in the doorway to the wardroom. The Spsom was a different creature now; the fine, short fur was streaked with damp marks—perspiration, and the Spsom's eyes did not seem to track completely together. Its ears were drooped and dispirited. Nonetheless he motioned to Flerdistar.

When she responded, Vdhitz immediately began in his own language—a seemingly endless series of hisses, clicks, dental stops and spittings. Without waiting for a reply, he slid back toward the bridge and vanished.

Flerdistar sat quite still for a moment, staring off into space, as if ruminating. Translating? She pushed her chair back from the table, and it slid, not along the floor, but according to some positioning mechanism. She stood, and said, distantly, abstractly, as if discussing some far-off exercise, "The situation is thus: *Ffstretsha* is finished. All the directional control projections are gone, blown out, torn away. Space-anchors are deployed sternwards and a single surface remains forward to stabilize us. The conditions outside have at the least stopped worsening; we have held together thus far—we should continue in one piece. We are approaching the system of Monsalvat at great speed, but fortunately, the planet is on the far side of the system primary, and the turbulence of the planetary system added to normal forces should slow us to a manageable approach. Shchifr believes he can make a clean planetfall, but that is all he can do. The ship is . . . broken, somehow. There was a lot in the other's speech I did not understand. We will have one shot at it, straight in and land. Once we go sublight, we'll start losing air. They got off a distress signal, which was heard and relayed by the *Thlecsne;* and answered by a Spsom craft called the *Ilini Visk,* which will attempt to approach Monsalvat after discharging cargo and rerigging for extreme duty . . . The *Ilini Visk* is a smaller vessel, but very spaceworthy. At the least, they will make the effort."

"How long will it take . . . the rescue?"

"We will see Monsalvat sometime tomorrow; it could be as much as a year until we see *Ilini Visk*."

"I don't understand. If they could answer a distress call, how could they be so far away?"

"Spsom communications systems have great range; the *Ilini Visk* is a great distance from us. There are a few others nearer, but none sufficient for Monsalvat. So, now!" Her manner shifted without warning, became peremptory. "Below, and make ready! Gather all we can carry. We shall have to survive there until rescue can be effected."

She made to depart the wardroom, and Meure did not hinder her. As she cleared the table, he could see the remainder of her clothing, which had been concealed below the table. Flerdistar had been dressed in *Dhwef-Meth-Stel** fashion, a mode of dress not ordinarily displayed, by custom, before Humans. The long lines of the *Dhwef* swirled about the girl's narrow hips, and then she was gone.

Meure slowly made his way out of the wardroom, down the ladder, back down the passageway to the suite of rooms. In his mind he heard the words of the girl about the fate of the *Ffstretsha*, and in his ears he listened to the now-audible creaking and groaning of the ship. He felt a slight vertigo from time to time, as if in a light earthquake; the motion was beginning to be felt. And at a deeper level, he remembered what he had gone to seek out Flerdistar for: the dream, and what she had told him about it. Possession. He snorted to himself. No, not quite that, she had said. Something like that, but conceptually more subtle. The ship gave a sudden zany lurch sideways, which could definitely be felt, and Meure occupied his attention with holding on.

In the common room, there was no one. Seemingly, Flerdistar had already passed this way. She had not stopped. The lights were turned down to minimum, and the doorpanels

---

* Basic forms of Ler clothing remained static, and were oriented toward one or another of the four elementals, Fire, Air, Earth, Water. *Stel* was a gauzy, translucent, loose blouse, tied with ribbons at the top, which was a loose, open neck; below, it fell about to the hips, where it was tied with another ribbon. *Dhwef* was a long, wide, trailing loincloth, the ends falling to the feet. The upper end was usually held in place by a string of beads, or in extreme cases, by a chain of flowers. The mode most common to wearing of the *Dhwef* could be politely described as the "mood conducive to amorous dalliance." It could also be construed as an invitation to the same. Needless to say, after the Ler manner this was behavior governed by the Water Elemental.

were secure. Meure turned into the right side, the compartment for the four Humans, entered, closed the panel behind
him. All seemed quiet, at least for the moment.

Meure climbed the narrow ladder to his own bunk, slid
within. He wondered if Flerdistar had intended for him to
awaken them all immediately. He thought not, listening.
Here, the noises of the ship were somewhat less than outside,
in the corridor. He could here no motion from the other side,
no sounds here, either. He reflected, somberly; surely a ship
as well-finished as the *Ffstretsha* had alarm bells, or horns, or
klaxons, or buzzers of some kind to alert passengers. After
all, Spsom had ears, too. Tomorrow, she had said. It seemed
time enough. Meure removed his clothing and turned out the
light.

He turned to the wall as he pulled the covers over him, settling into what promised to be an uneasy sleep. Then Meure
remembered that he had left the sliding panel to the bunk
open. The ship made a motion. He thought of closing the
panel, for he did not wish to be pitched onto the deck; it was
a good drop to the floor below. So he turned to close the
panel, and saw, silhouetted in the glow of the standby lights
from the kitchen unit, a dark, rounded shape filling the opening. The visitor slid into the bunk-compartment, and closed
the panel. Meure started to say something, but he felt a finger
placed over his lips. He could still see a little, for the compartment retained tiny indicator-lamps recessed into the walls.
Enough to recognize the shape as that of Audiart. He half-
rose, on one elbow, to sit up, but she pulled the covers back
and slid in beside him, almost before he could make the motion. Meure covered the girl, finishing the motion by embrac-
ing her with his free arm. Her nose brushed across his, and
the soft, fragrant hair trailed across his face. She said, below
the level of a whisper, "No words, is all I ask." Meure
nodded that he understood, feeling cool bare skin against his
own; warmth beneath. He knew what to do; now there were
no doubts. None whatsoever.

3

ACELDAMA

"This question 'who art thou?' is the first which is put to any candidate for initiation. Also, it is the last. What so-and-so is, did, and suffered: these are merely clues to that great problem.

—*A. C.*

Night it was: the terminator had long since passed its westerly way across the high plains of the land Ombur, which was an antique central portion of the continent Kepture. In the western sky, a first-quarter Moon could be seen, dim and small, casting hardly more light than that of the stars.

To the east, the roll and whoop of the prairies increased their pitch, culminating in a low, undistinguished range of hillocks, which fell away on their farther sides, down through broad swales and gullies, to the vast delta of the river Yast, the far side of which could not be seen even in the light of day. But down there was a great darkness, and the pinpricking of a multitude of tiny lights. The lights shimmered and flickered in the nighted gulfs, as if ripples were passing before the points of light; but overhead the light of the stars was steady and flickered very little at all.

The dim starlight resolved, at distance, few details of the plains of Ombur. Little distinctive could be made out, save a faint trace, a bare track, winding eccentrically from west-southwest to the east, where it wound between two knolls and vanished. North was an emptiness, where the plains stretched to meet the Yast as it curved to the west, unseen. In the south, a gradual rising of the land led to a series of hogbacks which obscured the view. Beyond were more of the rolling prairie uplands, more of Ombur, which extended far to the west and the south.

Those-who-used-Names recalled the name Ombur with

48

fondness, for Ombur had once echoed from horizon to horizon with the name of one lord; perhaps Ombur had possessed one lord before that, or many times: Time was long, in Ombur, just as it was in the other named lands of Kepture, which in their times had also known one lord of their own, once, twice. In the West of Kepture were the lands Ombur, Warvard, Seagove. Across the North, facing the Polar parts of World-Ocean, were ranged Boigne, Yerra, and tiny Urige; the East was Intance and Nasp. In the center were Incana, encompassing most of the highlands, and Yastian. Kepture bore the outline of two potatoes grown together, the western part being the larger, but the eastern extended somewhat more to the North, whereupon Urige was cold, and Cape Hogue at the southernmost tip of the western parts was tropical.

Ombur was neither lifeless nor empty, nor even free of movement across its broad swathes and textures. One such motion now was proceeding out onto the plains from the line of hills to the East, a motion which was that of a small cart, unpainted and weathered quite gray, moving along slowly and with deliberation, almost with leisure, pulled in no great haste by two gaunt creatures of anthropoid shape, heavy-framed and large, walking steadily, methodically. The cart rolled on two immense solid wheels, and featured a small roofed cupola at the front for the driver; the whole followed the irregularities of the track with a patient, rolling motion, swaying from side to side.

On a shelf attached to the rear of the cart sat a hulking, lumpy shape, motionless save for that imparted by the rolling of the cart; inanimate, or asleep. Or merely still. Inside the cupola at the front sat the driver, who now bestirred himself, looking carefully about the landscape, as if looking for landmarks. He paid little attention to the creatures pulling the cart. The driver appeared to be well-furnished about the midsection, fleshy but just shy of fat, a balding man approaching middle age.

The driver, by name Seuthe-the-Bagman Jemasmy, now nodded to the draybeasts, the Sumpters, whispering in a low tone to them, "Dur, Dur." The Sumpters paced on for a time, glanced at one another out of the corners of their heavy-browed eyes, and let the cart slow itself to a stop. The creaking and rattling of the springless vehicle continued, then it too stopped, and now only the breathless silences of the night could be heard. The figure at the back of the cart looked awkwardly over one shoulder, leering madly, teeth gleaming in the starlight. Jemasmy turned and leaned over, to speak into a compartment inside the cart, saying softly, "Morgin. Are you awake?"

A grunt answered him. Presently a stiff and slow-moving figure, a spindly man of no easily discernible age, phyle or sept, topped by a bushy, iron-gray stubble on his head, emerged and climbed into the vacant seat to the right of the driver. There was yet silence among the rolls and plunges of the land Ombur. Little wind could be sensed. All that could be heard was the deep breathing of the Sumpters, the gaunt, heavy creatures who pulled the cart.

Jemasmy volunteered, "Your wish was to be awakened when Sovin Hogback obscured Vatz Pinnacle, on the plain. We are here."

"What now the track, Seuthe?" queried Morgin-the-Embasse Balebaster, in a hoarse voice.

"The Lambascada Swathe, of course."

Morgin mused for a moment over the empty plains, at last getting to his feet, and leaning out and holding a roof-brace precariously, looked about, as if to reassure himself that he was where he wished to be. He stood thus for a long time, sometimes smelling the air, and also pausing to listen carefully. Morgin looked long into the empty, rolling distances; then he slowly and stiffly climbed down from the cart to stand thoughtfully in the track, alongside the Sumpters, who towered over him, long-legged, short-armed. The Sumpters stood quietly, shifting their weight from one splayed foot to the other in an unvarying, monotonous rhythm. Morgin patted the nearer one affectionately on the rump.

He said, "All seems proper for the moment. Very good. Have Benne feed and water the Sumpters." At this, the dray-beasts blew air through their cheeks, making a flapping, blowing sound. Morgin continued, "Here we shall pause; there is time to read the signs before we leave the swath and sojourn to the west."

Jemasmy queried, "Not indeed to Lambascade?"

"No. Not directly, although it was my intention that *they* so imagine." Morgin gestured with his head in the direction from which they had come. "First," he said portentously, "on to Medlight. Then, in turn, to Utter Semerend. We can turn south to Lambascade after that; I would speak with Ruggou first."

Jemasmy chuckled, "And not let the others know, eh?

Ayoo! Good old Gutsnapper! He may not rule over as much of Old Ombur as he'd like, may St. Zermille continue to thwart his plans, but you still have to account for him firstly. Rightly so, Master Morgin. To Medlight, then, and Utter Semerend."

Morgin winced at Jemasmy's use of the vulgar cognomen of Incantor* Ivak Ruggou, leader and chief of Sept Aurisman. He hoped that Jemasmy would not forget and blurt that out in the hearing of Ruggou, or one of his favorite henchmen. There were not many to call Ruggou Gutsnapper to his face, and remain ignorant of the procedures by which he had gained that name.

Jemasmy hung the reins upon a peg and also dismounted, making a sign to the hulking figure at the rear of the cart. Benne-the-Clone dismounted the cart awkwardly, as if it were the first time he had ever done it, and began to rummage under the rear quarter of the cart for barrels of water and bags of mash for the Sumpters. Standing back from the cart with a load under each arm, Benne displayed a short, bowlegged figure with excessively long arms corded with ridged muscles.

As Benne carried his load to the Sumpters, Jemasmy, now by the massive axle, could be seen to be carrying a large pouch slung over one shoulder, with something weighty in it. Jemasmy inspected the wheel-mountings of the cart, while Morgin walked about, apparently at random, an abstracted expression on his face. Finally Jemasmy straightened from the wheel, and rounded the cart to join Morgin in his perambulations.

Jemasmy waited a little for Morgin to notice him, and said, "By the Lady, let be a pest upon the Delta and all its ratfolk! I do believe that the bearing is going bad!"

Morgin appeared not to have heard the remark. He asked, still looking into the distances, "Were we followed?"

Jemasmy answered, "No. At the very least, not from the Delta itself. Up the swale, I saw nothing. All was innocent. But once on the plains, the Sumpters have been somewhat

---

* Incantor: a middle-ranking title-of-nobility from the Phanetical system, which included, from the highest, Phanet, Feodar, Incantor, Deodactor, and Sphodic. The suggestion was that the office was elective, despite the fact that it usually was not. Titles in the Phanetical system were not usually associated with dynasties, which were covered by the Phyacic system, listing from the highest, Phyacor, Erchon, Hospod, Peshe and Phreme. Both these were the ancient orders of nobility of Kepture and the other continents as well. An Incantor would equate somewhat to a Baron, or perhaps Warlord.

uneasy. Not from something close; perhaps a band of distant hunters, watching for a straggler from the Delta."

"One never knows," somberly reflected Morgin. "Perhaps you are correct; in any event, let us continue to hope. On the other hand . . . could be Haydars, or Meor. I should not care to meet either in the darkness of Nightside, although were the band small enough, we could probably stand off Meors."

"Three of us . . . Hm. We do have a ballista in the cart, and Benne is good with one."

Morgin reflected, "There is an immanence in the air which I sense with the Sumpters. As much as I would regret it under other circumstances, perhaps we should consult the Prote. Yes, have it decyst."

Jemasmy advised, "Morgin, you know it will be ill of temper. You did keep it decysted during the whole meet."

"Yes, yes, of course. There was little enough choice there. Yet here, too. I am uneasy, apprehensive. Something stirs in the nighted gulfs about us; there is motion, fear, and . . . hope. I know; I feel it. But not from whence it comes. Most certainly we must have a reading of the locus . . . I could not place it above Hospod Alor of the Lagostomes that he pay a Meor formation to harry us."

"Alor? But what could he pay?"

Morgin made an airy gesture. "What else? The usual, of the course: girls. Or a brace of gelded bucks for meat." He shrugged. "It's all they have."

Jemasmy said resignedly, "Very well. Now, I tell you, thusly never went events in Cantou when I was Bagman to Thrincule." He reached gingerly into the pouch, as if half expecting to find a live coal there. He felt along a cold, hard shell, feeling for a certain node. Jemasmy located the node, pressed, felt something gelid give a little. He withdrew his hand fastidiously, adding, "In Cantou, one could always trust the Cantureans to treat an Embasse and his Bagman rightly. No treachery."

Morgin agreed. "Kepture seethes with it, rightly enough. Just so came I from great Chengurune and the Dawnlands of the east; and there, too, we had Embasses in plenty. Here; there are never enough."

"Or in Glordune," added Jemasmy.

"Glordune," said Morgin, "will have to wait. It is not for me."

Jemasmy commented, "Nor for me. They still adhere to the old ways, so it's said."

Benne growled, from the general area of the Sumpters. "The old way, yes. 'Yoo, they keep it good, too, they do, the Glorionts, but they call on the Lady no less than we." Benne-the Clone had once been a sailor on the wide bent seas of Monsalvat, and had set port in Glordune, wildest of four continents.

Morgin said, half-irritably, "Respect to St. Zermille none the lesser, but the Embasses were not her doing, nor the folding of the tribes*. Those are of Cretus the Scribe."

Jemasmy added, ritually, completing the formula, "Before the treachery out of Incana that brought the Empire to nothing; that kept the Kleshmen from their natural home the stars."

Morgin mused, "Such a strange old dream, that . . . Is the Prote decysted yet?"

"Not yet, Morgin." Jemasmy felt inside the shoulder bag, exprimentally, gingerly. "Softening, but not open yet."

Morgin nodded, acknowledging. He expected no better, for back down in the Delta, he had pushed the Prote to what he had thought were its usual limits—and beyond. But it had not once broken cooperation. Curious.

One of the native life-forms of the planet, a prote was a creature of curious abilities and even more curious limitations. No one was quite certain exactly what a prote really was, nor had anyone stepped forward with knowledge of how it fed, lived, excreted or reproduced. If indeed it performed any of the acts which fell under those headings. Generally sessile, a prote could exude pseudopodia and move, very slowly, on occasion. It rarely did.

But while having no identifiable traits common to most life-forms, a prote did have two abilities recognized as uncommonly useful by all: The first was speech, via sound waves to Humans, and by some unknown method among each other, apparently with little or no limitation of distance.†

---

* An event in the far past of Monsalvat. It was said that Cretus spoke to all septs, tribes, phyles, directing them to be complementary to one another, rather than maniacally competitive. That this ideal failed was unimportant. Cretus was remembered for that he was the first of Monsalvat, which is of the Klesh, to say so and try to implement it.
† Not via electromagnetic radiation. The first explorers had confirmed intercommunication among protes, firstly by observing one prote act upon information only another had known. Later, when they could speak with protes, they had testimonial evidence. But they did not uncover how the intercommunication took place. The electromagnetic spectrum was searched, without success. The problem had not yet been solved when organized society abandoned the planet.

The second ability was, in the end, even more valuable, and even less understood; a prote perceived. With no identifiable sensory organs, and having no permanent characteristics save its own protean flesh, a prote was capable of perceiving the disposition and condition of everything about itself, on occasion to considerable distance. That was their inimitable key to survival. A wild prote simply watched its surround, and, at a certain threshold of danger, encysted, becoming impervious to any method of attack yet discovered on Monsalvat. Fire, sword, projectile: all were alike in their uselessness. Thrown into bonfires, they vanished. Thrown off cliffs, they were not found. Taken into space, the containers arrived empty.

There were no young protes, nor had ever one been seen to bud, spore, mate or perform any known category of reproductive act. And the communication that passed from one prote to another, while seemingly unlimited in space, was curiously circumscribed in content: descriptions of conditions passed effortlessly, but complex ideas, or rational discourse was blocked.

Protes were somewhat rare; and they were the jealousy guarded possessions of the Embasses* of Monsalvat. Or, perhaps the Embasses were the property of the Protes. Klesh did not trouble themselves with distinctions that made no difference to the order of things. And the protes? They found the Embasses to their liking, or tolerance, or to an emotion known only to protes. If they possessed any. Embasses who stepped beyond their function were quickly humbled, for their prote would leave them, or contrive to be lost, and found again by another mixed-blood. A prote could not be coerced.

Morgin had now been in Kepture for about twenty of the years of Monsalvat, and for the whole of that time, with the

* An Embasse was a person, usually of dubious origin and questionable race, who performed communicative functions between the various tribes, and other social organisms of the Klesh on Monsalvat. They could not be called peacemakers, for they arranged conflicts as often as they negotiated to prevent them. Rather, they functioned as leavening, controlling agents in the eternal racial ferment of Monsalvat. "Civilization," denoting desirable conditions of order, was related solely to the effectiveness of the Embasses of a given area, not to any arbitrary concept of order held by any tribe or group. In this context it may be noted that the continent Glordune was considered "wild" solely in that there were no openly-practicing Embasses there. The kinds of barbarisms practiced in Glordune were not more in kind or number than on other continents—just more disorderly.

services of several Bagmen, he had carried his prote. In the course of that association, never entirely pleasant, Morgin had learned much he could not always put accurately into words. But he had also become sensitized to unusual conditions, and had learned when to call upon the powers of the prote. An act he never did casually, for protes were both ill-tempered and rather oracular in their utterances.

Now in the soft plains night, in the silence under the stars, Morgin began to walk about restlessly, casting short, sharp glances at the horizons, the empty prairie distances, not so much looking for a sign as casting for some subtle something out of place. The sense of Immanence was becoming stronger; from its rate of onset, and the strength of the growing hunch, he could almost read it. Almost. *Haydars,* he thought. A Meor band would leave more obvious traces, hang back, probe, feel them out, and take days to make up their minds. Morgin could recall travellers who had been trailed by Meors for ten days before being attacked. Haydars, on the other hand . . . They would vanish, leaving a sense of terror behind, or suddenly come straight in without warning.

Jemasmy broke into his searching, "You suspect treachery of the Lagostomes? I shouldn't think they'd have it in them to dare to."

Morgin looked back, from the deep-blue darkness of the horizons, curiously, as if he were seeing Jemasmy for the first time. He answered, after a moment, "Lagos? What? Oh, that; yes, of course, of a matter of course, Seuthe. Of a certainty I suspect them. They are more desperate than most—driven into the Delta by pressure from surrounding tribes and Phyles, and now stuck there. Floods, and then storms from the Inner Water, nothing to trade and never enough food, and the highest birth rate in the whole world. And all around them the predatory races of Kepture, and an ancient compact which says that where a lance in the ground does not bring water, so there does the Lago become prey. And nothing to make a ship of, and no land to receive them, if they had, Inner Water or Outer*. So now they seek to buy a stone's throw at a time, slipping back up the Yast and trying to confound both Ombur and Incana. This, Ruggou suspected. And so likewise thinks Molio Azendarach of the Kurbish Windfowlers. A pact with the Meors to the south. The Lagos know

---

* The Four Continents enclosed the world-ocean into an Inner Sea and a much greater Outer Ocean, which in turn covered more than half the planetary surface.

that we must return to Ruggou, to the Ombur. If Ruggou knows, then so will Azendarach. And then all these careful moves for nothing, once more exporting slaves to Azendarach, while Ruggou combs their western bluffs and encourages the Haydars. Then the Meors will tire of them, too."

Jemasmy ventured, "Is it not the Embasse's part to be neutral?"

"Yes, yes, of course, but not to blindness. The Lagos are a plague. Unchecked, they would engulf all Kepture, and no less than Azendarach and Ruggou, I also desire to see them kept in the Delta, in their land Yastian. So have all the other Embasses." Morgin paused. "And the Prote?"

A flat, timbreless voice issued forth from the bag, sounding clearly, close at hand, but also as if the speaker were a vast distance away: "To the disturbance of One-Organ Morgin is this instrument come; speak, then, o singlet."

Morgin cast down an evil glance to the bag. "Address me not with such endearments; perform function, encyst again—this is all that I ask, not these repeated abuses." Morgin's vulgar cognomen arose from a fact pertaining to his anatomy, a lacking occasioned by an injury sustained in his more ribald youth. It was said that Morgin had engaged the attentions of a young lady whom, it would seem, had already been spoken for. Morgin never appreciated being reminded of this. Jemasmy looked away, concealing a ribald smirk. Benne-the-Clone stood by the feeding Sumpters and chuckled to himself, adding an insane giggle now and again.

Benne said, at last, calling across the Sumpters, "Give up the one, Morgin! It is only a goad! Emulate your loyal servant, disciple and retainer, and be liberated from the gusts of hot temperaments!"

Morgin ruminated to himself. "While I try to steer a course through storm and reef, one asks why, one calls names, and the last urges castratodom." He sighed deeply. He would never be free of the abuse of the Prote, nor the ignorance of Jemasmy, nor the inappropriate advisements of Benne. He spoke, now clearly, to the Prote, "East Ombur. Danger I query. Read place and tell."

There was no immediate reply, nor was one expected. The Prote said nothing, but after a moment, there began a slow stirring in the bag. Jemasmy removed the bag from his shoulders and carefully laid it on the ground. The shape-changing of the Prote was disquieting to him, an event he had never learned to like, or even tolerate. He walked away from the

bag, which continued to shift slowly, fluidly. There was motion on the ground beside the bag, a darker shadow.

After a time had passed, and the circling stars moved a
little way across the skies of Monsalvat, and clouds moved
over the face of the darkness, the voice spoke again in its
flattened, measured cadences, "The suspicions of Morgin the
Embasse transpose into the farsight of a prote."

Morgin now approached the bag on the ground, circum-
spectly; neither he nor any of the rest said anything, but
rather remained silent, to allow the prote to develop its oracular remark after its own fashion.

The Prote continued, "Darkness and light are one, but for
the shadowcaster; Ombur teems with movement, fierce life,
men, near-men, not-men. Korsors and Eratzenasters,* Haydars and Meor and Lagostome. To certain of these, such as
this band do not exist; to others, interest. To others, central
attentiveness. Lagostomes observe your movements from the
eastern swale, awaiting a small band of Meors arriving along
the hogback. All are persuaded by reasonable doubt: ahead
are Haydars. Their presence disturbs, makes resolve hesitant."

Morgin asked quietly, "Where are Haydars? How far?
How many? Why are they here?"

The Prote answered, "They see you in the present; you will
see them in the future. Afoot in their custom, they could
speak with you within minutes. A moment: sensing . . .
there are . . . fifteen. One is a girl, the omenreader. Another
is an Embasse."

Morgin paused, then asked, "The Embasse. Captive?"

"Negation. They seek new lands. This is a vanguard party,
who came by air to seek an omen. The Embasse is for order
as they pass through lands."

Morgin thought swiftly, trying to foresee consequences,
considering factors which would cause a band of Haydars to
come to the East of Ombur, far from their more usual
haunts. They preferred the west and north. Their presence
would certainly disturb things. . . . Ruggou might become
more demonstrative, but the Meor would certainly withdraw
farther south. He asked, "Is their prote decysted? Can you
read names?"

---

* Native life-forms of Monsalvat, both predatory. The Korsor was
somewhat bearlike in size and general shape, but much swifter and
more graceful. The Eratzenaster was a nightmare resembling nothing
known on any other world. They were large flying predators of the
upper air. Both forms were occasionally tamed and put to odd uses.

The prote answered, "They are . . . Talras Em Margaria, Rhardous N'Hodos, Kori D'Indouane, Zermo Lafma the Garrotist, Segedine Dao Timni . . ."

Morgin cried out, "Stop, stop! May the Lady prevent me from asking who might be found in the Delta! We would spend the next ten years listening to a recitation of all the full names of all the Lagos that are, plus all the little splitlips begotten while the first list was being delivered! Three I need, and of what clan. Phreme, Embasse, Omenreader."

The Prote answered in the same toneless voice, "In that order, *S'fou* Ringuid Goam Mallam, *Cland* Joame Afanasy, *Lami* Tenguft Ouarde. Dagazaram Clan."

Morgin straightened. There was no danger to them from this group of Haydars, and their presence might be an asset. Indeed. He reflected that neutral Haydars were the best protection available. And that to read names, their prote had to be decysted. He stepped back, so he could see better around him, and said, "Let them approach. If they haven't attacked by now, they've no intent of it."

The Prote said, "They come already . . ."

Morgin asked, "Are the Lagostomes and Meor the sole danger? If so read, then you may encyst. These will cover most contingencies."

The prote did not immediately respond, and the slow, fluid movements in and around the bag continued. The voice said, now as if from a great distance, "A moment, One-Organ. The currents are roiled and turbulent. Time is required for deeper reading. . . . There is an immanence somewhere . . ."

And the bag made further motions, as the prote made adjustments to its form to enable it to read more fully the surround. Morgin was used to this pause, and expected no more from the prote. Presently it would return to its normal encysted condition. Protes always read as far as they reasonably could; they were professional worriers. But a deeper reading did require time. Morgin walked away from the bag by the side of the cart, preparing to meet the Haydars.

In the front of the cart, the Sumpters began to move nervously, stamping their feet, wagging their ponderous shoulders from side to side, causing their harness to rattle and slap against the heavy drawbar. Benne spoke softly to them, trying to calm the draybeasts. Morgin and Jemasmy both looked about apprehensively, trying to see, to hear something, but whatever it was disturbing the Sumpters, it was more subtle than their perceptions could detect. The Sumpters became

even more agitated, almost as if they were in fear of their
lives. Minutes passed slowly, as hours. And then, without any
anticipation, the Sumpters became still, so abruptly that their
harness continued to rattle momentarily after they had
stopped. Morgin and Jemasmy looked closely about, trying to
penetrate into the darkness, the limpid and deceiving distances. On a low rise no more than a few meters away was a
small group of deeply hooded and cloaked shadows of the
night; the two groups nervously watched one another, neither
making a move.

Four of the tall, thin shadows detached themselves from
the distant group and began to approach the cart in a
measured, deliberate manner. Jemasmy shivered suddenly, as
in the grip of a violent ague, but Morgin, sensing the motion
out of the corner of his eye, smiled to himself. The motion of
the approaching Haydars reassured him; he knew something
of the Haydar way, and it was in just such a manner that one
suggested benignly neutral, if not peaceful, intent.

They came closer: now Morgin could discern differences
among the shadows, differences of outline, gait, tallness, posture. He glanced behind the approaching tetrad; the remainder of the band had vanished. Of those approaching—now
Morgin could resolve a pouch such as a Bagman might carry,
after the manner of Jemasmy. A Bagman. Another walked
directly, with businesslike stride, with his cloak flapping about
his shanks. Afanasy, the Embasse. One other was proud of
bearing, but deliberate and aloof: most likely Mallam, the
leader. And the last moved as any Haydar did, flowing, striding, using its incredible height to maximum advantage, but at
the same time, with a more fluid, more graceful series of motions. The girl? Morgin strove to recall Haydar lore. Yes.
Only one unwed could serve as tribal wisewoman. So: Tenguft Ouarde.

Now they were near, glancing over Benne and the Sumpters, passing them by. Jemasmy they ignored, and Seuthe the
Bagman was grateful for their inattention. Before Morgin
they separated a little, each facing him equally. The girl, if
Morgin's suspicions were true, bent, stooped, lowering herself,
and laid a spear on the ground. It was only slightly longer
than her height, which was well over two meters. The others
were taller still.

Morgin reached within his caftan, removing a poinard-like
knife-sword, with a wavy edge; by all accounts, a vicious
weapon. This he laid on the ground before himself.

One of the group spoke, a deep, hollow, mournful voice. "I am Afanasy. You would know me as Embasse."

Morgin replied, "I am Morgin Balebaster, Embasse of the Ombur. You surprise me. I ask without intent of offense; are you truly Haydarrada?" The allusion was to Afanasy's lineage; it was the force of tradition that an Embasse be mixed-blood.

Afanasy answered, the cavernous tone of his voice changing not at all, "Not Vere-Dagazaram Haydar, as are my associates. I am of the Techiascos. Mixed enough to take the prote of my predecessor, but somewhat true in form. How may we assist you in serving order, Master Embasse of the Ombur?"

Morgin said, "Lagostomes dog our trail from the Delta, and our prote reads Meors in collusion. I think dispersed along yon hogback. I bear reports, and desire only to pass unmolested into the west to the water-places Medlight, and then Utter Semerend."

"Are you not under warrant?"

"Only within the Delta country."

"Fear them not. We met a band of Meors at dusk when we landed. Those are not worthy of the name 'enemy.' Those who survived fled east. They were unworthy of running to earth. These will do nothing. We are here to feel out new lands. No Haydar range the East Ombur, save in rare hunts."

"You will settle here?"

"The Dagazaram will divide; Ullahi will remain in the ancestral huntlands. The Iasamed will range East Ombur. Who will oppose, Embasse?"

Morgin reflected, then spoke. "I understand that Incantor Ivak Ruggou of Sept Aurisman desires that his people extend somewhat to the east."

Afanasy replied, "Aurismen? We know Aurismen. They will stay in their little walled towns and break the sod around them. So long as they content themselves with their gardens, they will know no Haydar. We do not contest territory with men of the soil."

True enough, thought Morgin. *But hardly know them? Haydars were the legendary ogres of the night, on every continent. No place was free of them, entirely, for only the Haydar were fierce enough to break and ride, in the air, the gruesome Eratzenaster. Yet it might not be such a bad idea to have a small band settled permanently in East Ombur; Haydars reproduced slowly, and they would of a certainty di-*

lute the ambitions of Ruggou. Brave or not, only fools
willingly moved into an area known to be Haydar Huntland.
They ate trespassers. He added, aloud, "Molio Azendarach,
across the Great River, has thwarted the expansions of the
Lagostomes; since they cannot walk on water, Ombur becomes worthy of their notice; the more so since the Meor can
only be pushed so far southwards down the coast. I may not
speak for the Meor, being out of their favor in the present—
yet I could tell them that Ruggou has plainly stated he in-
tends to occupy the uplands if he senses any movement west
by Lagos. This issue is a perpetual one in these parts, usually
resolved by the Lagos remaining in the Delta. My reading is
that they are to the point of defying Ruggou—he is farther
away than Molio Azendarach and has notable supply-line
problems for an investiture of the East Ombur."

Afanasy reflected, not speaking, while Mallam stood back.
The girl, Tenguft Ouarde, stepped closer to Morgin, close
enough for him to make out individual features, instead of a
gaunt Haydar wrapped in a shapeless cloak and robe, further
covered by the soft night darkness: she was tall, indeed, tall
enough that Morgin had to look up to see her face. Under
the hood were bottomless, hollow eyes, a great blade of a
nose, a small mouth. Yet in her own way she was also
smooth and young, and full of the confidence of bearing that
only beauty brings. The beauty was not in gross shapes, in
structures, but in something deeper that animated those
shapes.

She spoke, a tracery of youthful boastfulness counterpoint-
ing the husky adolescent voice, a girl's voice, even in the
deep resonances of the Haydar throat, "Lagostome peoples
are only fit for the casting of omens; they are soft and weak
and have no sinew in their souls. I read your brow! You do
not know the Haydarada: *game* is that which fulfills us, not
those who spend their lives in breeding. You may rest easily
now, Master Morgin the Embasse of the Ombur and the Incana, and say the same to Ruggou and his Aurismen. Upon
the Sun's coming, I will walk along the ridgeline there in the
east in my hunt clothing, as I came into the world and time,
with spear and knife my only companion. And not one will
cross the river."

Mallam rumbled, "*Lami* Tenguft suggests a solution to affairs of these parts."

Morgin commented politely, "It is as you expound,
Ringuid Goam Mallam. I shall say as much to Ruggou; it

would appear to be to his advantage, indeed. And so the lands of the Aurismen will not change, nor those of the Lagostome. Upon what or whom will you hunt, may I ask?"

Afanasy said, "The outcast, those who have done great wrong in their own lands; the outlaw bands, robbers and murderers; and of course those who come to hunt Haydar . . . what should they expect."

Morgin reflected and was content. Yes, just so were things resolved, usually. Be patient and an answer would come. The Haydar band would bring stability, a continuance of the state of things. And Ruggou would not be brought into contact with the realm of Molio Azendarach, which would have the effect of keeping Molio on his side of the river, and would save Sept Aurisman for a more temperate leader to succeed Ruggou, one with more pedestrian dreams. Yes. He said, "I see no impediment to your coming here."

Mallam nodded, smiled, flashing white teeth. "A-ha! That is good. So, then, here we are, all of us." He signalled with one arm to the remainder of the band, and in response several dark shapes materialized, seemingly out of the very earth, out of shadows. Mallam called to them, "Talras, Segedine! Make the signs to free the beasts! We stay! Rhardous N'Hodos and Tesselade! To the south, for a fete, one Meor. One will be sufficient for us, for the stranger-Embasse is not of the blood!" He turned to Morgin. "I may proceed assuming you do not share our custom?"

"Without offense. I hope I give none in turn."

"It is as you say . . . there are few like us in the wideness of the world. But will you rest a while? Lafma has his tamgar, for the song, and the *Lami* carries in her mind the visions of the people. She will sing of our great hunts, that our young men may on the morrow feel the wind and see far, and make the motions by the firelight that they may have before their spirits the image of the perfect woman of the people."

Morgin answered diplomatically, "When I spoke with *Lami* Tenguft Ouarde, I could see with all my senses that she was indeed a worthy vessel of your dreams. Would that I could see and hear it all, that I, an unworthy Embasse of unknown lineage, might glimpse that which your people know in full. But yet I have affairs of my own, as well, which call. I would speak with Ruggou, that his mind be correct in the way of things."

"Just so . . ." He was interrupted. One of the Haydars

who had remained behind now approached, quickly, and spoke to Mallam. The hoarse whispers said, "My S'fou Mallam: I made the signs in their proper order, but they who fly do not depart. They continue to circle, and have been joined by wild 'Natzers as well!"

Mallam responded, "Into hunt-dispersal, then! Call in the hunt! Embasse! What of the Prote?"

Tenguft, having heard, had been craning her head back, hood falling off and back, looking at the sky and the stars. Morgin looked at the girl, then at the sky. He saw nothing, but a suggestion of motion nagged at the edge of perception. Something was up there, that was sure. Tenguft said, "When they circle and are joined by the wild, there will be blood. There are almost fifty 'Natzers now waiting."

Morgin turned to Seuthe-the-Bagman, but it was not necessary, for now the Prote of Morgin the Embasse had chosen to speak. The voice of the Prote was strained, full of wavers, and hesitations. It said, "The reading is complete, near and far. Danger! Encystment has commenced. Do not move, especially to the north or east. A star is falling, and one may not run from it. Impact by the breaks, east. Something burning, from the other side of the world, from deep in the night, from far away, around the horizon. There is energy! Something is interfering with placeread!"

Morgin started. "A falling star? Here?"

The Prote continued for a little, its voice now much weakened, "Not stone, One-Organ. Something that slows, that moves against the stream, that moves of itself. I fear." At the end, the voice was highly distorted. The Prote spoke no more.

Morgin said to Afanasy, "And yours?"

"Encysted already."

Morgin said, "That which moves against the stream is a ship! The true men are returning! The men return!"

Tenguft retrieved her spear. "Or the warriors, may they eat grass, such as shall lead them to." She lifted the blade to her lips, kissed it quickly, thrust the long spear upward against the night sky of the east. She repeated fervently, "Let the Warriors return and meet their creations!"

Morgin turned with the rest and looked now to the east: at first, they saw nothing—there was the night and the darkness; the lights of the Delta could not be seen from the plains of Ombur, where they stood. And down from the starry zenith, the near stars shone clearly, without flickering, but near the horizon, close to the planet, through the dense atmosphere, they winked and trembled as if ripples were passing before them. They marked out the familiar constellations of the proper season: The Reaper, The Crown, The Netsman flinging his sparkling cluster into the South. Close to the horizon, they seemed to go on and off, some winking out for moments at a time. But there was another star there, in the East, that did not go out, red-orange and burning in the night, rising from the east, a baleful star that neither wavered nor flickered out of sight. It cleared the horizon and vaulted into the sky, growing as they watched.

4

"I once examined the horoscopes of a number of murderers in order to find out what planetary dispositions were responsible for the temperament. To my amazement, it was not the secret and explosive energy of Uranus, not the sinister and malignant selfishness of Saturn, not the ungoverned fury of Mars, which formed the background for the crime, but the callous intellectualism of Mercury. Then comes a most extraordinary discovery. The horoscopes of the murdered are almost identical with those of the assassins. They asked for it!"

—*A. C.*

For a long time, in the warm darkness of the compartment, they did not say anything; no words seemed necessary. But after an unmeasured time, Meure could no longer contain some of that which was in him, and he said, simply, "There are words that I wanted to say before, then, now, for I came to remember."

It was quiet again for another time, marked only by breathing, by heartbeats, by a small, rare rustling of the coverlet. But in the end, Audiart spoke also; she said, as simply, "And I came to forget." And then, "To cast away, be rid of, be unencumbered of . . . but I see that even as I wipe away that which has passed, the marks of my wiping make a new record, and nothing will come of what I wished but more change."

"I am changed."

"And I, by no less." But she rolled away from him and curled her body a little, as if she wished to sleep now.

Meure remained still, listening, waiting, remembering. He let his senses return him to his surroundings, to collect the feel of the ship *Ffstretsha*. There was yet a dim light in the compartment, splayed along the ceiling, coming from the kitchen lights down in the space below. He remembered: he had intended to shut the compartment door, but that had been interrupted, and it was still open. His body was damp with sweat, and there was a warm, bare body next to his. And now he felt again the motions of the ship: rockings from side to side, damped, gentle, but reduced greatly from the true motion which must be outside. The ship moved on all three axes, sometimes simultaneously, sometimes by two axes, sometimes along one axis alone. The motions were random, unpredictable, now seemingly less severe, but broader in scope. The ship calmed, and almost became still, and then without anticipation began a surging motion ahead. To Meure, his inner ear system suggested a mushy acceleration ahead, as if pushed from behind, while the ship pitched upwards, nose-high; this was followed by an indescribable slewing, which rapidly altered into an angry shaking, a series of jerkings. He heard, from below, a hissing sound from the direction of the kitchen unit, and the lights went out. Not at once: they faded out. A red light illuminated in the ceiling of the compartment, and from a concealed speaker, a beeping tone began, interrupted at regular intervals by the breathy lisping of a recorded Spsom announcement. The compartment door began sliding shut. Meure half-rose to reach to stop it, rising at last out of the passive waiting, suddenly realizing; he reached across Audiart, who was also trying to move, but he felt a prickling along his fingertips, a numbing. He reached closer, and there was a bright flash of energy discharge. He drew back, rubbing his fingers, against the back wall. Audiart pressed her body back from the doorway, now fully closed. From somewhere in the framework of the ship, several metallic sounds occurred, strongly suggesting the operation of a locking mechanism. They were locked in.

They pressed close together; there was a sensation of pressure, of numbness in their limbs, and then there was no

motion sensible at all, and in one more instant, nothing at all.
There was no fading, no drifting, as in sleep, or unconscious-
ness. Time just ended. Meure had only time to start to say, "I
th-

STOP

                                    -ink it is some kind of protective
field." Time began again, the door snapped open, and from
speakers all over the ship, a gong began tolling, punctuated
by a Spsom voice enunciating at regular intervals, a single
word that sounded like 'Vv-h't.' The outer door of their
shared quarters burst open to the noise of much confusion
without, and at last the voice of Clellendol broke clear
through it: "Up! Up! All out of the ship!"

Meure and Audiart hurriedly retrieved their hastily-dis-
carded clothing from the places where it had fallen and
struggled to put it on, while below, in the compartment there
was the sound of doors and cabinets opening and closing, and
then quiet. Now they could hear the sounds of the ship.

The sounds were not so much in the air, as in the very fabric of the ship itself; there were long, sustained groans, punctuated by ominous pops, cracks; in the background, the
hissing of escaping gas could also be heard from time to time.
They took no time to gather anything, but dodged through
the kitchen into the common-room, where the lighting was
still working, but was flickering. The ship settled to a new
center of gravity with an easy, floating motion, which seemed
to start up a new series of creaks and groans. They balanced
carefully across the shifting compartment and attained the
hallway, where the lights were definitely out.

At the curving of the bulkhead, Clellendol waited for
them, looking nervously about. "Come on, come on," he fidgeted. "They are waiting for us at the port. We're down successfully on Monsalvat, whatever luck that is, but *Ffstresha* is
breaking up and we must get out of it. That Vdhitz tried to
explain it, but I couldn't make sense of it."

The three of them hurried through the swaying central corridor to the entry port, where the remainder of the crew and
passengers was awaiting them: three Lerfolk; Dreve Halander
and the slender girl, Ingraine Deffy; two Spsom, Captain
Shchifr and Vdhitz; and the single remaining slave, the dimin-
utive furry creature from Vfzyekhr. Vdhitz was anxiously
looking outside, half-hanging out the port. Without looking
back, he made a motion with his free hand to the rest, and

swung through the port onto the ground. Shchifr glanced quickly over the survivors, and gestured at the port. Then he stood aside to let them pass.

Meure was at the end of the line and could see little enough of the view outside the ship; he had an impression that the ship was somewhat tilted over on its side, so that the port was looking downward, rather than directly out, as would be the normal case. There was a peculiar reddish light, but he could not imagine the source, and he asked Audiart, "What time is it?"

She looked back over her shoulder, her face blank. "Time? It's the middle of the night, of course! When else shipwreck? Come on! We're here, that's what!"

Audiart reached the port behind Clellendol, grasped the edge-handles awkwardly, and swung through. And with Shchifr urging him from behind, Meure followed her onto the soil of Monsalvat.

Meure felt dazed and disoriented. He wanted to stop where he was, in the now comforting shadow of the bulk of the *Ff-stretsha*, under the tangle of the absurd Spsom conduit system, but Shchifr had now dropped out of the ship, and was hurriedly removing devices from his vest and tossing them back into the open port. Inside, all was dark. Here, there was a faint light, but the source was out of sight. There seemed to be vegetation underfoot, wiry and stringy, matted down by the ship when it had landed. He heard voices, sensed motion ahead, under the piping, and Clellendol's voice urging him to run. He ran ahead, ducked under a sagging conduit, whose paint was burned entirely off, and whose broken end waved loosely about like some live thing, and at last saw the group ahead of him, running from the ship. Meure followed, trying to catch up; Shchifr easily ran past him with the half-bound, half-leaping motion of a Spsom running.

Shchifr waved them on, and together they ran another distance, slightly uphill, not looking back. Meure sensed motions around them, in the air, along the ground, a great confusion somehow, but he could not stop to look.

Finally they attained a rocky knoll, where they stopped. Meure found Audiart, sitting on the rocks, knees clasped closely to her chest, looking, staring back, in the direction of the ship. No. Past the ship. At the morning.

He cast himself down beside her, looked back. In the east, the star of Monsalvat was rising into a new day. A double star called Bitirme.

The star rising out of the eastern horizon was a close double, the two component stars being of apparently the same size, both of a rusty-orange color. They were separated by what appeared to be something a little more than a diameter, and their position seemed to change slightly with respect to one another as he watched. The sun (*or was it suns*, he thought) was filling the dawn sky with color, bringing the day out of night with an impossible indigo color, while clouds tinted in oranges and reds floated in impossibly clear air; around both stars was an envelope of pearly radiance which was fading with the daylight even as they watched.

The ship lay partly on one side in a little hollow in what Meure saw to be rolling plains that fell away eastward; there were still lights showing in parts of it, but it also seemed to be settling into the ground, as if it no longer had some structural integrity necessary to conform its odd shape. Yes, that was it: it was relaxing, like some exotic, overripe fruit.

And Meure looked upward and saw now the source of the motion he had sensed, perhaps. There were shapes in the morning light, darting, gliding, impossible shapes his mind at first refused to resolve; and from behind the ship people were running, running madly for the ship. People! Humans, judging by the shape of them in the distance, and their gait. They ran like people across the bristly, grasslike vegetation, which Meure now saw to have a distinct blue tint.

The people surrounded the ship. Meure could see that most of them were smallish, slight of build, but most were carrying long knives, or short spears. They seemed to act like savages, capering and gesticulating madly, some rushing up to touch the ship, while others tried to wrench off a piece of dangling piping; it looked ridiculous, like ants attacking a ground-car. Meure felt a motion beside him, smelled a warm-cookie odor.

Vdhitz said, half-whispering, "Semtheng neuw to sirprese dem volk den dere; Tshchiff'r set the Pile to iverlode biffor hee kem den. Blew soon, heh, heh, heh."

Audiart heard the Spsom and started forward to her knees, half to her feet. Meure grasped one arm, and from behind a rock, the Ler girl Flerdistar stepped in front of her. Flerdistar said quietly, "Do not oppose this; you will only die without changing the result. Spsom do not permit aliens to capture a disabled ship, and of a certainty not on Monsalvat; those will be Shchifr's instructions, and he must carry them out. It is his last act as Captain of a vessel, forever."

Audiart settled back, but she said, "Those are people down there."

The morning was now coming to light rapidly, the color coming up through various blues into a rosy color. And by the ship, the crowd had become large indeed; but some, at least, were suspicious, and urged the others to withdraw. There prudence was soon rewarded when one end of the Spsom ship suddenly glowed, sagged, and began to melt, sinking to the ground. The throng outside drew back, and Meure could hear their voices, calling angrily, hissing their displeasure. They left a respectful distance between themselves and the ship, but continued to watch attentively, milling about, brandishing their weapons at the ship.

Flerdistar looked, and said, "There is no answer to that. We think those are people, but we do not know. This is Monsalvat, and the word has strange meanings here." And she looked away from Audiart, and did not meet her returning gaze.

Now some of the crowd about the ship were regaining their boldness, and were leaving their compatriots to make little forays to the ship, as if it were some live thing they could daunt with their boldness. Or perhaps they knew their gestures made no impression on the *Ffstretsha*, no longer a live thing to dance and flow in the currents of the oceans of space, and their demonstrations were for the benefit of their associates, more of whom seemed to be arriving every minute, so it appeared, from the east, from behind a low rise.

Some became bolder, after some moments passed with no further events aboard the ship, although the melted end continued to glow redly with no visible change; one especially bold darted quickly to the entry port, hesitated, looked back once, and swung upward and inside. Another followed closely behind, not wanting to be thought less bold or resolute, but the second one did not enter. The crowd edged closer, throwing rocks at the ship.

From the relatively undamaged end of the ship, a fluting whistle began sounding in short bursts, each of the same duration, equally spaced, an unchanging rhythm. No, there was a pause, and then the fluted tones began again. Broken by another pause, then starting over again. Something was changing . . . each time, after the pause, there was one less whistled tone. Meure counted as soon as he realized what was happening: seven, *pause,* six, *pause,* five, *pause,* four, *didn't the fools see what was happening inside the ship? It was counting down a warning. Pause*, three, *now the crowd sensed something was astray, and many of them drew back, pause*, two, and the one by the entryport was shouting something into the ship, *pause*, one, the one inside appeared at the port, waving his arms wildly, and then there was light shining behind him, the figure was a dark blot silhouetted in a doorway losing its shape, the crowd was running away, then the *Ffstretsha* became an instant, rigid, white, spiky flower, a hemisphere of thousands of white streamers that *came*, and hung poised, even as the punctuation of the explosion rent the air with a sound never before heard on Monsalvat, and then the magnesium whiteness left the streamers, and the rising suns lit them from behind, suffusing the dust with lights of rose and old peach. Pea gravel rattled among the rocks. In the morning light, Meure could see that most of the former crowd were prone, all laid neatly and radially away from the place where the *Ffstretsha* had been, but that farther away from the ground zero, many were beginning to stir, to pick themselves up, to feel their bodies carefully, and to call to others.

As explosions went, it was not worldshaking; neither was it extremely destructive. It did erase the ship completely. Where the ship had been was now a small crater, littered with small miscellaneous unidentifiable debris. Some were glowing, but their glow was fading even as they watched. The explosion cloud was now almost completely faded and dissipated.

As the crowd below revived the merely injured, Meure now looked upward, again, to try to see the shapes flitting overhead, a motion which had ceased just before the explosion, as he recalled. He saw creatures flying through the air in swift, zany courses that did not seem to be under too much control: the things zoomed and careened madly, sometimes barely avoiding collision with another by desperate, lurching maneuvers. Their speed and darting courses across his field of vision made details hard to make out.

Meure looked away from the east and tried to follow one of the creatures; found one in a labored turn back into the scene of the action, followed it carefully now seeing it in all its improbability: size was difficult to judge, for he did not know the altitude of the flying creatures, but they seemed large, much larger than a person, all leathery wings. The creature he was following with his eyes was long and narrow, with two sets of narrow wings, one very close to the front of the beast, and a larger set, about twice as large, far to the rear. Each wing was narrow, tapering and tipped with a knobby cluster; the wings seemed to be partially rigid, partially stretched along bony frameworks. The front pair were swept forward, while the rear pair were radically swept backward, beating slightly out of time with one another, the front pair downstroking first, the motion rippling to the back pair. Between the wings, the body was narrow, compressed, A third set of the knobby clusters was located at the narrowest part, about two-thirds to the rear, just before the broad rear wings. The fore end of the creature seemed to lack what could properly be called a head: the body, or central spine of the creature merely tapered down rakishly to a depressed point. There were features along that tapering, drooping prow, but Meure could not make them out. Sensory organs?

Out of its beating turn now, the creature pitched up a little, and smoothly halted its fore wings in their downstroke, locking them together under the projecting fore part. The rear wings increased their stroke, in amplitude and rate, and the speed of the flying thing accelerated. It passed overhead, a little to the north, and Meure could see that the rear wings were curved a little behind, joining at the very end in a smooth parabolic curve. There was a tail, but it was very small. From the front point to the wings in the rear, the curved outline of the shape was smoothly concave, expoential in shape. Aft of the rear wingtips, the curve was shallowly parabolic and convex. It seemed impossible and improbable, but there was no quality about it suggesting humor, or decoration. To the contrary, it moved through the limpid air of Monsalvat with strong, confident strokes, powerful and purposeful, alert and probably dangerous. It paused, gliding over the scene of the action, rocking slightly from side to side, making microcorrections in course with the huge rudder in front formed by the down-folded wings and narrow headless neck. Gliding away, it lost altitude, then opened its fore wings to help support it, and began another hundred-and-eighty degree turn, both wings beating again.

Now the folk who had survived the explosion seemed to notice the creatures flying overhead; indeed, some of them were making passes over the site where the ship had grounded, at quite low altitude. Meure could not tell if their behavior was caused by fear of the flying things, or rage at their losses to the explosion. But they seemed to go completely crazy, running madly back and forth, gesturing at the sky, looking about for something with lunatic energy. Clellendol whispered, "They are looking for us, I'll wager!"

Flerdistar said, from the side, "I'd not care to face that mob. But you're correct: They know the ship was essentially intact, and that it was open, and there were no bodies."

Clellendol added, "And that someone set a bomb and left it running. No, indeed; this is not to my liking at all!"

Meure volunteered, "The flying things distract them; perhaps they will overlook us."

Almost as if Meure's voiced hope had been a cue, the large beast he had followed overhead, which had circled around from the east to the south, now approached the shallow depression where the strange folk were gathered. Meure and the others, from their elevation, could see the flying creatures circling back, but those below apparently could not; they were oblivious to the creatures save those they could see overhead. It barely cleared a low ridge, both sets of wings beating madly, as if for speed, not altitude. Now they were looking down on one of the creatures as it set its wings to glide, its speed much too fast for conscious reaction by the people who had come to the ship. The flying beast had already calculated its trajectory. They could only glimpse parts of features along the narrow forward end: several paired spots that seemed to be eyes, and something else that emitted a deep red light in pulses . . . one of the people was running, and some sound, some feel, some perhaps sixth sense warned him. A single glance back over the shoulder, and he made his decision: run faster, turn to the left, there were some rocks not far away.

Meure watched helplessly; to run upright was clearly useless, as the flying creature was closing on the intended victim at a velocity easily ten times the man's top running speed, probably more. At the last moment, the man also recognized this and dove for the ground, almost under the forward-swept fore wings. The creature made a last microcorrection, dipped, covered the spot where the man would have been; something talonlike reached from the narrowest section of the creature, and it pulled up into a steep climb and began beating its wings again. No man was on the ground.

Audiart made a choking sound, turned away. The two remaining Spsom looked on stonily, saying nothing. Clellendol muttered something under his breath. Then he said, more clearly, "We needn't worry about any suffering of that thing's prey: acceleration alone would break every major bone in its

body, never mind any other trauma the creature might in-
flict upon contact."

Meure paused, and wondered what kind of structure the
flying creature had that was resistant enough to take those
impacts itself.

Now the creature was climbing to the north. Some of the
other creatures, mostly smaller, made half-hearted attempts to
pursue it, but soon returned to their circling overhead.

Below, the people now became wary and cautious. But
they retained their older sense of urgency and mad activity as
well. Now taking cover wherever it could be found, they
gathered in little knots, now and then shouting from one
group to another. These groups now began to spread away
from the spot where the ship grounded, some members
watching the morning sky, while others carefully looked over
the ground. None of the groups headed back to the east.

Flerdistar observed, "Now they are looking for the survivors. They already know we are not to the east, for they
came from that direction. Their activity has obscured any
track we might have made near the ship, but they will find it
farther out, soon enough."

At the onset, the cautious searching by the little people in
the depression, watching as they also were for attacks by the
flying creatures, seemed to gain them nothing. Others among
them began to see to the injured, helping some to their feet,
calling for assistance with others. Some were examined, and
left behind. But after a time, the results began to bear fruit.
The depression was examined carefully, and one by one, very
systematically, the possible hiding places began to be eliminated. Various groups called back and forth across the
natural amphitheater in harsh, nasal voices, coordinating their
efforts.

One industrious individual found something on the ground
that interested him greatly: others he called to his aid and
concurrence. Several more joined him, and a discussion ensued, accompanied by extravagant gestures and much waving
of the arms. They started out carefully in the direction of the
rocky eminence in which the survivors of the shipwreck were
hiding, occasionally looking up to the rockpile to verify their
progress. In the rest of the depression, others began drifting
over to join the group, while still others started back to the
east.

Meure said quietly, "I think they know we're here."

Halander added, "Fight or run, and I don't see how we

can fight a crowd of that size; besides, the action would bring reinforcements."

Audiart asked quietly, "Where can we run to? Do we even know what continent we landed on?"

Vdhitz held a brief discussion with Shchifr, and then said something more toward Flerdistar, still in his own speech. The girl reflected a moment, nodded, and said, "We're on the northwest continent, Kepture, somewhere in the middle of it. Neither Spsom got to see too much, coming in; Vdhitz thinks he saw a large body of water extending to the south, and it seemed too large for a lake. If that's true, then we're in the west of Kepture . . . I suppose it doesn't really make any difference which way we go. No native can be assumed to be friendly, so there's no reason to go in any direction save to retain our lives. They agree: we should leave this place immediately." Suiting action to words, she stood up to began climbing through the rocks to the west.

The motion was noted by sharp eyes below, and an immediate outcry was raised. Clellendol roughly jerked the girl to her feet, but it was, of course, too late. Meure could see them clearly now: the people below were now converging in their direction. Meure looked around, and saw Vdhitz bare his muzzle, exposing fine, needle-sharp teeth; he also drew a slender, dully finished knife. Audiart looked at Meure, her eyes blank, staring. Meure searched through the rubble, grasping, measuring, finally settling on a wicked, flinty shard of rock.

The vanguard of the mob drew closer, now rather silent. They no longer shouted back and forth, but said small phrases to one another, making gestures of anger. Now Meure could make out their features better; no longer were the people abstract and generalized human shapes, but identifiable, with perceptible characteristics. They were smallish in stature, rather ler-sized, but more angular. Their skins were light brown to pale, with an unhealthy pallor that seemed at some variance with the clear air and bright, ruddy sunlight. Their hair was lank and stringy, off-brown or dirty blond. But their faces arrested his attention the most, for in every face he could see the upper lip was cleft in two; more in some than in others, but never absent. The appearance of the people was dichotomous and contradictory; the cleft lip lent their faces an engaging, rabbity look, but the obvious expressions on those faces were, to a one, those of rage and hatred. They moved up the slope with maniacal, detached deliberation, always talking back and forth, watching each other carefully. They were a people used to joint activity, and to large crowds.

Their clothing seemed to be whatever scrap each one could have found, arising in a hurry; some wore patched, loose robes, hardly more than a sheet with holes poked in it, or perhaps unfair advantage had been taken of holes already in place. Others wore shabby leather breeks, made of some limp hide and held in place with rope belts. There seemed to be no leader, no order, no sense of formation. But they were approaching now quite close, only meters away. Meure was certain they could see them all.

Clellendol now stood, facing the group climbing up the scree, holding a slender rope in his hands. Meure also stood, holding his rock flake at the ready, thinking no thoughts at all. And the two Spsom now stood as well, stretching to their full height, both holding knives. No words were spoken, no gestures were offered.

The foremost of the crowd climbing the rockpile now stopped, carefully considering that which lay ahead. He could almost hear their thoughts, considerations of how many lay ahead, in the rocks. Perhaps a bad place to attack, with three aliens of unknown powers. Who among them knew what a Spsom could do? The front of the group crept slightly forward. Though now still, they emitted a palpable emotion of crazy ferocity, an utter disregard for personal safety. Short, rippling glances whipped back and forth across the faces of the crowd. Meure thought it would be any minute, now.

At the rear of the vanguard, they were beginning to crowd and jostle, their numbers being ever increased by those arriving from behind. But the ones in the forefront, who had been looking from figure to figure calculating, now looked as if through the survivors, and at one another again, and the feral light in their eyes began to fade, translating into apprehension, doubt, then badly-concealed expressions of fear and loathing. Some comments were passed up and down the line, quietly now, as if the members of the crowd wished not to disturb something. The crowd stopped piling on at the bottom of the slope. The members of the vanguard began backing down the slope, always keeping their attention on the rocky outcrop. Slowly and cautiously, the people began to retreat back down the hill. Meure looked out over the depression and now saw the others leaving, moving off in the direction of the east, not hurriedly, or in panic, but with many a backward glance.

Meure relaxed, breathed deeply, realizing that he could not remember the last time he had breathed. Something had changed their minds, but he hardly thought it would have been the Spsom. Alien they were, but there were, after all, only two of them, and armed with no more than knives at that. He looked down the slope now at a retreating mob, fading away as fast as they could in good order. He risked a glance at Audiart; she was still sitting, completely still, her face an expressionless mask. She sensed his gaze, turned to meet his eyes. They both wanted to see what it was that had turned the crowd, if they could. Together they met each other's eyes, and turned to see.

Meure felt ice in his veins. In the rocks behind the Spsom were standing, absolutely still, three elongated figures in hooded robes that swathed them from head to foot. He could see little of the shape of what lay within the robes, but the figures were Human, judging by what suggestions of facial outlines he could make out, and they were holding long spears tipped with leaf-shaped blades whose edges gleamed silvery in the morning sun. Their hoods shadowed most of their faces, but what Meure could see was no less frightening than the faces of those he had seen on the slope; save that these faces were thin and gaunt, and focused on large, bladelike noses. Above the ridge of the nose, heavy, hairy brows shaded deepset eyes that seemed to have no color at all— merely pools of darkness.

Two remained in the same unmoving posture, gazing eastward rather into the unfocused distance instead of directly at any particular object. The third, ignoring the mixed group in the rocks, moved fluidly and quickly around them to a better vantage point, the better to oversee the people now departing the depression. This third newcomer stepped out onto the slope and again became still for a moment, looking.

Meure watched intently. There was nothing about the figure he could identify as male or female, but he found himself thinking unconsciously, "she." Something about the effortless, flowing movement; or the appearance of slighter stature. He didn't know. The creature now lifted its free arm, shaking folds of the sleeve of the voluminous robe to reveal a slender and shapely hand of long, tapering fingers. This it lifted to its face, and emitted a long, piercing cry, an almost-soprano howl that set Meure's nerves on edge and struck fear into him.

Down in the depression, those departing heard, and looked

back, over their shoulders, not turning full around. As they heard the sound dying, most immediately broke into a quick-time trot; some began running hard at once. Atop the slope, the creature shrugged, made an indescribable wriggling motion, and the robe simply fell away, revealing a naked, slender girl of long limbs and wiry, taut muscles, whose long, black hair was tied tightly at the neck in a folded braid. Her skin was a rich olive brown. The girl tossed the spear she held to free the robe, recatching it, and stepped off onto the slope, letting gravity accelerate her, now guiding and controlling the motion, flowing down the slope in lengthening, beautifully exact, flowing paces. And below, in the depression, the entire field broke into a dead hard run, as if they were to a man stricken with the utmost in stark terror. The girl reached the flat ground and lengthened her stride into a ground-covering run, easily moving more than twice as fast as those who were now bent solely upon escape. Meure, watching, did not know what the girl was doing, but it certainly seemed as if she were hunting the rabbit-faced people, that they were prey.

He looked at the rest of the group, who had also watched the scene in the depression, and were now looking away, as if not to see the logical conclusion, turning also to look at one another and to the two remaining newcomers. Now there were five, the three additional newcomers indistinguishable from the first. For a long moment, each group looked at the other, making no moves. Then one of the hooded figures made a gesture with the hand, motioning toward itself and half-turning to the west, from whence it had come, seemingly. The meaning seemed clear enough. They were being invited somewhere. The gesture was made without motion of the weapons the creatures carried; indeed, it seemed that the leader went to some pains to avoid attention to his spear.

Vdhitz made an almost-Human Spsom version of a shrug, and sheathed his knife, followed by Shchifr. Clellendol coiled his rope, and said, half under his breath, "Does anyone imagine that we have much choice, here?" There was no answer, but the rest reluctantly got to their feet. He continued, "These are dangerous, as you see . . . but I prefer these and the unknown west to those who came from the east."

The one who had motioned did not understand Clellendol's words, but he seemed to comprehend the motion of the group easily enough. Without further word, he nodded, and turned back to the west, moving along an almost-invisible path with effortless, graceful motion. His compatriots stood aside to let

the group pass. And one by one, they followed the gaunt
newcomer down the rocks, and onto a rolling plain spreading
before them into the west, seemingly without limit.

5

---

*"It is not enough to dip the Magus in the Styx;
he must be thrown in and left to sink or swim."*
                                        —A. C.

Now it was getting on into the afternoon; Meure awoke
with a sudden jerk of his head. He was sitting in the shade
cast by an eccentric, two-wheeled wagon which was apparently pulled by two of what appeared to be very large and
very stupid men. The others were still about him nearby, in
similar positions; Halander was curled protectively about
Ingraine Deffy, more under the wagon, in the shade. It was
warmish. The rest were nearby, and Audiart was closer to the
front of the wagon, half in the sunlight, the orange cast to
the sunlight coppering her hair. She was awake, staring out
into empty prairies, her face expressionless, her thoughts
manifestly elsewhere.

Meure shaded his eyes against the brightness of the sky,
which was a deeper blue than seemed natural to him; deeper
blue, but also curiously opaque, instead of transparent like an
evening sky might have been on Tancred. . . . It was only
then that he began to understand that he was now in a different circumstance, truly on a new world, in a new world, a
different universe. In the ship, they could pretend that they
had retained the old with them, but without it, things were
different.

The land rolled away to the distances, covered with a wiry,
bluish vegetation that suggested grass, but wasn't. Here and
there, small, meaningless features broke the open spaces; a
dwarfed and stunted tree, a rockpile. Clouds drifted across
the sky, the kind he had always associated with summer and

fair weather; well-defined puffs, whose edges were as solid in appearance as the land beneath. Many were darkish along their lower edges, and one, far to the north, seemed to be trailing a veil of rain, which trailed out into nothing high above the ground.

One of the tall creatures they had accompanied was visible far to the rear of the wagon, squatting motionless and impassive in the sunlight, its hood completely shadowing its face. Meure thought it was not the girl he had seen in the morning, although he could not say precisely how he thought he knew this. He could not see the creature's face, nor its eyes, but he was sure it was watching them. Where was Flerdistar? He looked about in apprehension: where were the two Spsom? The furry slave?

Meure stood up awkwardly, stiff in all his joints from the hard ground, and the wheel he had been leaning on. If the guard cared, he evidenced no sign. Meure looked about; some distance to the front of the wagon, a frail sunshade had been erected, slung between poles driven into the ground at outward-leaning angles. Perhaps the spears he had seen the tall ones carrying. There were the rest; he could make them out clearly, and some others he had not seen before, different from the tall hunters. If he listened carefully, he could make out the distant hum of their voices, although of the hum he made no words. But the tone of their voices reassured him; they were neither hasty nor angry. Each seemed to speak in turn, carefully and slowly.

For an instant, the idea of escape crossed his mind; of just walking away, then perhaps running. . . . He did not know where he would run to, and he was certain that he would not get very far, should the hunters decide to follow him. Meure remembered how the people with the cleft upper lips seemed to fear even one of the hunters; perhaps this was justified by past experiences. He decided that he did not wish to test how tight were their invisible bonds.

He glanced toward the tent, and saw that the meeting seemed to be breaking up, casually enough; the tall hunters withdrew to confer among themselves. Meure could make out the angular shapes of the two Spsom, still engaged with a group of three of the tall ones, apparently communicating mostly through sign language. One of the hunters handed Shchifr his spear, which the Spsom captain hefted experimentally, then demonstrated his style of throwing it. The hunters seemed to think the style as odd as the alien shape of their visitor, but they could find no fault with Shchifr's accuracy, for he had hit the little bush he had aimed for exactly, the spear now standing, rigidly vibrating, driven into the wood. After a moment, more sign language ensued, which seemed to be an earnest discussion about hunting, or some similar activity. Meure had not known the Spsom hunted; indeed, he could think of very little that he did know about them, of themselves.

Flerdistar and Clellendol returned to the wagon, accompanied by one of the hunters, and two of the strangers, one stocky and beefy-faced, the other thin and rather stern in appearance, bearing a shock of disorderly iron-gray hair; both were dressed in well-worn garments resembling undecorated bathrobes—simple wraparounds with a cloth sash to hold the front closed, which fell to the knee. Both wore what seemed to be crude, but serviceable stockings and heavy sandals. Unlike the hunters, neither seemed to be a figure of fear or awe, although judging by the expressions and gestures of the hunters, and the Ler young people, they were certainly figures of respect, men of influence, at least locally.

Flerdistar excused herself from the group and joined those waiting at the wagon. She saw they were indeed attentive, so she began at once, "For the moment, we can relax somewhat, if any of you are inclined to harbor morbid thoughts. We are in no immediate danger from these, so long as none of us makes a rash move, such as an escape attempt. These people are nomads who call themselves the Haydar. The best I can tell, they are one of the original Klesh stocks, and their folklore is extensive and elaborate. They have maintained their way of life with little change since the beginning here; with them alone I should spend the remainder of my life. But that is neither here nor there. They bear us no hostility, but as nomads, they cannot keep us, and only the Spsom are capable of joining the hunt with them, so we will . . . not remain here."

Audiart asked, "Where are we?"

"On Monsalvat, on the continent Kepture, as we suspected. We are in a portion of Kepture, somewhat to the west and south, which is called Ombur. North and east is another land called Incana. It is there that we will go, I think. The names do not refer to countries, or governmental organizations, or anything like that. Time is long, here, and the various lands have collected names through the years. We await now the return of the girl from the hunt; she is, in effect, the Shaman of this particular group. She is the one who memorizes the epics of the Haydar and reads the omens. The leader of this band wishes to remove us from this area, but he must allow her to cast the omen and ratify his decision."

Flerdistar paused, then began again, "They seem amazed that we do not fear them. Even explained as simple ignorance, they still regard us as people of extreme self-control. By all means, do nothing to suggest otherwise. That way lies safety. And you may be sorely tempted to break, for these are an abrupt people who make hard decisions."

She continued, "These other two belong to a class of wandering intermediaries, whose function it apparently is to communicate between groups who detest one another. The general rule is that they may not be harmed, robbed, detained or made hostage except in very specific circumstances, upon which I would not now care to speculate.

"The speech here was Singlespeech at one time, but with the changefulness of Humans, it has undergone much development. I urge you to learn it as fast as you can assimilate it. There are also many other variants, which I would class as cult jargon, tribal lore-speech, and functional languages. Most of the people here will be fluent in at least three or four basic patterns appropriate to their station, and the intermediaries will of course be conversant in more."

Meure ventured, "Are there cities, towns? Or is the whole planet wild?"

"There are . . . cities, although when we see one, I think we will not call it so. Places where men gather. Communities, places of safety, of defense. No land is under the control of any one ruler, but is divided many ways. There are no borders here, no frontiers, no lines of demarcation, no customs-collectors. Things change on Monsalvat, which by the way, they call 'Aceldama.' They know the name 'Monsalvat,' but they prefer the other." She sighed deeply. "We have, indeed, much to learn, much to take with us."

Halander added, "If we survive to greet the *Ilini Visk*, a year from now."

Flerdistar looked away, and said, "We have to learn that, too; and it may be a hard lesson. Be perceptive. And flexible. It will be as hard on you as on us! Never have I met so much diversity suggested in their speech: each tribe here is as different from another as we are from the Spsom, and they know even more aberrant groups in lands farther away. But for the present, be as comfortable as possible. Rest. Events will permutate tonight, and we will see . . ."

Meure was not thinking anything specific, just listening to Flerdistar, but a sudden flash idea flickered across his mind, so rapidly he almost missed it; even so, having caught the fugitive thread, he struggled with it for a time to put it into speakable order.

"*Liy* Flerdistar, do you have any idea what we can do until the *Ilini Visk* comes for us?"

He knew as he said it that he had made it too general, too comprehensible. Thus she had missed it. What he wanted to say, his mind was screaming, and which he did not dare speak aloud for fear of alarming the hunters, was more. It was, *if the sample we see before us is accurate, there is not place for us here. Here, on Monsalvat-Aceldama, whichever it was, there are the various tribes, none of which we resemble, who heartily despise one another at the best, and eat one another at worst. Or perhaps that is not the worst. At any rate, we must survive. To survive, we must find matching tribes, and be scattered to the four winds. Rescue! The terrifying thing was that Flerdistar, now the ostensible leader of the group, did not even see that there was a problem. She was totally wrapped in what she was reading in these people.*

She answered casually, "In the land Incana is an historic strongpoint. We must get off these empty plains. Empty lands on Monsalvat are lands in contention. For the moment, we have powerful protectors, and we must contrive to keep them until we can reach a place of greater security. One step at a time."

Meure nodded, then looked away from her. It was reasonable enough, on the surface. Problem: get out of Ombur. Solution: get these natives to take them to another place. Then we figure where to go from there. Meure could not imagine it: He looked out again over the empty plains, the rolls, the bareness, the sky. He couldn't bring himself to say he liked it, but he was sure he wanted to live, and he understood something about Monsalvat immediately, without being told it: that whatever any of them did *here*, in this place and time, it would initiate consequences immediately. He knew nothing of what lay west and south; he feared the rabbit-faced people of the East. Wrong, wrong, to go north, into this Incana. And even as he became sure of the wrongness of it, he knew that they would go there.

Flerdistar gathered them all together, save the Spsom, and

the little creature who had been a Spsom slave, and commend-
ed them to the care of a third member of the negotiators, a
misshapen, troll-like man with enormous arms and a broad,
evil grin, who appeared from the rear portion of the wagon
at a motion from the gray-haired man, bearing a basket
loaded with flat biscuits and slivers of some cured meat,
which he began passing out, naming each item as he passed
it. This was to be their instructor. Meure turned his attention to the newcomer, began to listen with growing interest.
He did not care so much for the mission of the Ler, who had
hired them, nor the concerns of the Spsom, who had flown
and lost the ship. Here was survival. Meure saw in this troll,
not a freak, but a halfbreed, or even misbreed, who had survived. He would be worth listening to.

Now the day was softening into twilight; at first the
shadows had lengthened, but as they grew longer, they
softened and merged. Meure had been, for a reason obscure
to himself, avoiding the direct light of the star-pair Bitirme.
Somehow, he didn't want to see the close binary. Now he
thought he could, with a head full of Aceldaman lore, as
much as he could digest. He reflected on that, too. Of them
all, he seemed to pay the closest attention to the manservant,
Benne. The rest, Audiart, Halander, Ingraine, all seemed repulsed by the troll-like figure and crude mannerisms, but
Meure had sat and listened and repeated the strange words,
many with disturbing hints of the familiar in them, and listened closely to the meaning of what Benne was teaching
them. Eunuch and misbred he might be, but there was a fine,
honed mind behind that lowering forehead, and many years of
survival behind him. More, he was a natural teacher, starting
with the immediate and practical and expanding spirally into
steadily more complex ideas. Meure knew his new vocabulary
was insufficient, that his grasp of the structure of the language was equal now only to the most primitive needs, but he
had a little base he could now expand himself. The others?

Meure stood, stretched deeply in the cooling air, and
stepped out, away from the wagon, more properly, he
thought, into the environment of Monsalvat itself. The Haydar watching them turned its head to observe him, briefly,
then turned back to its original position.

Far off in the west, Bitirme was sinking into veils of high
cirrus clouds, spreading its orange-tinted light across a violet
sky. The star now appeared to be distinctly ovoid. Before him

ranged the seemingly endless plains of Ombur, rolling gently
away into the uttermost west. The plains were still and quiet,
supernaturally so; Meure could hear tiny sounds he would
not normally be aware of. He thought he could hear the grass
that was not grass growing. The strange men who had been
hitched to the clumsy wagon had been sitting awkwardly, still
in the traces of the wagon, but now they were beginning to
stir, to make little grunting noises to one another. They were
the most curious of all he had seen so far: giants in stature,
with heavy-boned, gross features, pale waxy skin, stringy,
limp blond hair, and expressions of blankness on their
homely faces. *Sumpters,* Benne had called them, enumerating
various creatures native to this part of Kepture, or domesti-
cated here. Odd, that: Benne had not referred to them as a
tribe, but had listed them with the animals. But then he had
not included the rabbit-faced people, the Lagostomes, in his
list of Humans, either.

Meure looked about, more widely—Flerdistar and Clellendol and the two intermediaries, and the Ler elders were still
holding an earnest converse behind the wagon, while over by
the sunshade, Spsom, Vzyekhr, and Haydar were carefully
taking down the covering which had shaded them in the day.
Audiart and the other two were still by the wagon.

Far off, from the southeast, he heard a series of howls, first
one alone, then that echoed by an irregular chorus. The Haydar remaining in the vicinity of the wagon immediately
stopped what they were doing and turned their heads to listen
to the howls. Meure could hear no words in the far-off faint
sounds, but he could hear a difference from the chilling call
he had heared the girl use this morning. Whatever information
the howls carried, it seemed to please the Haydar hunters, for
they returned to their task with seeming enjoyment, their
dour watchfulness changing into an odd joyousness. Some
gathered, and produced firemaking tools from their voluminous robes, and began kindling a fire. On this they laid long-
ish chunks of some dark substance. Meure searched the
horizon in the direction of the howls, but he saw nothing.
The darkness was falling fast, now. Bitirme was below the
horizon.

He looked to the sky in the east, sensing some movement
there, he thought. The first stars were beginning to shine
there. But he saw nothing. All was quiet. The distant howling
stopped. Now he turned back to the wagon and started toward
it, to rejoin the others. There was something he had to tell

Audiart, something she seemed to need, although it was obvious to him that she was older and more experienced than he.

It was still evening quiet, each sound magnified; in this quiet he heard a rushing noise high up, faint, rhythmic. Looking up, he caught sight of a group of the odd two-winged creatures he had seen this morning: about ten or so, in cruise configuration, with forward wings partially folded, heading westward. A sudden fear crossed him; but when he looked back down to the Haydars, they seemed unconcerned, looking up, then returning to the matter at hand, as if they had expected them. *Eratzenasters*, Benne had called them. Meure looked back. The eratzenasters were slowing, descending, and one of the larger ones seemed to be carrying something on its dorsal surface. The light was uncertain now, and he couldn't be sure.

The creatures expanded their forward wings now, and continued to descend, turning southerly, and then circling back, approaching the ground reluctantly, steepening their angle of attack, the lead wings beginning to flap at the air in anticipation of a stall. The smaller ones were now close to the ground, and settled onto it with an awkward motion, part fall, part glide, part stall. They seemed to kill their forward motion by running along the ground on unseen limbs beneath the stiff wings. The larger ones took longer, made more shallow approaches, landed with more skill. The largest one landed most delicately, as if it did not wish to dislodge that which was aboard it. The payload moved, sat upright, legs straddling the narrow midsection of the eratzenaster. There was no mistaking who it was: it was the girl who had hunted the Lagostomes, still as nude as she had been when she had begun the hunt.

The eratzenasters moved about beyond the perimeter of the temporary camp, looking for suitable places to settle, and folded to the ground, one by one, resembling irregular, long rocky outcrops. The large beast Tenguft rode continued to walk on its unseen limbs, slowly and carefully, into the camp. As it came closer, Meure began to see just how large a large one might be, and what an odd form it had; it was about thirty meters long, with the larger rear pair of wings extending outwards less than half that, although they were not fully extended now for flight. As it moved on the ground, the whole body flexed somewhat, as if the whole of the creature were partially rigid. At the ends of the wings, at the points, were stubby clawed appendages, whose function Meure could not fathom. On its walking legs the spine rode higher than the height of a man, even a Haydar, and the wings drooped almost to the ground.

Meure felt lightheaded, but he felt no fear. This one was obviously under control. He approached it, while the others stood respectfully back; save one Haydar, who came carrying a long robe for the rider of the eratzenaster.

It was almost complete night; details were difficult to make out. Meure looked closely, eyes straining; the front of the eratzenaster was just a front. It narrowed down to a bony point. No mouth, nose, nothing. Farther back, there were eyes, four of them that he could see, gleaming an oil black. Set in the middle of what he would have called a forehead was another eye, this one dull and with a suggestion of insect-like faceting. The creature now towered over him, turning slightly to perceive him; Meure felt an odd prickling on his skin, a vibration, and the faceted eye began pulsing, glowing with a deep red light from within. Meure felt heat on his face. The light faded, and facing him, the creature stopped. He was close enough to hear its breathing, a sighing, rushing noise emanating from somewhere under the wings; he could also smell its odor, an odd compound of something pungent, and also musty, like old fur. He felt the prickling on his skin again, and the eratzenaster folded itself to the ground, forward end first, followed by the rear. Settling, it arranged its wings as the others had done. Tenguft swung a long, slender leg over the spine of the beast and slid to the ground, where the hunter awaited her with her robe. This she tossed overhead with the minimum possible movement, and strode off to meet the other Haydars.

There was a stir beside him: Clellendol. The Ler youth said, softly, "A fearsome beast, that one."

Meure thought a moment, and questioned, "Which?"

"A-ha. Very good, very sharp. And you are to be the innocent one, yet you ask me which . . . well, I answer, *both, or either.*"

Meure said, "I fear both, this horrible flying nightmare with my instincts, and she with my mind."

"The former—that can be overcome, overridden, or utilized as a goad unto excellence; but the latter . . . we have spent much time overcoming instinctual fears, so much so that we have neglected the latter."

"Yet what I fear about her is that she's probably not the worse I will meet, here, on . . . Aceldama."

"Do you know the word?"

"No. I am no student of arcana, ancient or modern."

"It is from very ancient times. It means, so Morgin the Embasse tells me, 'A place to bury strangers.' Its usage is traditional; as are the words used to signify humans, or rather, beings of human origin." The difference in Cellendol's phrasing did not escape Meure. Clellendol continued, "They call all menlike creatures by the old word, *'Klesh'*; and humans that have managed to retain human ways they call *'Ksenosi.'* Strangers. An ancient discipline is operative here, one both your and my people have sidestepped, avoided, not resolved."

"Say on."

"In the ancient times, humans, *Starmanosi*, the old people, entered an ecological niche on the homeworld in which they effectively had no competition. Therefore they competed among themselves at a certain critical population level. This is basic principles. At the time the *Lermanosi* came into being, we would have done the same, but we blunted the issue in two ways: we avoided competition with you by leaving the area. . . ."

Here Meure interrupted, "Which postponed but did not solve."

"Exactly. Translated the problem into a different arena, larger scale in both space and time. Within ourselves, we made the avoidance of internal competition a cult essential by incorporating it into our family structure, always striving to better systems to ingest socially the outlander, the stranger, the Ler from steadily farther away. You, in turn, borrowed in part from us and made homogenization of population one of your goals. And in both cases, these things have worked to greater or lesser degree. To the contrary, here, these mad klesh have not sidestepped the issue, but have leaped directly into it—and chosen the path of internal competition. Selfness, sense of self, here will be extremely strong, more than you or I have ever seen. That the Haydar did not mark us prey comes from that: no one here will assume ignorance of this basic tenet on our part. It is much as Flerdistar has said— they think our sense of self, our confidence, if you will, is too great to fear them, and without fear, there is no game. That we came on a starship, which they saw, is of no moment whatsoever. They know other creatures live in the universe, but they think it's just like here on a larger scale: murder, mayhem, massacre, and the weak in selfness gather into masses."

"Why do you tell me these things?"

"I will be candid. I mean no offense. You are an innocent. That is not a bad thing of itself. But you are also active, you move around, see things, peek into things, get involved. As here." Here Clellendol gestured behind him toward the wagon. "Those two, the boy who came with you, and the slender girl; do you think either of them would walk here to see an eratzenaster up close? You know it's virtually helpless on the ground, regardless of what it does when airborne. You can see it directly. But they wait in the same place they were left this morning. And the woman with whom you seem to have formed an association . . ."

"Seem to have is correct. We have had little together."

"Just so. She is shocked, but you will recover and adapt. Mind, if she lives here fifty years, she won't like it, but she'll manage. That is her nature. But these three are not going to upset anything. You may. Before the landing. Flerdistar was the key member of this group; this was her project, her thesis, if you will. Now the thesis is unimportant."

"I understand that."

"I know you do. You are the only one who does. And the things you will do here are pivotal. You, sooner or later, are going to upset some balance point. I see it as my task to retard your entry into events beyond your capabilities."

"You see this, Clellendol, and do not want the position for yourself?"

"It can't be mine. This is, all appearances to the contrary, a *Human* planet, in the most ancient sense of the word. All the old demons are alive and well here, walking about naked and proud. I know many things—to what you would say a point beyond my age in years, but when it's all said and done, I remain, after that, a Ler thief. I have no instincts for the job and I have no knowledge of the internal field. But you do. And are active enough to learn to use them. These people, these Haydars and these halfbreed embasses and their servants, and all the others, they are all innocent, too, in a sense. You and they fit each other."

Meure said nothing. Clellendol let that sink in, and then added, "Of course, there is the matter of Flerdistar as well; there will have to be those who integrate her into their deeds despite herself. She, for all her disagreeable nature, is like yourself, an innocent activist, only she had purpose, and if unrestrained, could awaken things here I do not wish to see awakened."

"Understandable, that. With her pursuit of history she will reawaken legend-memories of the Warriors. They are gone, but I would suppose to a klesh it would make little difference . . ,"

"Although not the whole of it, that is enough for now. So, then: let us for the present associate and please listen to me."

"So that I can be . . . retarded, until the moment for release?"

Clellendol spoke more sternly, "You are not an arrow, but a disturber of equilibriums. My wish is that we survive here."

"Until the *Ilini Visk* comes?"

"You know little of the Spsom?"

"Very little. A little, from school. I have seen them, heard some tales. I know more of what I have seen."

"Meure Schasny, I must enlighten you in this regard: the Spsom are possessed of an elaborate sense of humor, of which we see little. They find many things amusing, that we would find terrifying, or sorrowful. You may recall, back on the hill before the ship blew, that Vdhitz thought it was funny that Shchifr had set the power system to explode. Well, so it has been with the tale of the *Ilini Visk*."

"In what way?"

"Flerdistar does not know them as well as she thinks she does. She knows the Spsom language well enough, but she knows very little *about* them. That is why I am here. I know, for example, that the *Ilini Visk* is a ghost ship from the Spsom past . . . all people have such legends, and humans are particularly rich in them, The Wandering Jew, The Flying Dutchman . . . *Ilini Visk* is such a vessel of legend among the Spsom. Vdhitz told Flerdistar that, and she had spread it to us all. What Vdhitz was actually saying . . ."

". . . was that only ghosts heard us."

"Was that only ghosts would come to rescue us. They heard us all right, but they won't come. Those Spsom would think it humorous that Shchifr lost his ship against his own better judgement, all for the higher payment he'd get from a charter instead of tramping it around."

It was completely dark, now, and Meure was certain that Clellendol could not see his face, but he was equally sure of what was showing on it. Marooned on Monsalvat. . . .

Clellendol said, "I think we'll be rescued, despite all that. Spsom have their humor, but their civilization is older than ours, both Ler and Human put together. And they are not barbarians. My own feeling is that the warship will go down for repairs, and come here. Less than a year. Maybe no more than a season. Moreover, I think Vdhitz knows it. It's in character. He also knows I know. It's his joke on Flerdistar and the perils of thinking you know more than you do."

"Does she know?"

"No. Not yet. I am saving it for the proper moment. I suspect Vdhitz is also savoring punch lines as well and is waiting for the proper timing. As far as I am concerned, it can stay that way for the time. Now . . . let us join the others." Clellendol looked to the small fire the Haydar had made, where tall shadows were beginning to stride back and forth, as if readying, preparing themselves. The Haydar seemed nervous, wishing for action, although none spoke a word, and their movements made no noise. Only one seemed to remain relatively still, one tall shape, graceful and slender, who stood facing the fire, directly opposite Meure and Clellendol, head bowed, her face deep in the shadows of her hood. Her hands fidgeted with what seemed to be a small bag made of leather.

There seemed to be more Haydar present now than had been gathered about the wagon during the day; they seemed to materialize out of the shadows too. Meure thought they were the ones who had been gone through the day, but he did not speculate upon what they might have been doing. The Spsom were there, and their slave, and the Humans and Ler were also approaching the group about the fire, urged in part by Flerdistar and their desire not to be left alone on the plains of Ombur.

Flerdistar joined Meure and Clellendol, whispering excitedly, "The one who calls himself Morgin tells me that events have been so extraordinary today that they are going to call for a divination by the girl . . . what's the more, they don't care that we watch, which is something I wouldn't expect in primitives."

Clellendol commented, "Perhaps they're not primitive. . . ."

The girl's face clouded with a most unhappy expression and she answered, "Of course they are—the wildest sort of barbarians and anthropophages too!"

"On this planet, Human society is old, and was imposed upon the native life-forms. The Klesh were considered to have low potential for survival, yet they have survived, even prospered, after their own fashion, with no help from either of their would-be helpers. There is either something operant here which we don't see yet, or can't perceive, or there is a highly sophisticated system of order in force; perhaps all three."

"I think you are reading data into random numbers."

Clellendol responded mildly, conversationally, "You have been trained to realize the condition of the past through its shadows in the present; not the less have I been trained to be suspicious about that same present, to perceive traps and snares. Just so can I tell you that I *know* we have already set off several alarms and telltales during the course of the day and our landing here: an entity—whether creature, organization, or thing—has become aware of us and observes us. I have the suspicion that it may have known we were coming. This—if true—falls into patterns of risk-assumption I do not wish to follow yet."

Flerdistar accepted the correction without retort, "Possible, possible, indeed. Talking to Morgin, I can sense something unnatural in their pasts."

"An event?"

"No, a presence. The sense of it is . . . smeared out through time, that's the way I'd say it. I'm only getting a little of it just yet, so I've had to allow for considerable error. That's all I'd say now."

"Remain alert, if you will, and share with me, as it was intended that we do."

"So I will. Now hush; they are to begin their rite."

The Haydars had ceased their pacing and settled into a loose circle about the small fire. Only the girl remained standing, still holding her head bowed, deep in thought, or trance. Meure also noticed, on the far side of the fire, that some non-Haydar had joined the tribal circle: Morgin and his party, and the Spsom.

The girl moved slowly around the fire, avoiding it while giving the impression that she was unaware of it, stopping before one Haydar who sat alone, separated from the others by a gap of respect.

Flerdistar whispered, barely audibly, "The girl now readies herself, and approaches the leader. Ringuid Coam Mallam. She will speak for the spirit world. This is a chancy time for us, for he will do what she says . . . Mallam has requested a divination, and he must abide by the oracle."

The girl said something, to Mallam, but Meure couldn't make out the words. An introduction, a preamble?

Flerdistar continued. "Now she makes the invocation; she mentions certain divine beings known to her, and others, pos-

sibly demons, or revered persons from the past. And at the
end, she invokes a St. Zermille . . . now she holds the bag
up, now she lowers it, and dumps it before Mallam, so that
he may see the disposition of its contents . . . something
white."

Meure peered through the darkness, dazzled by the fire.
What had fallen on the ground looked like bones.

"Now she speaks again . . . she enumerates the basic configurations, which Mallam knows as well as she. The objects
are bones from the hand and fingers of a sacrifice, I think of
one of their prey tribes . . . no. I hear it, now. The bones are
of one of their people, her predecessor. Now she studies the
positions. She points, and Mallam follows, agrees. They are
to go on a hunt . . . tonight. The Spsom will accompany
them; they are to be initiated. Under no circumstances must
they leave this band, the Dagazaram. If they do, misfortune.
Now she comes to the rest, and says as firmly that the others,
which is us, must depart immediately, not to be harmed or
hunted. Something about a talisman . . . I can't make it out.
Mallam concurs, and they discuss how to do it. The girl isn't
clear on this. Her reading only gives what to do, not how to
accomplish it. Mallam presses her now. He wants to take us
somewhere, a place I don't know. She looks at the bones and
says no. It's not far enough. He mentions another place,
Medlight. No. She is under some strain, now. She ventures a
suggestion, another place I don't know, something about flying. Mallam is angry, but controlled. It is resolved. She kneels
to retrieve the bones, and the others stand . . . something
else is going to happen, something dark . . ."

Meure did not really wish to see anything dark, but he
could not look away, either. Now the Haydar were getting to
their feet, slowly, but still maintaining the loose circle. They
were all staring intently at the girl, while she carefully retrieved the bones from their places. She finished, and sat back
on her heels, as if exhausted, her head thrown back, her eyes
closed. Then she seemed to come to herself again, and slowly
got to her feet, carefully avoiding looking at any one of the
surrounding group. They were all watching her intently as
she replaced the bones in the little bag, and pulled the string.
The divination was over.

Meure decided he'd seen enough, and slipped behind Clellendol and Flerdistar, to move to the place where the wagon
had been left. He did not look at the fire, or the girl, or the
tribe, but he could see out of the corner of his eyes that they

were still standing motionless, silent. He moved through the dark, unseen. All eyes were on the circle.

He walked across the springy turf to the wagon, where the Sumpters were half-reclining in their harness, unconcerned. Meure wished to avoid the Sumpters, beasts who looked like men, or men who had become bestial. He didn't know which. He stopped at the back of the wagon and looked out over the starlit plains rolling away to the east. Behind him, he could hear now fragments of conversation, motion. The firelight began to fade, as if it were being put out. He listened, despite his best intentions: nothing had happened. Meure breathed deeply. Now they were going to move again. Flying, Flerdistar had said. Probably a rattling fast run in the cart of Morgin, although it didn't exactly look like it had been built for speed. . . .

He heard the Sumpters suddenly start, snorting, rattling their harness. The wagon moved a little, creaking against its hand-brake. There was a soft noise, and when he turned to look around the corner of Morgin's wagon, he saw a darkness obscuring the dying fire, a tall, spare form approaching, one hand on the wagon's edge to steady herself, and Meure Schasny felt his hair prickling along the back of his neck, and ice running in his heart. He stopped.

She came within arm's-reach before she seemed to be aware of him. Meure stood absolutely still, afraid to move. He had no idea what these wild Haydars might do, oracle or no. Besides, she might be immune from her own words, might be under another oracle. This was a mythic figure before him, not a person he could comprehend, easily.

Tenguft was tall, about half a head taller or more than him; and at that she was slightly slumped, not at her full height. Meure could not make out any details of her, close as she was, for the darkness obscured everything.

She seemed to become aware of him slowly, as if still in the oracular trance. He could sense she was, however, staring at him intently. Meure wanted to turn and run, but he knew he had better not.

She studied him for a long moment, then said, in a soft, breathy voice, "You, it is to be." Meure heard the words, strange, but he thought he understood her. She continued, "Come with me. Now, fly. Tonight." She said something else, wearily, but Meure didn't understand the words. Only something about 'Incana.' Where they were going?

Tenguft extended her hand, took Meure's arm to guide

him. The contact was light, the feel of the hand unexpectedly soft, but he could sense steel under the softness, and impulses held rigidly in check. What? He was sure of it. Did she want to hunt him, and was restraining herself? She started him off, with her, repeating the word again. "Come." They walked around the wagon.

Meure now saw that there was a different air to the place they had been: the Haydar and the two Spsom were in one group, all staring at the girl and himself with opaque, flinty stares that he found intensely uncomfortable. . . . The Ler elders were standing disconsolately with Morgin and his associates, to the side. Other Haydar were walking among the flying creatures, prodding them with the butts of their spears, speaking to them in harsh, peremptory tones.

From the group close by the eratzenasters, Flerdistar hurried to meet Meure and the Haydar seeress. She spoke quickly, breathlessly, "We are being split up! Morgin is sending the Elders with his servants! He is turning over his function here to one among the Haydar who is also of that office, and going with us. We two, and you four Humans, plus Morgin and the Vfzyekhr will fly . . . northeast, to another land, Incana. A place they call 'Cucany.' It's a fortress, or a castle."

Meure asked, "Fly? In what? Do we whistle up an aircraft?"

"No," she said. "On those things." A tug on his elbow reminded Meure that someone was guiding him. Other Haydar were gesturing at the grounded Eratzenasters, moving Audiart, Halander, Ingraine. It was clear they did not wish to go.

Flerdistar and Clellendol were unceremoniously hustled off toward the beasts, now grumbling and making jerky, awkward motions as they were abused into wakefulness by the suddenly impatient Haydars. Flerdistar had time to say one more thing before they were separated, "Schasny, be careful. I think you have become part of some kind of rite . . ." Her voice trailed off. Meure and Tenguft were now beside the large one she had ridden in the evening.

The tall girl gestured. "Up." Meure reached to the semirigid surface, the leading edge of the aft wing, touched it. It was covered in a microfine fuzz, and felt cool to the touch. It, the skin, moved slightly, as if sliding over a harder structure beneath. On all fours, moving with extreme care, he negotiated the slope to the spine of the creature, which was slightly depressed, and bare of all coverings. The skin felt looser. Tenguft bounded onto the Eratzenaster, and mounted with an odd spanning locomotion, graceful from much practice, but also gawky and awkward. She settled herself just aft of the narrowest part of the creature, moving experimentally up and down, bouncing to find the right place. Her motions were transmitted through the creature's members, making it rock and vibrate slightly. Now she tossed her hood back with an abrupt motion of her head, and turned to glare at Meure. She made a peremptory gesture with her right hand, to a spot behind her. "Here."

Meure clambered forward along the spine to the girl, and settled himself close behind her, not touching her. She reached behind herself with one of her long arms, and pulled Meure up against her; then she reached with the other arm, took his hands and placed them across her thighs to the Eratzenaster's skin in front of her. She bent his fingers into the cool, flexible surface. She said, "Hold here." She did not wait to see that he had done so, but released her grip on him and slapped the creature hard across the spine.

Meure gripped instinctively and the Eratzenaster lurched forward, getting its drooping wingtips clear of the ground, then using them to help it along.

Tenguft was still sitting upright, looking back to see that the others were up and moving; Meure ventured a quick look. He saw others, precariously mounted, alone, holding on for their lives, while the Haydar stood aside and hooted encouragement and instructions to them. All the larger beasts had riders, but the smaller ones were up and moving, too. Apparently the whole flock flew together.

The girl tensed her body, dug her heels into the stretched membrane connecting the wings, and leaned forward. Meure moved with her, feeling the thing beneath him begin increasing its speed, turning slightly to find the correct azimuth, the heading into the wind. There was a breeze, he realized, and he felt it increase. He was also acutely conscious of the girl's body he was pressed against; he could feel the muscles beneath the thin cloak she wore, feel the heat of the wiry body. Her scent was sunwarmed, oily, aromatic and very slightly sweet at the same time.

Tenguft looked back at her passenger over her shoulder, a broad grin opening her lips to reveal white teeth that gleamed in the starlight. She slapped the Eratzenaster again and its awkward, loping pace increased, and Meure could hear a rhythmic, dry sound from underneath. He felt now tendons beginning to move in the creature's structure. It felt as if more than four limbs were moving, but he couldn't be certain. Now it began to bound, making a rocking motion, springing along. The wings began making synchronized motions; the wind now became uncomfortable. Meure could see little directly forward, for the girl was in the way, but it seemed as if they were approaching a rise, a low ridgeline. The Eratzenaster now began working its body violently, struggling for speed; they seemed to leap forward, the ground rose to the ridgeline, the wings beating violently, grabbing at air, a thrust, a lurch, a falling sensation, and Meure, from his vantage point near the thin middle of the creature, saw the ground sliding away underneath him.

The motions of the Eratzenaster were labored, carrying two as it was, and it gained altitude slowly, beating its wings in their odd syncopated rhythm. The wind in Meure's face became cold. It seemed they were moving to the east. He held on tightly. He felt muscles move in the hard body against him, shoulder and arm, buttock and leg. Now they began a slow, shallow turn to the north with almost no bank. He could feel Tenguft still pounding the creature's spine, urging it to greater speed. The flexing motions increased, and the wind hurt. He averted his face, and leaned closer to the girl. The motions became more violent, then the rhythm changed abruptly. Meure risked a glance ahead into the slipstream and saw the forward wings now set, opened wide in a shallow dihedral, the tips opened to wring the last gram of lift, while behind and under him, the rear wings thrust powerfully. The motion was violent, and he pressed as close to the girl as he could, feeling the contours of her body. She pressed herself down, almost prone. She moved, adjusting to him. Meure pressed himself against her, and felt a strong visceral pleasure in the motion. Tenguft turned slightly, although she could no longer turn enough to see him, and squeezed with the muscles of her hips. The message was direct and unmistakable, and required no words, which would have been torn away in the blast of the slipstream anyway. Then she returned her attention to guiding the Eratzenaster.

In the night of Monsalvat they flew, apparently not at any great altitude, although the speed with which the creatures flew seemed very great, judging by the blast of the slipstream and the violent motions of the aft wings, which made his perch feel unbalanced and precarious. He dared not look around to see if the others were keeping up, although now and again Tenguft would steer their mount from side to side so that she could see behind her. Meure guessed they were keeping up, for she did not divert from their northward course.

He sensed a darkened, empty land, the swales and rolling prairies of Ombur, passing beneath them. There was an area that seemed jumbled and rugged, canyons and gullies, and the land fell away and a great darkness spread beneath them. There was a chill dampness in the air, and the odor of a river; a large one, apparently, for these sensations continued for some time. Then the dampness faded, and a resinous scent replaced it. Meure could not make out any details in the country beneath, but it seemed more irregular than Ombur. They increased their altitude, and made slow detours around hills. The land seemed to be rising. Now they were passing over an inhabited land, for occasionally Meure could see yellowish lights, which were invariably extinguished as they passed overhead; but these were few, and scattered.

Now the scale of the hills increased, became low mountains separated by broad, open valleys. Tenguft made no attempt to fly over them, but followed the valleys as the openings presented themselves. The mountains were curiously isolated, in many cases steep and scarped. Meure's eyes were becoming adjusted to the starlight, and he could see more clearly to the sides. Many of the hills and mountains seemed to be crowned with structures, some large, some small. Castles? Fortresses? Some were nothing more than stone towers, others huts, and some more substantial. There were no lights below.

Meure sensed the Eratzenaster pitching up slightly, felt their speed decrease a bit; they were climbing, slowing. The forward wings still remained outstretched. Meure ventured a quick look over the girl's shoulder, and saw a great bulk ahead, surmounted by a dark, blocky mass, with pinpoints of yellow light in it. The mountain seemed to be steeper on the side they were approaching it from, swooping up from the broad valley floor, peaking like a wave, and falling off to the north more gradually.

The girl turned and shouted over her shoulder, "Cucany!" Now they were just below the mountain peak, turning onto it from the center of the valley, a shallow left turn. Meure's eyes were now adjusted enough to the darkness to make out the place they were making for; more or less, a fortress atop a long mountain that faced the valley in a steep scarp. He couldn't make out fine details of the structure, but it seemed to be a blocky castle or fortress that had developed whole families of erratic projecting additions, almost grown on like lichens on a brick: shelfs, turrets, towers of several mismatched styles and shapes; apartments, balconies. There was no city or town or anything resembling one about the structure—if there was a town here, the town was the fortress.

The Eratzenaster continued the long and shallow turn to the left, maintaining its altitude and dropping its pace somewhat. Now they were just below the summit of the mountain, looking up at the fortress; now they were turning back the way they had come, apparently to land somewhere else. Their mount now stopped the beating of its rear wings and set them, like the front pair, for maximum lift, pitching its nose down to keep airspeed up. Meure risked a look behind him, to his left; and there the others were, strung out in a loose line formation, all turning behind them and setting their wings into glide shapes. Meure could see on most of the larger ones irregular protuberances along the spines between the wings: their passengers. The riderless Eratzenasters continued to climb and began making playful, gliding passes beside the burdened ones before following the lead beast down.

Their speed now lost its driving force and the airblast gave up some of its violence. He felt Tenguft's body tensing and working again, instructing and guiding the creature they flew on. Now the glide angle pitched down more steeply, but the creature set its wings so that its speed did not build up. Meure sensed a definite holding-back, a pause, before they committed for grounding. The noise of the wind abated, too. Tenguft leaned around and shouted back, "Watch now; then stop!"

Meure shouted back, "People there?"

She answered, "No people; Korsors! Dromoni! Maybe a Selander!"

Meure did not inquire of the nature of the forms she mentioned. He reflected that on Monsalvat, not all Humans were human, and that there were probably stranger shapes on the planet than Haydar and Sumpters.

Now their mount, still holding back, slowing, made a sweep over the dark ground below, moving subtly from side to side. Apparently satisfied, it made an abrupt series of motions with its rear wings, rocking them from side to side rapidly: then it flattened out its wings and pitched down hard, a motion that almost threw Meure. He grasped tightly, pressed closer to the girl. The dark ground below rushed up at them slantwise, fast. Meure began to see quick flashes of details, bushes, small trees, a watercourse, and the Eratzenaster pitched up and began beating its rear wings rapidly, shallowly. They began to settle, and the front wings started beating, now in an entirely different rhythm from their take-off beat; the ground rushed up at them as the Eratzenaster made its final approach descent. At the last possible moment, both pairs of wings beating wildly, it broke its fall into an awkward glide, stalled out, and made contact, slowing itself with the unseen limbs of the underside.

Tenguft did not release her hold on the creature until it was almost completely stopped; then she abruptly sat back, throwing one leg over the side. "Off!" And she ran lightly down the leading edge of the right rear wing. Meure followed her, half-falling. All around them the others were landing in their semi-controlled crashes, dropping out of the sky like leaves in the Autumn. Meure saw Morgin the Embasse climbing most ungracefully off his mount, stumbling as his feet hit the ground. He did not wait, but ran to where the others were still huddling on their mounts, and began urging them off. Tenguft was doing the same. Meure followed them and ran to one of the Eratzenasters they had missed, calling, "Get down! They want all of us off!"

The rider sat up and began clambering down, like someone in a trance. Meure could see from the shape that it was Audiart; the last few steps to the ground, he had to help her. Standing, she was shivering. It was then that he noticed that he was suddenly hot, almost overheated. Of course, the air had cooled him, and he hadn't noticed.

Now the others were all off, and Tenguft ran from beast to beast, slapping them on the wingtips, tugging at them, but making as little sound as possible; and one by one, reluctantly, they began scuttling along the ground, climbing awkwardly over irregular places, and one by one, springing into the air, beating the dark night with their leathern wings. Meure watched them depart as they climbed into the night, wheeling back around to the southwest, climbing higher than they had when they had come, noiselessly, then fading dark spots, and then lost in the starry background.

Tenguft led them to a small, bare knoll, from which they had a good view of the surrounding countryside, and indicated that they should remain where they were. Morgin took Flerdistar aside and spoke earnestly with her. The Ler girl gained her feet and approached Meure.

"I come to you first. Morgin says that we are to remain here for the night; we will go to the city tomorrow. The Haydar will not approach a strongpoint at night. In those places they shoot first, and Morgin makes me to understand that in Incana, that may be the best policy. Morgin also says for me to tell you that you must do as the girl says, no matter how odd it may seem. . . ."

At the end, she trailed off suggestively in a manner Meure was not sure he liked. She returned to her place, between Morgin and Clellendol and the Vfzyekhr. Meure stood where he was, uncertainly. Tenguft, satisfied that all were placed as she wanted them, now turned to Meure, coming down the hill to him. He watched the spare, tall figure approaching him, a persona of mystery and power. And violence, he added. But he also remembered the tense feel of her wiry body when they had ridden the wind, and the suggestive motions she had made, once; and when she motioned for him to follow her, away from the knoll, he thought he knew something of what she had in mind, although he could not, for the life of himself, imagine why.

6

"There is, of course, extreme danger in coming into contact with a demon of a malignant or unintelligent nature. It should, however, be said that such demons only exist for imperfectly initiated magicians."

—*A. C.*

Two suns cleared the horizon and illuminated the land of Incana, dispelling the dawn twilight, replacing blue shadows with a winy tangerine light; Meure, breakfastless, found him-

self toiling up a steepening slope toward an enigmatic structure which became more, not less, peculiar as he drew closer
to it. The others climbed the slope with zeal or lassitude as
befitted their basic dispositions; Clellendol deliberate and
careful, Morgin tiredly, Halander and Ingraine awkwardly
and reluctantly, Flerdistar quite beyond her limits physically
but grimly determined to go upward and see it all. The
Vfzyekhr climbed easily, as if on an outing. Tenguft. . . .

Tenguft moved up the slope warily, always watching, listening; pause: then a step, another, pause, listen, look. She
watched the lowlands behind them out of the corner of her
eyes, never leaving it entirely, never losing the air of a preda-
tor in a strange land. The orange cast to the light seemed to
dull her, as it brightened the air, the rocks, the scrubby vegetation, waving slightly in a light, cool breeze. It had not been
thus in the night, when she had let her robe fall away from
her and calmly walked into the icy stream at the foot of the
valley, calmly motioning to Meure that he join her. He had
been chilled by the water and intimidated by the half-wild,
intense tall girl, more so by her manner, which became surprisingly passive past a point he was not sure had passed. Nor
had she spoken any words at all, not since they had dismounted the Eratzenaster, but the sounds she had made deep in her
throat would haunt his memory forever.

Audiart came last, going slowly and laboriously; she was
not made for clambering over pathless mountains and made
no apologies for her pace.

Now above him, Tenguft halted, motioning the others to
stop as well, while she scanned the structure looming at the
top of the slope. Meure found a secure place, and took the
time to look as well.

Now he did not have the panoramic view from the air,
wheeling high over the valley, nor the long, dim night-view
from the valley floor. Now, in the bright tangerine morning
of Monsalvat, he could only see one side of it, and it no longer looked quaint, eccentric, barbarian. To the contrary, it
looked ever more grim, although it still retained its erratic air
of improvisation. The basic lines of the structure leaned in-
ward, from a many-sided foundation merging with the rock
of the mountain, then gradually becoming more or less
square. It had, Meure suspected, once been rather flat-roofed.
No longer. Now superstructures covered it like lichens on a
rotten log; galleries, complete with tiled roofs, turrets, balco-

nies, many connected with masonry staircases, covered or
uncovered, Projecting cupolas leaned far out into empty
space, some with great open spaces staring out into the air,
others closed tightly up with only slit windows for illumina-
tion, or outlook. Higher up, it became more erratic, the turrets fading upwards into minarets, watchtowers, some
complete with crenelations and embrasures.

Clellendol negotiated what Meure thought to be a particularly difficult section of scree and joined him. Clellendol, too,
had been looking upward, at the strongpoint Cucany.

"Look yonder," Clellendol gestured toward the rising suns.
"You can see more of these castles on the peaks, all around
us."

Meure looked in the direction the Ler youth had indicated.
Far up the valley, true enough, was another castle perched
atop another peak, as precarious, if not more so, in its site.
Meure also saw something flickering, a reflection, or sheen,
about the dark mass of the distant castle. "What's the light,
there?"

Clellendol shaded his eyes and watched for a moment. "A
heliograph, sending code; it's regularly modulated. I can't
read it, of course. I should imagine that there's an answer up
there in Cucany on the sunlit side."

Meure looked up to Cucany, but couldn't make out any
movement, or indeed, any sign that the fortress was even inhabited.

Clellendol ventured, "I don't see much evidence on this
slope that they *do* much, up there, but everything suggests
that they observe and comment; make no mistake: they've
been watching us since we came out of the brush before
dawn. I can tell by watching the Haydar girl, if by nothing
else; her attention is now about seven-eighths on the city, or
fortress, or whatever it is."

"She was not afraid by the river, last night."

"Curious, is it not? Perhaps whatever she feared will not
approach water, although I cannot imagine it . . . but never
mind. There is much here which will prove beyond my experience." Then he changed the subject. "And you—I trust
you are learning to follow the wave of the present, to get into
the flow of it."

"I feel much out of my depth here, to be candid. I am
being offered much, but the reasons don't make a coherent
whole. It's as if I were being guided to something out of the
ordinary, for reasons I can't see."

"As you know, those were my feelings earlier. I am more suspicious now, as well." He glanced upward to the outcrop where Tenguft was sitting warily, her hawk profile outlined against the lighter tan color of the walls of Cucany. "That one, now; Morgin told us last night that Haydars do not enter Incana voluntarily. There is no specific prohibition, indeed, there is no government as such to prohibit them. And as you see, the land is open. But they do not come here except in extraordinary circumstances. They fear these people, these Kurbish Windfowlers, as they call themselves. Morgin either does not know, or is being reticent; but there is something about the past, and something these people did. Flerdistar is trying to plumb it."

"I see . . . but she brings us to a land she fears . . ."

"She has brought you, not us. We simply have no other place to go, and since she's on the way anyway . . . Moreover, Haydars are known for their refusal to enter any permanent structure. They consider such things to affront the spirit world; therefore a city is unclean; a fortress more so, since it is its permanence that distinguishes it. Yet I do believe she will walk into that pile up there to deliver you."

"To whom?"

"I am asking myself, '*to what.*' There is no people in the universe without a fear, or fears. Therefore to override hers she must be enacting a powerful shamanistic role, which is already hers within the Haydar tribe."

Tenguft stood and motioned to the rest of the party. It was time to move on. Clellendol stood, and turned to leave, saying quietly over his shoulder, "Still and all, friend, you must go forward, for here and now you own no back into which to retreat, as we might say in the House of the Thieves."

Meure said, also standing, "But I am the least of those to set out blindly."

"We seem to have gathered little choice, you the least of us. So go forward with faith; and with eyes open . . . you know that on the sea, one can still go anywhere one wants, even though the wind only blows one way, but in a canyon one can only go where the stream leads. But there are streams and there are streams."

"What is the meaning of that?"

"Some courses have carved themselves; others are guided by the skillful arrangement of rockpiles to either side, to provide a given destination. This thing we are on seems unnatural, all the more so with every step we go farther into it. It

becomes . . ." Here Clellendol hesitated, then continued,
". . . as if it didn't make any difference whether we could see
it or not. It will even become obvious to you in time. I sound
like I'm telling you to become a willing sacrifice, but I'm not;
you are to be given your chance. You must take it and act
innocently, which is to say, unpredictably. Only there lies
safety, in unsafety."

Then he turned and began climbing, and would say no
more. Meure followed, looking back to see if the others were
climbing again after their brief stop. They were, and most
were already past him. He looked up the mountain, and began climbing.

Rested a little, at first they made good progress, but they
soon slowed, doing progressively less walking and more
climbing. The slope became steeper, and dislodged pebbles
now rattled down the mountainside for a considerable distance before stopping. Meure could hear them clearly in the
calm air, bouncing and ringing on the stones below. He did
not look back, or down.

He did not look up; now Cucany seemed close enough to
reach upward a little and touch . . . In reality, the foundation courses were still a few meters higher than them. But he
was now close enough to see the structure in detail. There
was nothing particularly modern or sophisticated about its
construction: heavy basal courses of dressed stone, laid without mortar, skillfully, but not extremely so. Above that began
the masonry, timbers and rubble, projecting braces of stone
and wood. The masonry had weathered to warm pastel tan,
and the wood to a silvery-brown. Some of the balconies and
hanging galleries were almost directly above them, soaring
into the aqua-blue sky.

And Tenguft was nowhere in sight.

Now he was at the base of the castle, and saw there was a
tiny, precarious ledge that ran erratically about the base, disappearing to the east around a projection of the walls. To the
left, it followed a spine of the mountain upwards, up a flight
of rude steps, at the top of which Tenguft awaited them,
looking not at them, but out over the empty landscape, the
tremendous open distances of Incana. Meure looked where
she was looking: to the east, mountains rose in isolated peaks
and ridgelines like waves in a frozen sea, a dun sea illuminated by an orange star. Near the horizon, he thought he
could make out the shimmer of heat waves, or a mirage forming, but he could not be sure. The expanse of distance was

hypnotic; The horizon seemed much farther away than he knew it had to be from the size of the planet. And he also saw that what Clellendol had said was true: almost every point of high ground held a structure of one size or another. And that in a good number of them, a flickering, pulsing point of light could be glimpsed, a silvery flickering like sunlight being reflected off an unstable surface, perhaps water, although not necessarily so. Meure felt very uncomfortable, and wondered if he was catching some of Tenguft's wariness; or perhaps it was the overpowering nearness of this fortress atop a bare and uncultivated mountain, with little sign of habitation in the land, save the enigmatic castles. Inside, they watched, and discussed, and consulted with other castles. . . . Out of the corner of his eyes he could now sense the horizon flickering of the heliographs, first one, then another, then others.

Tenguft waited for the rest of them to come up on the path, and then continued up the rude stone steps, following the line of the last outcrop. Meure followed her.

The stairs made a few more blind turns, always upward, and then ended in a smallish stone-flagged porch, facing a tall, narrow doorway shaped in an ogive arch. Tall doors of dark wood and black iron barred the way. Beside the door, a stone gargoyle projected a leering, slavering face into space; stylized drops from its lolling tongue hung down: apparently a bell-pull. Tenguft pulled on the cord without hesitation. They heard nothing within, and waited passively.

It was only a few moments before movement could be heard inside, in response to the doorbell; there was an immanent thumping and knocking, as if a bolt were being slowly withdrawn, and then the arched, tall doors opened on a figure even more curious than Tenguft and the Haydars, if such a thing were possible.

At first, Meure saw a tall, spare figure wearing a helmet or headdress. Its body was concealed under a long black robe not dissimilar to the loose robes of the Haydars. Like them, it seemed slender and tall, the headdress adding to its height so that it seemed as tall as the Haydar girl. As far as he could see, it carried no arms of any kind. The headdress, however, attracted all his attention: It was as wide as the shoulders and easily twice as tall as the head within. It was shaped most curiously, being built up of a number of superimposed prisms; from a point resting on the upper chest, it rose up-

ward in straight lines to points just above the shoulders—
these apparently supported the weight of the contraption.
From the shoulder points, small shelves, triangular, stepped
back at a rising angle to meet another prism shape, which
was a continuation of the opening for the face. This inner
prism rose to a height above the head and also terminated in
a sharp point. Seen from the side, the lines of the helmet
formed a diagonal cross shape. The top was filled in with triangles, points down. The face opening lozenge-shaped, a continuation of the outer lines of the figure. The colors of it were
arresting, too: the sides were a bright, deep red, while the
rooflike top triangles were painted a flat black.

A face could be seen inside, but only dimly, for the over-
hang of the helmet blocked most of the light; the face was
heavily shadowed. Whatever was inside seemed bearded, and
the eyes were outlined with greenish-white circles, that
glowed? Glowed. Fluorescent paint. Meure suppressed an
urge to idiotic laughter. Suppressed it because the attitude of
Tenguft displayed unmistakable submission.

Morgin nodded politely to the silent figure, and turned to
the members of the party. He said, very seriously, "You see
before you the Noble Molio Azendarach, Phanet of Dzoz Cucany. You are his guests, but do not take the word lightly, for
travelers are few now in the land Incana and hospitality is
not offered to all. Proceed forward, then, with respect."

The helmeted person, Azendarach, made a slight motion, a
subtle nod, and motioned for them to follow; having done so,
he turned and proceeded into the depths of the castle without
waiting to see if they were following. Morgin went first, followed by Tenguft and Meure. The rest came after.

Another helmeted figure slid out of the shadows by the
door, to close it behind them, but they had little time to see
the second one, save that his helmet seemed almost as large
and impossible in shape as Azendarach's. The Phanet was
moving on, down a high-arched corridor which was in strong
contrast to the openness and light outside, for it was dark and
gloomy, the ceiling fading into shadows.

Azendarach led them a ways along the dark hallway, and
then turned into a narrow way, climbing a steep stairwell. Inside, there seemed to be the same construction as the outside—masonry over rubble braced by half-timbers sunk into
the material.

Now they climbed the awkward stairwell through many
abrupt turns until they were thoroughly confused as to direc-

tion. The stair was interrupted frequently by small landings with narrow doors fronting on them. None were open, and no sound could be heard; it was as if the castle were uninhabited. Yet the doors were well-maintained, and the sills were swept clean. People lived in Cucany, true enough; it seemed that they were very quiet about it.

The stairs continued upward, sometimes almost too steeply to be called stairs; rather more like ladders. Azendarach maintained the same pace, whether walking on the level, or on the sharpest ascents, always holding his carriage so that the helmet did not wobble or misalign itself in any way.

At the last, they emerged onto a broad landing where the ascent ended. All were breathing hard from the climb, save the Phanet, who was opening the iron-bound door with great concentration. While he was manipulating the mechanism, Tenguft leaned to Meure and whispered, "Wizards! Beware!" After she said it, she straightened and shivered slightly.

Azendarach opened the door and allowed it to stand ajar for them to enter. Light flooded into the dim landing from an enormous room alive with the play of light. The contrast was blinding at first.

They were obviously high up in the castle, or Dzoz, as Morgin had called it, probably near its highest point. This room appeared to be a single large area, with curtained alcoves along the walls; where there were no curtains, the walls were whitewashed carefully to a uniform flat white. One side was entirely open to the air, and seemed to be one of the projecting galleries Meure had seen from the ground. Facing the south, generally, it curved far out in a smooth line unbroken by supports. Its sill was even more curious, being a pool of water. The roof was stepped back slightly. There was no furniture in the room, save some antique cabinets or wardrobes along the walls, in the curtained sections, and cushions scattered around the floor, which was of flagstones. Air from the breeze outside whispered in the corners of the room, and light played there, some from the bright-dun landscape stretching away to the horizons, and from reflections from the wind-ruffled pool along the sill.

Another helmeted figure emerged from a curtained alcove and made motions of deference to Azendarach. They spoke then, ignoring the visitors, but Meure listened alertly. To his surprise, their speech was more understandable than Tenguft's, although to her ears it probably sounded archaic and cryptic.

Azendarach said, in a thin reedy voice, almost like nasal whispering, "What are the reports, Erisshauten?"

The one called Erisshauten answered, "Phanet, Dzoz Soltro relayed through Kormendy and Endrode that a party of Lagostomes attempted to pass Vakiflar Narrows, but were repulsed and punished. Dzoz Veszid and Orkeny in the Eastmarch report empty reflections. Lisbene likewise. Midre, Andely and Lachryma report through Malange Gather that a party of Eratzenasters departed the Reach for the Ombur, exiting above Torskule. Atropope had an incident with Korsors. Potale Dzoz has reflections, but they are not clear and a more expert reader has been summoned . . . shall we dispatch Romulu Bedetdznatsch?"

"What was their nature, at Potale?"

"Continuing, but weak. They want an evening reading . . ."

"Understandable . . . but we may not spare Bedetdznatsch. We will read tonight; have Onam Hareschacht posted from Lisbene. If he leaves now he can be there in time."

"Your will, Phanet," replied the man, and he turned and returned into the alcove from whence he had emerged.

The prism-shaped helmet turned back to them, and once again the eye-circles stared out of the darkness of the helmet at them.

Azendarach said, almost whispering, "These are the riders of the ship of space?"

Tenguft answered, straining to match the phrasing of the Phanet, "These people and a thing for which I have no word . . ."

". . . No matter. We have taken knowledge of it."

". . . Were the dunnage. Those who owned it remained with my people, now of the Ombur."

"Just so. I understand. I have read of it in the prodromic current; and so has its profluence been. We did not believe, for there is much that passes understanding in the reflections. Yet they continued so, even to their meeting of the Venatic People, on Ombur. And they were to be here, and so indeed are they here. We shall continue the eutaxy."

Meure suspected he was in the presence of a madman, or a lunatic cultist, or perhaps both. Neither were improbably on Monsalvat.

Apparently Azendarach divined his uneasiness, for he now said, "The Kurbish Windfowlers of Incana are reputed the strangest folk of all Aceldama, which you will know as Monsalvat." He nodded the heavy helmet toward Tenguft. "That child of open spaces, of the night, and murder, who is no small thing at the arts herself, and who practices divination using the hand-bones of the left hand of her own mother, given to her willingly, I might add, she fears for her very sanity in the halls of Cucany. But consider, civilized creatures. I call you creatures for I know that all are not human. Some of you are of the kind of the ancient enemy, he who made us as we are. Have no fear! For we know the ends of the things of the past, and the Warriors are vanished, faded away. Whatever vendetta might be left over we have more than expiated against one another these millennia. But consider, I say: Incana *is* an empty land, but no man will march on it, not even the pestiferous Lagostomes. We neither expand, enslave, nor disturb the rest of others with our machinations. We mine the peaks, we grow things in the roof gardens, we trade, we gather the wild things, we limit ourselves . . . altogether good neighbors. But," here his voice rose in volume, "we read truth in the reflections of the light of this world, and consult, and act, and if we are right, then if some say, 'there walk wizards on the parapet,' then so let it be as they will say."

"And so Bedetdznatsch and I so read what has come to pass. Here, in an isolated Dzoz in an empty land, and that one such would be brought to us who would dare what we dare not to ourselves. One from *Outside*. Embasse, tell him."

Morgin, said, "History. Only one man ever tried to unify this planet, knowing that to be the necessary precondition to our rejoining our human fellows. He lived long ago, and was called many things, but his name was Cretus the Scribe. He was not a soldier, or a warrior, but one who could put things together. He started at a location, by the great river of Kepture, which no longer exists, but he finished here, in Incana, in Cucany. The great work was under way, and even the mad Lagos were restrained once from their breedings, and then there was no more. Cretus expired, the heirs fell to disagreements, and the empire vanished. The Windfowlers from Inner Incana remained true to his memory, but the rest fled like scavenger beetles in the dawn. Here is where the Scribe worked, counselled, plotted, built. Here, below ground, is where his dust remains, and an artifact he used. He was the last of his Klesh-kind, and only a quadroon of that was his in truth. He had no tribe, no land, no hetman, no loyalty but to his own vision. He had a thing he saw visions in, which no one else knew how to use, or wouldn't. It is widely accepted that the guardians of the world saw fit to strike him down for stealing their secrets of the future . . . that is what the people know of it."

They were interrupted by a young boy, obviously an apprentice, who wore only a light open framework about his head instead of the full rigor of the opaque helmet. The boy issued forth from the same alcove Erisshauten had come from, without asking permission, bowed with his hands hidden in his sleeves, and said, in a high voice, "My lord Phanet, the Cellar Chamberlain Trochanter advises me that all is in readiness."

Azendarach nodded acknowledgment, dismissed the boy with a gesture. Close on the boy's departure returned Erisshauten from whatever observation point he occupied.

Erisshauten announced, "Phanet, Dzoz Potale respectfully withdraws their request for the boon of interpretation. They aver that their reading is now clear, to be passed to the Master Reader without delay. It is this: 'Say that they say to do it now.' "

"That is all?"

"Just so they sent, M'Lord Phanet. They said that there was rapid clearing during our last series of transmissions."

The Phanet shook his headdress from side to side slowly, a universal gesture of unsureness. He sighed audibly, then said, "I cannot doubt a clear reading, for they are rare, and even the inexperienced lad at Potale can read a clear; nevertheless, I would wonder why we read no such message here. . . ?" He trailed off, musing, seemingly innocently.

Erisshauten began to evidence sighs of nervousness. He spoke, now rapidly, "Perhaps, your surety, it might lie in the practices of our own reader, the Noble Bedetdznatsch. Having read at dawn, and having performed the 'clearing mind of distraction by horizoning' exercise, he now takes his rest in his chambers."

Azendarach chuckled to himself, and said, expansively, "So, indeed. And I suppose the apprentices read in the day."

"I should not venture to comment upon the practices of the Noble Bedetdznatsch, but it does sound highly probable that such might conceivably be the case."

"Well, we shall not disturb old Romulu. Doubtless he has earned some freedom from opprobrium. Ready the chamber, then. I shall read."

"Begging M'Lord's pardon, but . . . in the presence of outlanders?"

" 'Now' must be verified. There is risk in what we would try."

"As you instruct, then." Erisshauten then fussily began to prepare the chamber for what they called a reading. First he latched the doors from inside, then he carefully arranged the cushions and throws on the floor. Azendarach stood aside and waited without comment. Erisshauten then walked gingerly to the parapet, peering owlishly outside, determining the angle of the suns. Then he returned, went to another alcove, and extracted an iron rod with a crank, which appeared to be pivoted at its concealed end. This he began turning; the mechanism this operated worked without noise whatsoever, indicating long use and careful maintenance, but the effects were immediately apparent. A section of the roof over the parapet began withdrawing into the supporting structure, allowing the orange sunlight of the two suns to flood into the room.

Azendarach now seemed remote, uninterested. He looked off into space, at noplace. Meure could not be sure, but his eyes seemed to have an unfocused look. Azendarach said, in a monotone, "What is the mode?"

Erisshauten answered, "Coming up on Broadside, M'Lord Azendarach. Best possible conditions there are, clear sky, no wind."

Azendarach did not acknowledge that he had heard. Erisshauten continued cranking the handle. Now, besides the light streaming into the room from the sunlight, more light appeared, as if from an artificial source. Meure looked up, to the low ceiling, but saw only a reflection from the pool of water along the parapet. The pool was there to throw a reflection of the sun onto the ceiling, or perhaps the walls, according to the time of day. The room became very bright.

Now Azendarach carefully got down to the floor, and laid himself out, with as much dignity as he could manage. The purpose of the odd headdress now seemed clearer: it was to minimize distraction and reduce the flux of light. The chamber was so bright that it was uncomfortable, and the visitors squinted.

Erisshauten motioned to the visitors for quiet. Azendarach stretched out, relaxed, became quiescent. Stared at the reflection of the suns on the ceiling. Meure felt uncomfortable. Omens! These damn Klesh read omens at the least provocation, in front of others, and they seemed to consider such behavior normal. He supposed that most of them used some method; they could conceivably meet necromancers, geo-

mancers, palmists, dreg-readers of several classifications, de-
pendant upon the beverage employed, fire-leapers, the whole
gamut. He risked a glance at Clellendol and Flerdistar. They
stood respectfully, also accepting the behavior without comment.

Now he looked at the reflections on the ceiling; it was a reflection of the suns, side by side. Broadside, Erisshauten had
called it. The image was not perfectly still, but wavered ever
so slightly, in sharp, nervous little movements. The image
conveyed nothing intelligible to Meure. The time was now
midafternoon.

Azendarach watched the reflections for some time, without
gesture or sound, or indeed any sign of consciousness. Then,
abruptly, he waved to Erisshauten and began getting to his
feet. He seemed to have some difficulty in doing so, and Audiart stepped forward, her hand extended, as if to offer assistance, but she stopped quickly. On one knee, Molio
Azendarach fixed her with a glance of malign intent, so that
she looked away, and stepped back, avoiding the imprint of
those glowing-rimmed eyes.

Azendarach gained his feet, while Erisshauten proceeded
with the operation of closing the parapet roof. When he had
finished, the Phanet said, "Yes, it is so, just so. I would rate
the uncertainty factor at Purple. The admonishment is clearly
to proceed."

Erisshauten commented, "I will so inform Trochanter."

"Very appropriate. And also as you do so, remember that
our guests will require sustenance."

"Aye, I will see to it, as you have said before."

Erisshauten indicated that they should follow him, and set
off without ceremony, save silence. The members of the
group hesitated a moment, then fell in behind him. Erisshauten led them from the chamber of Molio Azendarach,
out onto the landing, and then down, down, quickly turning
off at a landing just below, and boring down into the bowels
of the castle through ways much different from the way they
had entered. Meure, pausing at the door before starting down
the steep stairwell, glanced back once—and saw Azendarach
standing at the edge of open space, staring out into the afternoon light and the distances, his hands carefully folded behind him, apparently deep in thought. What thought? What
weighty decision lay in feeding strangers? Or that the omens
should be consulted, unless all these Klesh people were
hagridden with them?

Then he turned and followed the others down, catching up with the end of the line, the ridiculous slave creature from Vfzyekhr, struggling with the stairs which were too great a step for its short legs.

They rapidly lost any sense of direction in the narrow warrens of Cucany; they traversed short corridors, went through ponderous wooden doors framed in black iron, which latched behind them. Light came from iron lanterns, burning an oil which made little soot, or from shafts cleverly let down into the body of the castle. And always down. Meure could not recall a single instance in which they went up. Nor were they greeted by any inhabitant along the way—it seemed the castle was inhabited only by those they had met in the upper chamber, and ghosts. They heard no noises, no conversations, no sound of life whatsoever. But judging by the passages they traversed, the castle had to be honeycombed, riddled with ways.

The scent and feel of the air changed subtly; a faint dusty odor gave way to a damper smell, and it felt damp. Meure tried to compare how far up they had climbed against how far down they had come, and decided that they were now below ground level. Still, the inner walls were of masonry, rubble, timbers of a heavy, coarse wood. Down one more stair, almost steep enough to warrant a ladder, and they reached a level where the walls were stone. There were fewer intersections.

Erisshauten led them to a room of moderate dimensions, furnished with plain tables and benches, motioned to the benches, and departed. Presently, another person appeared, still wearing one of the prism-shaped headdresses of Incana, bearing bowls of what appeared to be a stew or goulash. The food was steaming hot. The steward set the tables, left and returned with huge clay pots of a light, but very bitter beer. They all looked uncertainly at the lamplit hall, the rough tables, the bowls and jugs, and sat down to eat, one by one. Satisfied that all were setting to the fare, the steward left.

They were all hungry, and began at once, slowly at first, then faster, as the bland taste of the stew began to fill them. The beer tasted odd, too, but it seemed to fit the food. All seemed correct, all were eating, even Morgin and the Haydar girl, although in their cases they ate very sparingly, almost reluctantly. Nothing seemed out of place, unless it was the distance that their hosts kept from them. Meure concentrated on

the bland stew and the beer; it might be some time before
they had such an opportunity again.

The steward looked in once more, saw empty bowls, and
refilled them, also refilling the beer-pots. Yes, indeed, all did
seem well. There was no sign of hostile intent in the steward's
manner whatsoever. Meure attacked his new helping with
gusto. Underneath the bland taste of it, there seemed to be a
subtle flavor he couldn't quite identify, but which he began to
enjoy. And he saw the others were similarly engaged, and
that was good. This was turning out to be less hazardous than
he had imagined. Shortly, he imagined, they would be led to
plain but serviceable pallets somewhere in the castle, and
would spend the night. That sounded like a very good idea,
even better than the food, for, now that he thought of it, he
was very fatigued from the adventures of the last few days—
he wasn't sure how many since they had abandoned the ship,
but it seemed like a long time. He tried to imagine how long,
for something didn't quite fit, that it, the feel of the time,
seemed longer than his recollection of the number of days involved.

He looked around at the others. The Vfzyekhr had curled
up in Audiart's lap and seemed to be asleep. Well enough
that! Slaves would learn to sleep whenever they could, if half
of what one heard about the Spsom could be credited. He
saw that Morgin and Tenguft had not taken seconds, and
were sitting, quietly aloof, their eyes drooping. What odd
people, not to take advantage of hospitality. The others continued, just as he did, but in slow-motion, as if suspended in
syrup. He turned the beer-pot up and drank it clean. Flerdistar was across the table from him, staring at her bowl with a
most comical, wall-eyed expression on her thin and homely
face, although now Meure thought to see some previously
hidden charm in the aristocratic Ler girl. He looked again at
the plain face, the pale skin; the thin, boyish body. The
watery eyes. That was how she ought to be, he thought, but
she didn't look that way now, even though she was acting
very odd. Now he could see some of the intensity of her inner personality animating the physical features. Yes, of
course. She would possess extravagant emotions, and would
probably be fond of all sorts of odd practices. He saw her in
other lights now; saw the thin mouth as a giver of hard kisses
and fierce, passionate words in the dark. How could he have
thought of her as plain, even homely. Clellendol was a fool
for ignoring her.

The Ler girl pushed her bowl away and laid her head down on her arm, her eyes open, staring, but after a moment they closed, separately. Her mouth opened, and he could see her teeth behind the thin lower lip, white and pink. He felt emboldened, full of confidence. Yes. Tonight. If Clellendol wouldn't he would. Right! It was then that he discovered he couldn't seem to put his intent into motion. He wanted to get up and join Flerdistar, but somehow he couldn't move his legs properly. In fact, he could barely keep his head up. He looked around, and saw the most curious sight; all were settling at their places, their heads drooping over the table. And the oil lamps were so bright now! Even Morgin and Tenguft, although upright, seemed disconnected, not conscious. Only Clellendol, who was sliding off his bench with exaggerated care. Meure laughed. Let him! Now he could discern what Meure had in mind, with his superior intuition, such as Ler were supposed to have. And he would come to him and tell him, after the blustering manner of Cervitan, to leave the girl alone. Hah! It was not to be so!

Meure watched Clellendol crawling on his hands and knees around the table to him, as if it were the hardest thing he had ever done in his life. Each step forward was like climbing a mountain. It was fascinating. At last, Clellendol reached Meure's place, and struggled to support himself on the bench. Clearly, he was failing to do so. Meure leaned close; it could do no harm. Why, he'd even tell him what he had in mind. What the hell: he could watch, if so inclined. He leaned down until their heads were almost touching. Clellendol tried to look up, but couldn't make his eyes look high enough. And then he spoke, and it was not what Meure expected to hear.

". . . We've been drugged . . . be careful . . . beware Cretus. Don't look at it, whatever it is . . ."

But then the Ler boy could say no more, for he was sliding to the cold floor, with just enough coordination left to keep his head from bumping.

Meure laid his head on his arm and thought about that for a moment. He closed his eyes, because the light from the lamps was so bright, it hurt. *Don't look at it.* Flerdistar? That didn't sound right. Cretus? Why beware a man dead thousands of years, however long it was. Cretus was gone, something for Flerdistar to worry over. Drugged? Well, now, he'd have to look into that. That wasn't hospitable at all, but he supposed that the matter would keep until tomorrow . . .

Nightfall occurred coincident with the phase of the Sun Bi-tirme which the savants among the Windfowlers called, among the society of the Elect, *manefranamosi,* which they thought meant "broadening" in the ancient Singlespeech of their once-masters.* This was when one of the pair was rounding the limb of the other, suggesting an ovoid shape; the pair of stars, already broadened by the atmosphere, distorted by uneven refraction, and their orange light reddened further, assumed a bizarre, floating shape on the edge of the world, seemingly stopping for a moment, and then sinking unnaturally rapidly. This condition, with just the precise degree of ovality, precisely at the moment of sundown, augered in general success for deeds of questionable virtue, in the system affected by the Windfowlers. No doubt, for others somewhere on the four continents of Monsalvat, such an event might well have contrary interpretations.

No light illuminated the cellar refectory of Dzoz Cucany except the oil lanterns hung along the walls, with a slight added gleam coming from a pair of such lamps suspended from an iron standard carried by a helmeted and robed figure whose headdress identified him as Eddo Erisshauten. There were others; one, in the most angular prism-shaped headdress, was Molio Azendarach. Another carried a rotund figure beneath the dark robes, and answered to the cognomen of Romulu Bedetdznatsch. A fourth was doorward of the castle.

They entered in the refectory with a gait suggestive of two opposites: great ceremony, and the furtiveness of sneak-thieves. They came in procession, but they watched the sleeping, drugged guests carefully lest any one of them show signs of awareness. Morgin still sat bolt upright, but his eyes were half-closed, and his breathing was slow and regular. Tenguft, likewise, also sat upright yet, but her eyes were closed. The procession, led by Erisshauten, wound into the cellar, filing to that side of the bench where sat Schasny. There they gathered in conclave, conferring in almost inaudible whispers.

Azendarach whispered, "The inhalation will awaken him?"

The doorward answered, "Certainty. The subject will be ambulatory, but will have little will, other than to perform as he is instructed, and the instructions are not difficult. It is

---

* What the Klesh thought was Singlespeech was actually the degenerate form of that tongue as spoken on the planet Dawn. The correct construction would have been "mafranemosi (felor)", with the word for star, "felor", understood, but not said.

nothing new, this procedure," he added petulantly. "We have done this before."

Azendarach answered, after a long hesitation, ". . . As you say, so it is. But this one, now, this one is of the offworld *gorgensuchen**, and who knows what he might be carrying in his bloodline."

Bedetdznatsch interjected, "The underservant reported that the subject was more resistant than the others, but that his lapsing was well within the calculated tolerances. We should anticipate, if anything, only another failure."

"It is possible that he might have done it willingly. The drug may be a factor in our past failures."

"The concomitant use of the ingestant and the inhalant stupefies the will and renders the subject suggestible; so much is rote from the pharmacopoeia; even persons resistant to hypnosis perform marvels in the attained state. Remember, the drug was resorted to for the reason that no one would even look at it otherwise."

"We are, naturally, equally prepared for the other possibility?"

All moved their helmets ponderously, signifying affirmatively. Erisshauten summarized, "In the event of successful transfer, we must destroy the device immediately and overpower the subject so that we may interrogate him at our leisure, without fear."

Azendarach mused, "I fear this, each time we try it. I like it not, even though it was read in the reflections generations ago and reverified again and again. We are to attempt to revive the personality of Cretus the Scribe in the body of a subject. After that, nothing. No advice, no instructions, suggestions, absolutely blank. The best omenreaders have plied their trade and get no reading of advantage or disadvantage, blame or unblame."

Bedetdznatsch corrected the Phanet, politely, "Your pardon, m'lord, but the reading is always 'advantage/disadvantage, no blame.' "

The reply was icy. "In my workbook, that is the import of the null reading."

Bedetdznatsch whispered, "Of course, of course. But within a concept in which inaction is a form of action, and indeci-

---

* A word impossibe to translate simply. It meant, more or less, "the descendant of persons who deliberately perverted their racial ancestry and destiny." Moreover, who continued to do so. It was a word filled with connotations of shivery horror and singularly repulsive deviance.

siveness a form of decision, then a null reading has its wording and commands the same respect as the others. And we cannot overlook that this particular one was delineated. 'One will be brought from the offworlds. Use him next.' This is the one, according to the Embasse."

"The Embasse also said that the Star-boat crashed very close to the country of the Lagostomes. He could have been for them to use."

"They couldn't have done much. Only we possess the talisman. No, things have worked to bring the subject here. The reflections so read, and so it has been. I have faith."

"Mine is not in question. I am fearful, when I receive what can only be interpreted as specific instructions from the omens, and no resultant is revealed at the culmination of those actions. And no way has been found to weasel it out, either."

Bedetdznatsch mused, "Rapmanchelein the Mystic was reputed to have inquired in the reflections of their origin, to wit, were the omens, of God. In his opinion the interpretation was a negation of that idea. That is, while his sanity remained. He spent the remainder of his short life, muttering, 'they laugh their laugh, they do,' and sometimes, 'one in many, many in one.' I would not think of wondering what the source is. For the time, I will accept that it is not communication with the One, but perhaps something lesser, at least familiar with Aceldama."

Azendarach added, "And the region surrounding it, out how far we can't even guess. We read the instruction many days before the Ship could have landed here."

Erisshauten agreed, emphatically, "Yes, many days, indeed. One wonders, for a certainty."

Azendarach turned away from the group and looked at Schasny, reflectively. Finally he said, still looking at the unconscious body slumped at his place at the table, "We should be able to control that one in the event the transfer works . . . dare we mention the rest here?"

The doorward said, "This level is supposed to be free of bane or omen. All experiments conducted here approximate random to the extent we have been able to perform and record them. The conclusion is that this level is blind. . . ."

"No one knows why the readings suggest the reactivation of Cretus the Scribe. But in the archives it was reported that he was known to be not only a reader, but an activant. That implies control, or cooperation with some affective entity. If our suspicions are accurate, then we will possess either a key to our dreams, or else a powerful bargaining tool to work toward that. But it will have to be fast. We must not let him get away from us this time, eh? Like those fools of the old Incana, long ago, let him get away from them."

He stopped, as if the idea were too powerful to submit to the tyranny of mere words. He shook his head. "These adventurers and charismatics come along and think the world's their own toy to pull down or set straight! And setting straighter it's always needed, correct enough; but for it practical men are needed to guide the repairing hand, else all be broken along the way. *They* had the right idea, then. They insulated him in routines and functions and repetitious acts and got him pointed in the right direction. It's all in the archives. But they left him one way out. We must leave this one no way out, if it works. And then we'll subdue this proud Cretus. With fire and iron, if need be . . . What shall we have him set to rights first, my fellows?"

Bedetdznatsch muttered, "Potale has long been a hotbed of heterodoxy and should be brought to heel."

The doorward ventured, "Rid the wide world of Eratzenasters. And their riders. My cousin was taken."

Erisshauten said, thoughtfully, "The Lagostomes will provide ample manpower, properly instructed, for ourselves and associates to subdue Kepture; we can work from there."

"Let it begin, then."

Erisshauten withdrew from his robe a vial containing a clear liquid. This he poured onto a towel handed him for the purpose. The solution appeared to have no discernible scent. Then he seized Schasny roughly by the hair and covered the boy's face with the saturated towel. At first, there was no change; Schasny gave no indication whatsoever that he perceived what was being done to him. Then his eyes began moving under the lids, and he opened his eyes. Erisshauten removed the towel, and the boy sat upright unassisted. He asked no questions, nor did he look around, although he seemed alert enough.

Azendarach said sharply, "Test him!"

Erisshauten asked the boy, "What is your name?"

He answered tonelessly, "Meure Wendrin Schasny."

"Give your age and planet of origin."

"I was born on Tancred; I have twenty Tancred years. The correction factor for Tancred is .962215."

Azendarach asked, "What is a correction factor?"

The boy answered in the same toneless voice, "It is a ratio between a planetary year and the year of the suspected planet of origin. The period has been verified independently by biometric means, so the system need not be found to prove the concept. It provides a means to equate ages among persons from different planets, for statistical purposes, and also legal purposes."

The Incanans looked at one another. Azendarach asked, "The existence of such a concept suggests a community of many planets. How many are there inhabited by humans like us?"

Schasny emitted a short giggle. "None."

Azendarach asked, "How many inhabited by those like you?"

"I don't know."

"More than twenty?"

"Yes."

"More than a hundred?"

"Yes."

Azendarach looked at his companions. "That's a lot of people."

Erisshauten commented, "Homogenized *Gorgensuchen*. One Klesh would be worth any ten or twenty. They have not had to survive against their fellow Humans in the manner we have. They will reward equality and conformity. We pursue excellence. There is no correspondence between the two systems. We will gain an initial advantage at first, then enter a period of stalemate. After a time, their will will weaken and we will gain the victory. This will come later. Now, first things first."

Azendarach said to Schasny, "What is your desire?"

"I have no desire."

"Then arise and come with me."

He got to his feet, unsteadily, assisted by the doorward, who turned him in the direction he should go. The group left the refectory and passed through a small kitchen, Azendarach leading, Bedetdznatsch and Erisshauten bringing up the rear.

Bedetdznatsch whispered to Erisshauten, "Molio's not such an alert watchman as one might need."

"Precautions have been taken."

"I have it from my morning reading that this one will take."

"You kept that quiet, didn't you?"

"Azendarach assumed the Phaneterie by chicanery; he may read according to his abilities to do so."

"They say each reader sees a different truth, both ways. You know the saying."

"Aye, what you can see and what it says. I know: they can change, they can. I've caught 'em changing with the students, more than once."

"You know more?"

"They don't like Molio."

"Why?"

"Too much peace, not enough war. He's a parlor-Phanet, a politician, such as the filthy Lagos follow."

"Well, from what I hear, Cretus'll change all that. All the accounts say he was fond of action. Took the council almost ten years to get him under control. We'll accomplish that tonight. Or we'll put the legend to sleep for good."

"I'll give you a foretelling . . ."

"It's supposed to be bad luck."

"Throw that! Luck is made, not waited for. So all I'll say is give him room. not a lot, and be wary, but if Cretus makes the first move, let him make it."

"He'll get Azendarach, then?"

"There's a big uncertainty factor in it, but it looks like that's the probability."

"What's the uncertainty factor?"

"Orange."

"You're dreaming, not reading. Orange lies within the norm of random variation."

"I admit it was weak, but I say it was there."

"Very well. But attend! These steps are bad."

Now they were at the end of a long passageway they had been traversing, starting down a steep stairs deeper into the native rock. Erisshauten's caution was not in error; the stairs were dark, wet and treacherous, making several changes in direction and pitch; not enough to make a landing, but enough to make one stumble. At the end, they descended into a small chamber, quite bare, which led into a larger one. The lanterns they carried cast a yellow, flickering light to the dusty, underground rooms.

Azendarach was explaining to Meure what he must do; "You are to carry this lantern, and enter that room. There, you will find a shining object made of wire. You will pick it up and look at it in the light. While you are looking at it, you must try to imagine, and remember what you see."

"That is all?"

"That is all. If you see nothing, you will replace the object in the place where it was."

"Am I a fortuneteller now?"

"You may be a fortune bringer. Now!"

Azendarach and the doorward flanked Schasny and led him into the room, carefully averting their eyes from something out of sight to the left, using the headdresses to great advantage, as if they had been designed just for this purpose, to let one see where one was going, blocking the sight of something. The others lagged a little, hanging back at the doorway.

They saw Schasny, moving like a sleepwalker, look for something, and locate it; he reached for it, bending, and picked up something shining and glittering, something from which Bedetdznatsch and Erisshauten alike averted their eyes. Holding the object with one hand, and the lantern with the other, the boy looked blankly at the object for what seemed like an extended time; so far this had been identical to scores of other times. But this time began to go differently, and in a way none of them expected, without preparatory gesture, or motion, Schasny rapidly squeezed the object with the hand holding it, breaking up its shining glitters and transforming it into an uninteresting wad of metallic fibers. It was done fast. And then all hell broke loose.

7

"'Motion about a point is iniquity'. . . and 'Torsion is iniquity.' I understood that every disturbance, which makes manifestation possible, implies deviation from perfection."

—*A. C.*

There had been a passage of time so long that years could not serve to measure it; centuries would not suffice, for there would have been too many of them. And if the double star Bitirme had been visible from any other planet as a member of a constellation, then that constellation would have changed shape to the naked eye.

For one who called himself Cretus the Scribe there was no time, and the courses of the stars in space had no meaning for him. He was here; and then he was . . . *here*.

Cretus entered the chamber at the bottom of the stairs, carefully latching the door behind him. Not so much for security, he told himself wryly, because they could break it down in minutes, but for the little reassurance that he'd have a short privacy for what had to be done. The chamber was a storage closet, a good locker for times of siege. Empty now, the shelves bare, damp-smelling, dusty. There was a crate on the stone floor. Cretus placed the lantern he was carrying on the shelf, absent-mindedly, and then pulled the crate over to him. He sat, looking back up at the lantern, as if verifying its relative position.

He thought, *about now, they'll find out I'm gone.* He knew how it would go after that; they'd not waste time worrying about how he got past the guards, supposedly his protectors, but would check the gates of the stronghold Cucany, and find out that none had passed. But they'd put out a patrol anyway, supplemented with the filthy Derques*, and with daylight, there'd be a Haydar or two to cover the ground. No, they wouldn't be fooled long; they'd imagine he was somewhere in the stronghold yet, and they'd start looking. Very thoroughly, a room at a time. They were thorough, that was a fact. And that thoroughness would of necessity slow them down a little. Long enough, he supposed.

He reached into the plain robe he was wearing, and withdrew an object, shining and glittering in the lamplight, now in its inactive shape, mostly flattened into a shape that was disclike and toroidal at the same time. He looked at it carelessly; it didn't matter now, folded as it was. He could do nothing with it until it was opened up.

* Derques were a form of Klesh far removed from the original human form. A Derque supported its weight on its arms, which were greatly strengthened. The hands were atrophied into footlike appendages. The original legs were much reduced, and the former feet served as organs of manipulation. Derques were reputed to be less sentient than the average animal, and this was not merely another of the myriad racial slurs of Monsalvat, but carried more than a bit of truth. Derques in fact did roam wild in Chengurune, serving as scavengers. A Klesh Radah called the Ularid Khoze captured them and trained them as scenthounds, paralleling the free Haydar who were visually-guided predators.

The object was, to his knowledge, the last *Skazenache* in existence, just as he was the last Zlat. And at that, not a true-zlat, but a quadroon-zlat. One-fourth, that somehow had bred true. But he did not delude himself; he had looked deeply into time and the symbol that told stories which he now held in his hand, and he knew his appearance and zlat ways were only one expression of a probability formula that no one could change. The terrible magic wrought by the Warriors in the deeps of yesterday was coming unravelled in some of its parts, and the Zlat trait was being absorbed back into the common ruck and squabble. He also knew that the genetic distribution expanded its base by a factor of two each generation. Were he to sire one more true-zlat, son or daughter, they would only have one-eighth zlat in them. One could not maintain a pure line by oneself.

Cretus sighed. He had seen much, but he was not, so he imagined, much of a philosopher. A faint smile flickered across the sharp features, the deepset eyes, the lines and hollows of his face, the half-shaven stubble that had been his trademark. He thought, *it's this, now: I couldn't do anything for my people, because my people are gone, one by one. At least I could do for myself. At the least I could help the others keep their identity, and put a stop to this absurd race-crossing. What foolishness! To populate this world with bastards! Even half-breeds detested the idea, and would seek others like them to form the cores of future tribes. But I am a victim of my own program, am I not? 'Cretus,' they cry, 'who saved us.' Who had unified all of Kepture that counted, first from a base in Ombur, and then here in Incana.*

And who had felt his grasp leading men slowly leached away by government, by counsellors, by servants and toadies and politicians and professional hangers-on, who always waited for a leader to ride behind as long as they survived . . . and who they now cherished like a prisoner, to deflect along the shabby paths such running-Derques always wanted. What trash! He had offered them the stars, in time, ultimately. And all they wanted was something they could feel today: a woman, money, an eyrie in the castle with a view. But they couldn't seem to grasp the first step, that all Monsalvat had to be wielded into a whole of component Klesh races, everyone to his part, stronger than all the rest put together. Like crystals in a matrix. He had seen that.

He had seen much with his storyteller, once he had learned it was for more than telling stories; lives from the past,

worlds and their inhabitants spread across the sky, old humans, new humans, more, stranger creatures, some odd
indeed. He had nothing but the Klesh experience to judge the
universe by, and he suspected that it was an erroneous view,
but he didn't know where the error was. And there were the
others, whose location and nature, kind and numbers were
vague, shifting, unstable. Nothing remained the same but that
they spoke, indirectly or not at all. They had suggested (was
it he, she, or it had suggested?) this way out, *into* the
storyteller to wait for another time, another body. More than
once he had rejected the idea out of hand. Zlats had never
used the device that way, so his grandmother had told him.
Never. It was the unclean way. His skin crawled. Cretus, who
had terrified many in his climb from street urchin to titular
ruler of most of Kepture, was himself terrified by what he
thought to do.

They'd protect him until they found the right one, eh?
That's what they (he, she, it) said. But how long, that's the
rub. Only that all these coattail riders will all be dead, and
that they'd be considerably discomfited by his absence, since
their only genuine foreteller would be gone. Cretus had
learned to fine-tune his *Skazenache* to the immediate world-
line and the immediate future. And who could win battles
against one who could read the future, and not only choose
the ground, as he'd learned on the streets, but could choose
the time of engagement as well?

He unfolded the device into a shining spherical object
made of metallic wires, with thousands of tiny beads strung
along them, made a series of adjustments, now concentrating,
not careless or off-hand at all, and *looked* into it, face curiously empty of expression. Then back. He nodded, as if he
had seen more or less what he expected to see.

It was time to do it. His chamberlains were not far away,
proceeding with thoroughness. Cretus took a deep breath and
exhaled slowly. To be gone, this agile body, and what would
he continue in. A fat publican? A child? Perhaps a woman?
Now that would be something. He smiled to himself.

A last odd thought occurred to him, and he stood up to
look about the storeroom. A mirror, that was what was
needed. A mirror. He was not vain, but he wanted to have a
last look. And there, by the door, on the bottom shelf.
Cracked, and the frame damaged, to be sure, but serviceable
enough, if dusted. He retrieved the mirror and dusted it with
his sleeve. Then he sat it at the back of the shelf, opposite

him, sat back on the crate, and shook the storytell out, returning it to its null-setting. There was infinity set into it now. No escape. He looked at the mirror, and the mirror looked at him. He saw no more than he expected to; a street-tough, cynical face, bony and sharp, a little tired around the eyes.

He looked around, alarmed. The oddest sensation, as if he were being watched . . . the feeling faded, returned, then faded again. *Damn. I'm making excuses.*

He held the device in his lap, so he couldn't drop it, and looked into it. This time, the images didn't come swimming into his mind like an unusually-clear dream. There was nothing but the emptiness of the spaces between the wires. He couldn't *see* anything. He knew it was hopeless to force it: it couldn't be forced. He thought to daydream, to relax, the room grew dim a little; was the lantern running out of oil? Infinity. He had not dared to contemplate it before, but it seemed there was just a lot of nothing to it. Nothing. Crap and damnation! It wasn't working at all. He chuckled. The old tales and warnings of the Zlats were just that: old tales. The damn thing wouldn't work, it couldn't. . . .

. . . his mind had been wandering, hadn't it? To the storytell. Try again. But there was something odd now. The light was brighter, and he was standing, holding the lantern in his hand, and the storytell in the other. *Must have gone to sleep,* he thought ruefully, *and they have caught up with me.* The light hurt his eyes, it was too bright. Someone was in the room with him, behind him, keeping him between the device and them. He could sense them, hear them breathing. The door was open and there were more outside. He didn't dare look. His mind felt fogged, dulled by something, a drug. Cretus wasn't sure. Something reeled drunkenly in the adyt of his mind, a vertigo. Had it been that simple? Had it worked? He didn't know and couldn't ask. But he thought, *there's one way to test it, and that's to bet all on one throw. I don't know when I am, but I'll bet they don't want an uncontrolled Cretus among them, whenever they are.*

He felt the fingers holding the storytell, felt the wires against his skin. Sharp and cold. They would cut. He needed something to break down the fog he seemed to be in. It was distracting. He could think, but he wasn't sure he could act.

How many with him? More than one, for sure, in the room. Two definitely. A third? No, they were outside. Two. He could do it, if they were sloppy. He hoped they were.

Cretus squeezed the storytell as hard as he could, feeling

the wire cut into his hand, feeling the pain come rippling up his arm like a madman's shout, shooting sparks, and he crumpled it up into a shapeless mass, never to be used again. *To hell with it! If it didn't work, then my only escape's to the streets. And if it did, then transfer's occurred and we don't need the poor bastard who went-within. So long, sucker.*

First these two. Then the door. Cretus lifted one leg and let himself start to fall, away from the door, letting his arm trail behind him, and letting the lantern begin to drop. As he started moving, he started a turn to see his associates. Who would it be? Asc? Shlar? Osper Udle the First Servant?

They came into view, still drunkenly, although the pain of the cut helped clear some of the fog. He saw strangers with elaborate headgear which obscured their heads. But their faces were open, if shadowed and oddly painted. They had expressions of disappointment and disgust, as best he could tell. They thought he was fainting.

Now! He snapped out of the fall and let inertia swing the heavy iron lantern around under him, with a snap, and he threw it at the larger one's face-opening. The range was intimate, he could not miss, even with this clumsy, soft body. (*What the hell? Did I come out in a woman's body?*) The lantern struck, bottom first, direct hit. There was a satisfying, solid sound. That one was down. The other started forward, then hesitated, as if he might try to run. *Run where, you fool? I'm blocking the only way out of this dead end!* Cretus continued his motion, feinted to the side, and the other took the bait. Cretus stepped out, as if to trip him, and the other opened up. He backhandedly threw the crumpled mass of the storytell at the other's genitals. Another hit, but not a knockdown. The man grimaced, covering himself. Cretus stepped into him, extending his left hand rigidly, stabbing upward at a point just below the breastbone. The man crumpled over his hand, making retching sounds. Cretus chopped the neck exposed by the unsteady helmet falling forwards, hard, once, and as he slid to the stone floor, he flipped him over with his foot. As the body landed, rolling, he stamped on the windpipe, just to be sure. The other man he had hit with the lantern lay silent, crumpled in a corner. Dead? Looked that way. *That's two down.*

The first one didn't appear to have a weapon, and there was no time to rummage through the robes for one. But the other had a small sword in a sheath inside the robe, the hilt protruding through a slit. This Cretus took, straddling the body. By now the ones outside were reacting, sure enough. But now he had a weapon. Let them come!

One came into the storeroom, sword exposed, but Cretus could see he knew little enough of how to use it, and wearing one of those clumsy helmets to boot. The third man was pushing at the door with his free hand as if he anticipated Cretus closing it. Good. Cretus lunged for the door, as if to do just that. The third man pushed harder, opening himself up to Cretus' stroke without even a parry. Over the shoulders of the third, he saw the fourth, who was now looking about in total panic. What had become of the stronghold? Had they turned it into a roadhouse for tipsy wanderers and itinerant peddlers? This last one decided to run for it. *Oh, no. That one must not get away. He'll have to talk.* Cretus stepped over the body blocking the doorway, and started after him. The man had discarded his headdress, but had collided with the edge of the jamb leading to a set of stairs in their right position, and was only just now starting up. Seemed old and out of shape. Cretus raced to the stairs, seized a rising foot and pulled. A bulky mass responded, slowly at first, but like all things that fall, swiftly enough in the end. The fourth rolled back into the chamber with no ceremony at all.

Him Cretus rolled over, straddled, and laid the edge of the sword across the soft, jowly throat.

Cretus grinned down at the old man, jerking the sword suggestively, watching the dull edge indent the skin of the neck.

"Yes, it's dull, but even a fool can cut with a dull edge if he pushes hard enough."

The old man shook his head, apparently not understanding his words. They had sounded muddled, unreal, even to himself.

The old man said, shakily, "Who are you?"

"Cretus, of course! Now I don't care who you are. But I want to know when this is."

"When?"

"When! Is this place called Cucany, in Incana?"

The old man nodded.

"What year is it. I know it's been years by the look of the hats you wear."

"The year is that of the Korsor*."

---

* Part of a fifteen-year cycle which equated with a fifteen-month year. The Aceldaman calendar was solar, matched to the star-groupings visible along the plane of the ecliptic. The small moon was ignored.

"Does anyone number years sequentially?"

"Records are kept and years are marked as being so many from notable events, such as the assumption of a new Phanet, or a widespread natural event, or a war."

"I am Cretus, but I do not know what a Phanet is. Therefore the office came after me. How long have Phanets ruled Incana?"

"A long time, longer than I could say. Centuries, many. That is very far back, more than two thousand years."

"You knew about Cretus, but you do not know how long you've waited?"

"All I know is what I have read, been told, and seen. Cretus is known all over Aceldama; all men know Cretus."

"How is it that the *Skazenache* did not change any in that time?"

"The artifact? I do not know, save that it is said that it was handled only during the beholdings; at any rate, it doesn't appear to tarnish or rot. We do not know how to operate it, so it has been handled carefully . . ."

"A lot of good that's come to. I closed it, permanently. If you live to return to this place, come get it and melt it down; it's a valuable metal, pure like gold, but harder and it takes hell's own fires to melt it."

Cretus relaxed, stood up from the old man. He said, "Now lead me out of here. There were four of your hoodheads down here. Where are the others?"

The old man struggled to prop himself up on his elbows. "The others?"

"The rest of you. The guards, the attendants. You people don't go far without them. If you waited a millennium for a man from the past, it's a good bet you're not common folk. So where are they?"

While the old man stumbled, trying to make up his mind, Cretus allowed himself to relax a little, for the first time. *Now, this was going correctly, indeed. I come to the future, whenever the hell it is, and instead of steely men of power I meet priestly mumbo-jumbo and incompetents. Damn! They probably need me more now than they did . . . then. Yesterday? An hour ago? Centuries, he had said. That he did. More than two thousand years! Well enough. This body seems young, a little soft, male now that I care to notice it; it will stand hardening, and tempering to suit my style. And then, why then, we'll do it again, only this time we'll do it right, won't we, dear. We won't ever let us get tangled in a million threads again, oh, no. This time they'll feel the whip and the boot. They all want country villas and the love of nubile mistresses, but the only love they'll discover will be the kiss of the lash.*

The old man said, now standing, "There was a servant in the refectory above, at the head of the stairs. In the dining hall proper, there are off-worlders, of which you were once one. They should still be sleeping; they were drugged. What will you do with me?"

Cretus indicated the stairs with the point of the sword. "You can earn my pleasure by showing me the door out of Cucany. I was on my way to leave before, I believe, but I was interrupted."

"You will leave Incana, my lord?"

"Ombur lacked the concern of scope to carry out any program. Nomads! Worthless! Incana lacked will. What do they now call the land east of here, facing the Inner Sea?"

"Intance."

"I do not know the name." Cretus said it in an ordinary tone, but the old man, Bedetdznatsch, did not miss the hatred in his eyes, nor the lurid flame that lurked there. He thought, *To what purpose we have brought this demon to life again I cannot fathom. But he must be controlled, or killed outright. There is nothing in this world, this time, which would within him restrain him. If there ever was. He will build something he wants in this time, but he'll pull down the whole world to do it. If he'd walk out of here and put his wits up against the whole world, he'd have to be supremely confident or crazy . . . he had done it before, so went the legends.* The thought made Bedetdznatsch half-crazy with fear. But another thought intruded. *There's one consolation if we can kill him. Control is out of the question. And that's that he's cut off his escape route by destroying the artifact. Cretus is mortal, now, and we can rid the world of him for good. And let the past remain with the past. We want no saviors and changers!*

Cretus relaxed some more. *This was going to be simple. The old man was terrified, and slow to boot. He could do this half-asleep.*

Then something curious happened. Cretus saw himself raise the sword, to look at it. He had not done it, but there it was. He tried to stop it, but he suddenly felt he couldn't control the movement of his limbs; there was resistance. He staggered, and tried to keep an eye on the old man, who had noticed that something was amiss, but was still indecisive. He fell back heavily against the wall, still fighting for control, and now he heard from far away, somewhere deep in his mind, another set of voices, memories, something rapidly rising to the surface, emerging, parting. . . .

Meure Schasny found himself standing against a damp wall in a cellar, holding a sword, facing a man he remembered as Bedetdznatsch, who was looking at him with an expression of stark terror. Schasny tried to speak, stammered out, "How did I get here? Where are the others?"

To answer him, Bedetdznatsch turned and bolted up the stairs madly, robes flapping.

Schasny stood where he was, looking at the sword as if he'd never seen one. He hadn't actually seen a real sword before, and this one had blood on it. He felt unreal, drugged, half-stupefied, and when his mind wandered a little, he heard a voice inside him, speaking urgently, in words he could barely understand. The walls swung unsteadily. It seemed important somehow, but the words were in the way. He probed at it, but to no result; he relaxed and inwardly turned away from it, and then it came, pure ideas that something strung into words for him, like remembering a dream.

"STOP FIGHTING ME. YOU IDIOT! GIVE ME BACK MOTOR CONTROL! I/WE HAVE TO CATCH THAT OLD MAN SO WE CAN GET OUT OF HERE!"

Meure's skin crawled. He knew he was going crazy. He ventured, timidly, *Who are you? What are you? Are you me?*

This time the ideas came clearer, and he started moving toward the stairs, seemingly against his will, or *around* it, that seemed the more accurate word.

"That's right, relax a little, let me help you run!" Meure sensed an urgency to the odd voice, and a sense of truth in it, so he did as it suggested, feeling at the same time an impossible sense of separation-yet-unity with the odd, harsh voice, that spoke in his own recalled timbres and rhythms. Like a cinema, a newscast, where a speaker was orating powerfully, but in another language, and there was a lag, while the translator caught up with the sense of it, all the time the original figure mouthing wildly on the screen, waving his arms, spittle flying, urging what unnamed multitudes to what unknown deeds of valor or atrocity. He felt himself move, but he had nothing to do with it.

"Good, now. There's a lot to tell, but first we have to get out of this pile. They are going to kill you, do you know? You will want to live, and I, dear, have a most inordinate

desire to remain corporate. But later. You've released enough control now, so I'm going to put you to sleep for a while. Then we'll get acquainted. You won't like it, but neither do I, and neither one of us can do anything about it." Meure felt comfortable and reassured. The delayed, lagging sense of meaning carried an undertone of a sharp assessment of facts, and realistic plans of action. On that note, he faded out.

Cretus flexed his muscles, and made a motion like brushing cobwebs from his eyes. He thought, swiftly, *Didn't work quite rightly, did it? Well, no cure for that. First things first. That old buzzard will be raising the alarm even now while I stop to explain things to this mooncalf. Well, I'll show him some paces, now, and put this soft body through some changes.*

Cretus bounded up the stairs two at a time, pausing at the top only to be sure it was the same, and that no additional passages had been hewn since he had come down this way . . . how many years ago? He felt the edges of the boy's own memories, and found nothing. He had no memory of coming down the stairs. Cretus ran down the passageway, passed through a small cookroom, right. This had been the dungeons before. And into a larger common room beyond. Now he stopped and looked around, for there were changes. A lot of changes, in fact, the common room hardly looked the same at all. And there were a lot of strangers in it. He looked them over carefully . . . there was only one High Klesh present, a girl, a Haydar by the look of her, and . . . Cretus' skin crawled. Firstfolk! The creators. Strange oaths flickered through his mind like summer lightning: *Hell's highest demons! Vakiflar the Oathbreaker! Sammar, who lied and polished the cobblestones of the underworld. What did they here?*

Nothing looked right in this room. All these people were asleep, but at odd positions that said they were down fast . . . probably drugged . . . yes, that would explain why the boy had no memory of the stairs. Why drugged? It all began connecting. No time to waste, though. And he'd have to talk to one of them. There was a seasoned-looking man among the company, with gray hair, and the features of no identifiable breed. Cretus hesitated, weighing choices. He didn't trust mixers at all, but even less did he trust Haydars, and Lermen would be useless. This old man, now, he looked like a native. Cretus walked around the table, noting a young Ler sprawled on the floor, and stretched out on the bench, a smallish, white-furred creature he was unfamiliar with. He stood beside the one he had selected, and started to touch him. Then he stopped. *No. Not a mixer, first contact. I don't know what he is, therefore I don't know how he'll react. Now this Haydar girl, I know what she'll do. That's the virtue of having knowable types: we can adopt a known position from the start.*

Cretus turned and touched the girl lightly. Like all her kind, she was spare and stringy to the touch, her flesh being mostly muscle and tendon. She also seemed to be the one least drugged. The eyelids moved, wandered, opened. Closed, then opened again. The girl looked around, then to Cretus. The expression on her face suggested relief at first, but something must have tripped her hair-trigger hunting perceptions, for her expression rapidly changed to one of fear. *Whatever she had done with this one, there was someone else looking out of the eyes, now, setting the muscles of the face differently. He knew that, could feel it. He also knew that Haydars perceived all moving things that were alive as either co-hunters, or meat. And if co-hunters, then there were leader and led. It was all fairly simple. He knew what to do.*

He spoke first, "We are trapped and must escape this place of stones to continue the hunt. I know you to be a Haydar of the ancient High Klesh, one who does not mix the flesh, and I know you to be a noblewoman of high resolve, therefore I ask your good arm and eye, that our enemies may feel the thunderbolt. Is it to be so?" And suiting action to word, he gently put the point of the sword at her throat.

Tenguft swallowed, and said, haltingly, "I cannot deny one who invokes strong bonds in the language of the dead, that is spoken no more on this sad world, save by the initiates and the high. Are you a demon? They said. . . ."

"I am not a demon, although doubtless many would think me so. Come with me, then. There will be many of the helmeted ones to break through."

"These others must go also."

"There is need for haste. We cannot guide such a large party, especially those not willing to fight, or unable."

She shook her head, with great effort. "No. They must go. I have sworn a bond on their safety. I am responsible."

"Then I will speak of secret things, that the wisewomen of the Haydar see in the firelight by the bones of their mother's left hand: I am Cretus and I have returned to reclaim my

world. I see that you still obey that custom from the deeps of
time; I read it in your face. Four accompanied this body to
the chamber below, who were to capture me or kill me. They
failed, but I did not suceed, either. One escaped me, and is
now spreading the tale, recruiting his armsmen. There is no
way out of this chamber but up, and we must assume they
hold it now. Can these fight?"

"I do not know. They are offworlders and Firstfolk from
beyond the stars. The one with the gray hair is an embasse,
and he may not be attacked."

"Not good. It will be hard, this way."

"You invoke a force I cannot disobey; yet I will not leave
these. It is honorable to die in such circumstances."

*That was that. No point in forcing her further. Haydar
who survived the trials of adolescence would no longer have
a fear of death. It was just another option.*

"Demon or Cretus, I respect your obligations. But know
that I am a Hierarch of the Ludi, that I have seen Sara
Damassou with my own eyes, and walked along the Falaise."

"If you are Cretus, of whom it is spoken, you are not of
this world but of the past. Who was your master in the trial
of truth?"

"Tarso Emi Koussi."

She had tested him, and he had given an answer that rang
of the far past, and men who stood mighty in the legends of
the People. And Sara Damassou, the only city the Haydars
had ever lived in, the Forbidden One, the Holy Place, was no
more and none knew where it had been.

"E-eyeh! Let it be so! Let us awaken these strangers and
depart this place. It has come as was told to me, and I would
have you speak of these things with my people. It is said of
old that the Haydar were high in the councils of Cretus, and
would that it be so again."

"Indeed."

Together, they set to the task of awakening the others,
then, some easily, others with more difficulty, but after a
time, all were conscious again, and Tenguft had explained the
situation to them all. And not once had Cretus felt anything
from his unwilling host. He tensed himself slightly, hoping
that he would not until they could get out of this castle. Then
there would have to be some arrangement made, without
doubt, although there was no precedent for it anywhere in
Cretus' memory.

8

"Unless we live in the present, we do not live at all."
—*A. C.*

When they were all awake, Cretus explained briefly, borrowing the words and speech from Meure's memories; he spoke with wry authority and a fine sense of irony which left no doubt in any of their imaginations what he might do. And the situation was clearly as he described it; no one could argue against the necessity of escaping the castle immediately.

Clellendol regained his thief's ways, and assessed the situation they found themselves in. He observed, to Cretus-Meure, "We are far down in the rock. Then we shall have to go back up the narrow way, which they can challenge, no doubt."

Cretus thought a moment before answering. At last, he said, "They can. And I know no secret adyts, at least not near this level, such as we might use. And I assume that the inhabitants have delved more since my days. More, certain passages I remember may be blocked up, or be useless. No, the way out is not in stealth. But the narrow ways can work for us, too. And it also may be that they will not risk a direct confrontation; they do not know what I can do—or can't."

"You have lost the ability to read the future, that is true."

"I used it seldom, even in the first. My power was in decision and persuasion, in risktaking, and in minimizing losses. My opponents were dogmatists and safety-firsters. When I had the power to do so, I crushed them; when I did not, I manipulated their weaknesses until I could neutralize them, and deal with them at leisure. And besides, reading the future is uncomfortable; we do not have the reference for it, to understand what we see, so it is deadly; that is why I stopped early. And because also . . . that I saw that the act itself was just another system to build surety, as was theirs; so I returned to the ways I knew best. And what I have seen here so

135

far gives me hope that we can get out of here without too
much trouble."

Then he indicated that they should begin, and set out, up
the stairs and passageways of Dzoz Cucany. Cretus-Meure
led the way, and Tenguft covered the rear at his direction.
Close behind Cretus came Clellendol and Flerdistar. At first,
the Vfzyekhr walked with Tenguft, but as they entered the
maze of tunnels, it unobtrusively moved forward to stay close
to Cretus. It remained silent, and made no gestures or noticeable motions, yet it fell in behind Cretus quickly.

For a time, they followed a route that was the exact reverse of the way they had come; Clellendol could verify this:
the memory matched the present exactly. But soon, Cretus
turned off into a darkened section, which began to change
level rapidly. This passage seemed abandoned, judging from
rubble and debris scattered along the floor. Their only light
was a lantern carried by Flerdistar.

Clellendol ventured, "This air is live; flowing. There is a
draught. Therefore the passage is open, even though it seems
closed-off, disused."

Cretus-Meure answered, half to himself, "I searched his
mind and found that the way you came to the Durance Level
had not intersected the Grand Corridor. This way is the ancient Guardsway, and through it we should emerge at the
main door. They will be looking for us higher up."

"Why? If I were them, I would strive to contain a party
such as ours as far down as possible."

"They will think that I wish to hunt them down, and take
possession of Cucany. They have built the higher structures,
and so they will wish to meet me on their ground. It does not
occur to them that I only wish to get out of Cucany, and
indeed all Incana, as fast at possible. By the time that falls
into their minds, we will be at the door . . . this structure
was made to keep invaders out, not escapees in, once they get
to the door."

"Why didn't you just leave, before?"

"I had become more than a leader; I was a talisman for
their continued survival. So they kept me busy, filled my
hours with issues, loaded me down with hangers-on, sy-
cophants, toadies, counsellors of the Reach of Incana, and the
like. It is that way with all power; you set forces in motion
which later come to direct you, begin controlling your actions
. . . I saw that they would not move beyond Kepture, once
they had it consolidated. That was all they wanted; the rest

could come later, if their successors thought it worthwhile. They kept to the fine line, and by that I gradually became a prisoner . . . so I found this way, which is the trying of another time. Perhaps the situation now will be a matrix more readily bent to the original goal."

From the back of the line came a sibilant sound, from the Haydar girl. They fell silent, immediately.

Tenguft came forward to join Cretus-Meure and Clellendol, her hawk profile casting predatory shadows on the ancient stone walls. Now that the loyalty problem was temporarily solved and there was no contest between her will and Cretus', she had entered totally into the web of action. Now she whispered, but it was the oddest whisper Cretus had ever heard, for it had almost no volume, but it carried perfectly and none of the words were distorted. She said, "Above us, in the stone, men running, all together, in step. From behind, then overhead, and no longer do I hear them."

Cretus looked upward at the low ceiling, as if trying to see through it, remembering, trying to recover the layout of Dzoz Cucany. He said, after a moment, "It seems too early for them to reinforce the gate, but it could be possible . . . I wouldn't have given the old one enough credit to think that fast."

Clellendol ventured, "Perhaps he could have turned over matters to an underling with more initiative."

"Perhaps. In any event, the way we will come should lead us to the entry-corridor; and there will be only a few steps to the door."

"If things have not changed there, too, in a thousand years or more," added Morgin. To this Cretus did not respond.

There was more of the passage, much more going up and down, more of the narrow ways favored by the castledwellers of Incana, in many places partially blocked by rubble. In one place they had difficulty getting through, and there had to move some blocks fallen from the ceiling. Instead of leaving them lie, however, Tenguft carefully placed the moved blocks back on the pile of rubble, balancing them so they would fall at the slightest disturbance.

The passage now ascended abruptly through a series of short, debris-filled stairwells set at odd angles, and terminated at a small landing fronting on a panel which appeared to slide in a set of grooves in the lintel, and the sill. There was no handle on this side, and the dust on the floor gave no evidence of ever having been disturbed.

Cretus now whispered, "This appears to have been rebuilt since my day."

Morgin observed, "And not designed for exit, either."

Clellendol said, "Hst! Let me study this! Once we start to open it, it will have to be fast. That slab will make a lot of noise."

They would have continued to discuss the problem, save for the fact that at that moment a dull rumbling sounded up the stairwell behind them. Tenguft turned sharply, her mouth open, teeth gleaming. She drew a knife from beneath the folds of her robe. She waved with her left hand, gesturing them to silence. For a time there were some indistinct noises from below, but they soon faded.

Cretus asked, "Accident?"

Tenguft shook her head. "No. Something comes. Not soldiers. They rattle, and tread heavily. There was no metal-sound, but something live was moving after the blocks fell, I fear."

Cretus said, "Tenguft, you said you heard footfalls behind us and above us, but not ahead, yes?"

"It ended above us, and a little ahead. Then there was a sliding sound, like stone grating on stone, like a great mill-wheel. Be still!"

They all stood rigidly, not daring to breathe. Tenguft leaned out over the stairwell, ear turned down. Then she turned back, her pupils dilated to empty black pits and the muscles of her face working with fear.

Cretus shook her roughly, and whispered sharply, "What do you hear, hunts-woman?"

"In the darkness, something moving, making a snuffling sound, I hear the pad of its feet, the brushing of its fur on the stones, *O bi leberim, ao Dehir sherda!*" Her agitation was so great she lapsed at the end into the secret hunt-language of the Haydars.

Cretus turned to Morgin. "Speak, Embasse. What does this madwoman say!"

Morgin drew his own knife. "She says a Korsor comes. If you have weapons, prepare to use them now, for we must kill it, or be killed by it."

Cretus exclaimed, "Ai! Now I know; somewhere they opened a cage, to let a night-devil track us. That is why these pits have no exit from this side. Prepare for madness and fight for your lives!"

At the bottom of the stairs the darkness moved, and something immense and heavy and densely black solidified into form, a thing so large that when it turned the last curve of the stairs, the front seemed halfway up while the rear was still in the darkness. It neither waited nor threatened, but climbed the stairs like a destroying demon, and in an instant was among them. They all shrank back to the edges of the landing, seeing only blurred impressions of parts of the creature: something heavy and strong, black-furred. There were eyes, and stabbing teeth, and claws. Cretus it sought, and Cretus it found immediately, following its nose. Cretus raised the blade, although he knew it to be futile; his blade would only prick it. And the Vfzyekhr stepped within the circle of the monster's embrace and laid its hand on the throat of the Korsor, and the beast stopped.

Now they could see it: the tiny Vfzyekhr standing before the Korsor, a mountain of darkness. Bearlike it was in general shape, but there were many differences. It was in build as supple as a panther, and there was no fat on it whatsoever. The fur was a dull, flat black with no shine at all, and the muzzle had none of the doglike heaviness of the true bear, but was smooth and tapered. The skull was low, spreading out behind the brow ridges, but it was large and spacious. The eyes were set deep under shelved ridges of bone, and were seemingly covered by an iridescent film which showed shifting colors in the lamplight like oil on a wet roadway. Its presence and scent filled the landing: a pungent, musky odor from its body, and a raw-meat odor from its jaws.

The Vfzyekhr slowly turned, still touching the Korsor, and moved to the sliding panel. Allowing its touch to slide down the throat to the belly, still keeping contact, the Vfzyekhr caused somehow the Korsor to stand on its hind leges, and catch the edges of the panel in its claws. Then the panel began to slide open, enough to admit one human at a time. Then the small, white-furred creature slowly led the Korsor back to the stairs.

Cretus recovered first. "Through the door, you idiots! It will turn the Korsor loose!"

On shaking legs they filed from the landing through the slit, into an anteroom, and from there into the great hall, which stood empty. The guard room was immediately to their right, and beyond it, a simple wooden door with a bar across it. They ran to the empty room and slipped the bar from the door. Cretus hurried them out, through the narrow door, into the night. One by one they ran out into the darkness, down the stairs to the ground. There was wind, and a chill in the air.

Tenguft came last to the door, and stood by Cretus. "The furry one is still within with the Korsor."

"What is that little one, that it can stop a Korsor with the touch of the hand?"

"I know it not. The Spsom brought it with them from beyond the stars; it is their pet, or their slave, or perhaps something else we do not understand."

"What are Spsom?"

"A spaceship came. It was theirs. Star-folk they are. And they hunt. They remained behind, in Ombur. My charge was that the little one was to be 'as if people.' It speaks not."

"Shall we leave it? I fear a Korsor, just as you, but I fear more that-which-stops-a-Korsor."

"I cannot. And, I do not know if it can be left."

The Vfzyekhr emerged from the guardroom, looked down the grand hall, and then joined them at the entrance. It came to Cretus-Meure and grasped his hand like a small child. Cretus lifted the creature effortlessly, and set it on his hip, cradling it under his arm. He looked down at it and said, "Little one, we are in great debt to you." The Vfzyekhr said nothing, but it held on tightly. Cretus closed the door.

Cretus mused, "I wonder what it did with the Korsor?"

Tenguft answered, "We heard no noise, no cries of pain. Perhaps the Korsor now seeks other prey, for once it tracks, the hunt must culminate. How they pent it up is beyond my scope, but I . . ." She let the sentence trail off, looking sharply at Cretus. Something was wrong.

Cretus-Meure staggered on the last step, and was now looking about in the darkness crazily. The Vfzyekhr squirmed, freed itself, and dropped to the ground, where it took no further notice of what was now obviously Meure Schasny, not Cretus the Scribe.

The others continued walking into the darkness beyond the dim lighting of the porch of Dzoz Cucany. Tenguft took Meure by the elbow, bent and looked closely at his eyes, which were staring blankly into nothing. She said, softly, "Who are you. . . ?"

Meure . . . I think," he began uncertainly. "I have been

asleep, or not here, or something. I don't know. Why are we outside?"

She began, "There was something in the food, that made us dulled. I slept, but when I woke, I could not move of my own will. Then you came back, but it was not you. Another looked out of your eyes, and he named himself Cretus, the one they were trying to bring back. He spoke of things which I know *you* do not know, so that I knew it was not you . . . The others we awakened, and he led us through the stone to the door and we escaped. Now we must leave this place, before they recover and set the Korsor on us again."

"What is a Korsor?"

"You do not remember it, or the slave of the Spsom stopping it?"

"No. It's . . . there is something there, but I can't reach it. Like a dream you know you had, but you can't remember."

"You must remember. You must try; Cretus could remember things from your memory. True, it seemed he had to work at it, but he could recall from your memory how we came through the castle to the place where we were."

"I feel something there, but it's quiet now. I . . . talked with him, once, I remember that. He forced me to . . . then nothing. But now I can't feel him like then. It's like . . . something's wrong with him. There is a presence there, but it's veiled in layers I can't see through."

Tenguft was still carrying her knife openly. Now she grasped the blade and handed it to Meure. "Here. You must take this."

"Why?"

"I consulted the oracle when we were with my people. The vision was strong, not to be denied, one that foreshadowed my footsteps, my every act. I saw it, and could not but live it out."

"Can you not turn aside from a vision?"

"You are an offworlder and not one of the people, therefore I take no offense at your question. I cannot even frame such a question in my mind. To turn from such a revealed course. . . . I dare not force those-who-see to become manifest, to clothe themselves in flesh; they change. But see: I saw my way, and I walked in that path, and now I am free of it, this minute. I did not know it before, but I knew it would come. Now I am free. Now you must go your way."

"What is my way?"

"To meet Cretus the Scribe. I have done that which I was

constrained to do; thus and thus. So it was shown to me, and so I have done. But that I may be something more than a wind that has blown you to a strange house without warmth of fire, or to evil, I press my own knife to you. Take it! I took it in tongs living from the fire, and quenched it with my own hands, and as its light faded I laid upon it and my spear deep secrets only I know; therefore it will aid you. More I cannot give, and remain what I have been and am to be." She breathed deeply, and stood erect and tall against the light from the dark bulk of the castle, and her eyes were darker than the night.

Meure took the proffered knife by the hilt; it was made of many strips of leather wound around the tang of the blade. A rude weapon, one that had doubtless been used before. He looked at it intently for a long moment, almost as if he hoped some of what she put into it might speak to him. The spirits remained silent. Meure looked up, and felt a chill air moving against his face.

He said, "I know now much of which you have spoken. But I do not know why. As you said, to meet Cretus. So, then. I have met him, and it answers no questions. I do not know what he wants."

"Nor do I, beyond escaping from Cucany."

"Then you will return to Ombur?"

"Yes. We will go that way, and what will come to be will be."

"What of the rest of us?"

"I was commanded to bring you here and return you safely within the limits of my power. Thus I will do."

"And me?"

"You are no longer one of them, and I cannot protect you. You must become a hunter on your own account."

Meure felt a shiver pass along his body, one that ended in a sudden spasm of laughter. "Fine, then. I will take my first step. I will walk with you and your party for a time. But let us be gone from Cucany, and this whole land of towers and empty places. I sense that this spirit from the far past needs at least to meet some people from the present." So saying, he began walking into the darkness, where waited the others.

Tenguft followed him, and only one thing did she say: "It is said that of old Cretus was no prophet of the waste places, but one who went straightly into the press and the throng."

Meure said back over his shoulder, "And the Haydar? Are you a throng?"

She answered, curiously submissive, "We are but bands of hunters on the face of the wide world."

"Are there cities on this world?"

"In Chengurune the Great, and in Cantou, there are said to be cities . . . I know only Kepture. In this land are settled places, ports, trade-junctions, forts and castles."

"What about Glordune, the forth continent?"

"There are no cities in Glordune. But there is a place in Kepture where many gather."

"Where?"

"At the Mouth of Yast are the lands of the Lagostomes, and it is said that by the river docks can be found the sweepings and ends, and scraps of all peoples."

"Can we go there?"

"You can, if you will, but I will not take you. They are a vile people. We hunt them, and all true men of Kepture strive to keep them pent in the Low Country."

"Do they have a city?"

"Their whole land is city. There is nothing like it anywhere else. Ask of the Embasse; he comes and goes as he pleases."

At the end, she had seemed offended that he had shown any interest at all. And she had recommended him to Morgin with the distaste one would use for someone who performed a vital, but to her, a completely degrading act. But they were a long way from the mouth of Yast, and had more immediate problems for the moment. Meure felt a stirring in himself that he could not quiet. A stirring that was, for the moment, only a potential; but he wondered, at the same, if perhaps he would wind up there, whether he willed or not.

9

"The word of a Magus is always a falsehood. For it is a creative word; there would be no object in uttering it if it merely stated an existing fact in nature. The task of a Magus is to make his word, the expression of his will, come true. It is the most formidible labor the mind can conceive."

—A. C.

The Great River of Kepture, the Yast, began its journey to the sea toward the west, from the east of the continent, in a range of hills separating Incana from the land to the east, Intance. Except for the hills which separated Incana from Intance, the Yast was the border separating Incana from all other lands, as it passed westward, turned south, and finally ran back to the east for a shorter space before turning once more to the south and its delta between the two landmasses comprising Kepture. Within a frame of reference which could survey all known planets, Monsalvat was not a notable world in its landforms, nor was Kepture an impressive continent; likewise, the river Yast set no records. But it was the greatest river on the planet, and in its season struck awe into the Klesh who lived along its banks.

Meure vaguely remembered crossing the river; a greater darkness had passed beneath them as they had flown through the night; there had been nothing below to fix the eye on, no reference: the surface below had darkened, and dropped away, and later rose again into the dry hills of Incana.

Under one's own power on the surface, however, a viewer saw the great river of Kepture in different perspectives: from a low barge in the midst of its flow, it stretched away glassily to vague, low shores, or along its length, unbroken to the horizon. There was a current, requiring the bargemen, hybrids of unknown parentage, to take no action. The river was unruffled and waveless, but its calm surface was dark and opaque, and was pocked with upwellings, dimples, curious little whirlpools which appeared and vanished without apparent cause. There was an odor of something long-dead, and the sunlight lent no sparkle to the stagnant surface. It was the very image of a river in Hell.

No one had hindered their departure from Incana; for five days they had walked through an empty, unpopulated land, with the ridges and hills each crowned with a Dzoz of greater or lesser size. The land around them had been vibrant with the messages of heliographs, but they had neither been pursued, harassed, nor stopped. They had reached the river in sight of one of the castles, but such folk as lived along the Great River ignored it, and disregarded the influence of those who lived within.

Passage across the Yast was prohibitively expensive, owing, so the bargemen averred, to the labor of rowing the distance in the absence of wind. On the other hand, passage down the river was free, and should the Ombur bank be handy, they could debark as circumstances warranted. There was one barge currently in commission, due to leave, and so they boarded it, after bartering some trinkets Flerdistar and Clellendol had apparently hidden. Morgin procured some loaves of stale bread for them, on the strength of his office as Embasse, but without either Prote or Bagman, it was clear Morgin's influence was limited.

As for Tenguft, the bargemen-mongrels kept a respectful distance, but they were not awed by one Haydar. A band might have sent them into the water, howling with fear, but one alone? Let her pass, while they bided their time, for the Great River brought everything to the outcast bargemen.

There was a haze over the double sun, a film that Tenguft said meant rain. Meure sat atop a pile of faggots and watched the sullen flow of the river. The Haydar girl sat at the opposite end, chin on hands folded upon one knee, staring into the distance. The others had left him alone since the incidents at the castle, although Cretus had made no more overt manifestations.

Flerdistar and Clellendol climbed up on the pile beside him. The Ler girl broke the silence first. "Have you had any contact?"

Meure looked at her for a time before answering. "No. Not in so many words. He's there, all right; but not there, too. I think it's an effort for him to control me."

She nodded, as if she understood. "I see . . . that's an experience I have no words for."

Meure smiled, for once, finding her studiousness amusing. "Oh, yes, there aren't any. It's definitely out of the ordinary, rather unspeakable. You know that since he's the outsider, he is invisible to me . . . I mean, I can sense that he's there, but I can't catch any of his thought or memory. But he can see all of mine; I can tell where he's been, what things he's been poking through, because those memories are changed, somehow; as if they had been re-recorded. I suppose in time he could become me if he wanted, but that's not his way."

Clellendol picked up the thought and continued it, "And so Cretus could mimic you so perfectly we'd not know the difference."

"Right. But like I said, that's not his way. He doesn't want to become me."

Clellendol said, "Then you could become him."

"Not that, either. That would produce two Cretuses. I could suppress him entirely then. That's why he hides from me. While he learns."

"Learns what?"

"All about the universe we know, that he doesn't know and never did. Also Time. He wants to know how long it's been."

Flerdistar asked, "Does he know? Do you?"

"No, and no. Only that it's been a very long span of time, and that there's been little or no change in the nature of the Klesh."

She said, "That bothers me; for a long time it was so obvious that I overlooked it, but it's there, none the less. These people seem to remain essentially static, advancing neither politically nor technologically."

Clellendol added, "That and the prevalence of omens and fortune-tellers; they seem to be everywhere, and they also seem to work better than the usual sort one meets. . . . Morgin tells me that it's like that everywhere. The method varies, but the consultation is done and the answers are given. Except when a Prote is being used, the creature the Embasses use for perception and communication."

Flerdistar said, "It would seem we have two things to occupy our attentions, besides the original two—to resolve our old question, and get off this planet."

Meure looked at her incredulously. "You mean you still have those in mind?"

"I could hardly forget them. But the Spsom behavior was not to Clellendol's liking."

Clellendol explained, "It is true that Spsom are essentially carnivorous, and that they hunt. *However* . . . in their natural habitat, they prey on small game, and they are not built for heavy encounters. Moreover, they are inordinately curious, and they seek our Human contacts, the more bizarre the better. That they would stay with the Haydar, while we were off adventuring, makes no sense, especially when they let the Vfzyekhr go with us . . . we don't know exactly what the relationship is between those two races, but they simply don't let them go on their own. Flerdistar reads the past and smells a rat; I read the present and smell another. The Spsom wanted to stay in the same vicinity of the crash site."

Flerdistar finished, "Which means that a Spsom ship will come for us, sooner or later. And as for the other problem, the one we came here to resolve . . . That's not over, either."

"How could you ever hope to revive that, after what you've seen?" Meure stared at the girl blankly.

"All secrets leave their traces. We have always known that things were not as history had them, for us, the New People, but never what the true picture was. I said to you on the ship that we finally traced the echoes of that discontinuity to this world. We *know* that the truth was on this world at one time; and we *know* that historical truths like that leave traces stamped into the very gesture-language of the people who hide them, willingly or no. And at the last, as a reader of the past, I can feel the answer just as certainly as you can feel the presence of Cretus. It is here." Here she gestured with a hand all around the barge and the leaden, brassy water of the sullen river. "Here, all around us, if I could but get it out."

Meure said, "Which of our problems do you think will resolve itself first?"

Clellendol said, "Something on this world suppresses change. There are known rates of change for Humans, wherever you find them. When change does not occur, you look for the mechanism causing that lack. I am very concerned about it, because it implies a power on a planet-wide scale. It could be a natural effect, in which case we should not want to blunder into it. On the other hand, it might be something shaped by design. Then we are dealing with an entity, or entities. There is much here that strains probabilities; the lack of change, the success of omens, the isolation by stressed space, of the planet, preventing contact or effective integration with other worlds. And, like you and the Liy Flerdistar, while I can see that my problem's there, I can't resolve it any better than the two of you."

Meure felt his way along another tack. "About change, among Humans; I am not conscious of any lack of change . . ." He realized as he said it that he had just demonstrated the validity of Clellendol's concept. "At least, I know of no great changes in the people I'd heard of. And remember, I come from a colonial world. We had change, in the New Lands Program."

Clellendol answered, "So Tancred is a pioneer world, settled a few generations back, still being exploited. That I know. What about this fact, that for every new world Humans discover and exploit, they abandon three others, either to Ler, or some non-Human sentient, or in some cases, not all that rare, to the wind. Change is going on indeed, on a grand scale. Now Humans do everything right, but it doesn't work for them."

Meure laughed, "But it's right there: that we're right, according to your lights. Maybe we shouldn't be!"

"We are now discussing sanity itself," exclaimed Flerdistar.

Meure didn't answer her, but instead abruptly turned his head at an odd angle, and then looked about the landscape with a piercing glance quite at odds with his usual relaxed manner. Then he seemed to shudder, and resumed his normal appearance. Still, he kept silent, with his head cocked, as if listening.

After a time, he said, "Yes, that's right, though; it is no great secret. We have long envied the Second People and their ways. You get a steadier progression without the horrific ups and downs we seemed so attracted to in our history. And we always knew that *you* considered Humans primitive, uncontrolled, rude, unpotentialized. So gradually we quieted down, stabilized ourselves, concerned ourselves with homely things close to us. I had thought it was working."

Clellendol said, "That's the trouble with an interplanetary civilization. The consciousness of the far islands is lost. That's why there is a colonization program . . . but it has not halted the decline; only slowed it. What has been done has not been enough."

Flerdistar interrupted, "Was that Cretus, just now?"

"Yes. He's been listening to us. He left me a message to deliver to the two of you to add to your list of things to worry about. Clellendol: you said something was suppressing change here and isolating Monsalvat. Consider this—that we got in, and that a chain of circumstances leads from outside this stellar area right to Cretus."

"Cretus said that."

"Yes, and that he has his suspicions as well; that is why he is staying as hidden as he can. He says I screen him. From what, he doesn't say. But he said that his troubles in his original life commenced when he began to suspect the true nature of what Monsalvat harbors." Meure paused, and added, "I really don't like what he is suggesting at all. If it's true, none of this has been accidental; but not one of us knows to what purpose. Not him either."

Flerdistar asked, "What is it Monsalvat harbors?"

"I don't know. *He* doesn't know, although I sense that he has seen much more that we would like to know as well. It was not on Dawn, with the Klesh when they were made in the deeps of time, it did not come here with them. Somehow, they awakened it, here. But it was not of Dawn."

"Cretus has seen Dawn? Impossible. He can't have been an Original; Morgin talked about him, and Cretus appeared historically after the naming of lands."

"He looked. The thing that caused the transfer of him into me; with that he could see other places, other times. . . . He looked back to see where the Klesh had come from."

"Then he knows what we have come to hear." There was unmistakable triumph in the Ler girl's voice.

Meure smiled. "Perhaps. But until certain questions are resolved, he is as cautious of you as he is of Monsalvat."

Flerdistar assumed a more haughty posture, and said, "Neither you nor Cretus know to what lengths we would go to attain the final resolution."

Meure stood now, and looked down on Flerdistar and Clellendol as from a great height. And at that moment, they could not be sure which persona was speaking, for he said, "And you do not know what things Cretus has already done, over lesser issues than this one. He who was once Lord of Incana and All Kepture, come there from the street-wisdom of mongrelhood, will protect his refuge. And demand not of him, that he not demand more of you in return. For the moment, leave Cretus and your secret alone; he is capable of setting forces in motion we cannot imagine, the less control."

Clellendol said, with some heat, "He is mortal. Cut him, and he bleeds; strike him, and he pains. If worse comes to worse, he can be killed."

Meure now said, with chilling assurance, "Do not make the mistake of imagining either one of you could measure up to that." Then he softened a little, and said, almost apologetically, "You must not force him to activate before his time. Let it be! He knows what he must do."

Meure turned, climbed down, and went to stand by the side of the barge, looking out over the greasy reflections on the water. Flerdistar said to Clellendol, in an undertone, "It is clear to me what this Cretus wants; do you see it?"

Clellendol answered her, "This whole thing has been arranged to get Cretus the Scribe off Monsalvat. By whom or what, I cannot imagine, but it must not be permitted to happen. He is a unique type—a master of historical currents."

"Just so. And not only can he ride those currents, but he can, so it appears, steer them, and probably create them as well. He was schooled deeply in the barbarities of Klesh existence. The Humans will follow him into blood and iron again."

"It would, so to speak, solve their problem."

"Probably. But create others. This Cretus is an upsetter, and I want none of it; we have learned to do without them. I agree; Cretus must not be permitted to leave this earth; yet there are secrets we'd have of him before it comes to that, isn't it so?"

Clellendol turned his face, so that there would be no gesture accompanying the words, and innately Ler mannerism,* but his agreement was spoken: "Zha' armeshero," which was an affirmative that left little doubt, if any.† Clellendol would array against Cretus all that he possessed of the Ninth House of Thieves.

Now the great burden of Cretus pressed down heavily upon Meure, so that there was a darkness and a weight behind his eyes; and Cretus, who saw all things through the eyes and nerves of Meure, also felt these things and felt in his heart a kindliness, an affection, for one who had been given a burden unasked and undeserved, but yet bore it as bravely as he could according to his lights. And, bodiless invader though he was, Cretus contrived a way to speak more directly with him who bore him, as though they were separate.

This speech, if speech it could be called, passed faster than could be done with words, for it was made of raw thoughts,

---

* Ler gestures were muted, where present at all.
† Singlespeech, approximately, "It is indeed (most-)agreed." Past Indicative Passive Participle, superior comparison. Zha' is emphatic.

as were in men's minds before they invented words to symbol-
ize and transmit them. Yet it was speechlike, in that it was
directed thought, consciously shaped, not merely unedited
and uncontrolled mind-stuff. And there was much that Cretus
did not say.

Of the many griefs of the Klesh he spoke in summary, but
did not dwell upon those things; likewise he spoke of the bru-
tal weeding which had made the original Klesh pure racial
types in the beginning. And of the time before that, when the
pre-Klesh had been just ordinary Humans, men and women,
the Klesh only said, "That is now forgotten and unknown,
since we cannot reach it—the Time Before the Beginning. Of
that we know not, therefore we care not."

And when they had been freed of the Warriors, awaiting
the great ships that would take them from the planet Dawn
to some new home far away in the stars, they gathered, in
their many shapes and colors, and said among one another,
"We were slaves without hope of salvation, *since we were
slaves for the sake of slavery,* not even for a real purpose,
however shabby. Freedom, we had ceased to dream of it.
Now, we are free, and though we were made pureblooded
through no will of our own, pure we are, and pure we remain, and pure we shall remain by our own hands, for it was
the mixed men who were weak and allowed the corrupt Warriors to enslave them and mold their forms like wax. Thus
they set chains on them. Thereby let each cleave to his and
her own kind; let it be so until the end of time!" And it was
so. And they then all spoke strong and blood-curdling oaths
that never again, whatever befell them, would any Klesh,
even the least as the strongest, endure what had befallen
them in the pits of the Warriors.

They were taken to the planet the Mixed men called Monsalvat. And they also learned to call it Aceldama, a place to
bury strangers, learning that word from the awed and incred-
ulous administrators who came to guide them, meaning well,
no doubt, but failing as quickly as those who might have
meant evil. There, some flourished, even as others weakened,
faded, and their lines failed and their lights went out and
they were no more. Most of all they needed, and longed for,
stern teachers of men; but the Ler feared them, thinking of
the Warriors, no doubt, and of optative revenges by the
Klesh. And just so the men, who were from the stars, feared
them, seeing their tumults and the strife, and so both drew
back, missing much, and thereby withdrew altogether. And so

abandoned, the Klesh made do, and settled down to the long night.

In which, they suspected, they were not alone. Monsalvat was an old world; of that there was no lack of ample geological evidence, as discovered by the star-men, and the Klesh saw no reason to doubt their conclusions, for they flew through space, did they not? But nowhere were artifacts found, no ruins, nor any trace of any kind that speaking creatures had ever walked its surface. Here was an ideal planet, and one that echoed to the boundless silences of time throughout the ages, its native life forms few and bearing no trace of evolutionary relationship to one another. A world so old that the first explorers said that Monsalvat had known flowering plants before there was a Solar System. And there was no one.

But there was something to the clarity of the air, ripples just below the threshold of perception, motions seen out of the corners of one's eyes, lights in the forest, and the undoubted success of fortune-tellers and omen-readers. Here, the oracle spoke. And there was a brooding presence that could not be denied, even though the form it took could neither be defined nor perceived, a something older than the darkness, older than man, perhaps older than time itself . . . It seemed not to notice them that they could tell, and they hoped not to notice it, or them. And for a time, one could forget it, but always, in the back of the mind, there never failed the suspicion that one was being watched, and always the sensation was strongest at the most intense moments; so that in the midst of a great battle, when the horns called and the swords struck fire against their cutting edges, so it was that the heroes always paused, at the last moment before the battle-lust took them, and saluted, with their raised weapons, to the one unseen who was not to be named, and then fell to their deadly work.

Now in the beginning, the Klesh perceived that the type called Zlat could see farther than any of them, and they accorded them special place on Monsalvat; the advisers and counselors of chiefs and princes they became. But their service quickly separated them from one another, and their confidants cared little for the maintenance of any tribe save their own, so that in the course of their service, the Zlats faded slowly as a race, having to undertake long and perilous journeys for a bride or husband. Many had no descendant, and others mingled with other Klesh types, so that in the end they faded, and vanished. That some in that end stooped to evil deeds and false counsel cannot be denied, but however it was, they passed from the world, and were forgotten, with their secrets. Save in a few forgotten places, the Zlat Rada was gone.

Those few pockets lingered on a little longer, but in time, they too became single wanderers, itinerant fortune-tellers and omen-readers, and so mixed with half-breeds, renegades and worse, and so ended their line.

A generation after the end that was thought, there was born a boy, who by his marks was pure Zlat. His life was a chancy one, and soon he was orphaned by the incessant wars and mayhems of Monsalvat; he was eventually taken in by an old woman who claimed to be also a Zlat, and who possessed the artifact which lent them their far-sight, the *Skazenach,* the wire tangle through which the user could see places and times distant from himself, seemingly in the guise of stories and epics told on the settings of the *Skazenach** made by an ancient tradition.

The old woman took the boy to the fens of Yast, in the far delta of the great river of Kepture, where they made a living smoking meats, and the old woman cast fortunes for the nomads who came down from the heights of Ombur. Originally, the boy was sickly, and good for little in the camps of the nomads save for fetching water, and so he came to be called, in the common speech of those parts, Sano Hanzlator, which is bad Singlespeech, but which means, more or less, "Waterboy Last-Zlat."†

In time, the old woman's time came, and she died, having instructed him in the ways of the *Skazenach;* and she taught him in secret, and swore him to secrecy also, for the *Skazenach* was the most powerful of all oracles, and the possessor of one would be hounded for reading until he had no life left of his own, whatsoever.

Now the boy was grown almost to manhood, and the sickliness had been replaced by a grim wiriness. He left the delta

---

* The word is distorted Singlespeech, and means, "Betold-things." The correct form is, "maskazemoni nakhon," meaning those things which are spoken of in tales.
† Hanzlator = "last-Zlat" is correct, but Sano for "Waterboy" is the wildest sort of colloquialism. Literally, it would correctly mean, "most waterlike (in action)," an adverbial form.

camps of the nomads, and drifted north, to the great city
Yastian, a city grown exceedingly large, a vast mixing-pot
where all breeds met and mingled and detestation hung in the
air, stronger in its reek than the odor of the swamps. There
were bravoes and tarts, ruined beggars and kings, wise men
and fools alike, the rich and the educated, the ignorant and
the poor. There were also princes and fastidious clerks. Evil
was done in the light as well as in the dark, and a single life
was worth less than nothing. But being a fetchboy for the
fierce nomads, and the letters he had learned of the old
woman, and his secret oracle, all stood him well there, and
Sano became a scribe, transcribing petitions beside the palace
wall.

The boy Sano in the city survived and grew, even prosper-
ing after his own fashion, for he was wont to waste nothing
and live frugally; and as he grew he came to understand
many things from the life of the city in which he was im-
mersed. He came to understand that the great secret, the only
one worth knowing, was not that life consisted of haves and
have-nots, but that it consisted of doers and seers, the rub
being that the seers seemed unable to do, and the doers unable to see. That was the great secret and the division of
men, Klesh not the less. And more he saw clearly: that the
Klesh would never advance farther than they were at that
moment, if they failed to learn that they must cooperate with
one another, learn to complement one another, instead of
endlessly striving to outdo one another; and that the pride of
Rada that they took on so readily was but still another trap
from which there was in the end no escape, since each
remembered the crimes done to all, even to the whole of the
past.

Therefore in all his time, he studied, he dreamed, he
planned. He looked within, through his *Skazenach*, many
times and places, becoming skilled in aiming and directing his
thought through the symbolisms of the device. And his aim
became no less than to build the Klesh peoples into a great
people, such as they could be, but not by mixing them, which
they would never countenance, but by constructing a component system of interlocking dependencies, all respected, all
needed.

Now in Yastian the City there was a place somewhat below the palace where orators were wont to go and speak to
the people, and to that place Sano went to deliver his
message to whomever might give ear. When at last he had

spoken, many of those there mocked him, saying, "Sano the Scribe will deliver us from ourselves. And even as now. Whereupon he stepped down, saying, "Then I will be Water-boy Last-Zlat the Scribe no longer, but will come to you again as an avatar of Cretus, a fell hero of the old days*, but I will yet be a scribe until the last day." The mob hooted, and tried to stone him, unsuccessfully.

Sano, now Cretus, left the city of the delta and walked westward up into the land Ombur, where his words fell on sympathetic ears, but went, by and large, without action. So he crossed the great river Yast northward into Incana, where some listened, and acted, too. And first in Incana, it began to come together, not without strife, nor yet without war, but come it did, and soon all nations began to crumble before the newfound strength they seemed to possess as if by magic. But there was no sorcery, but varied skills being used together in concert for the first time in the history of Monsalvat. And at the last, Cretus commanded great variegated armies, and they marched over Kepture where they would.

Now there is something which must be told, which is part of the story of Cretus the scribe as well (and it was along these lines that Meure felt most surely that Cretus was with-holding something of it, not out of a desire for secrecy, but out of a requirement to protect Meure from something Cre-tus feared to face directly). From the beginning of his la-bors, which took in twenty of the years of Monsalvat, Cretus had been accustomed to consult his own oracle, and act thereupon, and it had not failed him, not once. But as Kep-ture neared complete assimilation, and the war at last neared its end, and even Yastian in its delta lands submitted, Cretus began to feel a subtle change in the oracle.

And in the circumstances around him as well. The coun-selors and advisers and court flunkies were closing in; he knew this to be natural, and moved to counter this trend, fol-lowing the correct course: and while it slowed the clotting of the great dynamic empire, it was only by a little. It was as if something offstage were purposely guiding all those people to a common end. And as he realized, or suspected this, he also saw that while they had indeed gained all Kepture, the re-maining three continents were as far away as other planets, and getting no closer; and that the invasion of Chengurune

* "Cretus" is a contraction of Koror Trethus, lit., "fear of the lance."

had been postponed so long that by now they must be waiting
on the beaches for them, to repulse the first overseas invasion
in the history of the planet.

There was more that disturbed him; his own oracle was becoming unreliable, unsteady, as if something was distorting it
even as he worked it. The visions it provoked were unclear
and vague, and he began to distrust them, for they always
seemed to lead to the path of more war, and more blood, and
even more strife. Then he used one of the ways of his people
and consulted their oracle, and the oracle told him that
within, as he knew the way, he would find rest, and be called
again.

—*Is that all?*

—No, not all. Nothing is ever all of it. But mostly. Yet
when I came again, it was to a world that had changed. Almost like another planet, but I knew that it was Monsal-
vat/Aceldama, and that a great, vast time had passed. The
empire came and went, and left little enough behind it. But
there was an equilibrium among the peoples, a quiet, as if my
war had been the last great one. What was it like, all those
centuries? Like a moment, in which I thought I felt some
ripples, and then I was you.

—*You think transfer was tried other times?*

—Yes. But no one knows how we Klesh armor ourselves,
save other Klesh. It wouldn't take, because it couldn't—we
won't accept transferance, because we hate too strongly. We
feel everything too strongly. So it brought a Mixed man from
the stars to me so that . . .

—*So that you would stir things up again.*

—I'll say it the old way: *Tasi mapravemo zha'*. Most correctly so. So that I would try to rebuild the Empire with
strife where none is now; therefore I hide from it. In bringing
me back, it has given a place to hide from it, where there
was none before. But you are exposed, of course; I will help
you as I may. (Here, the stream of onrushing thought paused
for a second, as if considering something Meure could not
see, or perhaps just wandering. He could not tell.) . . . yes.
It wants strife, so much I know. I know well; I have looked
through the *Skazenach* all the way back, to the beginning,
and beyond it. Ha! Beyond the beginning, I say! I know the
secret of the Ler, and what a joke it is; what fools they have
been. St. Zermille, our Lady of Monsalvat, protector of the
weak, defender of the defenseless, Sister of Mercy, on a

planet whose people confuse the word justice with revenge, and forget the difference. But we knew all along, and they were the ones who were misled. And knowing that we were right on that one, I wonder how many other things about this place we've been right about? Yes, about that. I know it's there. And yet, in a way I can't tell you, it isn't there . . . (And here, the thought almost faded out, as if Cretus was only musing to himself) . . . and the strife it wants I'll bring to it, if I can find it before it finds me.

—*You keep saying "it".* . . .

—I think that we are almost as hard for it to perceive as it is to us; but it can cause long-range events, large-current movements among the people. It can reach far, but it seems difficult for it to undertake fine detail work, except through the persuasions of the oracles it uses. . . .

—*It sounds almost like a God, but I.* . . .

—This isn't religion we're talking about . . . I'm not even sure it's alive, in the sense we'd call something alive, like a person or an animal or a plant.

—*But you talk about it perceiving; that's life, isn't it? And it causing things to happen* . . .

—Many things perceive, and even regulations can cause things to happen. Your machines have will and awareness, some of them, but for all that they are not alive. At any rate, the last time I looked, they weren't. The last time I looked . . . I looked across time and space to where a young man sat in a tower and wrote verses to the night. It doesn't matter where it was . . . or when, relative to you and I and now on Monsalvat the cursed. This he said aloud, repeating it until it felt right to him, and some of his words were strange, but I understood and remembered: 'Language is a chemical phenomenon, with atoms and molecules and complex superstructures, that, in a proper environment aided by proper stimuli, become replicating structures which lead to life-forms. Phonemes into words into ideas into chains of things. At the present, we who think are but in the bare-planet stage of life; the life-forms of the future are unknown to us who are to be their matrix, but in the future beautiful burning tigers will stalk through the nighted forests of our minds.' What do you think of that, hah? That things can assume life within our very thoughts!? Then do not be so quick to draw the line between the living and the dead . . . There are life forms, and there are other life forms. Size and scale, rates of time vary, perceptions vary. I am Cretus, what you think is a barbarian, but I know that to a creature who sees with radio waves, men are invisible, ghosts who probably aren't there. Yes?

—*You are a barbarian. Where did you learn these things?*

—I may be a barbarian, boy, but I was an Emperor. An emperor can do what he damn well pleases: he can stupefy himself with drugs, he can wallow abed with the court whores. . . .

—*He can indulge in gluttony, which is the only sin.*

—Very perceptive, that! Take it further, now that you've said it! All valid thoughts are endless chains, but you must follow them out as far as you can; there lies mastery.

—*Drugs, women, drink, food: just refinements . . . That the medium changes does not change the nature of the act.*

—Keep going!

—*One in power practices other indulgences beside those of the senses . . . I see, it still remains the same: Some fondle the position, and others the work that maintains it. Still others concentrate on the manipulations of power, plots, strategies . . .*

—Possessions, routines, obedience, flattery. The list is virtually endless, without changing the nature of it. And the others expect it of you and press upon you to seek those indulgences. I sought ways to avoid those traps. So much is basically natural, a part of us. It was when I escaped those fates that the pressure became unnatural, and at that point I was sure that there was an exterior . . . something . . . manipulating the people around me. Not by individual control, but by a kind of bending of the behavioral space to steepen the natural impulse. It damn near revealed itself, but it realized that I could then see its traces and was closing on its actuality; then it became more concealed. Shortly thereafter, I saw that the end was at hand in that time. I took what it offered, as a truce, because I could do no more there . . .

The voice stopped then, and remained quiet, as if it had admitted something unintended. Then it continued.

—So I know this about it: it isn't a God, because it has limited perceptions and makes mistakes. It is a life-form, not a machine, however odd it may seem to us, and it is single, not one of a kind of which there are others. It has continuation, but not reproduction, which suggests a kind of colony organism. But all that is nothing: what counts is that it has a single nature and it is fixed, immobile.

Meure could not deny the gloating he heard in the voice. And Cretus caught the fugitive thought, as well.

—That's correct. It is large, very large, but it is highly vulnerable. So much so that if I can touch it, I can kill it. And I intend to.

—*And you're going to use me as bait for it.*

—Not quite so. I am you, now. Rest assured that I will not recklessly endanger our mutual house. And remember this: it's hard to find, but I know that it can't move. I know that, now; because if it could have left, it would have. There are better opportunities for strife elsewhere. It's tied *here.*

—*It came here and was trapped, like you Klesh were?*

—No. Wait, I say that without knowing. If it came from elsewhere, it was very long ago. No, it has been here from the beginning. It is native, as far as I have been able to see.

—*I see it bringing others to it. It brought me.*

—And the Ler under circumstances that. . . . yes, I see. You are one step ahead now. It will bring in new contenders; the Mixed men from the stars, the Ler, those star-creatures.

—*And you-I are to ignite the mixture.*

—It would be here, of course. But I have an objection: though I do not care that the offworlders fight among themselves, I can see easily enough that it would be the end of the Klesh.

—*And the strife will not be limited to Monsalvat. I object to that.*

—Well you should, if you respect your origins; for it does not care about events outside. Only that they happen here.

—*There has not been in history a major interstellar war. Minor actions, yes, but nothing where the survival of a race or a planet was in question.*

—At the least, then, we can agree: you must let me do this thing.

—*We have little choice. Neither it nor the Ler will allow us to leave Monsalvat. And I fear what you might do there if you did leave.*

—You will keep me here, too? You will volunteer to remain on this most deadly world? Then you will assuredly need my help to survive here, now, for this has never been a gentle world. Up to now, you have been under the protection of a force, but that has now been accomplished which was intended, and I can no longer be sure it will protect you as fully as it has. Since Cucany, things have been easy. Do not be fooled by that ease. It has given me time to integrate myself into you. Now it will prod us a little.

—*You never did say what your indulgence was when you ruled.*

—To know what happened to us, why . . . and if there were any others. I will keep them to myself. Those times will not come again. I had my turn, and unlike others, was able to walk away from it.

And, abruptly, not finishing the thought-pattern, the Cretus presence withdrew, faded out, vanished. Meure felt freer than he had since the castle; Cretus must have gone deep within, to hide, or perhaps to sulk. He felt free; still, he knew he would never be entirely free of Cretus. There was no way he knew to reverse the thing that had happened to him. And he wondered, deep in his own thoughts, how they would eventually come to terms with each other. It seemed there was no way out.

10

"*It is hard to explain, and harder to learn, that truth abides in the inmost sanctuary of the soul and may not be told, either by speech or by silence; yet all attempts to interpret it distort it progressively as they adapt themselves to the perceptions of the mind, and become sheer caricatures by the time they are translated into terms of bodily sensation. Now the reality of things depends on their truth, and thus it is that it is not a philosophical paradox but a matter of experience that the search for truth teaches us to distrust appearances exactly in proportion as they are positive.*"

—*A. C.*

While Meure had been holding his internal conversation with the shade of Cretus, he had ignored the flow of perceptual events outside; and why not? For time on the river was a repetition of endless sameness, and within the group, relationships were now fixed.

But someone was standing beside him at the edge of the barge, who had come silently, unobtrusively. Ingraine Deffy, the other girl from the *Ffstretsha.*

Meure was fond of girls without desiring to possess them; still, he could appreciate how this slight girl, Ingraine, could incite possessiveness: seen from a distance, she was merely a pretty girl of no great distinction, not entirely real. Close by, however, she had a beauty that was remarkable—something not quite human anymore. Overall, she was fragile and delicate in appearance, with clear, almost translucent skin; and what he could see of her features had been drawn with a hand free of hesitation or doubt. Ignoring a slight childishness which the fineness of her features suggested, she was almost perfect, even after their escapades since the grounding of the ship.

Meure was not city-quick, after what he thought was the manner of Cretus, but neither was he an innocent yokel; he was perceptive enough on his own to see with his own senses that Ingraine was not as young as she appeared, nor had she been discomfited by some of the harsh exertions they had been through. He could see easily that she would inspire protectiveness by her appearance alone, whether she actually needed it or not. And that, having been favored by beauty, she had made herself the final adjustments in mannerisms to fit herself into a specific interaction with the people around her; feeling subliminally the undertow of others' emotions, she had turned herself to them, to her advantage. Now he wondered, what was the advantage?

He felt acutely uncomfortable; Meure and Halander had been only casual acquaintances, not particularly friends, and he had claimed her early aboard the ship. This action on her part could only cause problems which he did not care to add to what he thought were excessive complications.

Now she was here, when before she had scarcely noticed him, looking out over the water dreamily, brushing her soft brown hair out of her eyes, pursing her delicate, full lips pensively.

What had Cretus said? *Thoughts are endless chains, but you must follow them as far as you can.* He accepted without question that he would have to learn from Cretus. What did that learning tell him now? That Ingraine, sensing the stronger Cretus personality, had switched allegiances at the first appropriate moment . . . she could mean more trouble than all he had experienced on Monsalvat up to this moment. It was a most delicate moment; he felt, without looking, the beginnings of malice in Halander; what did the others feel? Tenguft? Audiart? Indeed, what about Cretus? Glancing about, internally and externally, he sensed withdrawal. He was on his own.

She asked, softly, as if for his ears alone, "What are you thinking about now?"

"I was thinking, as a fact, just now, why me? I had not hoped for so much adventure when I signed on the *Ffstretsha*, on Tancred."

She mused, "Yes, isn't it terrible, what's happened to us? Do you think we'll ever be rescued from this . . . Monsalvat?"

"Myself, I believed the worst; but the Ler think that a Spsom craft will come here, after all. If we can survive until then, they will surely pick us up." *Why had she hesitated over the word, Monsalvat?*

"But they sided with those hunters, so quickly."

"They think, only to allow them to remain close by the crash site; presumably the hypersensitive perceptions of the Haydar will warn them when the new ship arrives. In the meantime, they can enjoy themselves with a little sport, while they're waiting."

"While we wonder from minute to minute whether we'll be alive or not; I thought those hunters were preparing to eat us. And why didn't they?"

"They act under a system of oracles and revelations, as I understand it. The best way to say it is that their spirits told them to pack us off to that castle. Besides . . . I don't think they'd actually eat us: we're not 'game,' apparently. They might have disposed of us as excess baggage by dumping us somewhere, or selling us to another tribe. Who knows. We are certainly no threat to them, and they know that easily enough . . . of what we've seen so far, they appear to be the best. At the least, the most honorable, even though they are wild. I wish we had more of them with us where we are going."

"I thought we were going down this vile river only because it was away from the land of castles. Where are we going?"

Now Meure was wary, although he tried not to show it; Ingraine had spoken at the last to Cretus, not to him, Meure Schasny. Cretus-Meure had led them to the river and the barge; Cretus knew what lay at the place where the pestilential river drowned itself in the stormy gulf between the two southern peninsulas of Kepture, knew it far better than any of them, even Tenguft. And if he was bound there, to what purpose? Ingraine sensed that the land was just itself, but a city was a bridge to somewhere else, something else, change. He said, only, "To a city."

"Do they actually have cities on this planet?"

"So I am told, although they will not be cities as I have seen them. Like something from the dim past." Now he sought to deflect her. "Were you from Tancred?"

Ingraine shook her head briefly, as if shaking cobwebs away, sending waves flowing down her hair. "No. Didn't you know? Well, no matter—I suppose it never got around to you. I came aboard on Flordeluna."

Meure turned slightly away to conceal his surprise. "That's . . ."

She finished the sentence, ". . . a long way off. I know."

"Where did Audiart come from? Flordeluna?"

"She didn't tell you?"

"No. I hadn't asked . . ."

"She was there when I boarded. She hasn't told me, either. She has some mannerisms which suggest . . . perhaps a world like Tancred, something a bit out of the way."

Meure took no offense. He knew Tancred was more than a bit out of the way. But Flordeluna was on the far side of the central group; if Audiart came from a colony planet like Tancred, then it would be, very likely, on the far side, adjoining Spsom space. He asked, "You were hired on by the Ler as we were?"

"Hired, yes. Not as you were. She and I were aboard when the Ler girl chartered the *Ffstretsha;* we could have left the ship or taken employment with the Ler party . . . it was on a Ler world and I did not care to be so stranded." She finished with some heat, as if there was something offensive to her about a world inhabited solely by Ler.

"Was there not a Transiton?"*

"On Lickrepent? Indeed there was, but you would not care to have to work your way out of it. I did not." Here Ingraine looked coyly sidelong at Meure under her eyelashes. "I prefer not to work any harder than absolutely necessary, and so I thought being a scull for Ler aristocrats was better than slogging it in Transiton. I did not reckon on the disasters that have befallen us along the way, but all in all, things have not turned out badly so far . . . I will certainly have a tale to

---

* Contraction of "Transient-town," a common adjunct of spaceports.

tell!" Here she shook out her hair again and smiled up at the sky.

Meure thought, here stands a slight girl who looks like she should yet be in school, yet she is experienced enough to set out tramping rides alone across space, obviously an individual of considerable verve . . . Still, dangerous. Audiart had offered and given of herself with no thought of tomorrow; Tenguft had used him for some incomprehensible purpose, but had allowed him to share in it, however brief it had been; this one would have a price, which he was not sure he could pay. Or would. Not the least of which would be surrender to Cretus . . . He was not entirely sure Cretus would wish to pay, either, whatever it was. He was one who liked no restraints or obligations. But at the same time, looking at the smooth skin of her throat, at the slender body under the borrowed Ler overshirt, he could not but imagine. Meure looked around guiltily. He was acutely uncomfortable. And Cretus, of course, would sit back and let him make his own choices, and probably vicariously watch as well.

Halander was glaring at them from the bow, making small, indecisive movements. He continued glancing around at the others. Tenguft ignored the whole proceeding. Audiart caught his eye and looked away, with an odd flicker of sadness, or so Meure thought. As if she were worried for him, rather than jealous of the girl. He felt pressure to act, to make a decision. The only thing was, any way he moved, he would make an enemy, and he could afford no more. Cretus, however benign, had to be counted an enemy, and one such as no man ever had before.

One of the bargemen hybrids suddenly called out to the others, and began to jabber excitedly; the others hurriedly joined him at the stern, facing west, back up the river, where they conferred earnestly and gestured wildly at something out over the water which Meure couldn't quite make out.

The bargemen became more excited, and one climbed up on the rail and began shouting at the passengers. Meure looked hard up the river, but he could see no cause for their erratic behavior . . . there was an irregular spot far back up the river, seemingly moving toward them, but he could make out no details. It seemed to be moving, or changing its orientation. He could not make out a shape at all.

The bargeman who had climbed up on the rail emitted a long, doleful hoot that echoed across the water, an expression of emotions too complex to frame in speech, and then stepped over the side and began swimming for the nearer shore to the south. The remaining bargemen hesitated, looking fearfully first up the river, then at one another, then at the barge. Then, one by one, they, too, began climbing over the side, and swimming for the shore. The river had become ominously still, its surface like molten glass. The bargemen scarcely made ripples as they entered the water and began stroking mightily.

They all looked at each other uncertainly. The bargemen had abandoned the barge! Morgin had been dozing, but now he ran to stern to see what it was that caused such panic. Meure and Ingraine also hurried to join Morgin. They passed Tenguft, who hadn't changed position, but was looking intently up the river from under her deep brows.

South of the barge, between the barge and the south shore, the Ombur side of the Great River, the bargemen were still swimming for the shore; there was a sudden sucking sound and a swirl of water, and there was one bargeman less. Meure felt his scalp crawling. What was it, there, coming toward them that would make bargemen who supposedly knew the river brave it? The others took no notice whatsoever, but kept on making for the Ombur shore.

Now they stood by the stern rail and looked up the river; something was approaching, coming toward the barge, an irregular something which would not resolve into a perceptible shape, suspended somewhat above the surface without visible force. Meure looked at Morgin; Morgin looked back, blankly; here was something of Monsalvat beyond the experience of an Embasse.

Tenguft slid down from the pile of faggots, a silky, wary motion, and stood slightly behind Meure looking very intently at the approaching object. Meure looked at her also, but she did not return the gesture; she was watching.

Meure turned back to the object; it was closer now, still approaching, still suspended above the water without visible effort. He tried harder to make it out, but something about it continued to elude resolution. It was brownish in color, but it seemed to have no single outline, nor stable shape. It *changed* somehow, constantly; but it also possessed an inexplicable vagueness of size, for it seemed both very large and far away, and simultaneously small and close, no matter how it occluded the background it moved against. It was nothing he could classify into any known category.

He glanced again at Tenguft; the Haydar girl was still

looking at the object, her lips tightly compressed. Meure asked her, "What is that? Why did they fear it?"

She answered, not looking at him, speaking tonelessly and softly, as if she wished not to disturb some delicate equilibrium, "I have heard of such things in the most ancient of tales, but I have not ever seen one myself, nor has anyone I have known. Our rites exist to prevent the appearance of such demons. It is not good that we see it now; it is a sign of dire events."

Meure insisted, "What is it?"

She continued, "The *Lami* Sari Au Ardebe faced one alone for the sake of the tribe Tahiret; Gambir 'Am-seleb the holy man called upon one to end the holy war N'Guil-Ellem; Imrem Galtaru was said to have entered into association with one, but he was no longer of the Haydar after that, and was pursued as game by the great among the People—without success or trophy, indeed, many a fine warrior of the Haydar learned truth untelling in that quest. . . ."

"You mean they saw, but they could not speak of it?"

Morgin tactfully interrupted, "She means that the great warriors vanished in a manner strongly suspected of bringing great shame upon them . . ."

Tenguft interrupted Morgin, ". . . Ebdalla Yamsa returned to Illili without his spear, crawling on the ground in his fear. The people gave him the truth, and hunted after Imrem the unholy no more. His memory be cursed. But we do not forget, and we do not seek that-which-has-no-name; and what it does here is beyond me. I have not called it, and Morgin the Embasse does not know how, indeed, those who carry a Prote cannot see one."

The object, now measured against its background, seemed to have approached the barge closely, almost within stone-throwing distance. Its motion had ceased, save for that slight drift necessary to keep it near the barge, but not its mutability; its outline wavered constantly, and its shape and internal features shifted too rapidly for anything of detail to be made out. Meure strained at it, trying to grasp enough of it to make up an image, but he could not. It was as if the thing were mutating at a rate too great for his senses to discern any single state of it. It made no sound. And although he saw no evidence to support the suspicion, he strongly felt that it was a living thing, however imprecise it was, rather than a machine. Or a part of something alive. Where had that idea come from?

A voice issued from the thing, that echoed as if coming from a great distance, but also as if very close by from a tiny mechanism: "Where is Cretus?"

Tenguft raised her spear. "Cretus is not here! Begone! We are pilgrims driven by the oracle of Dossolem; I cast it, I read, I know! There is no place for you in it!"

It said, "Not so, Haydar. I give the reading. Cretus casts a shadow I can sense. For cycles he eludes me, and I do not know a way to that place. But his shadow moves in this time. I know the commotion at Cucany and the Invigilator speaks of it. They fear me much there. But Cretus is gone, casting his shadow. I seek the presence."

Meure said, "Cretus is not here. There is no such person!"

The thing seemed to regard Meure for the first time, although there was no perceptible change in its shifting mutability. It was a long moment shifting its attention, but Meure felt a great mass behind the object, a great momentum, a pressure. It said, "You I perceive, who move to Monsalvat. But the shadow you cast, it is of the cast of Cretus."

"Cretus attempted to possess me but I cast him forth! You must look elsewhere!"

"Can there be error? Not so. I review the course, and I follow the shadow of Cretus. There is a mistake but he is here; he must mingle his shadow in the I-ness—yes, it is so; he is all shadow now, a unit!" The thing moved slowly, closer to the barge. It was coming for Meure and Cretus.

Meure wanted desperately to be free of Cretus, but he felt a greater fear of this anomalous thing that he did of Cretus; what could it do to him extricating Cretus from him? Without particular thought he brought forth the knife Tenguft had given him, and threw it at the center of the object. The knife went truly and impacted point-first on the object, but it came back exactly along the same course to the hand that had thrown it, while Meure made the exact motions of throwing it, but in reverse order. He threw it again; this time it was off a bit, the blade moving as it came near the thing.

The knife was deflected off the surface, and was propelled violently into the river below the object, making a powerful splash which splashed water back up upon the object. A great gout of steam appeared and began to whirl rapidly about the object, making a hissing sound that grew in volume rapidly, reached a peak, and faded out rather suddenly, as if moving away. The whirling cloud dissipated, and there was nothing behind it. Whatever the apparition had been, it was gone.

Meure did not know if his act had been responsible; he thought that he had contributed to some instability in the thing; and thus it had withdrawn. But it would probably come again. He looked at the river surface, where the knife had entered the water. That was gone, forever; he hoped Tenguft thought it had been to good use. At the spot there was a swirling, as if something massive was moving just below the surface, and then, that, too, was gone.

It was afternoon, but the sunlight was waning under a high, filmy layer, through some illusion of the light and the reflections off the river, the light altered from its normal tangerine color to a greasy beige, a color, Meure thought, of repulsive substances. The mood was clearly one of apprehension and foreboding, and after the visit of the apparition, all fell silent. By shared impulse, each drifted off to maintain watch over the river, should it appear again.

The twilight deepened into a melancholy, depthless gray-blue tone, an oily, poisonous color, and the distant shorelines faded into first indistinguishability, then invisibility. Morgin and Tenguft distributed hard crusts and flasks of water, and as night fell, all found a shelter from the dampness that had come to the air, and slept a fitful sleep.

It was not yet light when something moved beside Meure, or a noise awoke him, and he awakened; a warm presence was beside him, one of the girls. He could not tell who it was, exactly, for she was wrapped up in a section of coarse cloth found on the barge. He thought it was probably not Tenguft; that one had a bony angularity about her that even heavy cloth would not obscure. Half asleep, he opened his eyes warily, suspiciously sniffed the damp air.

There was dense fog, not rising from the river, but pressing down upon it from above. There was no motion, either of the boat or of the fog; every surface was covered with a fine film of dew. There was also a different scent to the air, something laid over the persistent miasma of the dank water. It was weak, yet, hidden by the river's ripe odor, but it was there—smoke, and a pungent, toasty odor, that made his stomach turn over. It was not a fresh odor, but a stale one. They were nearing some kind of settled place. Meure looked for lights, but saw none; still, the darkness wasn't total. Something was illuminating the fog, although faintly.

He listened; the girl was breathing regularly, but he sensed

she was not asleep. Waiting. Far away, muffled by the fog
and distorted by the overripe airs over the greasy water, came
a suggestion of sound, a rhythmic tapping that proceeded for
a time, and then was silent. He could also hear, at slightly
less volume, the girl's breathing. The suggestion of body
warmth. The tapping began again, sounding fractionally
nearer, and continued.

Meure breathed deeply, and leaned against the warm
bundle to his left, feeling his heartbeat increase; who was it?
Where on the barge was Halander? The tapping became irregular and slow, as if deliberating each stroke, then picked
up its old pattern again, now a little faster. He moved his
arm, to enfold the warm body. The girl moved suddenly, rolling over and straddling Meure, at the same time moving the
coarse cloth around behind her so that it fell over them and
covered them. Good, he thought; that she knew the necessity
for concealment. But the folds and heavy weight of it made
motion difficult and distorted perception. He felt a hot
wetness on his neck, moving, on his collarbone, a sharp bite;
he felt cool skin where his hands moved, and the clumsy long
tails of the borrowed overshirts sliding upwards almost without effort, making him realize, curiously, that it was because
they had been designed to do just that.

She spoke no words, no endearments; neither did he.
Somehow, he thought words would shatter what was happening, deflect it into a mere entertainment. He searched with his
mouth, found an ear, a neck, a finely-boned shoulder, which
he kissed lightly, feeling hot breath and cool legs, and their
first shy contacts, delicate pressures, and their bodies slid together easily. They seemed to rest together at an odd position,
but this seemed to have no effect; the little motions they
could make seem magnified a hundredfold. There was no sensation of weight or force, just instincts which happened of
themselves, sensations, wet, light skin-kisses, things he did
without thinking of them, and a sudden, unanticipated hot relief matched in her an instant later by a timeless moment in
which she pressed her body against his and held her breath;
he listened, and he could not recall when the tapping had
stopped.

They did not move for a long time, feeling their heartbeats
and breathing falling back to their normal rates. He could
feel hers distinctly. Meure savored the sensations of the girl's
body, the slender wiriness of her, the warm spots where they
had touched the longest; cool spots they revealed by their

shiftings. A sharp, flowery tone to her scent, the way her
hands moved, one under him, the other holding the ball of
his shoulder . . . but he thought there was an odd pressure to
that hand, as she steadied herself to move, still adjusting, still
moving her body against his, as the hand pressed on his
shoulder at three points instead of two. He experimentally
flexed his own right hand, resting lightly on the girl's but-
tocks; it was difficult to set his own hand that way, because
he couldn't rotate his little finger far enough outward. A sudden suspicion nagged him, and with his other hand he
reached for the girl's hair, feeling his way around the cloth
that covered them, feeling. The hair was short, straight, and
silky-fine. Flerdistar.

Meure struggled with the cloth, finally managing to pull
away enough of it to expose their faces, to a light which had
now taken on a faint bluish tone not there before. He looked
directly into a thin, intense pale face whose lips were now
curved, slightly open, in a faint smile that held absolutely no
affection whatsoever.

11

---

*"The proof of a man's prowess lies in the invisible
influence which he has had on generations of men."*
                                        —*A. C.*

Meure hardly dared to move, or to make any sound whatsoever. Not even to look around; he listened, trying to pierce
the predawn bluish murk. All around him, but faraway and
delicately faint, so as to vanish at the slightest rustle, lay a
texture of noises, not at all like the silences and windsongs of
the wilderness. He listened for the tapping he had heard earlier; at first he could not hear it, but after a time it returned,
now much weaker, almost one with the background. The
river slapped the sides of the barge with small wavelets like
hands, irregularly. He could not escape the impression that he

was in the midst of a large settlement, isolated from it by the colossal flood of the river. And aboard the barge there was no sound whatsoever. This did not comfort him; he suspected that Clellendol could move soundlessly in the dark if he so desired. But on the ship he had denied having an interest in Flerdistar, and Meure had seen him ignore or deny her more than once since then.

Flerdistar seemed to read his worries. She leaned close, and said, in his ear, "No one has seen. I know; I can move in the nightside almost as quietly as Clellen. We have trained together for some time, and I have learned much of him."

Meure said, quietly, "And him, of you?"

"Thus, and thus. But he knows not the ways I have learned to reconstruct the past out of the noise of the present; there's a finer trick than slipping through the night and stealing. Have no apprehensions on that score. There is only one past-reader here."

"What about Cretus?"

"Cretus is one no longer, whatever he has seen in his own past. But of him I will be able to see the truth, that we have searched for so long . . . And of the here and now," and here she moved her hips suggestively, "you need not fear. Within my age cycle there is no jealousy to speak of for such events as these, and the circumstance of Clellendol and I . . ." She paused, either searching for a word, or reluctant to utter one. She straightened a little, and said, with some of the old authority he had seen her use, "He does not care what I do, or with whom. Surely you can perceive that as well."

"I do."

"And consider that Morgin is past his prime, and that Halander is a mooncalf . . ."

Meure interjected, ". . . And that I have Cretus."

"True. But not the sole reason, never fear. And also you must learn that I can rid you of Cretus, if you allow me to."

"How can you do that?"

"There are ways to manipulate states of existence like his. It is part of my training; we theorized that there was an entity here like him, so that we tried to reconstruct its characteristics from what we could learn of the planet and the trail of rumors which have come from here over the years . . . And having done so, we also developed certain practices to isolate and contain the entity."

Meure felt a spasm of humor, but his position would not permit him to laugh. He moved, shifted her weight, and chuckled. "And all that work for Cretus. . . . and you can't even get to him. Nor can he get to you."

Flerdistar leaned close to him again, and said, coldly, "We erred in that we missed the identity-persona in its exact state. We did not know Cretus; nevertheless, I can do so."

Meure shook his head. "You have erred further. Cretus is powerless—a creature of his times, no more. A man of the past. I admit to having become a victim of a singular misfortune, but he is nowhere near the elemental you seem to think he is. There is another entity here that has kept the whole planet at bay for thousands of years . . ."

"I know." She cut him off. "I saw the thing over the water. Although I don't think I saw the same thing you did. And I tell you—as a pastreader, what I am, that I can feel Cretus inside you, however well he hides, generating the kind of waves he makes right now. So much of the past vanishes into the backscatter, so soon. If you could but understand how insignificant most of your lives are! The whole of millions of existences adds up to nothing but a contributory tone in the background. But there are some you can read across time. Some of these identities can be resolved to personae known in recorded history, although their effects are different from what we imagined they were. Others . . . there is no trace of them, no name, no record, nothing, only the fact that they existed and that they changed the flow of time. At the beginning of the Ler, when we were created, there was a Human, just before that, who has deflected the entire course of Human history—a major turn in the long run. We know he existed, I have sensed his influence myself—finding him is one of our exercises. In a sense, he is more real to me than you are, now. But not once have our best been able to inrelate who he was in the real world, what his name was, where he lived, who were his descendants . . . he possessed the great mana, the power . . . and we think that he didn't even know it. We think that he didn't even care . . . He is one of the strongest in the pre-space period, although there are some further back who are very hard to read but who are as strong. But that one: he was obscure and unknown in his own time. Cretus, on the other hand, burns across my perceptions like some flaming comet! I must desensitize my perceptions in order to register him properly!"

"What is it that Cretus does that makes him so . . . visible to you?"

"It is difficult to explain; you are of necessity not

knowledgeable of the correct terminology or concepts; there is essentially not enough time to construct them in you. Nevertheless . . . what makes a life-form sentient, thinking, intelligent, as we say, is the way in which it stores the information necessary for it to act and endure. Many creatures store a program internally; thus is instinct; more advanced types reduced the instinctual preprogramming and rely on coding and evaluation and storage from the environment to the individual. At a higher level yet comes the ability to communicate pertinent segments of this data—this is the first great leap forward, and it is a major effort. Finally we reach the highest level, at which vast amounts of data are not stored in the individual, but in an abstract body of information accessible to all. We call this culture—our basic instructions, values, habits, standards of judgments, knowledge.

"The whole system here is based upon information and how it is stored and used, how one accesses it. To change behavior, it is only a matter of changing the informational base. You can see that to change the course of a people is a very great task—we find that these cultural entities follow courses of their own, according to laws pertinent to them. But in Human history we find . . . deviations along the course—sometimes abrupt changes in course. It is as if one were following the course of a star in space, and then it veers, for no reason you can see . . . some phenomenon perturbs its course. In the case of the star, the anomaly is resolved to an heretofore-invisible object; in the culture, the culture itself produces the disturbances."

Meure softly disengaged himself and said, "So far, I see; but could not the theory be unfinished? It would seem that a more finished version would also predict these . . . changes."

"We have followed that line of development; it leads nowhere. In fact, it leads to severe logical contradictions that render the entire concept meaningless. Instead, what we find is that certain individuals gain, at random intervals, the ability to change key sections of the overall assumptions, apparently by means of a process we do not understand."

"Are such people born to this? Genetics? Or is it that they learn to do it."

"The research we have done so far indicates both: the ability is inborn, but the facility to use it, consciously or unconsciously, is *learned*. Moreover, they act for no foreseeable reason. For example, as a Human culture approaches a hazard, a savior does not automatically arise, necessarily. Sometimes there is none; other times, one appears, too early. Some appear too late."

"You know early Human history . . . was Hitler one of these people?"

"Wrong. That one is an example of another phenomenon, even more complex . . . currents on the flow of assumptions lead to what we call nodes, which attract and capture exemplars. Apparently the node governs behavior to a fine degree. If we could go back in time and remove the physical person Hitler before his rise to power, we would find that another would snap into his place. That would be very dangerous, indeed, could it be done, for the next victim of the node might stand up to it better than the original. Hitler lost his great chance because he was flawed for the use of the node . . . it is a truism that political types tend to be node-fillers, rather than changers, magi, powers, whatever you should call them. Of course, there are exceptions . . ."

"Cretus, for example?"

"So much would seem to be the case."

"And what of the Lerfolk? What do you see in your history?"

". . . We work with an even larger component of culture than you, a picture of finer resolution. That would suggest that our stream would be more difficult to change, but in fact, according to this system, it means that for us, we have no random event, or happenstance; with us, it is simply Will and Idea. Anyone can alter the course whenever they please. The result is that . . ."

". . . You change constantly?"

"Wrong again! That we don't deflect the course at all. We are terrified of that act, because we cannot foresee to what it would lead. Only once in our history has one so seized the balance of the pendulum, and at that, the deflection was infinitesimal. Even so, the shock of it echoes through us yet. It is a contradiction implicit in that event that I am here to investigate, to resolve." She lay on her side with one bare thigh extended across Meure's knees. Now she moved her leg over his, slowly, softly. "I and this trip, here to Monsalvat, are the culmination of generations of work . . ."

"And you're going to dig Cretus out, whatever it takes . . . I am sorry; I have not tried to deceive you, but what you have gotten so far is just Meure Schasny, neither more nor less. What we just did was a . . . wonderful thing, nevertheless it was me, and not Cretus, who was your lover."

"I did not entangle my body with yours to tempt Cretus to come forth. At the first, that is unreasonable, for it would be the promise of joy, not the joy itself, that would tempt him, or you. I hope you will give him to me because of this in part, but I came for my own reasons, too." She breathed deeply. "Accept, ask not."

"I would know something. I am tired of groping in a fog, being used for others' purposes . . ."

"You possess a rare quality we call in my speech *wurwan*, which is best translated 'innocence.' . . . You accept what is offered you."

Here Flerdistar stopped, as if collecting her thoughts. Perhaps she would have elaborated further, but she did not. A voice from nearby on the deck of the barge interrupted her. "It might be more truthful to suggest, however impolitely, that the reason closer to reality lies in the fact that even a princess may lack suitors of the preferred numbers and types, and might be led to seek farther afield than would be the usual practice."

Meure turned and looked behind him, and found, as he expected, Clellendol, sitting on the rail, shrouded in streamers of fog. The light had brightened noticeably, but it was still not yet day; visibility close to the water, horizontally, was clearing in bits and vague open lanes, which still led nowhere. Above, however, the fog was, if anything, thicker. Its color was still bluish, but there was a hint in it of an orange dawn somewhere around the curve of the world.

Clellendol looked off across the water. All around them was a growing texture of sounds, wafted and misdirected by the odd atmospherics: sounds of animals, creakings, clatters, odd snatches of conversations, or calls. Somewhere, someone was singing an aimless tune, of which Meure could not quite make out the melody, or the words. It, too, faded. Clellendol spoke abstractly, as if to no one in particular, "You may have no cause to feel concern on my account; at the least, you have a certain gratitude of me, as this at last relieves me of a responsibility which I did not want."

Meure looked at Flerdistar, and then back at Clellendol. In the short interval, he had vanished back into the other part of the barge.

Flerdistar said, "There would seem to be no mystery here; Clellendol simply doesn't like me, nor has he ever . . . that is a mild way of putting it."

"Odd, then, that a mission of such importance would depend upon such an ill-matched crew. I know that your elders are fairly rigorous in their organizations . . ."

"We were pressed into it, by what we knew and conjectured about the surface conditions of Monsalvat, and by . . . that was what I was trying to tell you, along the way. Somehow, we were getting a dual reading from the trails that lead here: a Ler laid a heavy hand on this planet once, which is an event not repeated elsewhere. But the reading is . . . offset, somehow, as if that person weren't here. And then there was Cretus. Of course, we hadn't the name; but all the evidence told us that we'd find that out almost as soon as we landed, for here was the exceptional situation: a changer who was also a political figure."

She took a deep breath. "It helps if you know of the Tarot, here . . ."

"I have heard of it. I am not a practitioner."

"It is an ancient Human device. There are three levels of power in the types of cards—the ordinary numbers, the court cards, and the trumps. We have refined the system further, and believe that each persona corresponds to a card identity in the Tarot deck. So that ordinary people favor the ordinary numbers, and exceptional members of their number assume the identities of the court cards, which relate in part to the signs of the old earth zodiac, and essences of similar influence. Trumps are those who can change. They are rare. But what is even rarer is a single personality containing two trump identities; Cretus is such a person."

"Go on. What are the personae of Cretus?"

"According to my reading of the data, Cretus is a composite of two identities, The Magus, and The Hanged Man . . . there is much friction there, for the Magus holds power over the four elements, but the Hanged Man willingly sacrifices himself. There is in this system a pattern of flow, and in this case it is direct, but the sources and junctions add up wrongly along that path, so that inevitably, violence and accident are a by-product of that state."

Meure reflected a moment, and said, "If any Ler can change things, as you say, then all Ler are trumps, in this system of reference."

"That is so . . . but we do not attain multiple-trump identities."

Meure said, "Then let me guess, although I do not know the system well . . ."

"I will tell you, although it is a secret thing; I am trump

nine—The Hermit. Clellendol is trump fourteen—Art. But there is a thing which I read here that I had not before: besides Cretus, there is another double-trump on this planet, even just now beginning to come into influence . . . I have wondered if it was that thing that approached the barge. But it was not that one."

"What are its identities?"

"Cretus, being trump one plus trump twelve, controls all nodes directly or indirectly, save two . . . this other identity is trump zero, The Fool, and trump two, The High Priestess. That Identity controls everything Cretus does, plus the two he does not; and they both originate from the prime node . . . Where Cretus is a direct line of two segments, this other is split in two directions, with the Fool as the dominant side, although as I sense it, the High Priestess is the visible part. The dualities of this planet disturb and confuse me . . . things are moving to completion here fast, but I cannot see them."

Meure said, "Perhaps you are used to seeing these things from a distance, extracted out of the noise of Time; you may be too close to events."

"Perhaps you are right, there . . . but I cannot tell you how confusing it is. From a distance, it all seems to lead to an identity, which I can easily correlate to Cretus. But there's this other one, who is potentially stronger than Cretus, and could overpower him. But I could not see that one from distance, yet I know it is here. And it is aware of that which we do; it's an eye, seeking, open, but not yet fully aware. It has not yet focussed upon us, or anything I can see."

"Perhaps it's that creature, after all . . ."

"That creature, as you call it, has no identity whatsoever. Cretus in his own body could wish it out of existence. He fears it because he doesn't know the method."

"You do."

Flerdistar turned away, abruptly. Meure touched her shoulder. "What is it?"

"How did you know that?"

"I . . . guessed, from what you said. How could you know Cretus didn't know the way, unless you knew it yourself?"

"I know it, but I can't do it. This is a Human planet, and the governing system here is Human. I am, like all of us, a single trump and have the power, but it is only over my own society."

"Then you could tell Cretus how. . . ."

"Yes, if the Meure Schasny would allow him to do it . . ."

"I believe we have a common ground, Flerdistar; I think I could speak for Cretus without fear of contradiction, that he would speak freely of the things he knows about your people if you were to tell him how to erase his enemy. Thus things will resolve themselves in the easiest way."

Flerdistar looked at Meure fearfully. "What do *you* want, now?"

Meure shook his head, sadly. "I just want to go home and be left alone."

"So do we all, indeed. But the currents we swim in do not allow it . . . I sense it in the currents about us; the wind whispers of it, and the night-demons sing of it in their rites. I can almost see it, but it remains hidden, a potential coming onto the world. It is . . . Meure! The coming of Cretus to this time awakened it!"

"The thing over the water?"

"Something perhaps worse, but stronger for certain." She began moving under the tarpaulin, disengaging herself from Meure and their cover. She emerged into the bluish predawn fog, and brushed her overshirt down over pale legs.

She said, "Something is disturbing me, and so I will now leave you. I must go and meditate upon these circumstances." She abruptly turned away and walked quickly to the far rail, where she stared aimlessly out over the water, not looking back at Meure once.

Meure felt a fatigue creeping over him, but he knew sleep would not come. Something was stirring in him, too, but he could not identify it; Cretus? He thought not. Cretus had a certain *flavor* to his presence, and that essense also contaminated thoughts in himself influenced by Cretus. No, this wasn't Cretus, but it defied identification.

He slipped out from under the tarpaulin and set out toward the front of the barge. He felt an urge to talk to someone. Perhaps he could find someone awake. As he passed along the walkway down the side, he passed Tenguft, huddled beside a rude crate in an angular, uncomfortable position, but she was obviously asleep, and somehow he felt it wasn't her he wanted to talk to now; from one mystery to another: she would tell him horrific tales of the deeds of the Haydars, or worse, describe demons in the Haydar pantheon. No.

He reached the front. There he immediately found Clellendol, who was awake, but withdrawn and sullen. Not far away, Meure saw Halander, alone. Alone? He looked about for the two girls, Audiart and Ingraine. They were nowhere to be seen. Meure continued looking, circling the whole circumference of the barge, peering in every possible place. He found the Vfzyekhr in a tool box in a corner, its fur much the worse for wear.

Meure returned to the front of the barge, feeling a sense of unreality gathering about him. The girls were gone, without a trace or sound. Vanished. And when he came again into sight of Halander, Meure could see that Halander was staring at him with bloodshot, blank eyes. And the light around them was losing its blue color in favor of a ruddier shade. Day was coming. And Meure could see patches of water, farther away. The fog was lifting.

Meure started to speak to Halander, but something stopped him. Something in the boy Meure thought he had known had snapped, broken. Something had changed forever: this creature in front of him was no longer Dreve Halander.

It spoke in a rasping growl that made Meure's skin crawl, and also caught the attention of Morgin and Clellendol. Behind him, he sensed Tenguft come awake instantly. Meure felt pressure. Halander said, "You. You said come on this ship, and it came here. You wanted them all for yourself, when you saw them on the ship. Audiart you took, and you lured Ingraine. And when you had had your fill of them, they weren't enough, so you took the one no one wants, and let her practice her arts on you. And the girls, our own kind, you heaved overboard. Pervert! Monster!" The boy shifted position into a crouch, fingers twitching in anticipation.

Something moved in the edge of Meure's vision; Clellendol drew a knife, and offered it to Meure. Meure acted without hesitation: he waved the offer back. Halander chose that moment to spring.

Meure met the first rush and grappled Halander, saying, "Listen to me, you fool! I lured no one and threw no one overboard. I asked for none of this!"

Halander hissed between clenched teeth, "You killed them, you pervert, and you called to a demon of this planet to possess you, to teach you secrets from the past of this filthy world. Everyone has sat back and let it happen, watched it happen, and liked what they saw. These changling freaks, this mutant witchwoman from a tribe of savages who eat human flesh, this arranger of murder. But not I!"

Halander burst through Meure's arms and seized his throat, to choke him. Meure felt the same disassociation he had felt when he had noticed the girls were missing. A cool, analytical mood. There was neither fear nor panic. He was being choked. Noted. There was a cure for that. He stepped inside Halander's stance, and leaned back, hard. He began to fall; as he started falling, He let his body bend at the knees, drawing them up. Halander followed, still holding tightly to his grip, unwilling to release his victim.

Now they were falling together, and Meure's knees were up and ready; almost too late Halander saw what was coming: either release his grip, or hold it and be thrown. He released Meure and, off-balance, staggered forward over Meure clumsily. Meure landed on his back, rolling first to the side, then to a poised crouch, ready for Halander's next rush. It never came. Halander lurched to the rail, and seemed to try to lever himself up on the side of the barge to spring back, but he clumsily allowed his momentum to carry him too far up onto the low rail, and he went on over the side, hesitating only briefly at the top. A sullen splash told that he was in the water.

Meure rushed to the rail to try to help Halander back aboard, remembering all too well the fate of the bargeman. Clellendol and Morgin joined him. Tenguft did not, but said, "Nay! Do not save him! He is now under the power of the Changer! His course is written."

The three of them looked at the smooth, greasy surface, and saw Halander treading water, making no attempt to regain the barge. He was already beyond their reach, and drifting farther away. He glared back at them with the eyes of a madman. He began mouthing incoherent curses, fragments of expletives, none completed. His motions in the water became more agitated, and foam appeared at the corners of his mouth. Meure felt sick. What was happening to Halander? Suddenly Halander's face stopped its mad working, and assumed an expression of intense curiosity and wondering; he looked around himself, peering this way and that, looking at the water. Then his head slid under the water abruptly, leaving only a slight rippling behind to show where he had been. There was turbulence in the water, and then that, too, faded.

Meure felt sick with horror. A friend, a potential enemy, vanished, without a trace, or indeed a reason.

He stepped back and turned away from those at the rail. Beside the far rail, he saw Flerdistar, who was looking at him as if he were a stranger. And Tenguft had remained in her place, but now she was pointing, gesturing to the space around them, crying, "Look, an omen! The murk is the color of blood!"

Meure looked, and it was so. Sunrise was flushing the fogbanks of the river with an orange-brown tone. And the fog was lifting off the water as if it were delaminating, peeling up vertically, dissipating, fading. Day and clarity were upon them. Meure looked in astonishment and the scene that was opening up to them all: There, in all directions about the drifting barge, a city was appearing; a city of low, ramshackle buildings, narrow, dirty lanes, smoke and swirling clouds of filth. And in whatever direction they looked, it seemed to go on like that forever, to the limits of the horizons. It looked like a hallucination from the deepest nightmares of forbidden drugs. An enormous city of a depth of poverty far beyond anything Meure could have imagined in his wildest dreams.

Tenguft announced, "Behold Yastian, the city of the Lagostomes! See and understand why the Haydar seek the empty places!"

Meure felt the presence of Cretus, but it was a light touch. He was looking, through Meure's eyes. And the emotion from Cretus was even stranger than the one he felt himself: Cretus was struck dumb, appalled by the vast stinking city they saw about them. He was dismayed, and for the first time in Meure's recollection, completely at a loss for what to do. The phantom withdrew.

Meure felt Cretus withdraw, and felt safe enough, private enough, to think to himself, *What the hell good does it do one to be possessed when the possessing spirit quails from the reality he himself has precipitated us all into?* It was the most bitter thought Meure could remember having. But there was a resolve hitherto unknown contained in that, as well.

12

"Vitriol: Sulfuric Acid, H_2SO_4."

"VITRIOL: Visita Interiora Terrae, Rectificando Invenies Occultum Lapidem: 'Visit the interior parts of the Earth: by rectification thou shalt find the hidden stone.' The Lapis or alchemical stone is the True Self, which can only be found by rectifying one's attitude, by seeking inwards."

—*A. C.*

For the moment, the barge continued to drift with the main current of the river; there may have been other channels, for there was a suggestion of water all around, of distant canals and wharves. Meure could make out a mast, a mooring, a rickety derrick lashed together with bulky ropes, beyond the first line of buildings. Folk were up and about, stirring at their tasks, although there seemed to be no great urgency in their motions. He could see them moving along the shore, or an occasional rowboat stroking lethargically close to the shore. They seemed to take no great notice of the barge, although he thought they seemed to note their presence.

Meure asked Morgin about this. He now knew that Morgin was widely traveled, for a native of Monsalvat, and also that Morgin had visited Yastian often. Morgin now stood leaning over the rail, looking at the city with great attentiveness, and acknowledged Meure's question immediately, without looking directly at him.

"Do they know we're here? Indeed they do, but it's of no great moment to them. The Lagostomes . . . I must explain their ways to you, and to our Haydar friend as well, if she will be so good as to stifle her disgust for a time . . . Good, I have your attentions. Well, you see, in certain circumstances, they are nervous, excitable; I should describe them as both volatile and explosive, irrational and highly susceptible to mob-fever. In other occasions, they display the opposite virtues, exactly: they move through life with a placidity and a resignation which is astounding, and in that mood they are difficult to provoke. Then, also, they are totally self-contained, and almost immune from the influences of others."

"Are there other states? And when do they adopt them?"

"No, to the first question. Gratitude to St. Zermille for that, at the least. As for the second . . . there is no rule I could tell or teach you simply. Circumstances change, and they adopt what they think is the proper mode instinctively, according to transition rules known only to them. I am accounted as skillful as any outlander in the use of Lago mood, but I could not impersonate one successfully . . . As to why this peculiar condition exists, I would suppose it to relate to the condition of their lives, which are strict and disciplined in the extreme. They are severely overpopulated for the land they inhabit, and that land is a poor one for resource. They surmount the difficulty by an exercise of truly steely self-control. The other mode releases the tensions thus built up. Occasions exist within their social framework for the exercise of both in appropriate amounts. Here I must caution you: if a person performs what they recognize as a transition-act, that person can transform a staid and boring meeting of religious elders into a mass riot in a twinkling, which moreover will propagate. The only fortunate thing about this is that in the excitement, you may be overlooked. Also, the original cause is forgotten quickly, for the sake of action. Normally, the action will die of itself after a time, when a certain number have discharged their pent-up emotions."

Morgin ran his hand through the brushy stubble which covered his scalp, and continued, "Below the initiation of change level, they perceive the fading impulse, but do not act upon it. It, however, registers on the Lago consciousness, and they are aware of distant events in their society to an astonishing degree of accuracy, as they pick up the fading echoes of transitions. This perception includes what most people would regard as normal, ah, sexual activity, so I must caution you here not to respond to sexual invitations, and . . . er, innuendoes, so to speak, as you might be inclined to do by natural inclination; such events will precipitate consequences which will amaze you to the ends of your days."

Meure said, "You said 'aware of distant events.' . . . Telepathy?"

"No. Crowd-instinct, plus a hair-trigger sensitivity to very small cues in behavior, so most believe. By the way, I mean to ignore all sexual invitations, including those attachments which you might have with each other—such events are inflammatory."

Clellendol had been listening, and now he asked, "How is it that these overstressed people manage to reproduce and retain a viable society, then? How does one initiate a family?"

Morgin looked pained. "Like everyone else, they seem to manage their restrictions one way or another. Actually, they utilize an ingenious method, involving highly secluded establishments, where the necessary performances take place ... At any rate, it is my hope that you not see them in their release state; they are difficult enough as it is. The last time I was here, to preside over certain discussions, and to provide a Prote, it resulted in an attempt at my life. Nothing is sacred to Lagos, outside their own mores. They do not honor Embasses—only tolerate them, and in addition, they consult no oracles, which is the most unthinkable condition of all." Morgin shook his head, disbelievingly, as if no people could be so uncivilized.

Meure had a sudden thought, and followed it. "Why not consult oracles?"

"They say that in ancient times, they followed an oracle to the land Yastian, where they were trapped ..."

Meure said, "If that's true, then it's almost as if something wanted them where they are ... Who held these lands before the Lagostomes?"

Morgin mused, "Yastian, by definition, is the land of the River Yast. Peoples have come and gone. Yastian always has carried the stigma of a dumping-ground for the scraps and rag-ends of the peoples, from all four continents. They sojourned here, and they passed on, on their way to oblivion ... There is still a foreign quarter, in the neighborhood of the Great Docks, where exiles gather, but they are, all in all, few in numbers. Oh, indeed, you might well see all sorts there—Kurbs from the hinterlands of Incana, Aurismen, Meors from the Ombur and perhaps even Seagove; Maosts from Boigne, Garlinds from Intance and Far Nasp, which is just across the river-bottoms, to the east. Clones from Chengurune, for they are great seamen, and other races. I believe one even sees Haydar on occasion."

Tenguft asked, "They would not attack me here, when they could smother my spirit with their vile numbers?"

"No, most definitely. At least not while you were here.

You see, such an event would ignite the desire to settle every grudge each Lago had; the result would be carnage on a grand scale: of a fact, many Lagos would be killed, while the menace of the Haydar predation would only be diminished by one, hardly worth the price. No, you are safe—here. And since you can call Eratzenasters from the sky, I doubt if they would set brigands on us, either, although such events are probable."

Meure stood by the rail for a time, looking out upon the panorama of the city-state Yastian, the noisome city. Finally, he said, thoughtfully, "Cretus had once an impulse to come here; rather, to *return* here, since he grew up in the delta. But things have changed, so I believe, and Cretus shrinks from his future, our present. I see little we can do with such a people, save walk carefully and avoid entanglements with them. I share Tenguft's distaste for them. All the same, I do not wish to return to Incana, either, and Ombur is not a hospitable land."

Flerdistar said, softly, "There is no need for us to leave Kepture. We know that what we seek is here."

Meure looked sidelong at her, and said, almost inaudibly, "What you seek is where I am, and that is wherever I go: to Chengurune, Cantou, Glordune, or seek the sea-people on the face of the World Sea." The words came almost without having to think of them, although as he said them, they had a strange, alien taste on his tongue. Then, to Morgin, "You know your way about this place better than any of us; where should we debark?"

Morgin thought for a while, then said, "There would be no great profit in landing hereabouts . . . come, let us man these clumsy sweeps and steer as best we may for a proper channel. I will try to guide us toward the foreign quarter."

Clellendol said, "At least that is good. I would like to smell some sea air for a change."

Morgin said, "Do not hope, yet, for the sea. The Great Docks are nowhere near open water, and in Yastian is no boundary between land and sea, only a gradual change. You will only see the Blue Sea if you leave Kepture."

Clellendol added, "And also I have not forgotten the Spsom and their hoped-for rescue. No, it is not my intent to leave Kepture. I want to be where they can find us, when they come, not off somewhere else, roaming all over Monsalvat."

"Nor I," said Meure resignedly. "Now. Where are those sweeps?"

Morgin turned from the rail and sought for, and shortly
found, a locker which contained crude navigational gear: sec-
tional masts, ragged sails in much need of repair, and sweeps
for the steering of the clumsy craft. These last he distributed
among those remaining, save the Vfzyekhr, who was too
small to use one, and they began moving the barge according
to Morgin's directions.

For the remainder of the day, they worked at positioning
the barge as Morgin instructed them; although the Embasse
seemed somewhat vague at times about landmarks, as the day
wore on he grew more sure of himself. They did not make
for any particular point, so it seemed, but rather Morgin tried
to maneuver the barge so as to be moved by certain currents.
Once, he commented, "This is Upper Yastian; things in the
water are fairly constant. One can figure out where the currents are without too much difficulty. Below, however, the
matter is something of a different quality: the currents seem
to develop a mind of their own. We will not attempt that
part, and I hope to hit the edge of the foreign quarter, at the
least. Thus we will be spared the hazards of the river, as well
as the hazards of travel across Yastian among a pure Lago
population."

Flerdistar commented, straining with an oar much too
large for her fragile build, "I admit to confusion over your
attitude; you seem to dislike the tribes you serve. Is that not a
contradiction?"

Morgin answered plainly, without heat, "It is custom that
the Embasse be of mixed-blood, thereby miscastes also have
their chance to survive, where they would not otherwise. But
as we wander, we also see all the *Radah* within the limits of
our wanderings . . . Each people of this planet thinks themselves set above all others in quality, whereas the truth is that
each seems to emphasize certain traits at the expense of others. Some are simple and easy; others are rigorous and most
difficult. None have uncovered a universal truth. I myself
came to Kepture from Chengurune, and so am somewhat
more impatient than most. Yet I have my preferences. You
offworlders and Kleshmakers may think them arbitrary or ar-
cane, but they are mine nonetheless: personally, I never have
difficulties with the Haydar. They are, in my estimation, a
brave and honorable people. Yet it is sometimes hard to
strike agreements over territory with them, owing to their no-

madic ways. Here today, gone tomorrow. They are also fond of violence to excess."

He continued, "I would not wish to be an Aurisman, nor live like one, yet they are attentive to Embassies. Kurbs I find over-civilized and arbitrary in the extreme, but they have the quality of constancy—they remain the same this year as last. Garlinds are enamored of chaos. . . . I could continue, of course, but the central point is that all have some virtue. Save the Lagostomes: they change everything they touch forever. They utterly ruin land for future use, which is why they remain confined to the delta . . ."

While Morgin continued to declaim upon the negative values of the Lagostomes, Meure watched the city-state slowly drifting past, also observing the people when the barge drifted close by the shore.

As he did so, his anticipations slowly sank. Like Cretus and Morgin both, as he saw them, he could see no redeeming feature. This was not the place to be stranded, nor were these people the material from which to fashion the new millennium . . . Odd, that thought. It felt Cretusish, but he could not detect any leakage. Cretus was firmly hidden, completely withdrawn.

And the rest? Well, the Haydar certainly had a place, and as Cretus said, they had been 'high in his esteem,' and he in theirs. Otherwise . . . no. Not even the Haydar! He saw it! It came unbidden, unasked, but he saw it, clearly! He had reviewed each race he had met on Monsalvat, Lagostome, Haydar, Kurb, Rivermen, and Lagostomes again, and what he had learned of each of them, and he saw something of what Flerdistar had spoken of: Cretus *had* been a great character out of history, for he had set his influence and his logos upon the whole planet. Yes! They had attained it, once, under Cretus. Meure saw plainly that had Cretus endured and continued, he would have fused the warring factions of Monsalvat into the most dynamic human society ever fashioned. But he also saw that when this development was arrested in midstream, as it were, it had functioned upon the unique social conditions of Monsalvat like a virus, *to which the population of Monsalvat had developed a perfect immunity*, which went far to explain its changelessness, at least to a level from which it could be maneuvered into complete stasis by something else.

That was why Cretus had withdrawn: they were all immune to him now, something unforeseen by Cretus, or the entity who had manipulated events to bring Cretus back. And what was it Flerdistar had said? Another identity, a double-trump personality, coming into action . . . things moving quickly to completion?

The thought-pattern started moving, flowing, Meure could feel the answer coming; and there was a block. Something stopped him. He could not follow it.

He looked at the passing river shore, trying to redistract himself. Meure saw poverty of the most oppressive flowing past them, and more, it was a poverty without honor or chance to escape. The brownish river water washed flaccidly against a muddy shoreline, or against stained and rotting levees and pilings, while the people behind those borders moved about their affairs listlessly, or just sat and stared, or moved among one another carefully, carefully, more fearful of igniting one another than they were of the conditions about them that oppressed them. He saw it. Nothing held them here but themselves. They had built a mental-social refuge, which had become a prison. It was their values that made them distrusted and hated.

Meure looked hard at the reeking panorama of wretched huts, trash idly piled in random heaps, the careful motions, the ragged children which according to Morgin were procreated outside the home, which would go far to explain the extraordinary similarity of appearance among Lagos—they had the widest genetic base of any population on the planet.

Meure knew.

—*Cretus!*

There was silence and emptiness. No sense of presence at all. He tried again, this time more strongly.

—*Cretus! Cretus the Scribe! Come forth! You hear with my ears, so you know as I do, what can be done!*

One instant it was not there. Then it was.

—I hear. The "voice" was tired, resigned.

—*Magus and Hanged Man, she said. And what am I?*

—A most deadly combination, so I now see. I, too, know that ancient theory. My vice, you see; I looked far, I saw *Her*, and I saw beyond her as well, back to the beginning. I should have guessed it, but it's my nature, what I am, not to guess, do you see . . . that's why the transfers never took before: you can only transfer personality among likes, or upward, up the hierarchy. A double-trump personality could only shift to another double-trump. And to think that the entity projected itself across space to bring you, to house me.

Pardon me, but I must laugh to myself over that one. It has unleashed doom upon Monsalvat. You will change it more than I, and the entity will go, too. The Ler girl has seen far into it. I am, as she said, Magus and Hanged Man. The numbers are one and twelve. My symbol is their sum, thirteen: Unity.

—*And what are mine, Manipulator of Symbols and Giver of Oneself to a Unified Cause?*

—You know, nor would you ask. The Fool and The High Priestess. Zero and two. Equals two. Innocence of action and innocence of thought. Motiveless, resultless, energy. But Monsalvat lives on stasis.

—*No more.*

—You dare not ignite these pestiferous Lagos!

—*I will ignite them, you control them.*

—You have an escape, if you will but wait for it.

—*I no longer believe in escapes. I was brought here to stay here, forever. Do you think for a moment that that thing will permit any ship to approach this planet, with us on it? We have to go forward, now.*

—As soon as it learns what you have in mind, it may send you back without a ship, directly, though it would cost a lot of lives to do so . . . It may not be able to deal with us, on the other hand. I know it's not a God, or anything like that; it has limitations, although they are hard enough to find.

—*It sent a manifestation of itself, but it couldn't perceive you . . .*

—I don't believe it can perceive you, either, directly, though it can discern your effects. I mean, it knows something's there. That may be the adept's camouflage which my presence lends you: we muddy each other's image for it.

—*And for others as well.*

—Ah, well, it's just as you say, sure enough. Horny little beast, she didn't know who she was having, or why she was there in the first place . . . the light of a double star blinds those who have learned to see by the light of one.

—*However it was, she wants something of you, she came across the oceans of space to get it; I am not the source of these rumors about the Ler of long ago.*

—However polite the greeting, it always comes down to the matter at hand.

—*As you say, the matter at hand. How is it you are the source? And what it is you've seen?*

—To the first, I am not so much source, as focus. We

Klesh always knew something, do you understand . . . something from the old days that was never spoken of directly.

—*Something from Dawn?*

—Aye. Dawn. And who knows where *they* heard it. The Warriors were . . . secretive about it, so I understand. But it was before the Klesh, the secret, it was . . . but you can't keep a secret like that entirely shut up; you see, the Warriors performed a crime, and they never stopped trying to justify it among themselves, and so perhaps the very first slaves overheard something, and added it to other bits and scraps later on, and so in the slave grapevine, it was known. And if you had the power to look into a window upon all space and time, what question would you ask, Meure Schasny, what would you look for? The most important thing in the world to you, out of the basic facts of your life. And so did I. I looked through the *Skazenache*, I did; many times. I kept having to go further back, further and further. I have seen the exodus from Dawn on the great ships, the Great Warriors caged up and glaring like wild animals, the Klesh fearful; I saw the *Radahim* made out of human stock that the Warriors sifted, one by one; some had uses, some had esthetics, and some were just caprice: that was toward the end. I saw the Warriors make their first captures, I saw them find Dawn.

—*What they did, it was not on Dawn?*

—No. Before that. In a period when they were exiled and wandering, lost and trying to lose themselves, long years, visiting unknown planets, trying to find a place that suited their temperament.

—*What?*

—I am hanging on to life by one thread, and that's the one. And as soon as you know it, you'll sell me to her, you will . . . and so it was that I became the focus of what she's perceived out of the past, her past. I spread the story. We needed something to believe in, even an irony: Our Lady of Monsalvat.

—*St. Zermille, that I've heard them call on?*

—I invented St. Zermille. I, Cretus, will tell you that. If you can guess it yourself . . .

—*I would rather have you tell me; just as I would have you tell me what happened to the girls. Why was no one concerned? I wanted to ask, but everyone seemed to know except me.*

—And I wondered if you'd noticed. They were here, and then gone. It happens all the time; not as if an everyday thing, but often enough. It was so in my day, when I was a buck, and I would look no farther. Of course, ordinary foul play might be suspect, so you, say, might think. But not Morgin or Tenguft or I: we are natives. Not you or Flerdistar—you were otherwise occupied. This leaves the unfortunate boy, whom we cannot question, and Clellendol, who is so perplexed he is ashamed to ask. Him, a criminal, and a crime was performed under his nose. No—I do not wonder, because of what I remember. You would not suspect anything because you did not know what to look for. For example . . . the auburn-haired girl? Clearly, unmistakably a Medge of Urige. The other one? An Ellar of Holastri, which is an island off the southern tip of Glordune.

—*That raises more questions than foul play. It is not the most simple explanation.*

—Occam's razor, eh? Yes, I know about it. Well, that all depends upon what you know about environments, like Aceldama.

—*They were parts of it?*

—No. It can't hold a steady state in the world we perceive. No, they are, or were, or will be, real enough, real flesh and blood. It took them . . . or takes, or will take; and puts them out, under some control. Since there's a strain involved from the original, all it has to do is relax, as it were, and they return to the place from whence they came. I regard it as a most sinister symptom that this happened—it has dispensed with indirect controls.

—*That's not logical! If it could do that, then it could just reach out and pick who it wanted and transfer them here.*

—Wrong. First, it doesn't have fine control enough to work like that at a distance. Only here, and then, not all the time. Second, you would know it, and resist, which would make the transfer operation in Cucany worthless . . . No, it's as I've told you, it's control is very crude, and cruder with distance. When it came, I tried to perceive it, and saw a little—I am half in the shadow-world, anyway. It's been doing this for centuries, trying to lure the right type here. It made mistakes, you see. It helped the Klesh stay more intractable than they actually were, which frightened the others off, and it hemmed me in. . . .

—*I suppose you will say that it made up Flerdistar and Clellendol and the Spsom as well.*

—No—but it's been attracting them for a long time. I suppose you could say that it's kept an issue alive, that without

which, there would be no Flerdistar, and without her and her
family group, no expedition to Monsalvat . . .

—*But the space-stresses, the storms* . . .

—You got here in one piece, didn't you? And the ship you
came in was broken, wasn't it? I tell you, you must exercise
caution! It wants strife. What we provide for it isn't enough
. . . you see, when I was alive, what I did to Monsalvat was
instill a certain order into things; that remained, at least. It
stopped me too soon, but in actuality it was just right—for
us. To you, Monsalvat seems chaotic, but to me it's actually
quite orderly now, much better than the old days. At least I
did that! But for it, it's boring, like it was before the Klesh
came! No, I'm sure of it: it is leading you into a trap. You
must not set these Lagos off. I see repercussions that will
echo across time. It's prodding you, even though it can no
longer perceive you directly: that is a measure of its urgency.
Even at the risk of serious consequences to itself. It brought
you here to set things back as they were, and that must not
be.

—*Still the Hanged Man?*

—I am what I am. And you must be as true to yourself.
The Fool can bring any consequences, and The High Priestess possesses uncorrupted original wisdom. Already Flerdistar can feel your influence on this world, though she's a
pastreader—she's getting backscatter from the future . . .

—*I can refuse to act!*

—Fool! That's an action as well! Then you'll be led into
one situation after another, until you do the right thing . . .
you lose all initiative along that path, which means that you'll
do what it wants. And don't think that it will save you after
it has used you to ignite the change it wants—you're just a
catalyst. You have value until the moment, and afterwards,
nothing. It doesn't care if it kills you in the process or not.

—*What about you?*

—What so? It has already discovered what we know, that I
can't do anything anymore. So it is with all men out of time.
We are all creatures of our own times, and none other . . .
think of the irony on the entity: it brings me back, and I'm
useless for this world, this now-world. Then it turns out that
the vehicle is stronger than the cargo. Then it loses both of us
in the interference we create. Now it is tampering with reality
to the extent of its powers, even when there is potential there
to destroy it. You can be anything you want: you can be

Monsalvat's deliverer, or you can be an Emperor of Hell, for a short time.

—*We already have Brotherhood of Mankind, out there where I came from. It hasn't done us much good, so it seems.*

—Cain slew Abel, in the oldest story, and so much for Brotherhood. Your ancient Kleshlike forebears had the right idea. But peoples can work together, once they have the vision. So lead us! Finish the thing I tried to start! And we will go out and return to Man and teach, and all men will grow strange and wonderful—it's our diversity and our mutability that is our selfness—we've chased rainbows of ideology for millennia, but they have been wrong! All we have to be is ourselves, and work together. We all have different shapes, but we have congruent dreams; it will be that way, no matter how odd we become. Look how far Derques have gone.

—*I've heard of Derques, but not seen one.*

—What?

—*No, I remember them. I've seen them somewhere, but I can't place it . . . Yes, I remember them: they are odd Humans who walk on their hands and swing their bodies between their arms. Their legs and feet are atrophied and used as hands. They are not native to Kepture, but are sometimes brought here from . . . ah, Ch . . . Chengurune. Now it's coming . . . I can remember: men with robes and cowls atop a hill, in the wind, there's a pack of them, moving restlessly, and the men show them some scrap of cloth. They take it, show it to each other, holding it with their feet, which are hands. They are ugly brutes, grimacing and grunting, capering about; their shoulders are grown into their necks, and their faces are long; ugly, ugly. Now they begin to bound off down the trail, swinging both arms at once, and using their arses as a third foot, tossing bits of dirt in the air in their excitement. They are hunting someone! A fugitive; he escaped me and I set the Derques on him . . . That's not my memory!*

There was no answer from Cretus.

—*Gone hiding again? No matter, that: if I can remember Derques, I can remember the rest of it, what I need to know to buy free. . . .*

It was a little like trying to remember something he had forgotten, and also a little like trying to visualize numbers while working a mathematics exercise in his head. And a little unlike anything else. At first, he got results, but it was uncontrolled: a flash image, this, that. He remembered things

Cretus had thought memorable, the details we all remember without trying to do so. Meure remembered the color of afternoon sunlight on a sun-heated wall of stucco, amber-colored, a time when the city was just coming alive, and he, Cretus, anticipated nightfall and its darkness-blessed opportunities for larceny and vice. He remembered Nomads by a campfire deep in the fens, mysterious figures in dark robes who muttered among themselves in an incomprehensible jargon. He remembered a great battle, the end of it, men surrendering, others counting the fallen, while he stood in a hill overlooking a wine-dark sea, and one of the captains struggled up the hill and reported that it had gone just like he had said, and he saluted, not without a trace of awe, and returned, and he looked out over the violet sea into the unknowable Northern Ocean, and the deep blue light that flowed over it.

There was no key, it seemed. He could not control the chains of association. Things fell into his head, and fell out again, leaving disconnected echoes of themselves; the harder he reached, the more random the memories came, and the more erratic the duration of each scene became. Some were just instants—others lasted minutes, so it seemed. Still others were disconnected pictures, that made no sense at all.

Then there was a long one, a scene that must have made a deep impression on Cretus, for it lasted long and was recalled in meticulous detail. It was simple, in its own way—a view of a city through an open window, but there was something odd about it. Meure strained, a great force of will, and managed to halt the changeover of the memories. Now he had one. But there was an oddity about it, and he, Meure, didn't know what it was. Now he remembered as if it were his own, and he tried to see what was so extraordinary about this scene. Cretus remembered it as odd, alien.

The architecture of the city was unconventional, but that was not it. *That* didn't bother Cretus at all. But it bothered Meure: it was a city of slender towers, all set at different heights, all composed of ornate rococo cupolas set atop columnar bases of differing degrees of slenderness. Between some of the structures airy walkways were stretched, seemingly defying gravity, for he could not see how they were supported; there was traffic moving on the ways as well, but he could not make out any details of the figures. They were dark blots, moving, apparently walking or gliding with a motion rather like dancing, or skating, all without haste, very esthetically, as if Time had no substance. The creatures seemed manlike in general shape, but they were oddly jointed. Men? Meure couldn't tell. But Cretus wasn't bothered at all. He accepted that.

It was day, in the city. The sun was shining brightly in a clear blue sky, he could see it through the window, backlighting the scene . . . and it was a single star. That was what Cretus thought was the most alien feature of the scene he was looking at. It must have been a scene from his early use of the *Skazenache:* another world, perhaps another time, future, past, who knew. Now he had the association he wanted, a key to the vault within.

There still was no presence, but a voice seemed to whisper bodilessly in his mind, "This is the world Erspa, a planet located in the Greater Magellanic Cloud, a hundred million years in the past. It was the first time I tried to see another world inhabited by sentient beings, but neither Human nor Ler. I was astounded at the appearance of their sun. It looked incomplete, unfinished, naked. I have seen different shapes of living, reasoning flesh, but nothing so odd as that first time."

The voice faded. Now Meure had one association, and he pursued it. Now the images stayed longer, and were clearer, but they became very odd indeed. Meure saw empty planets illuminated by the violet glare of giant stars, doomed to oblivion hardly before decently cooling off. He saw things that swam, and others that flew; still others loped, strode, or hopped. Then, after many of the odd scenes had gone by him, he remembered seeing a Klesh, in the light of a single sun. Now he had the association he had been looking for, and he followed it, watching every scene closely, pressing for the conclusion.

He got the whispered rumor immediately, and it stunned him so much he almost lost the chain-thread he was following. But before he had time to digest the import of it, the source of the rumor Flerdistar had tracked across space and time, he skipped a score of similar images, that were Cretus' tracks back into the past, and then the final scene came without warning, and unfolded to Meure, as it had to Cretus. Everything was there, nothing was left out. And the oddest thing about it was that the memory was of a person telling the true story, as if to an audience. Perhaps it had been Cretus' viewpoint that had left that impression. But the memory was of someone talking directly to Cretus. And then Meure understood everything about the curious history of the Ler, and the Warriors, and the travails of the Klesh.

He was so surprised (for it was, actually, a simple story, despite its details), that he said, aloud, "So that's what it was, all the time."

Flerdistar, wrestling with a sweep much too large for her, turned and said, "What did you say?"

And with his mind still flickering and reverberating with the spillout of the memories of Cretus the Scribe, he looked at the Ler girl as if awakening from a deep sleep, and answered, "It was nothing. Nothing at all." And it was true: it was nearly nothing, considered in comparison with an uncountable number of acts, intentions, initiations, beginnings. Nearly nothing! But the consequences of that one act had left standing waves across time. Meure felt disoriented and deconceptualized. Nothing he had learned to assume about the consequentiality of acts, about the value of actions, had remained true after what he had 'remembered' from the memories of Cretus. He felt the conceptual universe shift along some unknown axis, adjusting to the new information, integrating it, although now it was the rest of what he thought he knew that shifted, rather than the new data. And then, prepared, initiated, ready, the realization following the exposure came rumbling through his mind, and he did not try to inhibit it, or deflect it. It, too, was a simple thing, almost nothing, but with consequences. It was: living creatures, being imperfect, unfinished, possess a flaw in their perceptions and reasonings which permits them to assign an entirely unrealistic set of weighted values upon their acts, so that what they think is a major decision, actually has close to zero value in the reality which includes the dimension of Time, and acts which seem unimportant, or even virtually nonexistent, assume major significance in that dimension. Oh, there was nothing wrong with the Theory of Causality—things were caused, all right—that was true beyond a shadow of a doubt. It was just that all reasoning creatures tended to assign the wrong values to the wrong acts. It was true, what the old stories had suggested, their authors half guessing even as they approached the real truth—that the death of a butterfly out of its sequence would determine the results of an election, and the form of government, and whether millions of those creatures would live or die, millions of years after the inconsequential butterfly. That the way a wind blows on a certain day would set the course of an empire spanning Time. That

an enormous commercial enterprise, spanning whole planetary systems, would vanish overnight, engulfed by its com-
petitors and its creditors, because one insignificant manager
of one operation could not manage his own mouth.

Cretus had seen that, and the examples that were its
foundation, in his view through the *Skazenache*, and for that
reason had left his work incomplete, short of its great triumph. He didn't care what his subjects might say, or historians from any planet or any period in time, before him or
after him. That was truly inconsequential; what mattered to
him were the things which seemed insignificant now, meaningless, valueless: the way a servant plied his broom; the way
a low-ranking minister looked out the window; and even
smaller things whose presence he could guess, but which he
could not see. From that data base, he had concluded that it
was time to disengage, that any of his idea at all be retained,
for if he stayed where he was, not only would the idea fail,
but its opposite would rise again in greater strength. *For Cretus to hold on to his Empire to the end, no matter what,
would have the consequence that Monsalvat would become so
filled with pride and rage and alienation that no society at all
would be possible, and that the Klesh of that planet would
disintegrate, and die off, and one by one, gutter and go out.*
But to step off the stage, voluntarily, at that moment, would
hold things somewhat as they were, and freeze them, for perhaps another to take up thousands of years in the future. *He
could only win by surrendering: that was what his study of
consequentiality told him.*

Now Meure understood Cretus very well. He understood
what Cretus had done, half-consciously at that. He understood the nature of things, because he had seen an excellent
example not to be denied. He had seen and understood the
secret of the Klesh. He had seen that Cretus had used his
knowledge to map out a rough outline of his unseen enemy,
the Entity. And now Meure felt a greater weight than Cretus
bearing down upon him; now he himself knew what Flerdistar had come light-years to find, but he did not know the
consequences of giving her that information. Or, for that
matter, of not giving it to her. But he felt the weight of his
decision multiplying, magnifying itself in resonances across
time and space: what he told her, and when, would have
results. That much was certain. And that was the least of the
decisions he had to make!

13

"There is no such thing as history. The facts, even were they available, are too numerous to grasp. A selection must be made; and this can only be one-sided, because the selector is enclosed in the same network of time and space as his subject."

—*A. C.*

The double suns of Monsalvat had sunk below the western rises leading to Ombur when Morgin announced that it appeared they would reach a section of the foreign quarter; how he knew was not apparent, as the city drifting past them had not seemingly changed, save to grow slightly more dense; in place of hovels and shacks, and seedy tumbledown sheds given over to all sorts of questionable enterprises, there were now small blocks of flats, with lethargic inhabitants leaning out of frameless windows, staring into space. There were also what seemed to be small factories, scrap yards, dumps. Peddlers roamed the streets, hawking various articles of food and commerce, with measured cadences, almost as if moving to a rhythm Meure could not either hear or imagine. It looked both dreary and impossible. The prevailing emotion was despair.

Now that the river had divided itself up into the myriad channels of the delta proper, the width of each stream was narrower, and they were drifting closer to the littered streets, and could see the inhabitants better. The Lagostomes in their city did not look any better than the ones he could remember from the incident alongside the vanished *Ffstretsha:* if anything, the ones who had come out after the ship had seemed to be better-dressed. They wore rags and tatters and castoffs whose original identity had long since been lost. Occasionally, one saw a rare individual in slightly better order, but that was seldom. A pervasive effluvia filled the air, of too many people, too long unwashed, mixed with all the substances which had been gathered by the Great River: waste, organic chemicals, other things not so readily identifiable.

Meure wondered what the others thought of it. For himself, he felt a great bottomless dismay; there was nothing in his experience or knowledge like this. Monsalvat seemed to be a way of life humanity had tried hard to forget. He said as much to Morgin, sharing one of the sweeps with the middle-aged Embasse.

Morgin ruminated long upon an answer, or perhaps whole families of answers. Finally, he replied, "I know Kepture and Chengurune by direct experience, Glordune by repute, which is adequate for my purposes, and Cantou by longing, which I do not expect to attain. Kepture is . . . rather harsher, shall we say, than Chengurune, but not quite so abrupt and unforgiving as Glordune. But these are differences of degree, not of kind. All peoples I have known seem to live lives of greater or lesser complexity, all deriving something valuable from the reality they inhabit. I have heard you off-worlders speak of things and thought that things sound more peaceable on your worlds, and it is a wonder to me, for even in Cantou, men strive and hate and slay. And in Glordune? Ah, that is beyond even some of us Aceldamans." He shook his head, as if something was beyond his ability to describe it.

And then continued, "But equally so, you have not lived as one of us." He favored Meure with a sidelong leer. "You saw the girl, who had taken up with the other boy? She seemed of the lineaments of the Ellar, and they are a most curious people, even for Glordune; all their lives, they make up, in their heads, an astonishing epic of some imaginary world, full of amazing events, monsters, magic, flashing swords, deeds of great valor and heroism. These personal legends are embroidered in fantastic detail—the more bizarre the better, and constructed according to a literary canon I could not begin to describe, it is so complicated and arbitrary. All this, you understand, in total secrecy: the epic is never committed to paper, nor is it repeated to anyone. Then, when the Ellar feels the approach of death, they summon friends and enemies alike, and all gather to hear the recitation of the Deathsong. And the Ellar do not expire until they have finished their story.

"I heard one in my life, and if I never hear another, I could vanish into eternity content. These stories are like nothing anyone has ever heard before, and they stir the blood with ancient longings; as a fact, after hearing one, the Ellar are prone to go out and perform some amazing feat.

"I heard the Deathsong from a mariner who had been the sole survivor of a shipwreck; he lay on the beach of Chengurune and recounted the real-world events first to us who had found him, broken and cast up. Those events made an epic in themselves: pirates, sea-demons, storms, Eratzenasters—astonishing! But those things were unimportant to him: he had to have an audience for the real epic he was to tell. We sent to the town for the people, that he might recite it, and not make his transition unhallowed. He was broken, tattered and bleeding, and quite beyond help, but he hung on until the people came, and then told his story.

"A man, more dead than alive, spoke from one dusk until the next, of events so ferocious it made his real-world tale seem like an ordinary trip to the market. And we sat there and listened, completely in his spell, neither eating, nor fornicating, nor moving restlessly until he had finished, which he did by including an elaborate curse upon all not of the Ellar blood. The curse I have long since forgotten; who listens to curses, when they flow like the air, everywhere? But the tale . . . ? I will never forget it, though I could not recount it if I tried; a savant in the crowd told me afterward that there were seventeen main plots in it, interwoven together in a manner impossible to unravel . . . spaceships were but the least of it. The Ellar live in small stone houses upon a rocky island, and cultivate things that grow on vines. By all accounts, they are rather poor and modest, except when attacked."

Meure said, "Then the girl Ingraine, whatever her real name was . . ."

"Most likely it was."

". . . had one of these stories in her all the time?"

"Of course."

"But it would have been unfinished . . ."

"According to the lore of the Ellar, Deathsongs of the young are reputed to be the best."

"I could almost understand that."

"There is one thing more to them . . . that they act out in their real lives, as best as they are able, a role selected from their personal epic. It is a major portion of the Ellar way to attempt to discern the outlines of that role and react properly to it. Such efforts fail, of course, but they occupy the Ellar well enough; I have not heard them complain of boredom."

"Cretus has told me that she was an Ellar, brought by an entity which oppresses Monsalvat . . . then she could have done so willingly."

"If she was a spy, I should suspect enthusiastic cooperation in such a proceeding . . . neither you nor Halander, of course, would appear in her Deathsong, in a form you would recognize, if at all."

"You didn't seem concerned about her disappearance."

Morgin shrugged, a gesture he could *see* Cretus making. "People disappear occasionally, that's a fact. Not everyone, nor even many, but some. I was not surprised . . . anyone on Monsalvat who seems unexplainable seems to vanish, sooner or later. Had it been one of you offworlders, I would have been surprised. Or the Haydar girl."

"Why Tenguft?"

"Haydar are never out of place, such is my experience."

Now Morgin turned his attention back to the sweep, as if he had spent too much time with Meure. But Meure understood what Morgin had been trying to tell him about Monsalvat: that its humanity was not muted and tamed. That if in Yastian there were pits of despair, in the hearts of the Ellar there lurked a poetry of soul-stirring complexity, an *Iliad* and an *Odyssey* waiting behind every pair of eyes . . . Cretus let an image through, and Meure recalled, that all the Ellar were small and delicate of physique, as Ingraine had been; slender, pale, self-contained, self-sufficient. A people who travelled little, who had fled from the tumults of Glordune to their rocky island, and who went no further, no matter what. Morgin had used them as a symbol for Monsalvat, and Meure could sense Cretus' agreement with that. The rest of the people . . . Meure understood that there was much in excess on Monsalvat, that the excesses and crimes had been trimmed, so to speak, from civilized humanity; but humanity had only one Homer, while on a small rocky island between the Inner Sea and the Outer Ocean, there was an entire tribe of them. What could an integrated Ellar have brought to Monsalvat, and what might they have brought to all men? And so it was with the rest. Perhaps, Morgin's opinion to the contrary, even the Lagostomes. . . .

Clellendol interrupted his thoughts. "Truly, I am in my own, here."

Flerdistar added, disrespectfully, "A blind dog in a meat-market would serve as excellent comparison."

Clellendol answered, unconcernedly, "A historian on a

planet where people remember oaths of revenge forever would not be far off the mark, either. But here, this city! I can hardly wait to land. It seethes with crime, of the most refined sorts."

Meure asked, "How can you tell that? Not that they don't look criminal to me, but then again, so do they all."

"I detect furtiveness, collusion, intrigue; it is in their motions, their gestures. I will need to get closer to discern the exactness, of course, but one can feel it in the air. There is burglary and chicanery here on a scale heretofore unknown! Cheating, conniving, and the taking of unfair advantages; all are represented in this paragon of vice!"

Meure said, "All those qualities you have enumerated; those would seem excellent reasons for avoiding such people—indeed, so feel the majority of the natives, so I hear."

Flerdistar added, advising caution, "And so much I would say as well. My ability allows me to feel the eddies stirred up by the mighty of this planet, in Time . . . but what I have felt does not make me wish to plunge into that stream and interact with such characters! To the contrary! Here we are the other way toward chaos, much too far to suit me—I only wish now to derive what I came to seek, and depart this planet. The wardens were correct an age ago: Monsalvat is no place for a civilized creature."

Meure said, "And so you are wise to wish no contact with the elementals, here; but to observe or communicate, you must contact some or many of them. How is it that you are affected here? You, Flerdistar, are losing your nerve at the last moment, and you, Clellendol, are gaining too much. Your purpose in being here at all is unraveling."

Flerdistar looked downward at the planks. "You must not speak of such things."

Clellendol muttered, "You are becoming a creature of this world too much for my liking."

"We are all merely responding to something archaic that has been preserved here and nowhere else; it was bred out of you at the start, and it's been slowly cultured out of *us*. But all legitimacies carry the seed germ of their destruction by themselves, if retained intact. That's just the problem: nowhere but here has the ancient dichotomy been retained, the paradox. And, yes, I feel it stir something in me, I didn't know I had."

Clellendol said, "Galloping across the plains with a spear

in one hand and an anatomical trophy in the other; or contributing to someone else's trophies? So much does not strike me as the goal of civilized Humans."

Meure replied, "The image is wrong from the beginning; for I am no Haydar, and they do not gallop, but ride Eratzenasters. And I know that neither here, nor on the Human worlds, has Man attained to his generic civilization. Not ever! It hasn't come yet! That is the great secret. Even now with so much Time behind us, it hasn't come yet! Spaceships and technology? They have buried it, not brought it closer."

Clellendol mocked Meure, "So here we have just another antitech."

"Because I said it was not the best answer as a whole system, does not mean I take a stand against it. You Ler are said to be folk of subtle distinctions: where in that is the subtlety?"

Clellendol asked, "Who speaks thus to us? Is it Cretus, or is it Meure Schasny, who could hardly lift his eyes from the floor not so long ago?"

Meure laughed, almost to himself. "For the moment, I am me, which is to say, Meure . . . although I am becoming less certain that such a distinction would be meaningful. And as for change . . . one is said to survive according to how one reacts to changing circumstances. Flerdistar, that is what we have lost, your people and mine: we have lost the ability to dance on the wind, instead, we built little closed cells in which change could be exempted. You say it yourself, with every statement you make: Ler culture hasn't changed for centuries, if at all. Since the originals left the Home planet, I suspect. And you said, no Ler would make any change, because they were afraid of consequences. But we inhabit a sea of consequences, and you read the waves on the surface of that sea. The faster the adaptation, the higher the creature. But building hermetically sealed closed environments does not increase adaptability."

Morgin cautioned them, "I sense dispute! This must now cease, as we are nearing our landing, and your words will doubtless unsettle some Lago, who will commit some atrocity."

Meure said, "Of course you are right. But would this not be reduced somewhat with foreigners present, as in the quarter we are in?"

Morgin said, "The foreigners are a minority, and of diverse background. There is not a single, coherent ideal to oppose and negate the Lago way; all this accomplishes is to make them more edgy, and less predictable. Soon we will land; we should find a place to run to earth until we can determine what is what. I have not the Embasse's protection, now."

"Do you know of such a place?"

"I know of several by repute. None of them are places I would choose in normal circumstances. We shall try."

Meure said, "And now I have another question, Master Morgin. How shall we get ourselves out of this city, into better lands? I know we cannot stay here forever, nor do I wish it."

Morgin scratched his scalp thoughtfully. "We have a Thief in our company, who claims to relish the aura of Crime exuded by the Lagos . . . And you have a most fearsome spirit locked up inside you; it might be worth consideration to allow these two identities to perambulate somewhat . . . There is no other way I know of to escape Yastian, save by this manner. I have no more good will left to draw on, and you cannot expect donations for a party which includes a Haydar, or Firstfolk . . . if you have not faced unpleasant choices before in your lives, you must prepare to face them now."

Meure observed, "You are casual enough about the choice you present us: Steal or Starve."

Morgin shrugged, "As an Embasse, I have spent my life telling lies of greater or lesser moment, for the good of all the people. I would act similarly to save my own neck as well. You may safely assume that all whom you meet here will already have made that decision. The ones who have elected to stand upon morality you will not meet."

Flerdistar asked, "They are not about much, then?"

Morgin again shrugged. "They are not alive, Lady. Not in Yastian."

With some currency they obtained through Morgin's sale of the barge and everything on it, at last, long after dark had fallen, they were able to secure an adjoining collection of poor rooms at the back of what would loosely qualify as an inn. They allowed Morgin to make the choices, although all of the places they had seen seemed equally bad. It seemed Morgin was using some standard other than cleanliness or style to select a place.

Indeed, he had told them after they were settled for the night, "One picks his place here with care, so it is; although you will not see so many open disputes in Yastian, when dark falls it is wise to seek shelter in an easily defended location, disregarding such niceties as comfort, or price, low or high . . . there are prowlers about in the nights, and they suffer neither resistance nor the bearing of tales, in short, they kill first, as silently as possible. I had heard of this place from certain outland bloods operating here temporarily, and believe it as good as any we could find . . . With a large, mixed party such as us, they will doubtless suspect a spectacular crime in the offing, and will leave us exceptionally alone. This place also provides street-wardens throughout the day and night—part of the tariff, so we should have a little space to breathe."

But that space was little enough. Morgin projected that the barge would translate very roughly into something less than a week*, allowing enough extra money to get them safely out of the land of the Lagostomes and into either Ombur, or Far Nasp, on the opposite side of the delta. Clellendol immediately went down to the tavern on the street floor, to orient himself for possible opportunities to practice his skill.

The rest of them settled down to rest for the night, with Tenguft volunteering to keep the night watch. Morgin found an obscure corner pallet and fell asleep instantly.

Meure was tired, but sleep would not come; he felt uneasy and agitated, for no cause he could determine. He knew he was not particularly concerned with safety, for he trusted Tenguft's hair-fine perceptions without question. Still, he knew from what he had seen of Yastian that it possessed distrusts no amount of confidence could still. Evening—sundown, had been typical of the city: the double suns had not set behind a horizon of faraway landforms or vegetation, but had slunk, bloated and gross, behind ramshackle buildings. From no point in the city proper could one see actual open land; and even the air itself seemed changed. Filled with a greasy, almost imperceptible haze, it distorted colors, washing them out, and shapes seen through it in the distance wavered and floated, appearing and disappearing.

Inland from the wharves, the physical condition of the city did not improve. Meure had seen no indication whatsoever that wealthy people formed a quarter of their own, or, for that matter, existed. Morgin had assured him that they were few, and so retiring as to be almost invisible. Meure had been somewhat surprised at that, for from the poverty he had ex-

---

* The "week" on Monsalvat was of six days.

pected to see evidence of at least part of a leisure class, but apparently in Yastian things had progressed much further than that; originally there had been a stratified class society, but that structure had eroded away long ago, by the operation of a sociological equivalent to Gresham's Law: once the low classes reach a certain majority percentage, their values swamp the entire society. A wealthy class was only possible where there was something left over for the poorest. Yastian had passed the nothing-left-over point early in its Lagostome history.

The foreigners Meure had expected to see had not materialized. He had imagined that the foreign quarter would have a raffish cosmopolitanism about it, with odd crowds, fragments of uncouth speech, restaurants catering to various ethnic identities. Instead, he caught quick glimpses of occasional persons, about which it could only be said that they were not Lagostomes. He had seen, in short, what appeared to him to be rather ordinary people, if somewhat furtive.

Meure knew his perceptions were not wrong—it was the data base he was using to interpret what he saw that was the problem. He himself didn't recognize the types he saw, and even the Cretus memories seemed uncertain. Cretus' picture of the tribes and septs of Kepture and other continents was an old memory—far back in the past. Also, Meure felt that he was seeing less than pure types, as well, for who else would wind up stranded in a vile city hated by all the rest of the planet, the city and its inhabitants. The hybrids, quadroons, octoroons and worse of the whole planet.

Cretus had remained quiet so far. Meure thought that his companion was now merely still, not so withdrawn as before, presumably observing rather than hiding out of dismay. He hoped he could keep Cretus quiet a little longer, for it would not do for him to take over in this place unless conditions were just right. Or required. He wished it, and had the curious feeling that it was so because of that, that somehow he was controlling Cretus. If it were true, he could be grateful for it, and might yet figure out a way to survive this experience.

The Vfzyekhr had settled itself down by Meure's hip, and after a long and elaborate toilet, gone to sleep, as soundly as Morgin. Now it was just Meure and Flerdistar again.

In the thick atmosphere of Yastian by night, light was refracted and muted, and so a steady glow illuminated the bare rooms, and Meure could see well enough; he suspected the diffusing effect of the city air helped Flerdistar and Clellendol rather than hindered them, as they would be able to see better in this half-light. Out in the open spaces, he had noticed that they were particularly careful about moving about after dark. He could see Flerdistar, by the window, facing it from her pallet, but not specifically looking out at anything; her face was blank and expressionless.

She abruptly rose and came over to sit beside Meure. She began speaking immediately, as if voicing something that had long been on her mind. "I had not wished to face this before . . . but it seems that someone must. Another expedition to Monsalvat has failed, and the remnants will have to decide what they are to do next; whether to wait upon a dubious rescue, or embark upon a hazardous future."

Meure said, "You cannot be said to have failed until you fail to get the information you have sought off Monsalvat."

"We have no ship, so I cannot go in person; we have no communications off-planet, so I cannot send it. Moreover, I don't have the answer to take or send, and our party of people—so well equipped and intentioned at the first, is now reduced to three, and one of those—you—is steadily growing more alien under my eyes, more frightening."

Meure laughed in a low tone, relaxed. "So you think Cretus is taking over? I can put you at rest on that account: Cretus is not me, and you would spot the difference immediately."

"Not Cretus. Something . . . worse I don't know . . . the present, the past, the future; they're all mixed up on this planet, and I'm finding it difficult to untangle the traces. I sense them, but I can't tell if they are from the past or the future. Shadowy powers moving, manipulating, in the background, point sources, which are people or people-like entities. Diffuse sources, or rather, one diffuse source, which I imagine is the entity; it is not coherent, but turbulent, sometimes many, sometimes one."

"Anything else?"

"Yes. I have feared to tell you, for the consequences."

"I don't understand."

"I . . . can't tell you how it works, but I *know* it: something I do initiates a major change here. I do something, and immediately there's a shift . . . in the world-lines. It's as if I create a character in History, but I can't see past that character into what it does; it masks the consequences, or blocks them."

Meure said, "Like an eclipse, where a smaller close body can obscure a larger distant one?"

"Like that, yes."

"How do you know *you* cause it?"

"This will be even harder to explain . . . but when I set out on this path, many years ago, I felt it weakly, even then. It became stronger with every step I took nearer here. It has now become so strong I can't see around it . . . the past and the future reverberate with echoes here, and somehow I myself am a momentary flicker in the time-line of this planet, and then unimaginable things happen; or I could deliberately thwart that by removing myself from life, because I don't know what it is that I do that sets it off. I can't see acts so well—only Powers."

"Having glimpsed Time, you now fear consequences of every act? That is no way to go forward, surely you know that, and do not need me to tell you. You could ultimately wind up a catatonic in a corner, fearing every act, and still be had by time, for that might be the thing that set it off. Nay! You must act as you would!"

"What I set off here makes Monsalvat different. All these barbarian cultures, preserved here as if in amber, they all vanish. What replaces them I don't understand at all."

"Surely not immediately, as if by Magic."

"No. It takes years, generations."

"Monsalvat could stand change; it is long overdue for it."

"You speak with more than an echo of Cretus."

"There are things Cretus desires, with which I agree, and would work with him to attain, without shame . . . what replaces the state of Monsalvat as it is now?"

"I think a civilization which is opaque to history-readers such as I . . ."

"So you fear to act, for fear of removing by improvement values of intolerance and hatred, because those acts perpetuate quaint barbarians for you to study at your leisure? Or that your profession be eliminated, while the rest of us slowly become relics of a former skill in adaptability and survival? Now you are something less than lacking in courage."

She replied, with equal heat to match his, "It is not those selfish things, but the fear for my whole people that stays me! We become enclosed, limited, curiosities . . . obscure, forgotten. We go on, but our stream is lessened. I will be remembered for this."

"In a sense, if you can read it, then you already are."

"Hmph. Time-paradoxes are idle play of every school-child!"

"And I will remind you once that a paradox exists solely because of incomplete perception, and for no other reason." And Meure stopped himself suddenly, afraid to say more, because of what it was revealing to him as the words unfolded. Because never in his life had he explored a paradox, created one, or thought about them. What he had just said, while no less true for that, was as uncharacteristic of him as it was possible to be. And it didn't feel like Cretus, either. That was the worst part.

A shadow detached itself from the other shadows in the dim room and floated silently to where they sat. The shadow approached, moved suddenly, and lapsed into an angular shape; Tenguft. She whispered, harshly, "On the stairs. Two come!"

Meure listened, but for a moment he heard nothing. He had not expected to. Then he heard scuffling, steps. Whoever was coming was neither slinking nor skulking, but coming openly, and he said as much to Tenguft. Nevertheless she drifted away from them to take up a position by the door, silent and invisible and deadly.

The steps came to the door, and there was a rattling at the latch, which opened the door, and in came Clellendol, assisting someone or something, they couldn't make out who in the light.

Clellendol said, whispering over his shoulder as he half-dragged his companion in, "Light, give us light, a little."

Tenguft secured and lit the reeking oil lamp, and by its flickering yellow light they saw whom Clellendol had brought: the Spsom Vdhitz, apparently none the better for his travels.

Vdhitz was not, apparently, fatally injured, but for the moment he was beyond speaking a Human language coherently. They made him comfortable, all the same, while he made half-hearted attempts to form Human speech formants. Flerdistar leaned close, and sputtered something in Vdhitz's ear in his own tongue. Afterwards, he returned to his own language, which Flerdistar translated in pauses as Vdhitz spoke, haltingly.

It was a tale that unfolded as a descending series of disasters and misfortunes. Things went bad, and then worse. The

Bagman and the servant had started for Medlight, as they and Morgin had agreed, assuming Morgin would catch up with them later, there, or farther on, at Utter Semerend, with the Ler elders in tow. Then Jemasmy returned, to report the Prote gone—who knew where? The disappearance of a Prote being a serious matter, they applied to Afanasy for a reading, using his Prote, upon which circumstance Jemasmy found his also departed—again, who could say where. The party departed for the west with foreboding, and Benne-the-Clone mounted and assembled upon its place on the wagon the powerful ballista with which he had such deadly expertise. Afanasy went with them, along with a buck called Tallou.

Mallam had studiously ignored these proceedings, but after they had left, he sent a small party to follow at a distance, sensing something on the wind. Mallam proved correct, if somewhat tardy. The following party returned with a tale of woe and heroic striving against great odds: Jemasmy's group had been jumped by the same Meor pack which had followed them up from the Delta, apparently circling far around the south. The Haydar had arrived at the end, too late to help, but they told a hair-raising tale, seen from a distance, of two Haydar covering Benne, while he dealt out deaths to the Meor with a speed and a resolve they had not seen before in one not of the blood of the hunt. Like lightning-bolts his darts flew among the Meor, and he did not miss, swinging the clumsy weapon to aim and loading and cocking simultaneously. But in the end, there were enough Meors, and not enough Bennes, Afanasys, Tallous . . . The relief party, led by Zermo Lafma, extracted a certain revenge upon the Meor band, but of course it was too late.

Lafma had allowed some of the Meors to escape, so as to spread the tale, and Mallam had them set out in the Hunt for these remainders, so as to leave the number to one witness. In the ensuing fray, somewhat south of the Yastian–Medlight track, Shchifr took a Meor dart and was killed. Perhaps it was the presence of aliens among them that stiffened the Meors, but they fought and stood their ground. Mallam had his revenge, but it cost him an amount he thought dear. Too dear; he had lost almost half his band, the Prote had abandoned Afanasy, and their spirit-woman had gone off into Incana on the word of the oracle. Segedine called down the Eratzenasters, to depart for the northwest, and the band they had left. They would have taken Vdhitz, for he had accounted himself competent in the fray with the Meors, despite his relative light weight and fragile build, but the Eratzenasters would have none of him, bucking and snorting and making odd blowing sounds from a concealed orifice along their undersides that made the Haydar warriors nervous and jumpy.

It was clearly an impossible situation: Rhardous N'hodos was called upon to make divination, and the portents were bad. They had a thousand kilometers to fly, perhaps farther, and to walk was clearly not advised. They were not convinced, further, that they could gain acceptance of Vdhitz by the other Haydar. Some muttered that the alien was bad fortune to them.

So Vdhitz left, and shortly afterward saw the band airborne upon the gruesome Eratzenasters . . . some stragglers circled back for a time, to keep him in sight, but in the end they turned back to the northwest and faded from sight.

Vdhitz hid by day and traveled by night across the wastes of Ombur, moving east toward the only place he knew anything about, Yastian. It was a city, and should there be a rescue attempt, it would be an obvious place to start for the rescuers. But in Ombur, night was no less hazardous than day: Korsors prowled the wastes, and other things as well, things that could be heard, but not seen. He became acquainted with fear. He saw things that were transitory and mutable, but emitted no sound, nor scent. It was puzzling. Vdhitz felt watched. But he could also feel the Vfzyekhr drawing him to that place, for the small furry creatures were not entirely slaves of the Spsom, but partners in a complex relationship for which no Human or Ler concept existed. Part of this relationship involved odd forms of telepathy, but only where certain combinations of Spsom and Vfzyekhr were assembled . . . he had wondered that the Vfzyekhr had gone to Incana with the Haydar girl, for Humans were not known to have exploitable telepathic ability, and the Ler were known to have none at all, save through their unique, and non-telepathic Multichannel Language, which acted like telepathy, but wasn't, being propagated by ordinary sound waves.

He starved and suffered; Ombur was Dry Steppe, with little open water, and little game. The Korsors and other nameless things that cohabited in the wastes haunted his wakefulness and his dreams alike. Men, stranger men than he had ever heard of, hunted him by day and by night, drawn by his alienness, his un-belonging to the land. And the adventure had passed—and what was left was a slender hope that in the mongrel diversity of the docks of Yastian he could remain alive, until a Spsom ship came again. One would come—the alternative was unthinkable.

In the marshes he left his pursuers behind, and came to the city, and made his way by night to the foreign quarter. That journey was worth ten across Ombur; the city was deadlier than the wastes. Still he continued, trading something of himself for survival, and wondering every moment when his supply of tradable Vdhitzness was going to run out, for no creature ever knows his own resources until the moment, the exact moment, of unchangeable failure. Test to destruction.

A trace element vital to the Spsom metabolism was lacking, or at best in insufficient concentration. That problem had begun immediately upon their landing, but it became more apparent in Ombur, more so in Yastian. He had finally allowed himself to be exhibited with a traveling circus that was now passing through this part of the Delta, representing a type of Klesh never before seen in this part of the world. Clellendol had picked up his rumor-trail on the street, immediately, and run the rumor to earth. How he had secured Vdhitz was not said.

Meure listened to this story and heard hopelessness in it, and mounting pressure, on him. Things were coming together fast now, and he hardly could imagine what to do . . . Then he laughed to himself. *Of course I know what to do. The only question is, do I dare do it?*

He stepped off into space, as it were, with a sense of abandon to the flow of time, and somewhere offstage, on the periphery of his imagination, or perceptions, something shuddered at the necessity of what it now had to do. Meure said, "Ask him what it is exactly that the Vfzyekhr does, Flerdistar."

She looked oddly into Meure's eyes, and the sudden authority that had come into his voice. But she turned without comment and put the question to Vdhitz, in his own sputtering speech. After a time, the answer came, marked by faltering and hesitations, first on the part of the Spsom, and then with Flerdistar's translation.

But the answer went: "They are not animals, as they seem, but rather the other extreme, the relicts of a race which was once both sapient and great, long ago, before Spsom, before man. Perhaps before everything . . . *(Not before everything,* went off a silent alarm in the back of Meure's head, but he already suspected that answer.) . . . No one knows how they came to be the way they are . . . the way the Spsom found them. They themselves had forgotten, and did not wish to remember. They had had everything, so the Spsom scientists deduced. Telepathy was only the foundation of what they had become; they were on the edge of becoming totally free of material life-support whatsoever. Then, they . . . changed themselves, and declined, voluntarily. But they retained some things, or shadows of former abilities, as they never attained complete control."

She continued, haltingly, ". . . This is difficult for me to understand . . . it seems that they can still communicate, telepathically, but not their own thoughts . . . they are not aware of what passes . . . like a part of an assembly of communications equipment, but only when the proper stimulus is present, which is, in Vdhitz's concept, at least two Spsom at each end . . . they don't know how it works, they never discovered the propagation medium, but it proved to be instantaneous, as far as they could detect, and unlimited in distance.

"They became, not so much oppressors, but guardians, preserving the Vfzyekhr carefully, for they were few. There were hints to the Spsom Vfzyekhr-students that their former power had been great indeed, and they feared greatly any reawakening of that, as oppression might cause, so they invited them along, as it were, and gave them the piping to clean to give the bored creatures something to do, something within the bounds they had set for themselves. . . . The Spsom told other races they met that the Vfzyekhr were their slaves, but the relationship's not like that at all; they maintain a spacefaring culture solely because of the Vfzyekhr, and in actual fact have no way to coerce them, should it come to that . . . and now with only one Spsom on the planet, the communications ability is gone . . . It's too late, that we know this. If we had known, we could have preserved Shchifr for a complete circuit . . . we could have brought an army in here, if needed . . . all for nothing, now."

Meure ventured, "There are two Klesh here; there are two Ler; why not them?"

"Vdhitz has said that between the 'components' there must be a certain empathy, a sense of sharing . . . at a threshold level. Use of the Vfzyekhr capability then increases this radically. We saw no sexual relationships suggested among the Spsom because . . . transmission so empathizes the participants that they become a social unit similar to a family . . . they tune to each other. There's no sex in it—it occurs several steps up the hierarchy of needs, and pre-empts that, along with several other drives . . . sexual experience among the 'components' distorts or prohibits use of the Vfzyekhr, because sex itself is multiplex and includes negative factors that upset the resonances . . . apparently this explains the Klesh end of it, and us as well . . . the use magnifies things among the group, so that Morgin's fear of Tenguft would no longer be rationalized away, but would dominate Morgin's personality. Like that. I would not attempt it with Clellendol after what I have heard . . ."

Meure nodded. "But I am twofold, unsexual, and our conflicts have been resolved, more or less . . ."

Flerdistar started violently, and said, "No!"

Vdhitz apparently understood some of what was going on, and he began making a series of gestures. Flerdistar said, "See? He says no as well. You do not know the consequences of such an act. At the least, if it worked, you would be put in direct communication with a Spsom Crew-entity. No! The potential for loss is too great. The experience could make both of you raving madmen. You and Cretus have to get along—you've been forced to it."

"What is any relationship but that it's forced to it by one circumstance or another, *whatever we say*. You institute selfishness into the core of your social order, Flerdistar, and the Klesh set up a racial selfishness in place of it, similarly. But Cretus was a mixed-blood, a remnant of a departed Klesh Rada. No . . . I think it's the only course. Now ask Vdhitz how it's done."

Vdhitz said a few words, and then turned away. Flerdistar translated, "He says it's just Will and Idea, and physical proximity. The Spsom unit holds hands with the Vfzyekhr in a circle . . . sometimes they just sit close together."

Meure looked for the creature, momentarily, and found that it had not moved from where it had settled for the night: by his hip. He looked down at the ball of off-white fur. Was it sleeping? He did not, he realized, know anything about its temperament. He felt, gently, along the body, curled up in rest; it was not so different from the basic physical shape of a Human, or a Spsom: two arms, two legs, a head, a body . . . By Meure's prodding, the Vfzyekhr stirred restlessly, and turned under Meure's touch. Then, as if realizing something, or sensing something, it turned to face Meure, although there was not much of a face to look at. Just fur, and suggestions. Deep within the thick fur that covered the face

Meure thought he caught a suggestion of something dark and shiny, like eyes, reflecting the light from deep in sockets protected by bone, flesh, fur. Something disturbing looking at him. The Vfzyekhr moved, to stand on Meure's knees, and faced him directly; he felt a disturbing sensation of being under acute observation. What was it Vdhitz had said? Will and Idea? Will and Idea.

But how did one wish the unimaginable? He dragged Cretus with him, wishing . . . what did he want? To communicate? To whom? Who was available? Some Home-planet Spsom Communications relay team? A tramp freighter across the universe? Cretus, overlooking Meure's memories, suggested, *Try Thlecsne Ischt, the warship. We could use firepower, and rations for the long furry one. His kind will . . .*

Meure concurred, wished, tried. Will and Idea.

Cretus wished, too. They made an effort, together.

Then they heard voices. No, not voices. Meure's mind substituted voices for what he was sensing. It, they, were not voices, but raw thought-stuff, but with no soft edges. It was precision, steely, ruthless, all-powerful; and once connected, grew stronger without effort on his part. Will and Idea.

Something was waking up.

He/They heard: *Threshold attained, empathy index 7A4×551AT&* (a string of symbols totally meaningless to Meure, so his mind substituted a coded number in place of the reality, which was untranslatable) *require adjust to #*+555DF$aa-3—feasible, now executing synchrony, to contact unit 9923A445-F, initiation will commence upon attainment of level A . . .*

There was no pain, no fear, no foreknowledge. Instantly, both Meure Schasny and Cretus the Scribe ceased, ended, terminated, and to themselves, vanished.

14

---

*"The idea of the Universe in the mind of a modern
mathemetician is singularly reminiscent of the ravings
of William Blake."*

—*A. C.*

Thesis, Antithesis, Synthesis. A persona was formed who
did not exist before, but yet who possessed two complete
memories of all events perceived by those two persons who
went into its formation; to it, there was no break in continu-
ity, no sense of change, abrupt or otherwise, but the natural
culmination of events. In the same sense that it was quite neither Cretus nor Meure, it was also both of them, combined.
At the first, it was not particularly conscious of a named-
identity for itself, but it was totally aware that it was a
unique being, possibly with unique powers. And where before
the two had suspected a great Game being played out far
above them, on the borders of perception, this new persona
suddenly perceived the whole Game, the players, and dealt itself into a hand, all in the single first instant of its existence.
It became aware. And simultaneously became something to
become aware *of*.

There was no time to waste; these first moments required
realization, but more, action and initiatives based on that realization. These things had to come before naming.

He saw a room in a pestilential city on the planet Monsalvat, dimly, as a faded hologram. There were concerned
people there, people who were entangled with him intricately,
who were afraid that they had set something in motion to
cause harm. Yes, harm. There would be change, and it would
be seen by some as negative, a change in state.

He was, in the primal perception, aware of the vast network across the universe maintained by the Spsom-Vfzyekhr
gestalt: a four-dimensional continuum of glowing nodes

spread across the darkness. But there was, of course, much more. Entities, beings, odd composite sapient forms . . . some contact was possible, he could see, and between other sets, antipathies. Space was distorted from what he thought it would seem like in this projection. Things did not fit, here, their distances in light-years. His target contact, for example, aboard the Spsom Warship *Thlecsne Ishcht*, in flight between the stars, which showed as dull pockmarks, had a shimmering quality, as if its place were somehow indistinct. There, but not now, really. Other places-points showed a specificity, a hard glitter. Far away, so it seemed, there was an odd pattern, unique. He could focus on it, examine it in detail, just by wishing it so: it was uncontestably alien. Alien to him, and alien to the norms of the network he had tapped into. Something was wrong (?), malfunctioning (?), contrary-to-expected-progressions (?). Moreover, it was aware of him, and moving sluggishly with a sideways-sliding motion which he could not translate into the physical world of human bodies. It moved, in this perception, but he sensed or guessed that it did not move at all, physically. But however it occurred, he was aware that it intended to threaten him.

He had *Thlecsne Ishcht*. To the transponder-entity aboard, he sent, *Bring the ship to Monsalvat and do what is necessary to rescue the survivors of Ffstretsha. And subdue a hostile entity which has been preying on the people of this planet.*

Thlecsne answered, *We come in strength, and are prepared for violence. As before when we tried to approach, we are experiencing flight difficulty. This time we are stressed for it.*

He: *I will attempt to weaken that influence. It is caused. You are part of this network; it is the alien presence at coordinates 23@¢# = +667, which is either on this world or immediately adjacent to it.*

The presence aboard *Thlecsne Ishcht* sent back: *You are seeing at magnitude G. We cannot perceive at that level. All we see are the other Spsom points, indistinct patchy areas, and you. You are not Spsom. What are you, and how did you tap into the Vfzyekhr network?*

He said: *I/We are/were Human. I now, under this method of data transmission, appear to have gained a single nature, but I do not know what that nature is, nor if it is lasting. I am now going to a higher level, to contact an alien entity threatening our mutual effort. You must take all Spsom terminals off this network for a time, as there is perceptual danger to your system. Have you Vfzyekhr use pattern 2#3,*

*shadowing and filtration applicable. If I do not recontact you,
enter this planetary system and destroy the entity. The
Vfzyekhr can locate it.*

Now he broke contact with the *Thlecsne Ishcht,* and tuned
his Vfzyekhr contact up into a higher band, higher, higher
still. It protested, like long-disused machinery, being forced
into configurations close to the limits of its own parameters.
He sensed, far back in the Vfzyekhr collective consciousness,
a protest. But it responded. They responded. The Spsom
gestalt vanished, and was replaced by other receptions he did
not understand, or could not resolve enough to comprehend.
The universe was full of aware, communicating entities. And
the Vfzyekhr were his only key to it.

His target entity now became the center of attention, and
as he progressed up the abstraction ladder, he found he could
begin to understand it. But perception and understanding, in
this conceptual universe, involved contact, and interaction.
There was great danger now of losing . . . what? Losing his
nerve, and being subsumed into the entity now facing him
with calculating malevolence.

Far back in one of the two life-lines he possessed, there
had been a contact with a projection of this entity; that had
held a superstitious quality, a dreamlike unreality, a tentative
instability. Contact now differed greatly; the entity existed, if
the word could be used at all, on a conceptual, communicative plane. It had roots in physical reality, but they were ten-
uous, deceptive, almost invisible, after the fashion of fungi.
And inasmuch as the visible part of the fungus was only a
fruiting body thrown out by the real structure of subsurface
filaments, so then the physical manifestations of the entity on
Monsalvat were not the thing itself, but contact-bodies, temporary sensors, communicative devices grown by an advanced
colony organism to interact with creatures it deemed primitive and inferior.

That much he could now directly perceive; what he could
not translate was where it was in what little physical body it
had left.

Of course not, it broadcast at him. And in that directed
communication he realized again the danger he was in, for if
Monsalvat was within the influence of the entity, here, within
a communications concept, he was existing within its proper
domain. He felt single and whole, but at the same time the
echoes of Cretus and Meure, the old individuals, still rang,
and of course there was the Vfzyekhr, whose amplification

powers made this contact possible. They together were a
shaky threefold organism, held together by a Vfzyekhr per-
forming near its limits, while the entity was . . . he strained
to focus down, to *see* . . . thousands, no, millions of units,
no, more than that, linked, interconnected. And those parts
were not individual wills, with their own conceptual lives to
match against one another, but fitted parts, each smoothly
matched into the enormous construct of the whole.

At last, it sent, *I can speak directly with one I labored over
so long to bring back from the house of the dead.*

The Meure portion contributed, *And also one whom you
brought from afar to serve as a new container for the Cretus
you brought back. But neither of us has gratitude for what
you have done to us, or to the people on Monsalvat.*

It replied, *What of that? Even artificial and temporary as
you are now, you have attained an exalted state; in that, you
will come to comprehend that when you become as I am, you
live through the actions of others. Animals are unsatisfactory,
because they have no idea of Time. Likewise, organisms similar to me have the power to be aware of me, resist me, perhaps attack me. No, the men of Monsalvat, full of glorious
passions, hates, revenges, detestations they were both convenient, and at the perfect state of intelligence. Loneliness
and boredom increase with awareness. Physical limitations
hamper the climb into this state, so they become reduced, so
one can reach farther and farther . . . no, We'll not give up
on Monsalvat. All those knives, and so handy to use. No, that
won't change. And since you couldn't come to me physically
even if you knew where my basic units were, there's little
enough you can do to change things.*

He sent, *What about me/us, then?*

*The transfer didn't work, and the two of you were stuck in
Limbo. Now, to contact me, you have further integrated with
another being; this process is not reversible. As for the entity
you have become, I have no use for that; you are aware of
me. You will have to adjust to your new state . . .*

What are you?

*A community, a colony, a gestalt . . . long ago, very long
ago, I was made up of units who had individual wills . . .*

Humanoid?

*Not particularly. Although my units had bones, organs,
limbs and all requisite appurtenances. Life follows basic patterns; only the details vary. But the universe has physical limits. The only way around these limits is to stop trying to beat*

*them in their own domains. To see, to realize, is all. It is not
necessary to actually go to a planet to perceive it . . . and
once we understood what we had to do, we started it in
process. We took control of our planetary ecology, to tune it
perfectly to us, and we undertook to guide our ongoing evo-
lution into forms that would maximize the intercommunication and reduce the friction of individual wills. This goal was
attained before your planet, the home of Man, had life
forms.*

He asked, *You say we and I. Which is it, properly?*

*How interesting! No contact body ever asked before. It is
both, of course. I do not exist in the physical universe; we are
an assembly of creatures which can be seen, felt, weighed,
measured, and anything else one would care to perform upon
them. In fact, it is possible for entities such as myself to . . .
transfer to another base population, where conditions permit.
This is the only sort of long-range mobility I have. We, as we
are now, have none, except local movement on the planetary
surface.*

You have not done so . . .

*No. But it would cause problems. The base population
would lose me; this is a form of budding, where the bud is
the continuation form and the stock is the infant. The base
population would retain the physical base of an entity like
myself, and would grow another. Such a creature would not
share my learned cautions.*

*And you want no competition. Obvious and understand-
able.*

You, it said, *are a creature of movement, which means you
are immobile with respect to Time. Conditions are reversed
with forms like myself. My intent, as you would translate it,
for Monsalvat, is to transfer my selfness there once the base
population has reached a certain level . . . they would be
space-mobile, under my guidance, and then I will be mobile
in both realms.*

(Aha, he thought. It's not on Monsalvat, because it said,
'transfer my selfness there.') And he said, *Spread and multi-
ply?*

No, came the answer. *Once transfer was done, we'd elimi-
nate the old base population, and travel together . . . density
to a certain level is a requisite of this kind of existence.*

(Aha again, he thought, shielding the idea. It has to have a
large population, probably confined to a single planet. Other-

wise it would have already invested Monsalvat. At least with a beachhead.) *Why move?*

The long view of time. Stellar systems eventually lose their habitability to any life-form. I shall be forced to leave this system in order to continue . . . I had quite given up hope until the Klesh came.

(Now he thought deeply. Why did it have to have a Human-Klesh vector?) *You control an entire ecology, an evolutionary sequence; re-evolve your original host population.*

All life forms, however powerful, have limits. That is one of mine. I can make forms coalesce, and specialize them, but I cannot renew to the old form, or evolve forward. You would call my host form so highly evolved as to be degenerate, a side-branch. I cannot make marble, only make statues of what marble I find. My Hosts, we are individually small creatures, grass and seed eaters, who are the distant descendants of what I might call 'Stem Epiprimates,' somewhat better integrated than the creators of the Klesh.

But you'll be coming down, to transfer here, to the Klesh . . .

True. But I won't let them go so far, either. They'll retain an ability to make technology, so we can move . . .

He said, *That's like the transfer you did with Cretus-me.*

Cretus was an experiment, that's true. I discovered him in Time, and laboriously tracked him down in space. And you, too, after others failed.

Have you thought that the same thing could happen again? That the Klesh-Monsalvat host might possess some concealed, untested strength? That it could turn on you and exploit you, with your knowledge of Time, your ability to move in its medium? I cannot see any beneficial effects of such an entity. It would impose change upon the universe in the same sense that I am going to impose change upon the Klesh . . .

What kind of change? There was a note of alarm in its contact, now.

To start with, I'll make them immune to you. Human legend is filled with the fear of demons. You'll do, well enough, although you're not exactly what I have always had in mind . . .

And for the first time, the eagerness for contact which had characterized the entity was gone. He probed, he listened, he searched. But for a time, there was silence, darkness.

He ventured, *I see . . . things like you were what we called demons. But those attempts never worked, or. . . .*

It responded, *No or. They never worked. I know. I have seen. Transfer has never been done successfully. It's always been tried from too great a physical distance . . . they were running out of time on their origin-worlds and had no nearby possible host.*

One race turned back from what you are, a third part of him contributed.

More than one, it answered. *Those I have seen as well. One of them is now the switching part of your collective entity. But they had my experience to draw on, and they saw before their forms were past the evolutionary point of no return. We had contact,* ago *as you would say it,* there *as I would say it.*

What was another?

Those whose ship brought you here.

Ths Spsom?

Indeed the Spsom. They feared amalgamation more than the Vfzyekhr, and so in time they forgot it . . . until they met the Vfzyekhr, and enough remained to key the association. By forming the communications network they do together, they mutually protect one another from going further again along that path of development.

What of Humans; of Ler; of Klesh?

The situation will seem paradoxical to you, so I will explain: all sentient populations develop toward unity. That process is an analogue of the way individual cells become multicellular creatures. So much is the general rule. There are exceptions. The Ler do not develop this way, because all their combinational drive has been translated into an equal society of perfect individuals within the limitations and attributes they have. The original DNA manipulators did not know this, and did it unaware. In turn, the Ler have influenced mainstream humanity by social feedback into a similar, but artificial, state. On the other hand, the Klesh, isolated from both by accident, and later deliberately so by me, are far into large-scale integration.

—But the races detest one another!

Never mind what they say. It's what they do. They react to one another in well-defined patterns. These patterns are the precursors to the large-scale integrations necessary to attain an awareness like mine.

Or, become the host for one.

Just so. To one other point, the Klesh are reachable, and many of them exhibit threshold sensitivity. Cretus, for exam-

ple, although it was his forebears who first caught my attention. I was almost too late.

Cretus fought you . . .

Some of that. He had his own ideas, as well . . . at the least, he set up conditions where I could implant remote sensors on Monsalvat, and prevent things from falling back further. It costs me a great deal to maintain those sensors there; they are like myself, not completely material, although they seem so at your perceptual level.

A Cretus part of him said, *Protes.*

Correct. The word itself is from an ancient Human word, protean. That is why they could never discover how Protes communicated. They don't; they are parts of me. There is no waveform between them, but a continuous state of being.

Protes were before Cretus.

And I am a creature of Time. I planted them before Cretus, so they would be there to use after him. It was both the most I could do, and the only thing I could do approaching direct intervention.

That's the best you can do in the material universe.

It's the only stable form I can attain in the material universe.

He would have asked it more, thinking to let it ramble and reveal itself; he knew it was nearby, near enough to come within range of the weapons of *Thlecsne Ishct*, whatever they were. But suddenly the perceptual universe he was sharing with the entity vanished. It did not fade out, or withdraw; it was shut off, switched off. And he had lost contact with his dim outside reference as well! He was walled up in Limbo, a nowhere, a nowhen.

A tiny voice spoke to him then, exquisitely faint, yet also of a piercing clarity so precise that he could have heard it over the hum and drill of the noises of the city, and of the entity's universe. Then everything had been shut off for another reason. The voice told him.

"We," it said, "are now drawing upon the resource of the entire Vfzyekhr population to shield you from that. It is shrewd rather than intelligent, but it is beginning to suspect you are trying to find out where it is. We know it from long ago, when we found it, or it us, and knowing it, turned back from becoming an entity like it. It is currently located on the second planet of this system, or based there. But this is a creature of Time, and so it anticipates you by commencing transfer now. During this duration-sequence, it will be es-

tablishing control of its new base population, and other functions will lapse. Already the warship finds clear space, and
approaches under full power. The entity, as you call it, is settling upon the population of the city we are in, before you
can set them off. But it must be stopped, for the aberrant Human population of this planet will increase its power by a
factor of two to the tenth. Then it can move out of this system where it has been pent."

He thought, "I thought it grew here."

"It is native to this system. But long ago it tried to move
out. It was the firstborn within this cycle of creation, and the
strongest. All other entities like it united to block it. There
was a great battle of wills . . . the perceptual universe you
have shared with it was ablaze with fire and thunder. Some of
the material universe responded as an echo to those conflicts.
We . . ."

"Go on."

"We did a shameful thing, a crime. We, those who were,
blotted all stars around Monsalvat—Bitirme out. We saw, for
we were creatures of Time, too, that some nearby systems
would develop life-forms which would serve as expanding
bridges for it, and it would grow forever. We arranged eddies
in the galactic structure to keep this region free of forming
stars, resonance nodes. The starforming shockwave spiral un-
forms itself in this region."

He sensed a guilt that could not be plumbed. He said,
"You destroyed much to pen this creature up here."

"Half of what we were then was lost forever. They went
willingly, knowing what future would come otherwise. Time
demands great life-energy to move it. That is why we disasso-
ciated and became what you see Now in Time: furry little
animals who use the artifacts of others. We were secondborn
after it, and we chose unknowledge rather than become like
it. That is the way of it. And we have come back from the
dead to make sure that we do not have to do this thing again,
for it is stronger now than it was then."

"You came to tell me what to do."

"You are an accident, a one-time thing, powered by the
Vfzyekhr collective will. When that has been withdrawn, you
will have only what is native to the Cretus-Meure combined
persona. Innocence and shrewd knowledge of men. You must
accept the responsibility for guiding this people to sanity. Perceive, and follow the vision. And you must tell this creature
what we will do to stop it, forever."

"What can you do?"

"The two stars that are the primary of this system are old and contain considerable helium by mass. Enough for a singularity to be created with the proper nudging, should they be merged; these events are not set in motion by wishing, but by realignments of basic forces in the universe. There are considerable side effects. All will suffer, even beings you do not know, whom Humans will never know. We have already now in your reference started the process. But you have the craftiness of Cretus and the dreams of Meure, and you have the ordinary weapons of *Thlecsne Ishcht* to use upon it, if need be. When you contact the entity again, you will have only a clear channel to it, and one other to *Thlecsne*. They will be mutually shielded from each other—secure. Even I-we will not be in contact. All I-we will see is what happens. If you fail, then we act." And as the voice spoke, he could sense a growing power behind it, a swelling of multitudes, as suppressed abilities lain dormant and forgotten for centuries, millennia, geological ages, began to awaken once more. The voice faded, faded, grew distant, and suddenly winked out.

Then the perception of the entity returned, and with it, superimposed on it, a sense of the warship. But only he could see them both. They were mutually invisible to each other.

He thought, it's on the second planet—Catharge, but it's already started transfer here, to Monsalvat. But to what population? It could be anywhere on the four continents, anywhere. But as he desperately tried to recall all the lore of Monsalvat he knew, from Cretus and Meure alike, one fact seemed to stand out. That nowhere on the planet was there enough of any one group to dominate even a single continent. That the Embasses, though widespread, were mixed bloods and few in numbers. There was nowhere for it to go . . . except here, to Yastian, to the teeming numbers of the Lagostomes, individually weak, but properly organized and motivated, unbeatable. And only they seemed to have the remarkable empathy for crowd-emotion that they did. He thought, *The nerve of the damned thing! It has to be here, right here, and under our very noses. But what will we give to stop it?* The Meure part of him was unsure, but Cretus had no such ambiguities.

He put the connection aside for a moment. Returning to the world was like dreaming. He saw through a distorting glass. He arose, carrying the Vfzyekhr, and made his way to the window, ignoring the others, who stared blankly at him.

He looked out into the night of the city. And though each point of light in that city was weak, by itself, together they made enough light to block the light of the stars. He found himself yearning for the clean uplands of Incana, the rolling swales of Ombur, wind in his face. Here at last was the real giver of visions, the oracle, who had been tinkering with Monsalvat for uncounted years. And coming here itself, at last.

The city of the Lagostomes had not quieted with nightfall, but it was quiet now, for no reason. It was as if everyone had stopped in those moments, paused, and anticipated . . . something. They were waiting for something. He could almost feel it, himself; a hidden emotion, a desire to let go, to flow with the collective will, to do what *they* wanted and said. Something heavy and lethargic was settling upon this land from out of the sky they could not see, something whispering to them sub-thought, *I come to release you, I come giving freedom at last, license to shout and slay, to eat and breed as one will. I will make you the great people, who will go to the stars, who will live forever* . . . and on and on it went, promising, promising, the heart-balm to a losing, desperate people. It was hardly perceptible, but the more deadly for that. Words would have made even the Lagos suspicious. This was something more than propaganda. Of course they answered, unknowing, *Yes, Master, we are thy people. Verily we come unto you.* It was happening even as he watched.

The air grew heavy with expectancy. He turned, to motion to Tenguft, now fighting the influence of the thing himself. She responded as if in slow motion. Dreamily she arose, and drifted to the window, not fast enough. She should have moved instantly. The window overlooked a small court, where people were gathering, looking guiltily at one another, and up at the sky, waiting. Here he would strike, whatever the cost. He would throw the spear of Tenguft at one of those in the center of the yard, and let precipitate what would among the volatile Lagostomes.

He felt a sharp jolt along his nervous system, like a shock, followed by a pain and an emotion he could not name. And the entity spoke, blotting out his perception of the present: *The ship came with fire, and has done great damage. My units panic with the fright of it, and this has made a difficulty. It is no matter. I am now budded. Let them gnaw at the bare bones of Catharge. In moments a great fist will rise into the sky and erase that metal thing. These people have*

*great strength, and with them I shall bend space. I could not
know until I felt them with the touch. We will not need to
train these to build spaceships. Wielded by me, they already
have the native power to reach out and have the ships
brought to us, there is no limit to what shall be mine.*

He tried to contact the *Thlecsne Ishcht*, felt the channel
open momentarily, then close again. It was as if there had
been no need to *say* it.

There was a glow on the horizon, in the East, where one
had not been before. A growing flame, rising out of the East.
Something was approaching at furious speed. And in the city
below, flickers of alien emotions began racing back and forth
among the Lagostomes. The glow became a fireball, white-
hot, burning, flaring across the sky like some meteor of incredible size. It came faster than the sound could catch its
passage, growing, and the people cringed, and it stopped,
dead, directly overhead, looming over the waiting city like
the angel of Death. The fire of its passage flared, bloomed,
and went out, leaving behind in its place the awful shape of
the *Thlecsne Ishcht*, its tubes now glowing from the intense
heat of its passage. The light from it cast shadows in the
streets below. It seemed to be at low altitude, hovering by
some unknown means. Lights, burning actinic points of light
began to flicker and sparkle along the network of the tubes
surrounding the slipper form of it. And the sound of its passage arrived and smote the streets and alleys and canals of
Yastian. Below, people were thrown off their feet by the
blow. Glass fell out of windows, and fragile sheds collapsed
in turning heaps of dust.

He sent at it, *It is not to be here, now. The ship is here
and ready to do worse than it did on Catharge, whatever it
did. We will not allow you the Lagostomes, nor Monsalvat,
nor the Klesh. As we love and revere all life, we would not
hound you to oblivion but we will prevent your parasitizing
us. If we are to have an overmind, we will grow our own.*
Then he waited for an answer.

For a time, there was none, although he could sense dimly
something happening out of sight, offstage. Dire events, no
doubt. There was a subtle perception of great energy transfers, roiling currents, struggle and strife. He hoped the entity
was having difficulty with the Lagostomes. Yet he could not
tell what exactly was going on; everything was muffled, indistinct, distant, and growing fainter.

Then everything cleared once more, and the entity spoke.

Betrayed! Trapped! And its signal was fading even as it sent that.

???

Cretus! I prodded Cretus until he became aware of me in his limited way, and he disengaged himself. But he promoted a stability which I took for preparation, when the right catalyst came again. Now I know what he did. He created a dormant, primitive multicellular consciousness, which I awakened in trying to transfer to it. I transferred here and let the other go, and the warship disorganized my old base population. They run wild now. And here now, the organism resists me, while the fear of the ship disrupts it. And another entity moves in Time to block that avenue. Fading. . . .

The transmission had become very weak at the end, halting, strangled, he would have said, had it been words. Choking on its own plots. And he sensed the Vfzyekhr shifting down from its higher levels, letting itself go, fading, too. It sent, *It is gone. We should have dealt thus with it the first time, but we thought what we did was enough.*

It, the Vfzyekhr mass consciousness, had briefly willed itself into existence, but now it was letting itself fall back into the oblivion from whence it had come. It had awakened with his prodding. . . . The Spsom had not responded at all.

He sent, *No! Not yet! I know neither what to do nor where to begin.*

Even as he sent, it was dissolving, disassociating back into its component parts, rustic, simple, rare folk who occasionally went to space with a race with whom they had formed a telepathic symbiosis *to prevent its natural formation and continuation.*

A last answer floated out of it: *You are Cretus who has been tamed by a persona-substance not available on Monsalvat: lead yourself. You know what to do. The spark still lives on Monsalvat, your people's ability to bypass the trap of the overmind. Strive . . .* and he could no longer receive it.

And with the quiet, came the end of the Vfzyekhr contact: it winked out an instant later, with a finality that told him he would never have it again. They, it—whatever it or they was or were—had locked him out, forever. Now he was left as the contact had made him, an unpredicted fusion of two disparate personalities. There was no model for this, no legends, no tales; he would have to feel his way along the road to come, blindly, sensing, reacting, building his own working diagram of the universe, and of the men who must know of what they so closely missed.

He was in a shabby room, still dimly lit from the glow of lights from outside. And outside, there was the sound of confusion and tumult, of despair and panic. He saw the others looking at him, and in their eyes he read something of his own strangeness to them. He thought that it would do to be careful, and deliberate, for of his words and actions he felt the stirrings of a newer conceptual universe being created; events would radiate from this room, this moment in Time, in ever-expanding circles, sometimes assuming strange forms. He would need to choose his moments carefully.

He looked down at the Vfzyekhr, that had set up the contact that had fused him, touched it absent-mindedly, as if for reassurance. The creature was cool and did not move. It was dead. Whether this was so from its overextending itself, or voluntary, he knew this to be the underlining of the last intent of the Vfzyekhr collective: that he would never again have access to the power he had gained to energize a system that had once turned itself off. He stroked the still form lovingly, feeling a great sadness. And thought, *They have paid their admission and initiation fees many times over, and still do not demand, nor compel. Now mine begin.*

Clellendol leaned closely, and said, "Morgin and I have been watching the people from the window; they are agitated enough, but not reacting at all like the Lagostomes of old, so Morgin says. They seem to have lost their sensitivity to one another. There is a general tendency to abandon this particular neighborhood, and after a bit, it should be safe to venture outside."

"Where is the ship, now?"

"Not far. The Lagos ran from it, and it is clearing an area for landing, now, not far away. They seem to know someone is nearby they should look for . . ."

"Let them finish their work. Afterwards, we will go to them."

"And we can leave, at last."

"You and Flerdistar can leave . . . there is much I have to do here that has been unfinished."

Flerdistar now settled beside him, wonderingly, and said, "Something happened to you, to us . . ."

He answered, suddenly tired beyond his ability to ignore, "To all of us; the waves of the past must pass through a place, here, that will mute their clamor . . ."

"Who are you? Cretus, or is it Meure Schasny?"

"It is neither, and it is both."

"How shall we call you?"

"As you will; or according to what I do."

"What have you come to do?"

"To help find the way we have lost, I think . . . I will bring a message to those who will listen; some will."

"I know not what to call one such."

"There is no need. Say 'Cretus,' that something be continued from that which could have been, but never forget that the other is an equal part, too."

"You will remain on Monsalvat?"

"Just so. It will begin here better than anywhere else . . . they can come here now. The stormy spaces about Monsalvat are smooth, and the terrible oracles are gone. It will truly become what its name means—'Mountain of Salvation,' rather than what we have called it—'Place to Bury Strangers.' "

Flerdistar snorted skeptically. "Salvation! And from what? Salvation is to save."

"From our worst enemy—you and I alike: ourselves. I will lead my people, here, and we will show the way . . . to be truly Human."

"What powers have you gained, that you could do this thing?"

"In terms of what you mean of power, I have not gained, but lost. Yet by that, I have become unique."

"As you are in your duality."

"Former. I am one, now."

"And so Monsalvat will again know the tread of the armies of Cretus . . ."

"Not that, again. This must be grown, not forced; cultivated with the loving care of the husbandman."

"I do not miss that inference; the husbandman culls, prunes, burns clippings, eradicates pests."

"Indeed that is; and so will I . . . but we will learn to do those things for ourselves. We need no master; we know the way already, but we fear it because it is simple, direct."

She said, cynically, "And the millennium will come, no doubt."

"Neither you nor I will see it; but Historian, you will see change of this day, far from now."

She said, "I have sensed it beforetimes, that it was coming; is it truly to have been this simple?"

He thought then back to his contact with the Entity, with

the Vfzyekhr collective overmind, with hints and visions of
the other lights that were, farther away than they had found
yet, but they too would come in the future and the men that
were to be must be ready for *that* . . . He said, finally,
"Simple? Yes, simple, like the matter of timing in music, that
meets the median between clashing noise and pedantic
formalism, that perfect timing, and the funniest part of it all
is that much of the time it's mostly by accident."

"An accident?"

"It's so simple, and so hard to say; the words aren't right.
Now we will make them so. It is accidental, random; also it
is implicit-consequence of everything that has happened here
since the beginning of Time. This system, with its dual stars,
teaches us much about the nature of things: everything seems
to possess dual aspect at the first level of penetration. That
the universe appears accidental and predestined at the same
time is not so much a measure of the qualities of the universe, but of the limitation of the perceptive system applied
to it."

"You are rather more oracular than the Entity, now. They
have not lost their oracle here, only traded."

"They never had one, nor have they one now. Do you not
understand what you saw here, what you perceive of this
world's past? That thing was no oracle. In that conceptual
framework, it was not an oracle, but a demon, a succubus,
that had fastened upon this world to suck it dry. It manipulated to the extent of its powers, for its advantage. They have
traded a taker for a giver. It was almost to have been that
way before, when Cretus walked in his own body, but for the
thwarting by the Entity. Fear not. History will not speak here
of the days to come, as the conquests of a conqueror, whose
name lives on in infamy; but they will note something happened here that changed Men forever, and they will never
know who did it. You said it: Monsalvat will become opaque
to your kind of analysis in History. First Monsalvat, then the
rest. We will be pariahs no longer, and I will be anonymous,
a face, a body that wanders. They will know me by my
words, and the dreams I launch them onto."

Morgin now leaned near, and said, softly, "You have spoken for the offworlders who do not know, but I see your
meaning as a native. You will need a knowledgeable companion on your long road . . . and a scribe to record a scribe's
words."

He smiled, a gesture barely visible in the dim light. "You

will never catch it as it is to be . . . but I will be grateful for
your knowledge. Come with me, then."

He got up, pausing to lay the Vfzyekhr softly on the pallet.
Tenguft towered over him, and she said, in a throaty voice, a
tone he had not heard in her for a long time, "I, too, will
come. As Morgin knows people, so do I know the markers of
the world itself. And of course," she added slyly, "you
should not have to worry over finding a new woman every
night, either."

"You know this is going into the darkness."

"Just so. I know the path well; the way of the Haydar warrior is into the darkness of unknowing. Otherwise, why would
there be warriors. Any city-man can walk in the light among
the known."

"Let it be so, then. But in this is neither fame nor glory.
Just hard strokes."

"But we will change it all. I understand. Forever. The rest
does not matter. I see that much I have known and loved will
pass from sight—and for others, too. But I also know that all
we have done before has been the illusion of change, that in
our hearts we were still beasts, no matter that some lived in
the bellies of machines . . ."

He looked out the window now and saw the *Thlecsne
Ishcht* settling onto a place not far away, still clearing the
ramshackle buildings under it with what seemed to be swift
strokes of light. At each stroke, there was no fire, only dust
and debris. The people had long since cleared that part of the
city. He made a gesture curiously like a shrug, and said,
"Come along, then. It's time."

15

"The art of progress is to keep intact the Eternal."

"Complete mystery surrounds the question of the origin of this system; any theory which satisfies the facts demands assumptions which are completely absurd."

—*A. C.*

They made their way to the ship in silence, not because they each had nothing to say, but that they each had too much to say; or that what was there would not fit the words they had to say it.

By the time they had reached the place where the *Thlecsne Ishcht* was to ground itself, it had completed its clearing process and was resting lightly on the bare ground. The ship was not shut down now as the Meure Schasny of long ago had first seen it resting on the field by Kundre, on Tancred. Here, it rested lightly, its bulk not quite touching the earth. It did not move, but they could sense that there was little holding its power leashed. And along the lengths of the tubes that surrounded its basic shape, infinitesimally remote colored sparks crawled spiral paths, like burning fuses.

It had been night; but now, far away across the flats and the river steamings, the eastern sky was beginning to color slightly. He thought, *There, over the hills of Intance or Nasp, the sky will be pale over the black seas, clearer than here. And now the shimmer you always caught out of the corner of your eye will be gone. Forever. We saw it so long, not knowing what it was, that we managed to forget it. Only offworlders were troubled by it, and thought things were watching them. Something was there, that we suppressed. And like a man, leaning on a wall, we'll fall now that the wall is gone, unless we build another one—or recover our proper balance.* And in his mind, before *thought*, he knew which one was the only acceptable choice.

Ferocious-appearing Spsom, dressed in what passed for uniforms among them, swarmed down the boarding-ladder, to retrieve Vdhitz, and take the still form of the Vfzyekhr from Tanguft, who had carried it to the ship, back to its own kind. Clellendol hesitated for a moment, but a moment only. He glanced at Flerdistar, at the rest of them, and climbed the ladder into the ship. The part he had come for was over. He was merely a passenger now.

Flerdistar stepped onto the first rung, steadying herself with a thin hand on the safety rail, pausing uncertainly. She said, "I came to study the past—instead I received an answer about the future, which I neither knew existed, nor wanted to know."

Cretus said, "Once you learn to hear answers, you hear all kinds of answers to questions you have not yet asked; this is as it should be, but it is hard to live with at first."

"I did not learn the answer to my project query."

"You haven't asked it plainly enough."

"Written history says Sanjirmil led the Warriors, as did the legends of the Warriors themselves. But through Monsalvat we suspected that this was not the truth. What was the truth, and why did it come through here?"

"As the Cretus of old, I spent much time with the *Skazenache,* learning the mastery of it. Once I saw a thing I did not understand, not at all. It was so odd I memorized the settings so I could come back to it—something extremely difficult, even for a master of the instrument. Later, when I had learned to interpret what I was seeing, I turned the *Skazenache* to those settings again . . . and the scene was replayed."

". . . it was odd because after I had learned all the major part of the legends about the Warriors and the Klesh, I found that I was looking at Sanjirmil herself, at great age. But listen: she was on another world—not Dawn. And she was acting, in this scene, as if she expected that someone would be able to see her—somehow."

Flerdistar asked, "What . . . ?" but Cretus held up a hand, gently, to hold her question.

"She spoke aloud, in simple Singlespeech, as if reciting. Now you will hear it from me as I-Cretus saw and heard it. When the First Ship was to have left home, Sanjirmil was the leader of a minority faction of your people who wished to exercise domination over the Humans. She was one of the elite

—the flying crew, and so was not seen on the first part of the voyage. And when the mutiny occurred, and that faction stole the ship, those Ler who were left behind assumed it was she who had led them.

"Not so. She had changed. Her views were part of a mental dysfunction caused by an overload she received as a child; and after her actions had set everything in motion beyond the point of no return, she was cured, by one who loved her greatly. The cure set her mind right again, and removed the radical view she had cultivated from her, but it also removed her ability to fly the ship. She kept to her quarters and secluded herself, doing some minor astrogating, some teaching, and trying to undermine the very thing she herself had started.

"As she was at the age of the onset of fertility, she entered into family relationships after the manner of your people. She had her two children on the first world your people landed on. And raised them there. She led a gentle, retiring life, indeed, almost a secretive one, practicing all the virtues of the Ler and trying quietly to obviate the evil she had done so much to invent in an earlier part of her life."

Flerdistar said, 'This modest person you are speaking of, this paragon of Ler virtues, is credited in Ler history with the invention of our own sort of evil, as a force. She is an historical character whose shadow casts itself longer than any other. She made us what we are now. And you say she recited that she retired?"

"Did you think I would not verify all that she said? Or that I could not? It was as astounding to me as to you. And afterwards, I did verify it. I studied Sanjirmil off and on for almost ten years. I know more about her life, almost, than she did herself."

"But of course, things do not always go as we want them to; where before she had been a Power, a shaper, in her affliction, cured she was a simple woman of the people, and the Mana was gone. She could no longer steer history. The conspiracy simmered underground, was passed from mouth to mouth, in secret covens . . . and almost a generation later, a band of desperate amateurs stole the ship and took off into space, marooning the majority faction, now colonists.

"They took her with them, since she was the prophetess of their whole movement, the one who started it—before any of them had been born. They only knew that she was Sanjirmil the Great. But it was against her will that she went; they kidnapped her when she resisted, knowing in their hearts they could not leave without their own legendary source, knowing that they could not endure the shame of having their own prophet denounce them, perhaps even seek revenge upon them.

"But her cure had been too complete; she proved no more able to justify the Sanjirmil of old aboard the ship again, than she had while raising her family. They had their talisman, well enough—but it was a talisman that would not accept anything short of complete surrender, and the return of the ship. They were at an impasse of the worst sort: she wouldn't cooperate, and they couldn't take her back, and to have killed her outright would have made them totally depraved, and to their credit, they at least saw that in that future.

"So, on their way away outward from their place, in their rush to the darkness of the Rim, they passed a curious planetary system, with a choice of habitable worlds within it. One proved to be a gentle and pleasant world, more or less, and so they landed there, and labored for a time, to build her a house by the shore, and left her tools, and seeds, and some animals. This world had no intelligent life, and was bare and lonely; here they could honor her with a small castle, but they could also abandon her there in good conscience, knowing she would never betray them. This world was so far out they knew it would never be found while any artifact of hers existed—they didn't know where it was for sure, themselves. Besides, she was then Elder phase, and couldn't have all that much time left, anyway. And so, after doing her honors, they departed, and left Sanjirmil on an uninhabited planet, whose location was not known and soon forgotten—mislaid—by its discoverers.

"But when she had been cured, it had been complete. Sanjirmil was then, I think, probably the sanest Human or near-Human, or Ler that has ever been. Alone in a stone castle by an empty sea, caught at last by the thing she had created and then abandoned, and at last fought, she did not despair, but called on strengths she had possessed all her life. She survived. First, the first year. Then a second. Then it got a little easier; she was falling into the rhythm of the planet.

"She expanded her little country, began exploring the land about her. She learned about certain dangerous forms of life, and how to avoid them. She took long excursions along the seashore, explored the interior. She had been overstressed, for the ship. But as a generalist, as a survivor, she was superb; she recreated a community, and all its necessary handicrafts, totally within herself. Hope she had none, but she would not give up, even where there was none to see it.

"She lost count of the years, for she could not know what they were in the years of the home planet. It no longer mattered. Her hair was streaked with gray when they left her; it went all gray, then white. She became careful of her strength, and stayed closer to her castle. It was then that she thought something was stirring, something aware, but unseen, unknowable, something evil, something that had been, for all practical purposes, dead. At first she dismissed it as hallucination, or simple old age and loneliness. But it continued, and the impressions became stronger. It began to leave traces she could objectively measure. Even doubting herself, she devised subtle little test-traps for it. It became the major objective of what remained of her life—to prove this suspicion a real, although subtle thing, or a figment of her own failing mind and body.

"She finally decided that whatever it was, it was real, not a phantom, and that somehow it was intelligent, powerful, and awakening. She feared it, but in a very limited way, she communicated with it; enough to hope that a day would come when someone would be able to look across time and space and see her who had set the events in motion that would lead to that person's vision. And so she set a particular scene, where she told this whole story, so that someone would know it, no matter whether the Warriors, as they had called themselves, continued or ended. And in the end she had the victory over them, for the Warriors are indeed gone, them and their line alike, and the lie they told of her, that she was their prophet, their leader, their ideal. She told me, and I. . . ."

Flerdistar said, "You as Cretus alone, long ago, spread the tale over Monsalvat. . . ."

"Edited, changed a little, embroidered to fit the people it served. . . ."

". . . That Sanjirmil. . . ."

"St. Zermille, our Lady of Monsalvat."

". . . though a Ler, had hated the Warriors and would love the victims of their persecutions."

"Just so."

"A fine tale, that, Cretus. Good for your people, and the answer I came for. All is well! But why here? What makes her important to Monsalvat?" And even as she said it, she knew. Her face shouted it. She knew.

"They left her here, on Monsalvat. She lived in the west by the Great Ocean, in the land we call now Warvard. Not so far from the Ombur. And she awoke the Entity who still lived on Catharge . . . and told me how to recognize it, and escape its influences. It could distort space and time, but somehow it couldn't deflect that message she arranged as one of her last acts, nor could it perceive it except dimly . . . it was through her that I disengaged, knowing that my dream could go no further as long as it was awake and alive, and that I could not reach it. . . ."

He had let it trail off, but now he continued again, "She walked into the sea and went for a swim, and the Great Ocean took her. And the seasons and the waves and the years slowly undid what she had done there by the sea, and the traces of it grew dim, and then invisible to untrained eyes. And then they came, the Warriors and their former slaves, who built, and tore down, and built again. And governors, and colonists, and all traces of her were erased. And why should anyone have thought to look for her here? They all thought she had gone with the Warriors—but when they were taken off Dawn, no Warrior mentioned her grave, nor any memorial to her, or indeed anything of her. No—it was here she lived her last days. And so we made her a saint, and I suppose in a way, that it's true, after all . . . in the end, a long way around, she did save us, and show us the way. For what I now reveal is not Cretus, nor Meure, but what she told me long ago—what we all must do. I have known it all this time, but could not transmit the idea of it. Now, after these final strokes—I can. And through me, she will at last expiate her crimes of centuries ago. She thought it all out— she had nothing else to do, and she was the only Ler at that time who was totally mind-clean—purged and humble. She had the clear sight that I lacked, even though I had a great dream. I was dreamer enough to recognize hers was the greater."

Flerdistar took an uncertain step on the ladder, words beyond her.

He said, as if in parting, "Say these things that you have heard and seen here to your sponsors, to your people . . . that you no longer will have to probe subtle concepts and study dusty manuscripts to travel to her who was your greatest seer, but that we will bring her to you, after a time, and that our lives will change, and we all will grow strange and wonderful and we'll look at all that went before this, here, as the initiation we had to have accomplished. Good-bye."

Flerdistar obeyed without thinking about it, walking up the inclined ladder into the belly of the *Thlecsne Ishcht*, without looking back.

And the ladder folded back into the ship, and it was covered and the hull became smooth and without seam. It lifted, moving hardly at all at first, then faster, rotating to a different heading, orienting itself according to the unseen Captain and astrogator, rising into a sky gone rosy-fingered with the approach of dawn, yet also with that tincture of tangerine that was the mark of Monsalvat and its double star—Bitirme. Noiselessly, and the sparkles along the tubing faded, and the ship rose, and diminished, and moved away, becoming a dark smudge, a spot, and then nothing.

It was said of the three remaining behind, by those who made it their business to watch all events in Yastian, that they remained in the cleared area for a short time, but then left. And that in the day that followed, made their way to the great docks along the south end of the foreign quarter, where they spoke with several captains, and at last went aboard a ship rigged with flowing triangular sails, and crewed by slender men who wore striped, form-fitting shirts and turbans, and whose faces were thin and skins shiny brown, identifying them as of the Radah Horisande, the dreaded pirate-mariners of Glordune.

There were those who averred that the three were welcomed there, with the grim reserve characteristic of that Klesh Radah, and that afterwards, the Glordune ship dropped its mooring lines and began drifting down the estuary, toward the sea. And as it faded into the growing dark of evening over the marshes, that they could be seen by the rail for a long time, as if relaxing, and that strange songs floated back over the water, not the usual bloodthirsty chants attributed to the Horisande by their few survivors. These things were noted, and put away in the press of daily events, but not forgotten; they were remembered as proper portents when after many passages of the double suns across the floor of the Inner Sea, many sums of such passages, Cretus the Scribe returned to Kepture, last of all the continents. But that is another tale, which may be summarized by the saying, there came a great change from the East. Which finished its course in Kepture, where it started, and passed onward, to all men and salamanders and gnomes.